Praise for the novels of Jill Sorenson

THE EDGE OF NIGHT

"With an emotionally charged romance, heart-pounding suspense and characters who resonate long after the book is finished, *The Edge of Night* delivers! You are guaranteed a dangerously addictive, gut-wrenchingly tight paced read."
—STEPHANIE TYLER, *New York Times* bestselling author

"Sorenson paints the graffiti-lined streets and the gang scene with broad strokes, and makes her characters realistic, flawed, and appealing. Deftly handled violent action and red herrings rush this thriller to a believable ending."—*Publishers Weekly*

"A spectacular story. The non-stop action and the budding romance between April and Noah made for a fast-paced tale, which I was unable to put down until the very end. I highly suggest blocking off a good amount of time when you pick this book up, because you're not going to want to put it down."
—Night Owl Romance

"Riveting! *The Edge of Night* is taut with emotion, suspense and danger. Sorenson expertly weaves the two stories into a heart-wrenching conclusion."
—*RT Book Reviews*

"An exciting romantic suspense, fast paced and well written. *The Edge of Night* is an entertaining story to read in the cold days of winter."
—*Romance Reviews Today*

CRASH INTO ME

"Sorenson's sleek sensuality and fresh new voice are sure to score big with readers."
—CINDY GERARD, *New York Times* bestselling author

"Beautiful characters, true-to-life emotions, heart-stopping action, and a bona fide bad guy—it doesn't get any better than this." —*RT Book Reviews*

"It was definitely hot. Sooo hot. Jill Sorenson is my new favorite romantic suspense author!"
—VICTORIA DAHL

"*Crash into Me* has so many unexpected events and twists that readers will be hooked all the way to the final page. Jill Sorenson is an author to watch!"
—The Romance Reader Connection

BY JILL SORENSON

Crash into Me
Set the Dark on Fire
The Edge of Night
Caught in the Act

Caught in the Act

JILL SORENSON

BANTAM BOOKS • NEW YORK

A Bantam Books Mass Market Original

Copyright © 2012 by Jill Sorenson

Published in the United States by Bantam Books, an imprint of The Random House Publishing Group, a division of Random House, Inc., New York.

Bantam Books and the rooster colophon are registered trademarks of Random House, Inc.

ISBN: 978-0-553-59264-1
eBook ISBN: 978-0-345-53209-1

Cover design: Jae Song
Cover photographs: Dundanium/shutterstock (man), Carlos Castilla/shutterstock (street)

Printed in the United States of America

www.bantamdell.com

9 8 7 6 5 4 3 2 1

Bantam Books mass market edition: March 2012

Acknowledgments

As always, many special people helped to make this book possible.

Heartfelt thanks to Junessa Viloria, my editor, for the fantastic insight, and to Laurie McLean, my agent, for the enthusiastic support. High fives to the Bantam Dell art department for a smoking hot cover. Meow!

Thanks to my husband, for helping me brainstorm, and to my mom, for always offering to babysit. I'm so grateful for my beautiful children and wonderful family.

Special thanks to the Department of Homeland Security for allowing me to tour the San Ysidro Port of Entry in San Diego. Public Affairs Liaison Angelica De Cima took the time to answer my questions and show me around the facilities. The technology, professionalism, and dedication to security inspired me.

Thanks to the Customs and Border Protection officers who protect and serve this country.

Caught in the Act

1

Karina Strauss approached the San Ysidro border crossing at a snail's pace, her cargo van idling among a thousand other vehicles.

There were twenty-four lanes on the Tijuana side, a massive snarl of traffic that found order in the last hundred yards. Before the inspection booths were visible, the dividing lines were ignored. The more aggressive drivers made their own lanes, squeezing into narrow spaces and zigzagging across the chaos. Everyone else lurched forward in semiregular intervals while street vendors navigated the shifting aisles, selling everything from *chicle* and cold drinks to silver jewelry and colorful hammocks. Some of the peddlers were children whose shoulders barely cleared the hoods of the cars.

Kari let out a slow breath, removing her sweaty hands from the steering wheel. She'd turned off the air-conditioning and rolled down the windows in hopes that her van wouldn't overheat. At just past noon, the summer sun was blazing. Her left shoulder, exposed by her sleeveless cotton top, felt burned.

As the crush of vehicles evened into single rows, Kari

became aware of impatient drivers angling toward the right. Her lane seemed more backed up than the others—not a good sign. Some of the inspectors were very thorough, checking the contents of each and every car. Normally she appreciated their diligence.

Today she was desperate for lax security.

She put on her signal and tried to merge into the next lane, with no luck. A woman in a midsized sedan stole the spot, her radio blaring Juan Gabriel.

The space in front of Kari cleared and she was forced to move ahead in the same lane. Now there were only a few cars between her and the inspection booth. She met her startled reflection in the rearview mirror, swallowing dryly. Her heart slammed in her chest, beating too hard, too fast.

Stay calm, she told herself. Act cool.

The officer stationed at the booth ahead didn't appear lax in any way. His dark blue uniform fit well. He had short black hair and a stern face. She couldn't see his eyes behind the lenses of his authoritative sunglasses, but she'd bet they were brown.

Kari watched the officer walk around a dusty Oldsmobile, gesturing for the owner to open the trunk. His short-sleeved shirt stretched across his back as he leaned forward to glance into the trunk's recesses. He looked strong, broad-shouldered, bronze-skinned. There was nothing unusual about him, other than an eye-pleasing physique, but she sensed that he was sharp and precise.

Sweat trickled between her breasts.

Too nervous to sit still, she unfastened the top buttons on her blouse, searching around the front seats of the van for a tissue to blot her perspiration.

The line crawled forward again. Damn!

She used the hem of her skirt to wipe her chest and left the buttons undone. Maybe she could entice the inspector to look down her shirt rather than inside her vehicle. Tapping the gas pedal, she eased the van closer.

She'd been waiting in traffic for over an hour and the final moments were the most intense. Blood pounded in her ears, her temple, her throat. She took a small sip of water and fiddled with the radio, trying to disguise her fear. Her pulse was racing, her hands trembling. She didn't dare glance back into the cargo space.

At last, it was her turn. She pulled up to the inspection booth, which was underneath a shaded structure, and prayed for a wave-through.

"Citizenship?"

"U.S.," she murmured, handing him her passport. Most of the stamps marked her visits to Mexico. Others were from the Czech Republic, where she'd been born. She watched him handle her paperwork, fixating on the almost indiscernible grain of stubble along his jaw, the smoothness of his taut brown throat.

Officer A. Cortez, the name tag on his shirtfront read. He was Hispanic, but that didn't relax her. There was no room for mixed sympathies in his profession.

"Anything to declare?" he asked.

She fumbled for her inventory list. His voice was low and even, no trace of an accent. He was also disturbingly handsome. As she passed him the handwritten account of the items in her van—well, *most* of the items—she remembered her gaping blouse. The flat expression on his face suggested that he'd noticed but wasn't impressed.

"It's all just stuff for my store," she explained, flushing. "Zócalo, on E Street?"

His gaze dropped to the insignia on the side of her van. *Authentic Arts and Crafts from Latin America*. The accompanying image was whimsical, a dancing skeleton in a sombrero. In Mexico, even death was a fiesta.

"Please turn off the engine and step outside the vehicle."

Her stomach dropped.

She switched off the ignition and removed the keys, curbing the urge to ask if she'd done something wrong. Better to stay mum. With numb fingers, she opened the driver's-side door. The instant she climbed out, her rubber flip-flops soaked up the heat of the asphalt, and a warm breeze rippled through her calf-length skirt.

She followed Officer Cortez to the rear of the vehicle, her heart in her throat.

"Open the doors, please."

Oh no. What could she do? Refusing to cooperate was not an option.

As she approached the double doors on shaky legs, her keys slid from her slippery grip, clattering to the pavement. She bent to pick them up, aware that her thin cotton skirt was clinging to her backside.

Cortez waited patiently, making no move to assist her.

Straightening, she unlocked the doors. Although her eyes had trouble adjusting to the dim interior, she could make out a few shadowy boxes and piles of textiles, her usual haul. She stepped aside, not allowing her gaze to linger.

Cortez glanced into the cargo space and then squinted down the line of cars, assessing the rows of vehicles. When he looked back at her, she shifted her weight from one foot to the other, self-conscious. He touched the radio at his shoulder and spoke into it, engaging in a clipped conversation she couldn't overhear.

Kari had to do something to distract him from the contents of her van. As he dropped his hand from the radio, she saw that he wasn't wearing a wedding ring. He had a lean, muscular build, and he was medium-tall, maybe six feet. Under different circumstances, she wouldn't have to feign interest.

"This must be an exciting job," she ventured, trying to sound fascinated.

He perused her cargo. "It has its moments."

"Have you handled any big loads?"

That got his attention. He gave her a bald look, obviously wondering if she meant to be suggestive.

She smiled, fanning her cleavage with one hand. "Hot, isn't it?"

Behind the dark lenses of his sunglasses, his eyes followed her movements. Although she'd dressed for comfort, not seduction, the outfit flattered her figure. Most men liked breasts, and hers were half-showing. Cortez was also fairly young, which worked in her favor. He might be an exemplary officer, but he wasn't immune to the stuff.

To her disappointment, he tore his gaze from her chest and continued the routine inspection, a muscle in his jaw flexing.

Her mind whirred with ridiculous options, like pretending to faint on the hot blacktop. Then a loud noise stole Cortez's attention. Several lanes over, a trio of intimidating-looking German shepherds were barking up a storm, straining at their leashes. Alerting officers of illegal cargo.

Officer Cortez stepped away from her vehicle. "Have

a nice day, ma'am," he said, handing back her paper-work. After calling for another uniformed man to cover his station, he walked toward the commotion in long strides.

Kari shut the back doors of the van, dizzy with relief. She went around to the driver's side and got in, ears peeled for a shout to halt. Thankfully, it didn't come. She turned on the engine and pulled forward, crossing the border into San Diego. Clear, organized roadways and a clean ocean breeze greeted her.

Freedom.

She stepped on the gas and inhaled deeply, letting the wind whip through her shoulder-length hair. Even after she'd gone a few miles, her heart wouldn't stop racing. She didn't dare glance back into the cargo space for fear she was being followed.

"Oh my God," she said finally, letting out a nervous laugh. "That was close."

Normally she went straight to her store, which was near Old Town, to unload the van. Today she drove to her quiet little house in Bonita. The tiny San Diego sub-urb was only a ten-minute trip from the San Ysidro port of entry. As soon as she came to a stop in her driveway, she scrambled into the cargo space, wading through cardboard boxes.

She tore open the largest box. "Maria?"

Her stowaway was hidden in a very cramped space, her slender limbs contorted in an uncomfortable posi-tion. As Kari lifted the top flaps of cardboard, Maria Santos moaned, insensible. Her eyes were closed and her head lolled to one side.

"Oh shit," Kari said, grabbing her bottled water. The box must have been hot, stuffy, and intensely claustrophobic. She poured water on the young woman's dark hair, trying to rouse her. Maria choked and sputtered, shaking her wet head. Kari put her arms around her slight body and heaved, pulling the woman from the box. Although Maria was slim, she weighed at least a hundred pounds and it wasn't easy for Kari to get her out. When she was free, they lay together on the floor of the van, panting from exertion.

"*Aire*," Maria rasped. "I need air."

Kari leapt to her feet and shoved open the back doors, glancing around the deserted neighborhood. There was a vehicle she'd never seen before parked across the street, but it looked empty.

"This way," she said, helping Maria out of the van. They stumbled across the driveway and collapsed on the front lawn. She rolled onto her stomach and retched, her slim back bowed, her arms trembling.

Kari retrieved her bottled water from the van and waited for Maria's nausea to pass, wincing in sympathy.

After a moment, Maria straightened, wiping her mouth with her hand. She accepted the water and took a small sip, studying their surroundings with wet eyes. Her gaze moved from the vibrant green blades of grass beneath her to Kari's front door. "This is your house?" she asked, pronouncing *this* as "thees" and *your* as "jour."

Kari nodded. "Do you like it?"

"It's beautiful," she said, blinking the tears from her eyes.

Kari glanced around the front yard, surprised. The neighborhood was middle-class at best, and her house a modest two-bedroom. It was Maria who was beautiful, with her lovely dark hair and serene smile. She had a slightly crooked tooth in front, a tiny imperfection that added to her appeal.

They'd met in La Bufadora, a poverty-stricken tourist spot near Ensenada. Powerful waves met steep cliffs there, creating a gust of ocean spray known as "the Blowhole." Kari bought crafts from the local women, but she also dropped off donations. She'd been a volunteer for a charity organization called Hands Across the Border for years, delivering clothes and school supplies to the needy.

Maria worked mornings at a nearby hotel and afternoons at a pottery kiln. The black clay of La Bufadora formed a very unique type of stoneware, and Kari was happy to pay a good price for one-of-a-kind creations. Whenever Kari came to the kiln, Maria went out of her way to accommodate her. She was charming and loquacious, a natural saleswoman. Over time, the two women had become friends.

Kari knew that Maria was supporting her widowed mother and younger siblings. Last week, over lunch, Maria had confessed that her family was in dire straits. Her sister needed medical treatment, and her brother, who was only fourteen, was threatening to cross the border to find work. Maria had begged Kari for a ride to the United States. In San Diego, she could make a week's wages in a single day.

Kari looked Maria in the eye, preparing to say no. It wasn't possible to assist every person in need, and trafficking was against the law. She couldn't save the world. But there was something special about Maria, an inner strength. She was desperate, and she was determined. Kari had heard the horror stories about single women who attempted to immigrate illegally, and she feared for Maria's safety.

So she said yes. Kari had always found it impossible to turn her back on those in need. Hoping she wasn't making the biggest mistake of her life, she made plans to transport Maria the following week. This morning, as Kari was loading up her van, Maria had grabbed a beat-up duffel bag and climbed aboard.

"You've never been to the U.S. before?" Kari asked.

"Just once," she said, her smile fading. "I walked through the desert with a group. It was a long journey."

"What happened?"

She swallowed a few times, as if sickened anew by the memory. "I got separated from the others at night. I was lost for many days, I think. *La migra* picked me up and sent me back to Mexico."

The story wasn't at all uncommon. Dozens of illegal immigrants died every year making the same arduous trek.

Kari had never imagined that she was capable of smuggling a human being. And although she wouldn't choose to repeat the experience, she couldn't regret her decision. For some reason, Maria reminded Kari of her troubled little sister. She sensed a hint of sadness behind her disarming smile.

"*Muchísimas gracias*," Maria said, giving Kari an enthusiastic hug. "I have waited years to return to the U.S. I am so happy to be here, to find work and send money to my family. You are angel from heaven. Bless you."

Kari returned the embrace, remembering the last time she'd hugged Sasha. Her sister had tensed, holding herself at a distance. For years she'd been closed off from Kari emotionally, a stranger with a familiar face.

When they broke apart, Maria noticed Kari's dishabille. "Your blouse needs repair. I will sew for you."

"Oh, no," Kari said, blushing as she buttoned up. "It's fine. I was just trying to distract the vehicle inspector."

Maria's elegant brows rose. "It worked, yes?"

"Maybe," she allowed, thinking about Officer Cortez's searing gaze. She wondered if she would see him again. Hundreds of officers guarded the San Ysidro port of entry, so she doubted it. "What are your plans, now that you're here?"

The young woman shrugged. "Find job."

"Do you need to use the phone?"

"I have no one to call. I don't know anyone here."

Kari stared at her, incredulous. "Where will you stay?"

Maria smiled. "Good question."

"How old are you?"

"Twenty-two."

She looked about eighteen, far too young to be wandering the streets, and much too pretty to go unnoticed. Kari didn't want her sleeping on a sidewalk. "Why don't you stay here? I have an extra bedroom."

It was meant for her sister, of course. Kari had finally come to terms with the fact that Sasha wasn't going to leave her drug lord boyfriend.

Maria's jaw dropped. "A bedroom? For me only?"

"It's nothing fancy, a small bed and some basic furnishings. Would you like to come in and see?"

"How much I pay?"

She tried to think of an amount that sounded reasonable. The house had been a bank foreclosure and a steal, so her living costs were low. Now that Zócalo was turning a comfortable profit, she could afford to keep Maria for free. "Half of the utilities," she offered. "But don't worry about it until you get a job."

Maria was already on her feet, eyes bright with excitement. "I do housework. Laundry your clothes. Whatever you need."

Kari laughed, closing up her van and walking toward the front door. During the summer months, she worked about sixty hours a week at the store, so she wouldn't mind a little help around the house. "Can you cook?"

"Oh, *sí*," Maria said. "Anything you like."

They were discussing plans for lunch as Kari unlocked the door. The instant she crossed the threshold, a dark figure leapt out at her. Before she could draw a breath to scream, the man slammed her against the wall and pressed the cold barrel of a gun to her cheek.

Adam Cortez had been propositioned at the border before.

Every CBP officer had seen more than his share of exposed flesh and sultry smiles. Sometimes it was silly teenagers, coming back from a wild night on Avenida Revolución, Tijuana's underage party central.

A more disturbing trend was for the Mexican cartels to use pretty girls as decoys. While a couple of slack-jawed officers were gaping at young ladies in short skirts and low-cut tops, they smuggled a shipment through another lane. Officers were trained to be aware of these tactics and respond accordingly.

Adam hadn't responded accordingly to Karina Strauss. Yes, she had a knockout body, and her unbuttoned blouse invited a man to take a closer look, but he shouldn't have surrendered to temptation. She'd been acting suspicious, attempting to divert his attention. He shouldn't have let her drive away.

And he definitely shouldn't have used government resources to do a background check on her *after* he clocked out for the day.

She'd made quite an impression on him. It wasn't the low neckline or her clumsy attempt at flirting that had captured his interest, although he'd taken note of both. What stopped him dead in his tracks was the familiar name—Strauss—and her arresting face.

Her sister, Sasha, was a platinum blonde and thin to the point of emaciation these days, but the resemblance was striking. Karina appeared to have more substance. With her honey-colored hair and sun-kissed skin, she looked like . . . the really hot girl next door.

Although Sasha had a couple of marks on her record for drug possession and public intoxication, Karina had never been arrested. That didn't mean she was innocent, just that she hadn't been caught.

Adam wondered if the siblings had similar lifestyles. Sasha was the longtime girlfriend of Carlos Moreno, a Mexican-born drug lord. He'd seen her with the crew leader on numerous occasions, making the rounds at nightclubs, partying until dawn. As far as Adam knew, Sasha wasn't involved in the smuggling operation.

Was Karina on Moreno's payroll? She made frequent trips across the border, supposedly to buy items for her store. It was a good cover.

He stared at the information on the computer screen in front of him, which included her home address. The next logical step would be to take his suspicions to the investigations unit and let them do their job. Carlos

Moreno had a very high profile. The DEA, ATF, and ICE all wanted a piece of him.

Adam wanted a piece of him, too.

A rap at the open door startled him out of his reverie. It was Officer Pettigrew, his superior. "What's up?"

"Nothing much," he said quickly, closing the screen he was viewing. "Just a routine background check."

Pettigrew gave him a curt nod. "See you tomorrow."

Adam logged off the computer and pushed away from the desk, his mind in turmoil. For several years he'd done unofficial surveillance on Moreno, waiting for an opportunity to get close to him. He'd spent too many nights chasing shadows, seething in solitude. At long last he'd abandoned the pursuit.

Seeing Karina Strauss had taken him back to a very dark place.

He knew he should file a report on her and walk away. Instead, he decided not to mention their chance meeting to anyone. Pulse pounding, he left the San Ysidro port of entry and headed north, filled with thoughts of violent retribution.

2

Kari gasped as the man wound her hair around his fist, pinning her against the wall.

Her first instinct was to try to get away, but the cold bite of metal at her cheek was a strong incentive to stay still. She braced her hands on the wall behind her, frozen with fear, wincing at the pain in her scalp.

A second intruder grabbed Maria. He locked his arm around her slender waist and yanked her inside, clamping his hand over her mouth to cut off her scream.

The man holding a gun on Kari kicked the door shut, keeping the barrel pressed to her face. Although terror had scrambled her senses, she recognized him as one of Moreno's top crew members, Jesús "Chuy" Pena.

God help her.

Every man affiliated with Moreno was a violent criminal, and Pena was one of the most intimidating figures she'd ever seen. His head was shaved bald, and he had a stocky, muscular physique. With his broad face and heavy features, he wasn't handsome. There was a teardrop tattoo high on his left cheekbone.

Kari didn't know Pena's companion, who had easily

overpowered Maria. His medium build and dark, poorly cut hair appeared common, nondescript. He would blend in with the crowd on either side of the border.

Maria stared at Kari, her eyes dark with fright.

Kari returned her attention to Pena. She waited for him to act, her chest rising and falling with each breath. His gaze followed the movement, lingering on her breasts. She'd fastened one or two buttons, but the neckline was still low.

Pena moistened his lips, making a murmur of approval. Kari's flesh crawled where his gaze touched her. Against her will, she flashed back to a horrible night when she and Sasha were teenagers. Kari could see her sister in the hospital bed, her mascara smudged, dress torn.

She squeezed her eyes shut, dispelling the disturbing image.

Pena dragged the barrel of his gun down the hollow of her throat and over her collarbone, sliding it between her breasts. "Nice," he said, nostrils flaring.

Kari was too afraid to react to his sexually charged threat, but Maria went wild. She bucked in her captor's arms, sinking her sharp teeth into the palm of his hand.

The man winced in pain, fighting to keep her under control. *"Basta!"* Unlike Pena, he didn't appear to be enjoying himself. He endured Maria's struggles, his expression reticent. *"Ya,* Chuy. We didn't come here for this."

Pena's eyes narrowed at the quiet admonishment. He didn't like being told how to do his business. But after a short pause he took the gun away from Kari's chest and relaxed his hand in her hair. "Who's the girl?"

"M—my friend," she stuttered, surprised by the question. "Maria."

"What are you doing here?" he asked Maria in Spanish.

Pena's partner removed his palm from her mouth gingerly, allowing her to speak. She had his blood on her lips and tears in her eyes. *"Busco trabajo,"* she said. *Looking for work.*

Pena forced Kari toward the living room couch, shoving her hard. The other man was more polite with Maria but just as firm. He urged her to sit down next to Kari. Kari stifled the urge to put her arm around Maria and cower against her.

"We have a message from Moreno," Pena said.

Kari eyed him warily, waiting for it.

"You sister has become a nuisance. She's been stealing his money, sneaking around." Pena waved the gun in the air. "He can't allow it."

"Bring her to me," Kari said. "I'll take care of her."

"Her debt must be paid first."

Her stomach twisted. "How much?"

"Two fifty."

It took a moment for Kari to realize that he didn't mean $250. "Two hundred and fifty . . . thousand?" she asked, stunned. Even if she sold all of her assets, she couldn't come up with that much. She didn't own her house or her business outright. There was no way she'd be able to pay the amount.

Pena's gaze fell to her breasts once again before moving up to her face. "Perhaps you can do us a favor."

"What kind of favor?" she asked, dreading the answer.

"Next week, during your next trip to Mexico, we'll

arrange for you to pick up an extra shipment and bring it across the border. In exchange for the safe arrival of those packages, Sasha will be delivered to you, unharmed."

She wanted to say no, but thought better of it when she saw the sly look on Pena's face. He stroked the barrel of his gun lightly, relishing the power he held over her.

Kari closed her eyes and took a ragged breath, reliving the last few hours. She'd been a nervous wreck as she crossed the border. She couldn't imagine carrying a large amount of heroin or cocaine for Moreno. Her anxiety level would skyrocket. And if she got caught, she would do serious time in prison.

But what choice did she have?

"Maybe I'll make an anonymous call to the border police," Chuy said. "They would love to meet your new friend."

Kari felt the blood drain from her face. Maria clutched her hand, her short fingernails biting into Kari's palm. Maria didn't want Chuy to report her. Kari was worried that Chuy would punish them in other ways. If she refused to cooperate, their lives would be in danger. Chuy had no qualms about harming innocent women.

"Okay," she said, her voice trembling. "I'll do it. Wh—whatever you want."

Pena smiled, putting his gun away. "We'll be in touch. And we'll be watching you, understand?"

She gave a miserable nod, acknowledging the threat. If she told anyone about this visit, she'd never see Sasha again. Moreno was not a man to cross. For the hundredth time, Kari wished her drug addict sister hadn't hooked up with that monster.

Pena turned to Maria. "Do you speak English?"

"Very little," Maria said, her accent thick.

"Come to the Hotel del Oro tomorrow morning," he said in Spanish on his way out. "We could use another maid."

Maria knew it was a command, not an invitation. She wiped the blood from her lips, flinching at the bitter taste.

"*Mil disculpas,*" Pena's partner said, bowing. *A thousand pardons.*

"*Mil maldiciones!*" Maria shot back. *A thousand curses!*

The men exchanged a startled glance and laughed, shaking their heads as they walked through the door.

As soon as they were gone, Kari jumped up, rushing to the front window to peer through the blinds. The men climbed into a sleek black SUV and drove away. "Oh my God," she said, massaging her aching scalp. "What am I going to do?"

Maria just sat and looked down at the coffee table. The fire she'd shown a moment ago was gone, and she appeared to be in shock. Although Kari wasn't too steady on her own feet, she hurried to the kitchen and grabbed a cold soda from the fridge.

"Drink this," she said, popping the top and handing it to Maria. The woman had been sandwiched inside a cardboard box for three hours and attacked by strange men five minutes after getting out. It was no wonder she was catatonic.

Maria sipped the soda and stayed quiet. After a few moments her eyes lost the faraway glaze.

"Are you all right?" Kari asked, putting a hand on her arm.

Maria nodded. "The last time I crossed the border,

I came with coyotes. They were bad men, like those. Rough . . . with women."

Kari understood what Maria was saying, and she knew all about abusive men. They were the reason Sasha couldn't handle sobriety. "I'm so sorry," she said, letting her hand drop. "I never would have brought you here if I'd known they were coming."

"They have . . . come before?"

"No. I've seen the bigger one with my sister's boyfriend. Carlos Moreno."

Maria recognized the name. It was well known on both sides of the border. "We are in very much trouble, yes?"

"*I'm* in trouble," Kari corrected. "You don't have to be. I'll take you back home."

Maria put her soda on the coffee table. "Tijuana is not my home. It is just a middle place."

"Where are you from?"

"Southern Mexico. And I cannot return with empty hands. My family needs the money I will send them."

Kari furrowed a hand through her hair, frowning. Maria could disappear in the city, get a job elsewhere. She didn't have to go home—but she couldn't stay here. "These are dangerous men, Maria. Cold-blooded killers."

"I waited four years to return to the U.S.," she said, her voice quiet with determination. "I saved every peso for the trip."

"You can find a different job, a safer place."

Maria reached out, grasping her hand once again. "I don't want to leave," she said, meeting her eyes. "You helped me. Now I help you."

Kari glanced away, uncomfortable. She felt awful

about bringing Maria into this, but she didn't know what else to do. Going to the police wasn't an option. She couldn't tell her mother or phone a friend. As horrible as it sounded, she was glad for Maria's company. She didn't want to be alone right now.

"Everything will be okay," Maria insisted, patting her hand.

Kari gave her a wobbly smile, feeling the hot pressure of tears behind her eyes, along with the endless well of guilt in the pit of her stomach. "I hope so."

Sasha was the only family member she had. Their mother had died when Kari was eight, their father ten years later. Kari had been responsible for Sasha since they were teenagers, but she hadn't been a very good caretaker. She'd let her sister down in the worst way, and she'd do anything to make things right between them.

Adam drove by Zócalo first, noting that the store was closed on Tuesdays.

He continued to a quiet neighborhood in Bonita. Strauss's van was parked in her driveway. Afternoon shadows stretched across the front lawn. Less than an hour had elapsed since she passed through San Ysidro.

He parked a few houses down and waited, easing back into secret surveillance as if the job had been tailored for him. It felt good, like lighting up a cigarette after years of abstinence. Right and wrong and oh so illicit. The best bad habit.

When Chuy Pena strolled out the front door, laughing, Adam couldn't believe his eyes. He grappled for his cell phone, pretending he'd pulled over to make a call, and watched Pena climb behind the wheel of a black Cadillac SUV. Pena and his companion, Armando Villarreal, managed the seedy Hotel del Oro.

Both were connected to Moreno.

Adam followed at a distance, his thoughts racing. He didn't know what he'd expected from the doe-eyed Ms. Strauss, but this wasn't it. For some reason, he felt disappointed. Part of him had hoped that she wasn't mixed up with Moreno.

Several parts of him, actually.

He swore under his breath, adjusting his bruised ego. Why was he surprised? She hadn't unbuttoned her blouse because she *wanted* him.

Moreno's men went to the hotel, their central location for drug sales. Neither carried a package, but that didn't mean anything. Adam passed by the Oro without slowing. He couldn't afford to be seen by Pena or anyone else who might recognize him. The DEA probably had undercover agents working this area.

He headed home to Otay, brooding over the sequence of events. As soon as he arrived, he saw a tall, scruffy-looking man with a duffel bag at his front step. He pulled into the garage and got out of his car, feeling surly. He wasn't in the mood to be panhandled.

The instant Adam rounded the corner, the stranger jumped to his feet. "Got any spare change, mister?"

Adam did a double take, letting out a low laugh. It was his best friend, Ian Foster. "Fuck, man. Have you been sleeping in garbage?"

"Pretty much. My base has rats."

Adam unlocked the door and gestured for Ian to come in. His friend's dark brown hair was longer than usual, curling around his collar, and he sported a scraggly goatee. With his sweat-stained T-shirt and ripped jeans, he looked like hell. Only his smile was clean. "You're a disgusting mess. Don't stain my couch."

Ian took that as an invitation to sit down.

Adam went straight to the fridge, grabbing a bottle of Pacifico for himself and a Penafiel for Ian, who didn't drink beer. He opened both and brought them to the living room, taking a seat next to his friend.

Ian accepted the imported soda and stared at the bottle for a moment, turning it in his hands. Adam's mother had always bought this kind of soft drink when they were growing up, so it carried a kind of sentimental value. He knew Ian missed her—they both did.

"Thanks," he said, taking a long swallow.

Adam thought that Ian had lost a few pounds. He was leaner than ever, all ropy muscles and sharp elbows. "How's it going?"

Ian shook his head. He couldn't talk about the specifics of his assignment. A visit like this was rare, and Adam was glad to see him, despite his broken-down appearance. "I find myself practicing, even when I'm alone. Staying in character."

"Come back to CBP," Adam said, naming the Department of Customs and Border Protection. Ian used to work border patrol, hunting coyotes in the desert.

"It's not that bad," he said.

Instead of pressing the issue, Adam drank his beer. Ian had never loved CBP like he did. Adam's family had been here—legally—for several generations, so he felt very strongly about enforcing immigration laws.

Ian didn't have the same conviction. He'd told Adam that he didn't feel right about arresting good, hardworking people. Four years ago, Ian had reached the end of his rope. He'd found a girl on the dunes, raped and beaten within an inch of her life. The attack hadn't happened on U.S. soil, so they couldn't investigate. After the girl was sent back to Mexico, Ian resigned from his position.

Adam had seen his share of tragedies, but he wasn't as conflicted about the job. The department he worked for stopped terrorists and arrested drug smugglers. They protected the country from attack. It wasn't a lost cause.

"How's your sister?" Ian asked.

Adam smiled, leaning back against the couch. "Pregnant again."

His face lit up at the good news. "Goddamn, man. How many kids is she going to have?"

Adam laughed. This was only number three.

"Tell her congrats for me."

He promised he would, and they caught up on other family members for a few minutes. The only person they didn't talk about was Ian's mother. Adam already knew how she was doing—poorly.

Ian shot him a canny look. "Are you ghosting again?"

Adam froze. "What makes you say that?"

"Just a hunch," he said, meeting his gaze. "Something I saw in your expression, right before you recognized me."

Adam rubbed a hand over his mouth, uncomfortable with the assessment. He didn't want to be so transparent. And his obsession with Moreno was an ugly thing. "I saw Karina Strauss at the border today," he admitted.

"Who's that?"

"Sasha Strauss's sister."

"Ah."

"They look alike," Adam said, getting defensive. He didn't run a background check on every Strauss he met.

"Pale and skinny?"

"No." The resemblance was in their facial features, he supposed. "Definitely not skinny. She's more . . . healthy-looking."

Ian's brows rose. "Sounds like you did a thorough inspection, officer."

"Her shirt was unbuttoned down to here," he explained, touching the middle of his chest. "And she came on to me."

"Really?"

"I think she was trying to distract me."

"Maybe she just wanted to jump your bones," Ian said, smirking.

Yeah, he wished. The presence of Moreno's men at her house killed that fantasy. Adam was almost sorry he'd driven by.

"Was she carrying?"

"I don't know," Adam said. "There was a disturbance down the line, and I let her pass through."

"You didn't check her vehicle?"

"No."

Ian stared at him, astounded. "Why, because you liked her tits?"

"They were pretty spectacular," he said with a smile, evasive. He didn't want Ian to know how easily he'd fallen back on old habits. Keeping secrets from the department, ghosting suspects after hours. He had no business following Karina Strauss.

"You need to get laid," Ian decided, scratching his chin.

Adam made a scoffing sound. "Look who's talking. I know you haven't gotten any lately. You reek, dude."

"I could use a shower."

"Go ahead," Adam said. He also offered his spare bedroom, which was always open to Ian when he needed it. His friend worked so much deep undercover it didn't make sense for him to rent his own place.

"Don't mind if I do," he said, rising to his feet. "Is there a game on?"

Adam grabbed the remote to check. "Padres."

"Sweet. I'll be out in a few."

They spent the remainder of the evening watching baseball. It was a comfortable, bachelor-style existence. At one time Adam might have suggested an outing to liven things up. Now they both preferred to stay in. Ian had never been a fan of the club scene, anyway. He wasn't the no-strings type. While on assignment, he wouldn't engage in a one-night stand if a woman threw herself at his feet.

Adam, on the other hand, had no qualms about casual hookups. During his self-destructive phase, he'd often trolled for women at bars, searching for someone who wasn't there. Like tailing Moreno, it was a pointless exercise. Sleeping with strangers was almost as unsatisfying as sleeping alone.

No one could fill the void Penelope left.

The last woman he'd gone home with had resembled his ex in a superficial way. He'd stayed later than usual, studying the way her dark hair spilled across the pillow. For several moments he was awash with memories, his chest aching.

He hadn't been with anyone since.

Karina Strauss didn't look like Penelope. He considered that a plus. There was also no danger of him developing feelings for a drug smuggler. Anyone involved in that business had earned his contempt.

Using her to get to Moreno would be his pleasure.

He said goodnight to Ian, who was already dozing on the couch, and went to his room. Tucking his hands behind his head, he stared at the ceiling, ignoring the empty space beside him. He'd relegated his favorite photo of Penelope to the top drawer.

Instead of taking it out, he conjured a vivid mental image of Karina Strauss. Although he couldn't fault her face or figure, he resented her for being clear and vibrant, while his memories of Penelope had faded.

3

Kari awoke with a plan.

She rose and dressed quickly, looking forward to an early jog. Morning was her favorite time of day, cool and quiet. She stepped out on the sidewalk and took off at a steady pace, gaining momentum as she rounded the block. Soon her body felt strong and her mind alert, ready to conquer any obstacle.

She completed her usual three-mile loop and came to a stop in the front yard, panting lightly in the shade of an overgrown ficus. Feeling renewed, covered in a light sweat, she went back inside.

Maria was standing at the stove, her hair mussed. An oversized nightgown hung from her slim frame, almost touching the floor. Her bare toes peeped out from under the hem. "Is okay if I cook?" she asked, spatula in hand.

Nodding, Kari poured herself a glass of water. After slaking her thirst, she said, "I thought of something."

Maria turned off the burner. "What?"

"I'll talk to my sister. Convince her to leave Moreno, enter a witness protection program. Whatever it takes."

"Witness program?"

"It's when the government gives you a new identity, new name. She'll have to move away, and I might not see her again, but she'd be safe."

"And you will be safe also, yes?"

Kari didn't think she'd be relocated. Once Sasha was out of Moreno's clutches, he couldn't blackmail her. Problem solved. "Yes."

Maria looked doubtful. "Your sister wants to leave her boyfriend?"

Kari took another sip of water, deliberating. Sasha wanted to do drugs, go shopping, and party all night. "When I tell her we're both in danger, she'll come around," she said, optimistic. Her sister would see reason. She had to.

They sat down for a light breakfast of eggs, fresh fruit, and toast. "This looks good," Kari said, digging in.

"You talk to sister today," Maria said, taking a bite, "and I go to work at hotel."

"Are you sure?" she asked, surprised.

"Yes. I need money, and it is better to act . . . *tranquilas*."

Kari smiled, remembering Maria's hostile attitude toward Moreno's men. She hadn't looked very peaceful yesterday afternoon. "Okay," she said. "I agree that pretending to cooperate is a good idea."

"This job is for maid, nothing more?"

Maria's trepidation was warranted—many illegal activities occurred at the Hotel del Oro. "I think so," Kari said, "but that place is full of bad men. If someone tries to grab you, run away. My store is close by."

"*Bueno,*" she said, fearless. "I don't mind cleaning hotel rooms, but I have never worked on my back."

Kari wished that Sasha had the same amount of self-respect. She finished her breakfast and left the table to get ready, hoping her sister would realize she'd hit rock bottom. After a cool, soothing shower, she slipped into a white cotton peasant dress, adding a colorful woven belt and brown leather sandals.

When she came out of her bedroom, she saw that Maria had also transformed her appearance. She was wearing baggy jeans and a drab T-shirt, her long hair pulled back into a sleek knot at the nape of her neck.

"What do you think?" she asked Kari.

"You still look pretty."

She squinted at her reflection in the hallway mirror. "Really?"

"Yes."

"Maybe I need a hat."

"I have one," Kari said, rummaging through her closet for an army-green baseball cap that she'd never worn.

Maria donned it with relish, pulling the bill down low on her forehead.

"That makes a big difference," Kari mused. The cap didn't turn Maria into a troll, but it disguised her best features. Her elegant, wing-shaped brows and thickly lashed brown eyes were cast in shadow, and her shiny hair was hidden.

"I am Ugly Betty, yes?"

Kari laughed. "Not quite."

Maria turned away from the mirror, her gaze wandering over Kari's dress. "You would not be able to hide from men."

Kari made a rueful agreement, acknowledging that

her curvy figure attracted attention. She didn't try to downplay her femininity anymore; it was a lost cause.

"Why no husband or boyfriend for you?"

"I'm always working," she said with a sigh. "And very few eligible bachelors come to my boutique."

"What is bachelor? *Un soltero?*"

"Yes. I met my last boyfriend at the grocery store." Brendan had been a firefighter, handsome and charming. They'd hit it off really well at first, but their opposing work schedules made spending time together difficult. Neglected too long, the spark burned out. "We broke up last summer," she said, frowning at the memory. She couldn't believe it had been so long. "How about you? Do you have someone special?"

She shook her head. "There was a boy in my village, but he found another."

"Men," Kari muttered, understanding exactly how Maria felt. Brendan had started seeing someone else *before* they split up.

"They say that Tijuana is a city of heartbreak."

She imagined there were just as many failed relationships on this side of the border, if not more, but she knew that TJ was filled with men who'd left their wives behind. It also had a booming sex industry and rampant crime. Every year it became more dangerous for Kari to shop for inventory there.

"Then maybe San Diego is the place for starting over," she replied.

They left the house just before 9:00 a.m., opening time at Zócalo. During the summer season, Kari kept extended hours. On Tuesday, her only day off, she locked the doors for her weekly trips to Mexico. It was a hectic schedule, but business was good.

Zócalo had started to turn a healthy profit for several reasons. First, she was picky about the merchandise. She carried a wide range of figurines and folk art, many inexpensive, but none poorly made. Some of her pottery pieces were gallery-worthy.

The store also had a choice location. It was close enough to Old Town to draw in tourists, but far enough to avoid the traffic gridlock. A few blocks south, the neighborhood deteriorated into seedy hotels and run-down apartment complexes, but Kari didn't mind. She liked the hustle and bustle of downtown, the noise and vibrancy. There were several parks and historic buildings within walking distance.

The third reason for increased sales could be attributed to changes within Mexico. Passports were required for all U.S. citizens now, so fewer shoppers were walking across the border to browse. Tight security made traveling by car more time consuming. And an upswing in violent crime, compliments of the drug cartels, discouraged tourism to Tijuana.

Kari sold a lot of items online, and she'd been attracting plenty of foot traffic as well. This summer had been her busiest yet.

She parked the van in the loading zone, near the back entrance. Maria helped her carry the boxes into the storeroom. When that task was done, Kari unlocked the front door, flipping the OPEN sign around to face forward. "Hotel del Oro is just three blocks down, on the right," she said, pointing.

Maria nodded, looking in that direction.

Kari remembered the extra can of pepper spray she kept under the counter, near the cash register. "Take this," she said, handing it to Maria.

"For the eyes?" she asked, mimicking a spraying motion.

"Exactly."

Maria clipped the small black canister to the waistband of her jeans, flashing Kari a thankful smile. Her chipped tooth gave her a cute, quirky edge. As she straightened her blouse, bells chimed at the entrance, signaling a customer.

Kari watched, her mouth dropping open, as Officer A. Cortez walked through the front door. He was wearing dark sunglasses again, but she recognized him instantly. The man was an eye magnet. His white T-shirt fit well, hinting at a flat stomach and hard chest. The jeans he was wearing were the comfortable kind, wash-faded, and saved from riding too low on his hips by a black leather belt.

Kari stared. Maria stared.

He removed his sunglasses, hooking them to the neck of his T-shirt.

A couple of thoughts occurred to her. First, he had brown eyes, as she'd suspected. Second, he wasn't in uniform. He might not be here to arrest her. "Hello," she said, pasting on an awkward smile.

He nodded, browsing the shelves.

Kari dragged Maria out the front door, which was difficult because her new friend was still gazing at A. Cortez.

"Good luck," she said to Maria, meaning *get lost*.

Maria didn't ask who Kari's customer was, but she seemed to realize it was time for her to leave. "Thanks," she said, giving Kari a warm hug, followed by a friendly kiss on the cheek. "You too."

Maria took off in the direction of the hotel, and Kari

went back inside, her heart pounding. Although Cortez was still perusing the inventory, she got the impression that he'd watched her say goodbye to Maria.

What did he *want*?

Maybe this was a coincidence. A bizarre, untimely co-incidence.

As she made her way to the front counter, she felt his eyes following her, and it dawned on her that his visit might be . . . personal in nature. She'd almost flashed her breasts at him yesterday. He hadn't seemed impressed, but he'd been on duty. It wouldn't have been professional of him to ogle her.

A different sort of tension filled her body, making her skin flush and her hairline tingle. This was not good. She had to get rid of him. But what excuse could she give for coming on to him one day and snubbing him the next?

She fumbled for a bottle of water behind the counter, taking a quick sip. There was only one thing to do: feign innocence. Encouraging him would be very stupid. Her sister had drug cartel connections, and she was harboring an illegal alien!

Squaring her shoulders, she pushed away from the counter, approaching him as she would any customer. He was studying the Day of the Dead figurines, her most popular items. Again she noticed how handsome he was. Her last boyfriend, Brendan, had also been nice to look at, but she couldn't remember having this strong a reaction to him. Maybe fear had heightened her senses, causing her to fixate on irrelevant details.

As she stepped closer she detected a hint of spicy soap. His clean, masculine scent unnerved her. She stared at his smooth brown throat, trying not to breathe him in. The fact that he was attractive made her more nervous.

She was both drawn to and repelled by him. This man was a threat to her livelihood—and her libido.

"Is there anything I can help you with?" she asked, her voice wavering.

He gave her a speculative glance. "Do you remember me?"

She moistened her lips. "Yes."

"I saw the sign on your van," he explained, gesturing to the dancing skeleton figurines. "My mother collects these."

Kari almost sagged against the shelves, giddy with relief. Apparently he wasn't here to arrest her *or* to flirt with her. He was just a nice guy buying a gift for his mother. How embarrassing.

"Now I realize that I should have studied her collection before I came in," he said, rubbing a hand over his jaw. "I'm not sure which ones she already has."

Her brain kicked back into gear. "The figurines are fairly common," she admitted. "No two are exactly alike, because they're handmade, but many are similar."

"Some of them look familiar."

"All of the pieces in the display case are one of a kind," she said, trying a different tack. The skeleton-embossed stemware and blown-glass skulls were unique, original, and much more expensive than the papier-mâché sculptures.

"I think she only collects the figurines."

"If she's been here before, I can access her previous purchases," Kari offered.

"No," he said quickly. "She always shops in Mexico. I'll take a look at her shelves and come back."

Kari walked toward the register, picking up her newest catalogue. "Many of the skeleton figurines are shown here, and I have a bigger selection online," she said, flipping through the glossy pages.

He didn't glance at the catalogue, but another display caught his eye. Between the Day of the Dead memorabilia and the impulse items at the front counter, there was a wicker basket full of baby gifts. Tiny little socks, alpaca wool mittens, soft knit caps. Grandmothers couldn't resist such adorable things.

"What's this?" he asked, fingering a colorful silk-blend garment.

"It's a *rebozo*," she said, moving forward to demonstrate. She draped the fabric around her neck, fashioning a sturdy knot at one shoulder and leaving a little pouch over her belly. "For a baby?"

He nodded, recognizing the traditional infant carrier as soon as he saw it on her.

"Some women wear them on their shoulders, as a shawl," Kari explained in a rush. "It can also be used in many different ways."

His gaze met hers, curious. Her cheeks heated under his examination. She'd been self-conscious before; now she was squirming. There was something unbearably intimate about modeling an infant sling. She felt more exposed than she had been yesterday, as if her secret desires were written all over her face.

He seemed intrigued by her discomfort. "I'll take it."

Kari removed the sling with care, untying the knot and folding the garment neatly on the glass-top counter. Maybe he was picturing his wife or girlfriend in the *rebozo*. Although he wasn't wearing a wedding ring, that didn't mean he was single. He might be happily married, the proud father of a half-dozen children.

"Would you like it gift-wrapped?" she asked in a formal tone.

"Sure," he said, his mouth quirking into a smile. "It's for my sister. She's expecting."

"Oh," she said, smiling back at him. A pregnant sister was much less disturbing to her conscience than a pregnant wife. She ducked below the counter, where she kept the tissue paper, and tried to squelch a tingle of excitement.

"Is this her first?" she asked.

"No, her third. She has a boy and a girl already." He said this with affection, his eyes crinkled up at the corners.

Kari's heart melted at the sight. She put a bow on the gift bag and turned to the cash register, ordering herself to stop staring at him. One of the reasons she'd been attracted to Brendan was because he'd seemed like excellent father material. She saw some of the same qualities in Officer Cortez. Heroic job, athletic physique, rugged good looks. He appeared to respect his mother and love his sister.

She named the price, and he took a wallet out of his front pocket. It was black leather, like his belt, embossed with an eagle. He placed two crisp bills in her upturned palm and she processed the transaction, watching him put the change away. His hands looked strong. She wondered how they would feel against her skin: callused or smooth, rough or gentle.

Blushing, she pushed the gift bag across the counter. "Have a nice day."

He picked it up, glancing around the store. She thought he might ask her another question about the figurines, but he didn't. "You too," he said, putting his sunglasses back on. Carrying the package under one arm like a football, he left.

Kari wasn't sorry to see him go. At any other time, she'd have enjoyed the attention of a good-looking guy. Right now Cortez was a dangerous distraction. She couldn't afford to keep company with a border protection officer.

Her sister's life was in danger.

When her pulse slowed and her breathing returned to normal, she picked up the phone to call Sasha.

Maria entered the hotel's front lobby, studying her surroundings while the receptionist gave a key card to an amorous couple.

The man palmed the woman's backside, giving it a firm squeeze.

Cheaters, she guessed, dropping her gaze. Only newlyweds and teenagers groped each other in public like that. But these two weren't young, and this place was no honeymoon getaway.

The Hotel del Oro had "good bones," she believed the term was in English. It was Spanish-style colonial with an open courtyard and stucco exterior. The exposed beams and arched entryways were a nice touch, but there were also signs of corruption and disrepair: chipped paint, broken tiles, outdated light fixtures.

Maria felt right at home. She'd worked in hotels like this before.

After the couple paid for their room—by the hour, she noted with an inward shudder—Maria stepped up to the front desk.

"Can I help you?" the receptionist asked in Spanish, a

bored look in her eyes. She was young and pretty and glamorous, trapped in an easy, dead-end job she felt was beneath her. Maria imagined that she wanted more from life. Her name tag said Sonia.

"I'm Maria, the new maid."

"We're not hiring."

"I spoke with Señor Pena yesterday," she explained. "He told me to come in."

Sonia gave Maria another once-over, her smooth brow furrowing. Maria got the impression that she was summing up the female competition. Perhaps she was Pena's girlfriend. Maria slouched a little, trying to look unattractive. Dismissing her as a threat, Sonia picked up the phone to check out her story.

Maria relaxed a little, glad for the "disguise." This receptionist might have turned her out on her ear had she looked halfway decent, and Maria needed this job. Kari seemed to think she could convince her sister to leave Carlos Moreno, but Maria was skeptical. She had a backup plan—to collect dirt on Moreno's men. They didn't know she understood English. Maybe, while she was cleaning up after them, something would slip.

At the very least, she could earn money to send home.

Sonia hung up the phone and busied herself with paperwork, not bothering to tell Maria her fate. After a few moments, an older woman in a blue smock appeared. She had sturdy black shoes, a round face, and graying hair.

Maria stepped forward to introduce herself.

The head housekeeper, Irma, was no friendlier than the receptionist. Ignoring Maria's greeting, she led her away from the lobby to a laundry room that was overflowing with sheets and towels.

Irma handed Maria a uniform shirt, gave her a supply cart, and took her up to the second floor. Then she lit a cigarette, gesturing for Maria to get started. "You've worked in a hotel before?" she asked in Spanish.

Maria nodded, her arms full of cleaning products.

"You should take off your hat."

"I'd rather not."

Irma shrugged, puffing on her cigarette. She didn't care.

Maria went through the motions quickly, collecting the dirty sheets and towels, emptying the trash and ashtrays. When the room was spotless and stocked with the meager amenities available, she stuck her head out the open door.

"Finished?" Irma asked.

"Yes."

She inspected the interior, offering no praise or criticism. "*Bueno,*" she said finally. "You're responsible for this entire floor."

Maria didn't complain, although it was a huge amount of work. There were ten or twelve more rooms that needed service, from what she could tell, and it wasn't even checkout time yet. She'd have to move fast to keep up.

"Don't poke around anywhere else," Irma continued. "Put your trash in the dumpster, and do your own laundry."

She only had one question. "When do I get paid?"

"Friday."

Irma left her alone and Maria got down to work. By noon, she was sweating, resenting the itchy baseball cap on her head and the voluminous T-shirt under her smock. She didn't stop cleaning for lunch, but she drank plenty of water.

At the end of the day, when the work was done, she felt drained but satisfied. After returning her cart to the laundry room, she trudged across the courtyard, almost bumping into a man who'd walked in off the street.

"Excuse me," he said in a low voice, going around her.

He was tall, dark-haired, sort of rough-looking. His T-shirt was dingy, his jeans were torn, and his goatee was scraggly. He seemed on edge and a little scary. Not the kind of person she wanted to stop and chat with.

And yet she did stop. Because . . . she *knew* him. His appearance had changed dramatically, but she knew him. When he glanced back at her, their gazes locked for a moment. She'd never forget those eyes, a calm hazel, fringed by dark lashes.

This was the last place she expected to see him. The man who'd saved her life.

4

Maria.

It was almost as if Ian's subconscious recognized her first. He'd noticed the slight figure in the baseball cap but he hadn't studied her closely. His job was to focus on the men who came and went here. Chuy didn't have any female customers.

He was aware that she'd stopped in her tracks, which was odd. These days, women crossed the street to avoid his path. Sensing her stare, he'd glanced back. Their eyes met for a split second before she turned and kept walking, her head down.

Maria Santos.

What the hell was she doing at the Hotel del Oro? Cleaning rooms, apparently. There was a pale blue smock slung over her shoulder.

Ian didn't think she remembered him. He hardly knew his own face in the mirror anymore, and years had passed since she'd seen him. She'd also been only semiconscious during most of their interactions. She might have fuzzy memories of a clean-cut border agent, but he doubted she could reconcile those images with the man he appeared to be now.

Maybe she'd paused to size him up as a possible safety threat. Or, worse, a messy hotel guest.

No worries on that front. Unlike Chuy, he didn't live here.

Ian was almost certain she hadn't recognized him, but he felt pretty confident in his identification of her. Even with the hat pulled down low on her forehead and a shapeless T-shirt disguising her slender curves, he knew her. He knew the shape of her face, with its fine features and dramatic eyebrows.

He'd memorized every detail.

The last time he'd visited her, the bruises on her neck were fading and the swelling on her cheek had gone down. He remembered holding her hand, rubbing his thumb over the delicate bones in her wrist.

Ian shook his head, impatient with himself. He'd done this before. There were thousands of young, pretty Hispanic girls in San Diego. More than once he'd thought he'd seen Maria, only to realize his mistake when he got closer.

That's all it was. His imagination. A remnant of a dream.

As hallucinations went, this was the most disturbing to date. If it *was* her, his cover might be blown.

Brushing the matter aside for now, he continued through the dilapidated courtyard, toward Chuy's apartments. The dealer inhabited two rooms on the first floor, a manager's suite and small office. It was a cover for his real business, which included distributing black tar heroin to a variety of buyers.

Chuy's partner, Armando Villarreal, did most of the

dirty work. A jack of all trades, Armando managed the seedy hotel, watched Chuy's back, and provided a bit of extra muscle when the situation called for it.

At the moment, Armando was leaning against a stucco pillar outside Chuy's office, whittling a small figure out of wood. His movements were quick, silent, precise. He had a sharp knife and a good eye for detail.

"Don't fuck with the maids," Armando said, not glancing up.

Ian realized he'd been caught staring. It wasn't a big deal—most men noticed attractive women. Damned if he was going to apologize for it. He nodded vaguely, wondering if Armando had staked a claim on her.

A few seconds later, the office doorknob turned, and Sonia Barreras walked out, straightening her pencil-slim skirt. She had little bumps on her knees from the carpet. It was a telltale sign, like her worn-off lipstick.

Ian felt a twinge of envy. He hadn't had a blow job in ages.

Sonia avoided his gaze, but he saw the hard glint in her eye. She was the kind of woman who enjoyed the reward, not the task. Or perhaps it was more accurate to say that Chuy didn't care what women liked.

Both Ian and Armando watched her go, appreciating the view. Armando didn't bother to issue another warning; only a man with a death wish would touch Chuy's property. Armando lifted his chin, gesturing for Ian to enter the office.

Chuy was sitting behind the desk, sweat dotting his forehead, his face languid with satisfaction. Lucky bastard. "What do you want?"

"The usual," Ian said, tossing a wad of cash on the surface of the desk.

Chuy didn't rush to fill the order, and the wait was nerve-racking. Ian never knew if he would end up looking down the barrel of an AK. Undercover officers got killed in the line of duty all the time. Whenever Ian made a buy, he was risking his life.

But he was also collecting useful information. Earning trust. Practicing mannerisms, playing his part. An anxious cop and a craving addict would exhibit some of the same behaviors, so he didn't bother to hide his natural reaction to the stress. Chuy expected him to fidget, sweat, and stutter his words.

Ian had been raised by a junkie, immersed in a world of chaos and dysfunction, so he knew what dopesick looked like. For his mother, every day revolved around getting high. Ian had been surprised to discover *straight* people as a child.

Now he lived in a hovel apartment like a hard-core addict, under conditions similar to those he'd known as a kid. It would have been a nightmarish existence for anyone, and it was especially hard on Ian, but he had to stay strong.

He chose this. He liked living on the edge.

Finally Chuy handed Ian a small balloon, which he shoved into his pocket, not having to feign impatience.

"I'm getting a new shipment in soon. Some primo shit."

Ian moistened his lips, torn between wanting to get the fuck out of there and needing to hear the scoop. "What kind?"

Chuy smiled lazily, his eyes half-lidded. Maybe he'd been chasing the dragon himself this afternoon. Either that, or Sonia did a lot better work on her knees than in the front lobby. *"Blanca nieves."*

Snow White.

White powder heroin was unusual in this area, where black tar ruled. Some addicts believed that one type was stronger than the other, but it really depended on the batch. All users were tempted by a unique mix that might take them to staggering heights.

A shipment of *nieve* could also be traced back to its source more easily. Different drugs meant new connections, new alliances . . . new leads.

"When?"

Chuy laughed at Ian's eager expression. "You junkies are all the same. Freaking slaves to the high."

Ian let his face go blank. "I prefer black myself."

"Okay," Chuy said, leaning back in his chair. He could bluff, too. "No problem."

"My customers might want a sample," Ian conceded.

Chuy shrugged, making no promises. "We'll see."

Muttering his thanks, Ian left the office. Armando was putting the finishing touches on a fist-sized wooden donkey. The animal was often referenced in the dealer-buyer relationship. Coyotes ran mules across the border, backpacks loaded with drugs.

Armando glanced up at him, arching a brow.

Ian's mouth twisted at the implication. Chuy had just insulted him, and now Armando appeared to be suggesting that he was a stupid animal. If Ian didn't feel the same way about drug slingers, he might have been offended.

"Later," he said to Armando, walking away.

Of the two men, Ian would much rather wrangle with Chuy. He was a ruthless son of a bitch, straight up. Chuy Pena would shoot you in the face. Armando was quieter, harder to read. He'd slide a knife between your ribs and you'd never see him coming.

Ian went "home," his steps heavy. He didn't want to dwell on the possible Maria sighting. Maybe he was cracking under pressure. His appetite was down due to low activity and high anxiety. He hadn't been this lean since he was a teenager.

He felt weak, physically and mentally. Working out was his favorite stress reliever, but he couldn't look too fit for the role. Most addicts didn't lift weights, and the only time a junkie went running was when the cops were after him.

The apartment building Ian lived in consisted of standard, economical units. There were a few decent people here, trying to save money and get ahead, but many of the residents were addicts. On the outside, it was basic, cheap-looking, and worn down. Inside, the conditions deteriorated sharply. It wasn't unusual to see a group of kids smoking pot or a prostitute taking a john up the stairs.

He locked the door, shutting them out, and lay down on his unmade bed. Staring at nothing. Thinking of Maria.

Kari didn't get in touch with Sasha until late afternoon.

Her sister ignored most of her calls, and sometimes they went weeks without speaking. Kari was careful not to leave too many messages or hint at any trouble; Sasha avoided emotional drama like the plague.

When Sasha finally picked up, her voice was scratchy from sleep. "Hello?"

"What are you doing?"

"Nothing," Sasha mumbled. In the background, cellophane from a cigarette pack rustled, followed by the flick of a lighter. "I have a headache."

Kari's spirits plummeted. Her sister complained of frequent migraines and often stayed in bed for days. So much for getting together right now. "I'd like to see you," she said anyway. "Are you free tomorrow?"

Sasha took a drag of her cigarette, mumbling something about being tired. She was always tired—or busy. For a girl who didn't work, go to college, or have any meaningful hobbies, she managed to stay very busy.

"I thought we might have dinner, do a little shopping."

Sasha was quiet for a moment. "Shopping?"

"Yes," Kari said, struck by inspiration. "I need a new dress."

"For what?"

"A date," she said, fingers crossed.

If there was anything Sasha was still interested in, besides shopping, it was Kari's sex life. Or lack thereof. Whenever Kari expressed disapproval about Sasha's relationship with Moreno or concern about her dangerous habits, Sasha was quick to criticize Kari's solitary existence in return.

"With who?" Sasha asked, intrigued.

"A really hot guy," she said, picturing Officer Cortez. "We just met at the store. He asked me out."

"What does he look like?"

"Black hair, brown eyes."

"How old?"

"Late twenties, I think."

"Is he built?"

"Mm-hmm. Athletic, but not bulky. Kind of like a soccer player."

"A soccer player?" Sasha exhaled with a rough laugh. "Sounds promising."

"I don't have anything sexy to wear."

"That's for sure."

"Will you help me? You know so much more about clothes than I do. And we're going out on Friday, so it's kind of urgent." Sasha used to dream about being a designer, so a fashion emergency was right up her alley.

"I don't know. . . ."

"Come on, Sasha," she said, almost there. "You cancelled our beach plans last week, and after I agreed to that awful bikini wax appointment—"

"Okay, okay," she said, laughing again.

Kari clenched her hand into a fist and brought it closer to her body, a silent expression of victory. "You're a lifesaver."

"Anything to keep you from buying another shapeless hippie dress."

She glanced down at her current outfit, frowning. It was a little bohemian, maybe, but not shapeless. She'd always favored comfortable, lightweight fabrics and simple styles. Her peasant blouses and gypsy skirts suited the store's ambiance. Kari didn't think she needed to change her work image. "Are they that bad?"

"They aren't exactly cutting edge."

"Next you'll accuse me of wearing muumuus."

"It's a slippery slope," Sasha warned. "This year loose frock, next year flowered housedress."

Kari smiled at her sister's wry tone. Sasha sounded sharp today, and upbeat despite her headache. It was a refreshing change from her typical drug haze. Sometimes she slurred her words and nodded off in the middle of a conversation.

They decided to meet at the mall after work, and Kari hung up the phone, feeling optimistic. She hated lying to her sister, but it was the only way to get the job done. She had to speak with Sasha in person. Moreno often screened Sasha's calls and monitored her activities. Kari prayed that her sister would show up tomorrow.

She turned the sign in the window to CLOSED and went outside, crossing her arms over her chest. The setting sun bathed the storefront in bright gold, and the still-hot sidewalk warmed the soles of her leather sandals. Although rush hour was almost over, the neighborhood was far from quiet. Cars passed by at full speed, while women carrying groceries shuffled home.

Kari cupped a hand over her brow and glanced down the street, toward the Hotel del Oro. Maria was walking in her direction.

For some reason, the sight brought tears to Kari's eyes. She'd had a long day boxing shipments in the storage room. Maria must have had a longer one, doing hard manual labor without the luxury of air-conditioning.

Kari waved, blinking away the tears. She realized that she'd been afraid Maria wouldn't come back. They'd only known each other a short time, and Kari was already attached. Maybe some of her fears and concerns for Sasha had transferred to Maria. She'd been trying, and failing, to reconnect with her sister for years.

On impulse, she gave Maria a hello hug. Her body felt slender but not delicate. She was like a reed that bent but wouldn't break.

"How did it go?" she asked, studying Maria's tired, pretty face.

"Fine."

Kari released her and went inside, gesturing for Maria to follow. "Did you see any of Moreno's men?"

"No. I saw laundry, and bathrooms, and beds."

Relieved, Kari locked the door behind her and grabbed her purse, setting the alarm before they stepped into the back alley. "I talked to my sister," she said, walking toward her van. "We're having dinner tomorrow."

Maria climbed into the passenger side. "That's good."

"You remember the man from this morning?"

She closed her eyes with a sigh, as if pleased to be sitting down. "Who could forget him?"

"He's the border officer I met yesterday."

Her eyes flew open. "No!"

"Yes."

"That is not good."

Kari agreed that it wasn't. "He said he was looking for a gift for his mother."

Maria's expression was doubtful. Then she narrowed her gaze on Kari's décolletage. "Maybe he wanted another look at your *pechos*."

"I don't know," Kari said. "He was very polite."

"He did not act . . . strange?"

She pulled out of the parking lot, deliberating. If he suspected her of breaking the law, why hadn't he questioned her officially? His behavior hadn't been that of a man in search of an easy lay, either. She shivered, remembering the way he'd stared at her when she tried on the *rebozo*. Something weird had happened between them. For a moment it had seemed as though he'd been picturing her with a baby. *His* baby.

Kari gave herself a stern mental shake. That idea was

ridiculous. It was far more likely that he'd been imagining her naked—or in handcuffs.

"I saw someone also," Maria said, letting her previous question drop.

"Who?"

"A guest at the hotel. I knew him."

"You knew him?" Kari glanced from the road to Maria's face. "How?"

She seemed pensive. "I told you that I came to the U.S. once before. I was lost in the desert. He . . . found me, I think."

Kari's mouth fell open. "You *think* he found you in the desert?"

"I was not well," she explained, touching her throat. "I went to hospital."

"My God," Kari said.

"He was *la migra*, but very kind. I remember his eyes."

"You're sure it was him at the hotel?"

"No. He seemed different. Like a thief, or . . . *una sombra*."

A shadow.

Kari was chilled by the description. For the first time, it occurred to her that Officer Cortez might be on Moreno's payroll. The drug lord had deep pockets—of course he bribed members of law enforcement.

"Oh my God," she repeated as the gravity of their predicament sank in. Would Sasha be safe in a witness protection program? Maybe she should cash out her bank account, kidnap her sister, and make a run for it.

"Don't worry," Maria said, rubbing her shoulder. "You talk to sister, I go back to hotel. We will be okay."

Kari took a deep breath, trying to stay calm. She

wished she could borrow half of Maria's equanimity. "Do you think these men are working for Moreno? The one you saw at the hotel, and the border officer?"

She shrugged. "Who knows? In Mexico, some policemen are worse than criminals. We hide from them."

"What do you do when you need help?"

Maria gave her a level stare. "We help ourselves."

5

Karina Strauss didn't act like a drug smuggler.

Adam watched her house from a distance, annoyed by the squeaky-clean image she presented. Yesterday her behavior had been friendly and professional. She'd even seemed embarrassed, as if the sexy vixen routine at the border had been a joke.

He shifted in his seat, picturing the expression on her face when she donned that baby sling for him. She'd looked sort of . . . bare, and vulnerable. Emotionally naked.

Jesus.

There must be something wrong with him to find that appealing. She liked babies—so what? Lots of women did. Usually a ticking biological clock was a major turn-off. His libido must have its wires crossed.

While he pondered the anomaly, she returned from her morning jog, cooling down on the front lawn. She was wearing a snug sports top and nylon jogging shorts. A fine sheen of perspiration was visible on her forehead and upper chest. Breathing hard, she bent forward, resting her hands on her thighs.

Adam acknowledged that she was in great shape. He'd noted this several times now. She had a body like a Playmate. She was curvy and feminine, but firm in all the right places. Drug users didn't have taut thighs, bouncy ponytails, or flawless skin.

Maybe she was innocent.

In the past two days he'd collected some basic information about her. She'd graduated with honors from the University of San Diego, earning a degree in cultural anthropology. Her arrest record was clear. She volunteered for Hands Across the Border. Her father had once owned a chain of popular furniture stores.

On the surface, Karina Strauss was a real Goody Two-shoes.

But criminals didn't always look like lowlifes. Carlos Moreno was handsome and fit. If he used drugs at all these days, he did it sparingly. Addicts broke the law to fuel their habits. Other people had more complicated, and often very compelling, motives.

After she went back inside the house, he took out his laptop, accessing a criminal information database. Chuy Pena had a checkered past and a long record, but Adam already knew that. His partner, Armando Villarreal, was more of a mystery. The Mexican national had been an armed guard in the capital city. Interesting.

Karina came out less than an hour later with the slender Hispanic female he'd seen yesterday. Her companion was wearing light-colored jeans and a pale blue smock. The cap, pulled down low on her forehead, seemed incongruent with her otherwise neat appearance.

He waited a full minute before following, keeping

several car lengths between them. When her van turned into the Hotel del Oro parking lot, he passed on by, swearing under his breath. Doing extracurricular surveillance was a real bitch. He had to worry about being seen by both sides of the law.

About a block away, he pulled over and waited. Karina's van reappeared a moment later, without a passenger.

It dawned on Adam that the smock was a maid uniform. The girl worked there.

Karina parked behind the store and went inside, flipping the sign in the front window, opening for business. Adam lingered a few minutes and drove around back, idling next to her parked van. He had an inexpensive GPS device ready. There didn't appear to be any security cameras in the immediate area. After a quick glance around to make sure no one was watching, he got out and affixed the GPS to the van's chassis.

Now he could track her movements.

The device would need to be recharged eventually, but Adam could triangulate her location until the battery wore out. The tactic was frowned upon in court, but this wasn't a legit investigation. He didn't have to worry about justifying his behavior to a judge. The moment he'd started tailing her, he'd thrown ethics and proper procedure out the window.

It felt pretty good.

He drove around to the front of the store and parked, as if he'd just arrived. His heart started thumping hard in anticipation of seeing her again, and not just because he was here under false pretenses. He liked her.

As he walked through the entrance, a bell chimed to

alert her of his presence. She was behind the counter, staring at a sheet of paper and nibbling on the end of a pencil. Looking up, she met his gaze.

"Back again?" she said, her brows rising.

Yesterday she'd been flustered by his presence. Today she seemed cooler, more reserved. Perhaps it had occurred to her that he was lying about buying a gift for his mother. And he was—sort of.

"It's on my way to work," he said, going straight to the papier-mâché skeletons. "Besides, my mom's birthday is this weekend." That part was true, although no one would be throwing her a party.

Adam picked a tambourine-playing character in an elaborate hat, his mouth twisting at the irony. He was buying a *dia de los muertos* figurine for his mother. Maybe he would give it to her on that day, when Mexicans celebrated the memories of their loved ones.

He brought it to the counter and took out his wallet, glancing at the clock on the wall. His shift started in twenty minutes.

"Gift wrap?" she asked, avoiding his eyes.

"Sure," he said, perusing the store. As a cover for a smuggling operation, it was pretty elaborate. Somewhere between a fine arts museum and a quirky curiosity shop, Zócalo managed to look authentic *and* classy. A lot of the crafts sold in Tijuana were crap, but her inventory looked hand-selected and high-quality. He recognized Oaxacan black pottery and Guatemalan textiles, along with hammered metal jewelry from Copper Canyon. She stocked some inexpensive novelty items, but none of the bobble-head Chihuahuas or faux velvet paintings that were an insult to his culture.

It was a nice place. His sister was going to love the *rebozo*.

With her back to him, Karina folded the figurine in colorful tissue paper, placing it lovingly in a simple brown gift bag. Her dark blond hair was caught up in a tidy knot, leaving her shoulders bare. She was wearing a soft white tank top with a gauzy green skirt. Her skin looked smooth and tanned.

As she reached under the counter for a ribbon, his gaze was drawn to her curvy backside and the lacy outline of her thong panties.

"How's that?" she said, tying the ribbon into a jaunty bow.

Adam managed to avert his gaze, but it took him an extra second to process her question. "Uh, perfect," he said, clearing his throat. She told him the price and he paid in cash. "I like your store."

Pride warmed her honey-colored eyes. "Thanks."

Adam looked around, seeing gleaming shelves and spotless glass. "What's a girl from the Czech Republic doing in a place like this?"

"How do you know where I'm from?"

"Just a guess. I saw the stamps on your passport."

"Oh," she said, flushing at the reminder of their first encounter. She must know that he recalled her passport, the sign on her van, and her unbuttoned blouse—in exquisite detail. "I was eight when we came to San Diego. I didn't speak much English, so they put me in ESL classes. Guess what I learned there?"

"Spanish," he ventured.

She smiled, pleased he understood. "Right. Every student in my class spoke it, so I picked it up quickly. I learned English, too, of course, but Spanish was easier at first."

"Is Czech a Romance language?"

"No," she said, her gaze flitting over his mouth. "But the structure is similar. Feminine, masculine."

Adam hung on her every word, moistening his lips.

"I couldn't go back home often, but Mexico was within reach. I went to college there for a year, immersing myself in the culture. I liked the artwork, the bright colors . . ." She broke off, seeming self-conscious.

"Which college?"

"San Miguel de Allende."

"I took a summer session there."

She tilted her head to the side. "Really? When?"

"Eleven years ago," he said, thinking back. "I was eighteen."

She'd attended more recently, but their experiences had been similar. They spent the next few minutes reminiscing about the quaint colonial town and its nearby attractions. Adam had done quite a bit of barhopping while he was there, and they both remembered a cantina that was famous for its dirty-talking parrot.

He laughed at her impression of the barkeep, who charged patrons for every epithet. Karina Strauss was full of surprises.

"What courses did you take?" she asked.

"Spanish for native speakers," he said. "I grew up here in the U.S., so I never learned to read or write it."

"I suppose that comes in handy at your job."

Adam nodded. He was paid at a higher rate because he could translate documents and converse fluently. But he didn't want to talk about work. A tiny crease had formed between her brows at the mention of his profession, suggesting that the subject made her uneasy.

It made him uneasy, too. She seemed smart, sweet, and genuine. He wished he wasn't here to deceive her.

"You own this place?" he asked, switching back to a safer topic.

"Yes," she said, her troubled expression clearing. "Well, the bank owns more than I do. But I'm getting there."

He wondered how she'd managed to come up with a down payment. Property values had fallen some in the recession, but prices were still astronomical in historic areas such as Old Town. If Zócalo wasn't doing well, she wouldn't be able to afford the mortgage.

Not without help, anyway.

Karina Strauss had a successful business right out of the gate. Either she was incredibly savvy and hardworking or she'd made a deal with the devil.

"I haven't been totally honest with you," he admitted.

Her lips parted in surprise. "What do you mean?"

"I didn't come here just to buy gifts."

While they were talking, she'd leaned forward, getting closer to him in a subconscious indication of interest. Now she retreated a step, wary.

Adam didn't have to pretend he felt awkward. He wouldn't normally pursue a woman like her. Drug smuggler or not, she was the commitment type, a certified nice girl. She reminded him of Penelope, in a way. Passionate, ambitious, beautiful. He could tell that she needed a steady guy—and he wasn't one.

"I wanted to see you again."

Color rose to her cheeks.

"I feel this connection to you," he added, forcing himself to meet her eyes. It would have been easier to lie, but he knew intuitively that she couldn't be swayed by half efforts. "I was wondering if you'd like to go out sometime."

A pulse fluttered at the base of her throat. "I can't."

"Why not?"

"I'm dating someone," she said in a rush.

Adam studied her face, searching for signs of deception. Her actions at the border weren't that of a taken woman. He hadn't imagined the eye contact they'd made over the *rebozo*. She wanted a man, a family.

She wanted *him*, damn it.

"It's kind of a recent development," she explained. "We just met."

Over the past few days, Adam had watched her interact with a handful of people. His mind balked at the thought of her with Chuy Pena or Armando Villarreal. The only other person he'd seen hanging around was the hotel maid.

Her roommate.

"Oh," he said, finding that mental picture much more palatable.

She flushed darker, avoiding his gaze. "Sorry."

Adam had noticed them touching yesterday, but he hadn't read anything into it. Women were always hugging and kissing each other. Now he found himself wallowing in speculation. Even with a boyish cap on, the maid was young and pretty. Were the lovely ladies more than friends?

"Well," he said, thrown for a loop, "good luck with that."

"Thanks."

He grabbed the gift bag by the side, ignoring the delicate little handles, and said goodbye. Outside, when he was thinking clearly again, it occurred to him that she was probably not having a lesbian affair. Anything was possible, and he'd enjoy reflecting on the matter at his leisure, but he suspected her of lying to get rid of him.

Just as she'd unbuttoned her blouse to distract him.

Again Adam reevaluated his opinion of the very sexy Ms. Strauss. Perhaps she wasn't so innocent after all.

Although her sister was always late, Kari rushed to get to the mall before sunset, dropping Maria off at home on the way. If Sasha showed up on time and Kari wasn't there, she might not wait.

The store Sasha had recommended, Smash, offered an eclectic mix of ripped jeans and punk rock couture. Kari glanced around for her sister, wincing at the ear-bleeding music an employee had turned up full blast. No one else seemed to notice the noise. Two teenage girls with pierced eyebrows were browsing the racks, heads close together. At the front counter, a young woman flipped through a magazine, her arms sleeved in tattoos.

Sasha wasn't here.

Kari shifted the purse on her shoulder, feeling out of place. She liked skulls as much as the next girl—Zócalo was decorated with them—but these clothes didn't suit her at all. Metal-studded bracelets and black leather miniskirts weren't her style. On the back wall, there was a giant poster of a woman screaming into a microphone, her mostly nude body covered in sweat. She was wearing combat boots, black panties, and electrical tape.

Kari slipped back outside, checking her phone. No messages.

The smell of hot pretzels made her stomach twist, but the smoothie stand looked inviting. She was about to cut through the crowd to buy one when Sasha appeared, all smiles. Kari made a sound of delight and embraced her, holding tight.

Sasha felt painfully thin in her arms, almost brittle. Unlike Maria, there was no hint of strength or sinew. Sasha held herself stiff and aloof, seeming uncomfortable in her own skin. She didn't like being touched anymore.

Kari pictured one of the fashionable skeletons on her shelves and her throat closed up. She released Sasha with great reluctance, her eyes flitting over her. She was wearing designer jeans with a low-cut tank top and a fitted jacket, the sleeves shoved up to her elbows. Her breasts were the only substantial part of her body.

Lifting her gaze, Kari pasted on a friendly smile. Even scary skinny, Sasha was gorgeous. Her cheekbones stood out in sharp definition, and her pale blue eyes were striking, accentuated with charcoal shadow and sooty mascara. Kari didn't mention Sasha's noticeable weight loss. "What did you do to your hair?"

Sasha lifted a hand to her shaggy mane, which now sported black and platinum streaks. "Just added some extensions. Do you like it?"

"It suits you," Kari said, feeling hopeful. Sasha experienced periods of depression, in which she didn't leave Moreno's compound for weeks at a time. The fact that she'd showed up at all was a good sign.

Sasha gestured toward Smash, moistening her lips. "Let's shop."

"Can we go to another store? I already looked in there."

A crease formed between her brows. "I thought you wanted something sexy."

"I do," she said. "But nothing black. It's summer."

Sasha stared at the racks inside Smash, her eyes glazed. Kari knew she was high; she always was. At one point Kari had refused to see her unless she was sober, but she'd given up on that ultimatum. Sasha's company was unbearable when she needed a fix.

"What about there?" she said, pointing Sasha toward another trendy boutique. Kari didn't really care where they shopped—there was no date to go on—but she wanted to talk to Sasha, and loud music made that impossible.

"Will you try on the slinky red dress?"

Kari followed her gaze to the next store over, Hot Mess. There was a bald mannequin wearing crimson in the display window, but the store didn't look half as outrageous as Smash. "Sure," she said, compromising. "Let's check it out."

The red dress wasn't available in Kari's size, so they kept looking. Sasha paused at another rack, making a murmur of approval. "This one," she said, holding up a floor-length burgundy silk gown. "The color suits you better than red."

Kari agreed but thought the dress was too revealing for her. She couldn't leave the house in any garment that dipped that low in the back. "Why don't I just go naked?"

"You'll have to, underneath," Sasha murmured, fingering the material.

Kari gave her sister an incredulous look. "People do that?"

"Sure, with certain fabrics. It's no big deal, unless you're a prude."

She glanced at the price tag. The dress wasn't more expensive than the others, and she didn't have time to be selective. If buying this glorified lingerie would put Sasha in an amenable mood, it was worth the investment. "I'll try it on," she said. "Do you like that red one? You should get it. My treat."

Sasha's face brightened. "Really?"

"Sure. See if it fits."

Her sister made a beeline for the red dress, grabbing one in her size, which had probably whittled down to less than zero. Kari, who'd always been curvier, no longer envied her sister's rail-thin figure. Sasha needed to gain at least ten pounds to look healthy.

They went to the changing room together, choosing side-by-side stalls.

"Tell me about this guy you met," Sasha requested.

"Well, he came into my store twice this week. We struck up a conversation and he seemed nice."

"Nice? I thought you said he was hot."

"He is," she said, pulling off her tank top.

"Scruffy or clean-cut?"

"Clean-cut."

"Tall or short?"

"Tallish."

"Athletic, you said?"

She unhooked her bra, picturing the hard muscles under Adam's soft T-shirt. "He looked very fit."

"What was he buying?"

"Gifts for his mom and sister."

"Are you sure he's straight?"

"Of course," she said, affronted. "Why else would he ask me on a date?"

"Did he check you out?"

"I think so," Kari said, almost certain she'd felt Adam's eyes on her backside. She glanced over her shoulder into the mirror, wondering if he'd liked what he saw. When she noticed her panty line, her cheeks heated. She hadn't realized the nude lace was visible.

"I told you the bikini wax would work," Sasha said.

Kari slipped out of her skirt, embarrassed. Sasha had insisted that Kari would feel sexy and carefree, and attract men like bees to honey. It had the opposite effect. Being almost bare down there had only made her feel lonely and self-conscious.

Desperate to be touched.

The silk dress was cool against her skin, slippery smooth. A plunging neckline revealed the inner curves of her breasts. The skinny straps that held up the bodice looked unreliable. Crossing her arms over her chest, she checked out the rear view. It dipped low in back, almost to the point of indecency.

"Are you going to stay in there all day? Let's see it, hot stuff."

Flushing, she walked out to show Sasha. There was a three-paneled mirror at the end of the changing area. When Kari saw their reflections, she forgot about modesty. Sasha looked like a ghost. The crimson dress fit perfectly, accentuating her pale skin and spare physique. Kari could see her ribs, her shoulder blades, the jut of her hip bones.

More important, she could see the telltale bruising on the crook of her arm, along with tiny red pinpricks. Track marks.

"Oh my God," Kari said.

Sasha smiled. "Isn't this dress fabulous? I love the color. Yours looks great, too. So much sexier than your usual style."

Kari couldn't speak; her heart was breaking.

"What's wrong?"

"Nothing," she managed, swallowing hard. "I'm just . . . really hungry. Let's buy these and go to dinner, yeah?"

Sasha's dress was twice as expensive as Kari's, but she paid for both without complaint, and they walked to one of the nicer restaurants at the end of the mall. They talked a little about Kari's work, a subject that never failed to bore Sasha.

Kari didn't mention the track marks during dinner. Sasha needed every bite she consumed, and often refused meals when she was upset. After the plates were taken away, Kari accompanied Sasha outside to the smoking terrace. "Some of Carlos's men came to see me," she said, watching her sister light up.

Sasha took a quick drag. "Why?"

"They said you owe a lot of money."

Her eyes darted around the deserted terrace, making sure they were alone. Kari had been on edge all evening, for obvious reasons. Now she wondered if they were being watched. Every piece of shrubbery looked like the outline of a man's shoulders. "That's bullshit," Sasha hissed. "I pawned a few pieces of jewelry. So what?"

Kari's head swam with nausea, although she hadn't been able to eat much. "Whose jewelry?"

"Carlos gave it to me."

Kari didn't know how these arrangements worked, but she suspected that Carlos intended for Sasha to wear the jewelry while she was acting as his mistress. She couldn't take it with her when she left, or pawn it for drugs.

"They demanded that I pay your debt."

Sasha smoked more of her cigarette. "How?"

"The next time I go across the border, I have to bring back some packages. If I do that, they'll let you go, free and clear."

"What the fuck is that supposed to mean?" She threw down her cigarette and smashed the cherry under the toe of her spike-heeled sandal. "I'm free right now. I can leave anytime I want."

Kari stared at Sasha. "Do you really believe that?"

"Of course."

"Then why don't you? Come with me, tonight. We'll check you into rehab, somewhere far away. Maybe we can use a false name."

Sasha laughed harshly. "I'm not going anywhere."

Kari grabbed her by both arms, refusing to let her off easy. "Carlos is going to kill you. You're going to kill *yourself*. I saw the needle marks, Sasha. You look like a skeleton. If you don't get help, you'll die."

Sasha jerked out of her grasp. "Don't be so melodramatic. I only started shooting because it's cheaper. Carlos has me on an allowance."

"Do you want to live like this? Do you want to *die*?"

She looked over Kari's shoulder, into dark space. "Sometimes."

Tears flooded Kari's eyes. She wrapped her arms around her sister, hugging her thin body. Guilt overwhelmed her, because she knew why Sasha didn't value herself. Kari took some responsibility for that. "I'm so scared for you. Please."

Sasha accepted the hug for a moment before disentangling herself. "Carlos isn't going to kill me. He loves me."

"I love you."

Her sister's face crumpled. She shook her head, sniffing back the tears. Deep down, Sasha was still that little girl who'd sucked her thumb, the towheaded toddler who'd followed Kari everywhere. "I love you, too."

"What am I supposed to do? They expect me to smuggle drugs for you."

"Tell them to get fucked. Nothing's going to happen to me."

"I'll go to the police, then."

Sasha's eyes widened. "You can't do that."

"Why not?"

"Carlos pays them, you idiot. He won't kill you, but they will."

"We can enter the witness protection program—"

"Are you insane?" She glanced around the terrace, lowering her voice. "Threatening to testify is a sure way to die. Promise me you won't do that."

"You care about me, but not yourself?"

"I'll be fine," she insisted. "Carlos doesn't hurt innocent women."

Kari thought she saw movement in the parking lot, a shifting shadow. "What about that reporter in Tijuana a few years ago? Penelope Mendes."

"She was in the wrong place at the wrong time."

"So are you, Sasha. So am I."

Her sister crossed her arms over her chest, closing

herself off. She had only one concern: getting high. Everything else in her life, including Kari, was peripheral. "Don't worry." Sasha gave her a dismissive peck on the cheek. "I'll talk to Carlos." She left in a hurry, anxious to get back to her boyfriend, her drugs, her slow suicide.

Kari stared after her for a long time, feeling hollow. "Goodbye," she whispered finally, wiping the tears from her face.

6

Kari overslept the next morning.

The night before, Maria had been waiting up for her when she came home from the mall. Kari was too upset to discuss the details, only saying that Sasha refused to leave Moreno. Maria seemed sympathetic but not surprised.

She'd tossed and turned until late and was unable to drag herself out of bed on time. Missing her run made her cranky. Tears hovered behind her eyes, threatening to spill over at any moment. She picked at her breakfast and took a quick shower, applying minimal makeup. After throwing on a soft gray tank dress, she pulled her hair into a messy ponytail and shoved her feet into black rubber flip-flops. She didn't feel like cute shoes or colorful accessories today. If she'd owned a housedress, she'd have worn it.

"Maybe you won't get caught," Maria said on the way to work. "Maybe everything will work out for best."

Somehow Kari doubted it. "Officer Cortez came to the store again yesterday."

"Oh *sí*? What happened?"

"He asked me out."

Her eyes sparkled with interest. "*De veras?*"

Kari nodded.

"What did you say?"

"I said no."

"Too bad," she murmured. "He is very handsome."

"Yes."

"And you like him."

"How do you know I like him?"

"Your face, when you speak of him."

Kari glanced away, sighing. She *did* like him, and she felt awful about turning him down. "I told him I'd just started dating someone, and . . . well . . . I'm not sure, but I think he thought I meant you."

Maria frowned. "Me?"

"I know he saw you at the store. I might have given him the impression that we're . . . ." She swirled her hand between them, a vague gesture. "Together."

After a moment of confusion, Maria smacked a palm over her forehead. "*Ay, Dios mio,*" she said, laughing in surprise. "My mother would be very upset to hear this. No husband, no children, and now I am a lesbian!"

Kari laughed along with her, almost until she cried. She felt a little delirious from stress. "I'm sorry. I didn't know what else to say."

"It's okay," Maria said, grinning. "You own home, business. I could do worse."

Kari smiled, shaking her head. "How's your new job?"

Maria shrugged. "Very much like Mexico. Hard work, no breaks."

"Better pay, though."

"*Claro que sí*. Ten times better."

"Have you seen that man again, the one who found you?"

"No."

Kari pulled into the parking lot at the Hotel del Oro, glancing around. It was a little run-down, but many of the older hotels in this area were. "Be careful," she said as Maria exited the vehicle.

"You too, *mi amor*," she said, giving her a saucy wink.

Kari continued on to Zócalo, trying to look on the bright side. It was a sunny morning, breezy and warm, no hint of June gloom. Traffic was busy, as usual. Summers in San Diego were unparalleled, and the tourist season was just beginning.

She relaxed her hands on the steering wheel, anticipating a good day of sales. Immersing herself in work always calmed her nerves. Maybe Maria was right. If Moreno kept his end of the bargain and broke up with Sasha, this could all work out for the best.

She could also take Sasha's advice and ignore the threats. It seemed like a risky proposition, but they couldn't *force* her to cooperate. Although Kari felt responsible for her little sister and wanted to keep her safe at any cost, Sasha was an adult now. Maybe it was time to let her pay her own debts.

When the store came into focus, Kari knew refusing wasn't an option. Zócalo was trashed. Someone had thrown eggs at the front windows and left garbage on the sidewalk. Gang graffiti covered the side of the building, thick black lettering against the white-painted bricks. Debris littered the parking lot, and the sign at the front of the store had been demolished. The Plexiglas façade was shattered, leaving an empty metal frame.

Her heart stalled in her chest.

Smothering a cry of shock and frustration, she parked in her usual spot and hurried toward the back entrance. The alarm was still on and there was no evidence of a break-in. Thankfully, her inventory was safe.

She glanced around the store, knowing how much worse it could have been. She would have to order a new sign, which was a considerable expense. But the graffiti could be painted over—she'd done that before. Her most valued pieces of merchandise were one of a kind and couldn't be replaced.

Taking a deep breath, she went outside to assess the damage. Smashed eggshells clung to the front windows. There were broken beer bottles everywhere. Although she couldn't decipher the graffiti, which looked like a foreign language, its message rang loud and clear: *Don't fuck with Carlos Moreno.*

He'd sent some angry young men here to make trouble for her. Next time they might burn the place down.

Straightening her spine, she walked back to the storage room and grabbed her cleaning supplies. Reporting the vandalism to the police would get her nowhere. There was nothing to do but take care of this mess herself.

Last night Adam had followed Karina to the mall, watching from a distance while she had dinner with her sister.

After they'd engaged in an emotional discussion on

the outdoor terrace, Sasha had walked away from the argument, leaving Karina in tears.

He hadn't known what to make of the exchange. He couldn't get close enough to hear what they were saying, and he'd noticed another tail. Chuy Pena had also been strolling around the mall, lurking in the shadows.

Adam had returned home, wondering if he was any better than Pena. Getting caught up in Moreno's world felt dangerous, illicit, and exciting. It was an adrenaline high, as addictive as the drugs they pushed.

And he always came down hard afterward.

This morning he'd spent an hour at the gym, trying to cleanse his soul with sweat. After he'd whipped his conscience into submission, he drove down E Street, slowing to a stop in front of Zócalo. Karina was outside, scrubbing the windows. It looked like vandals had broken the sign and tagged the hell out of the brick siding.

Chuy Pena must have reported Sasha's activities to his boss, who had disapproved, for whatever reason. Moreno had extensive gang connections. He didn't run the crews, but he was in charge of the drug supply, so he owned the streets. At the snap of his fingers, a hundred violent criminals would jump to do his bidding.

But what had Kari done to deserve this?

He got out of his car and walked toward her, frowning at the yellow gunk on the windows. Egg yolk. Although she noticed him approach, she kept scrubbing, her mouth grim. She looked upset and a little tired.

"What did the police say?" he asked, glancing at the graffiti. Otay Mesa South symbols covered the wall, claiming the territory. The upstart crew's membership had been increasing at an alarming rate. There were thousands of possible suspects.

"I didn't call them."

He thrust a hand through his hair, surprised. "You know who did it?"

She shrugged. "Kids."

"City maintenance would send someone out to re-paint the wall."

"I have paint."

"Karina—"

"It's Kari."

She pronounced it "Kah-ri," not "Carrie." Adam realized he'd never introduced himself. "Adam," he said, offering his hand.

Tossing her scrubber into a bucket of soapy water, she pushed a lock of hair off her forehead and accepted his handshake. "Pleased to meet you."

Adam tried to ignore the jolt of excitement he felt at her touch. He released her hand, studying the eggshell on the window. "You have another brush?"

Her brows rose. "What are you going to do with it?"

"Help you, if you'll let me."

"This is going to take hours."

"That's fine. I don't have to work until later this after-noon."

She gave him a large brush and resumed scrubbing with the smaller one. "You think I'll change my mind about dating you?"

"No."

"What's your deal, then?"

"I'm just being neighborly," he said, feigning innocence. "And maybe it won't work out between you and that other . . . person."

She returned her attention to the window, her cheeks pink. She was still nervous around him, which was fine. If she suspected he wanted to fuck her—well, he did. He wasn't the kind of guy who wouldn't take no for an answer, or thought he could convert lesbians, but he was always up for a new challenge.

They cleaned the glass in silence. Adam was there to do reconnaissance, but he felt bad about it. A few instances of odd behavior didn't make her a criminal. Considering the wrecked state of her storefront, Kari Strauss needed protection rather than prosecution.

"Tell me about your job," she said, dipping her brush in the soapy water again. "Why the border?"

"Why not?"

She glanced at him. "I don't know many boys who say they want to be border patrol agents when they grow up."

"I'm not a border patrol agent. I'm a Customs and Border Protection officer."

"Oh, sorry," she said, seeming amused by his correction. "I didn't realize there was a difference."

"There is. We don't do patrol work."

"Ah. So . . . why did you choose that?"

He scrubbed at the higher part of the window, realizing she couldn't reach it. "I wanted to be a cop, actually. I entered a criminal justice program when I was nineteen."

"Then what happened?"

"September eleventh."

"You wanted to enlist?"

"Very much. But my brother was already in the military, and my mom asked me to finish college first. I was on an athletic scholarship."

"For what sport?"

"Soccer."

A corner of her mouth turned up. "Go on."

"By the time I graduated, we'd invaded Iraq. I wasn't as intent on going there as Afghanistan. That same year, Al-Qaeda operatives were caught in Mexico. It seemed natural to work for Homeland Security, right here in San Diego."

"Are you sorry you didn't serve?"

"I do serve. Just not overseas." Penelope had also begged him to stay, and he didn't regret a moment he'd spent with her.

"What about your brother?"

"He went to Afghanistan *and* Iraq."

"Came back safe?"

"Yes," he said. "Safe, but not unscathed. It made an impact on him. He's like a stranger. Or a shell."

She paused to study him, brush in hand. Maybe she hadn't expected him to be honest about that. They hardly knew each other.

But—he felt like he knew her. And when their eyes met, an understanding passed between them. It reminded him of the time she'd put on the *rebozo*. He saw something in her that he recognized, an unfulfilled need.

Instead of continuing the conversation, they finished the windows. She rinsed the glass with clean water and let it drip dry. "I have to scrub the brick wall, too," she said, taking her bucket around the corner.

Adam followed, content to assist her. He could imagine how devastated she'd been when she'd seen the vandalism, and cleaning up the mess made him feel better about his ulterior motives. Watching her work was no hardship, either. The soft gray dress she was wearing clung to her curves. As she bent to refill a bucket of water, the fabric stretched across her bottom, drawing his attention.

Again he could see the outline of her panties, though he doubted she meant for them to show. Her style was feminine and understated, not an invitation to leer. But leer he did, tantalized by the hint of lacy material and rounded flesh.

When she handed him a clean bucket, he thought about pouring it over his head. The sun was beating down on him, and he didn't trust himself not to stare at her ass. Normally he wouldn't have considered that a problem. He liked relating to women on a physical level rather than an emotional one. For some reason, he couldn't separate the two with Kari. To his alarm, he wanted more than sex from her.

Adam frowned, disturbed by the realization. They needed to stop having candid conversations and meaningful eye contact. If he couldn't imagine her naked beneath him without extending the fantasy to cuddling afterward, he had a problem.

"Are you up for this?" she asked.

His mind faltered, swimming in sexual connotations. "Up for what?"

"Scrubbing, painting. It's going to take all day."

"I'm up for it. I'm enjoying it, actually."

"Are you always like this?"

"Like what?"

"A random do-gooder?"

"No," he said honestly. "Sometimes I do bad things."

She arched a brow. "Such as?"

He let his eyes travel down her body. The front of her dress was damp from soapsuds. "Skipping church," he said, lifting his gaze to her face.

She laughed and shook her head, knowing damned well he hadn't been considering religious pursuits when he looked at her. But she also kept an arm's length of distance between them, as if aware that he wasn't quite what he seemed.

Maria's third day at the Hotel del Oro unfolded much like the previous two.

She had too many rooms to clean, too many piles of laundry to wash, and too many trash cans to empty. But the rhythm of housekeeping wasn't difficult to sink into, and she could stay on top of her duties as long as she kept moving.

Irma had told her to mind her own business, but she wasn't blind. Maria had noticed the constant traffic of disreputable young men coming in and out of Chuy's suite. She'd learned that Sonia visited his office every afternoon for a little private time. There was only one real secret at the Oro: Armando Villarreal.

Although Chuy Pena exuded power and violence, his partner didn't have the same presence. Armando was more of an unknown entity. He stayed behind the scenes. Irma never mentioned his name. The two other maids, smart girls who worked hard, scurried past him. Sonia pretended he wasn't there.

Once, in passing, Maria had met his gaze boldly, wondering why everyone avoided him. There was nothing sinister about his appearance. He wasn't handsome, or tall, or interesting to look at. With his coarse haircut and weathered face, he resembled a common *vaquero*. His eyes were like black stones. He could have been anyone.

Maria wasn't afraid of Armando, though she found him strange. At Kari's house, he hadn't hurt her. He wasn't abusive, like Chuy.

Around noon Maria slipped down to the first floor, taking a circuitous route to the laundry room. A secluded area in the back of the courtyard offered a good view of Chuy's apartments. She lingered there, watching a lanky man approach.

Him again. *La migra.*

He obviously wasn't on the same side of the law anymore. His hair was too long, as if he hadn't bothered to cut it in months. An uneven beard shadowed his face. The shirt he was wearing looked worn and stained, and his jeans were ripped at the knee.

She almost couldn't believe it was him.

The man she'd known had been quiet and kind. He'd spoken her language with a bad California accent, but it had sounded like music to her ears. His presence—his touch—had brought her back from the dead. She could still feel his hand in hers, strong and warm, and hear his rough-soft voice, reassuring her in broken Spanish.

Maria watched him cross the courtyard, entering Chuy's office through the open door. She inched closer, trying to listen in on their conversation. She heard something about *blanca nieves* and Tuesday.

That was the day Kari would make her trip to Mexico.

Pulse pounding, she moved forward another step, her ears straining for more. Chuy's customer requested an amount of the *nieve*, using drug slang Maria didn't understand. His voice was harder than she remembered. Less patient.

After another exchange she couldn't quite make out, she heard Chuy's office chair rolling backward as he stood up.

Maria turned to flee . . . and saw Armando. He was standing in the spot she'd just vacated, lounging in the shade. Cool as ice.

Chingado!

Although she'd just been caught eavesdropping, she held her head up and kept walking, deciding to brazen it out. As she continued toward him, she looked into his empty black eyes, pleading silently for him to let her pass by. He showed no indication that he felt any sympathy. If he had a soul, he hid it well.

And yet she had the strange feeling that he wasn't going to stop her. Then Chuy came out of the office with his customer, and she made the mistake of glancing over her shoulder warily. Chuy summed up the situation in an instant. Maria was sneaking away from his office, having never passed by it.

"*Agarrala,*" he said. *Get her.*

Armando stepped into her path, blocking her exit.

Maria's first instinct was to run, but she couldn't barrel through Armando, and Chuy was at her back. Instead of panicking, she forced herself to stay calm. She would pretend to cooperate. Wait for a better opening to escape.

She whirled to face Chuy, her heart clanging against her ribs. The former border agent stood beside him, his expression guarded. He couldn't help her this time.

Armando put his hand on the small of her back, guiding her toward the office, and the next few seconds went by in a blur. She walked forward like a robot, staring at her long-lost savior. When Chuy grabbed her by the arm, dragging her into a back room, her haze broke. She screamed, kicking wildly as he threw her down on the bed.

"What the fuck were you doing?" Chuy asked.

"*Nada.*"

"You heard something."

Tears leaked out the corners of her eyes. "*No hablo ingles.*"

He slapped the cap off her head and fisted his hand in her hair, pulling hard. "You know what I'm talking about."

"I was just trying to help my friend," she said in Spanish. "She's scared."

Chuy accepted that answer; it was the truth. "Your friend better watch out. The next time she talks to the boss's lady, we're going to come after her. Break up her store, and her house, and all of her pretty little fingers." He punctuated each threat with a tighter grip. "*Entiendes?*"

"Yes," she gasped. "I understand."

He released her hair, watching it spill down her shoulders. Her chest expanded with each frantic breath, drawing his attention. Although her breasts were too small to notice, he looked at them. Her fear seemed to excite him. His gaze returned to her face and his hand to her hair, fingering the fine threads.

"Maybe you need to be taught a lesson," he said.

She turned her head to the side, shuddering with revulsion. At the same time, she slipped her right hand under her smock, reaching for the pepper spray.

7

As an undercover agent, Ian had a protocol to
follow.

If innocent people were in danger, protecting them
took precedence over his investigation, with one caveat:
he wasn't supposed to jeopardize his own life. Instead of
jumping into the line of fire, he was encouraged to stand
by. It was always better to wait for an appropriate time
to act. Dead men couldn't save anyone.

Ian knew he would be killed on the spot if he broke
cover at the Hotel del Oro. He wasn't armed or wearing
a wire because Armando patted him down on a regular
basis. His only recourse was to walk away and call for
backup. He doubted that his colleagues would get here
in time to prevent Chuy from harming Maria Santos,
but it was worth a shot.

Even as his mind formed that decision, his heart re-
jected it. He couldn't leave the scene while she was
screaming. Ian hadn't been able to prevent her previous
assault but he wasn't going to let the same damned thing
happen all over again.

He'd wondered about her for four years.

While he weighed his options, Armando stared at him in an openly antagonistic manner, begging him to make a move.

Don't fuck with the maids.

It occurred to Ian that Armando's anger was directed at Chuy, not him. He liked Maria enough to warn Ian away from her. Armando probably didn't want to stand here and listen to Chuy rape her, either.

Armando was a cagey bastard, impossible to read. When their eyes connected, Ian could only hope they were on the same page. Throwing caution to the wind, Ian lowered his shoulder and charged.

For a lean, average-sized guy, Armando was deceptively solid. Ian felt like he was ramming a brick wall. He slammed his opponent's back into the office window with enough force to shatter the glass. The entire building seemed to quiver as the crash reverberated through the courtyard.

Ian grunted in satisfaction; he wanted Chuy to hear the commotion and come out to investigate.

Armando was a tough son of a bitch, barely fazed by the impact. He jammed his knuckles into Ian's midsection, striking a ferocious blow, and it was game on. Ian didn't worry about being stoic or fighting with finesse. Wincing in pain, he retaliated with a hard left. Although Ian had a slight weight advantage and a longer reach, Armando came up swinging, giving as good as he got. He advanced, socking Ian in the stomach.

Ian fell into a potted plant, breaking it in half as Armando tackled him to the ground. Fists flying, they rolled across potting soil and shards of glass. Ian's elbow scraped the cement, leaving a bloody trail. Armando grabbed him by the front of the shirt and started whaling on him. He wasn't pulling any punches, but he wasn't going for the kill, either. It was more of a no-holds-barred sparring session than a battle to the death.

If Chuy hadn't intervened, Armando might have beaten him unconscious, just for fun. "Quit fucking around!" Chuy roared, pulling them apart.

Armando rose to his feet, brushing dirt and glass from his clothes. Still stunned from the final blows, Ian stayed down on the ground, trying to catch his breath. To his intense relief, Maria slipped out of the office and hurried away, her long hair spilling down her back. Chuy watched her go, saying nothing.

Chuy turned to Armando, his eyes blazing with anger. *"Que pasó?"*

"He jumped me," Armando said.

"You were stepping up?" Chuy asked Ian, incredulous.

Ian glanced at Maria's retreating form, feigning confusion. Chuy wanted to know if Ian was challenging his authority, questioning his treatment of women. "No," he said, straightening to a sitting position. "Oh, hell no. I don't care what you do with the maids. If I were you, I'd be getting my dick sucked all day long—"

Chuy slapped him across the face. "Shut the fuck up. What the fuck is wrong with you? How dare you attack one of my men on my turf?"

Ian stared at the mess they'd made of the courtyard, wondering if this was the end. Chuy might take him into the back room and shoot him in the head.

"No me importa," Armando said, spitting blood into the bushes. *It doesn't matter.*

"Fuck you," Ian said, pointing at his rival like a schoolboy who'd been caught brawling. "This motherfucker is always taunting me, carving little animals and shit. Everyone knows he's a shady bastard."

Chuy glanced at Armando. "Did you carve something for him?"

"*Un burro.*"

"You are a shady bastard," he agreed, seeming amused.

Armando spat blood again, not denying it. Other than a minor scrape on his cheek, he looked no worse for the wear. Ian wasn't so lucky. His shirt was torn down the front, his knuckles were scraped, and his left eye was swelling fast.

He'd gotten his ass kicked.

Chuy reached out, helping Ian to his feet. "Next time he'll carve your face," he said, squeezing Ian's bruised hand hard enough to bring tears to his eyes. "Now get the fuck out of here, and don't come back until Tuesday."

Ian didn't have to be told twice. He limped away with a pocketful of dope and a heap of new troubles, feeling more alive than he had in weeks.

Kari watched Adam out of the corner of her eye while they painted the brick wall.

Over the past few days he'd become even more attractive to her. Maybe because she knew he liked her, or because she couldn't have him. He was nice, but not *too* nice. Confident, but not self-important. It seemed impossible that a man so good-looking could have an equally appealing personality.

He was wearing casual clothes again, jeans and an old T-shirt. His skin was bronzed, his hair a shiny coal black. The grain of stubble along his jaw invited her to touch. She liked his lean muscles, his strong white teeth, and the way his jeans fit. Every time he lifted the paint roller, his biceps flexed, and her heart twittered.

His T-shirt got damp at the center of his back; he was working hard for her. He smelled like clean sweat and spicy soap.

Kari wiped the perspiration from her own forehead, trying to concentrate on painting her section of the wall. It was blazing hot out, at least 90 degrees in the direct sunlight. She felt like turning the hose on herself.

God. This was torture.

He wasn't making much conversation, which was fine. She appreciated the fact that his offer to help her came with no particular agenda, no specific expectations. He didn't seem to care if she never went out with him. His ego could handle it.

Adam's relaxed attitude made him harder to resist, ironically. His quiet assurance, that hint of mystery—all very sexy.

"So . . . fighting terrorism is your main objective?" she said, picking up the thread of their last conversation.

"Most of our day-to-day efforts involve drug smuggling prevention and detection," he explained. "But yes, terrorism is our top priority. And sometimes the two are related."

"How so?"

"Drug smugglers and terrorists use the same technology, the same weapons, the same methods of entering the country. Terrorists have been known to work with the cartels. Their activities are funded by selling drugs to U.S. citizens."

Kari tried to smother another wave of guilt and anxiety. On Tuesday she'd be doing her part to fund terrorism. Hooray. "What about immigration?"

"What about it?"

She glanced at him, wondering if she should drop the subject. Surely their opinions would diverge on this topic. "Do you ever feel bad for the people you catch? The ones who don't make it?"

"No," he said. "I hate seeing kids get hurt, but I don't have any sympathy for the coyotes who put them in danger, or the parents who cram them into tiny, airless spaces. What they're doing is criminal."

Kari cringed, thinking about the box Maria had crossed the border in. "Okay, but I have a hard time judging anyone for wanting a better life. I mean, I'm an immigrant myself. My family did the same thing."

"Legally, I assume."

"I wouldn't tell you otherwise," she said, only half joking.

"You know who I feel bad for? The legal immigrants, who still get treated like second-class Americans. I feel bad for the ones who do their paperwork, play by the rules, and wait at the back of the line." He finished painting, dropping his roller into the empty bucket. "You know, some asshole spit on my mother once at an anti-immigration rally. She was there to stick up for Mexican American *citizens*. Because the drug smugglers, gang members, and violent criminals give the rest of us a bad name."

Kari couldn't imagine the rage she'd feel if a man spat on her mother. So she could sympathize with him, even though he was wrong. "Why is the immigration debate always about dark-skinned people? No one seems to think that Canadian and European immigrants are ruining our country."

"The overwhelming majority of illegal immigrants come from Latin America. It's not a race issue."

"Of course it's a race issue," she countered. "It's also a humanitarian issue. We have a responsibility to be good neighbors, and to help those in need—"

"What do you suggest to solve the problem, open borders? Could your store survive the economic crisis that would result?"

She sighed, shaking her head. He had her there.

"I suppose you think we should legalize drugs, too."

"No," she said, frowning. Despite her current predicament, she didn't want street drugs to be more accessible. Immigration had made this country great; illegal substances were destroying it, little by little. Kari hated drugs, and what they'd done to her sister, with a passion. "I'd never support that cause."

"Really? You look like a medical marijuana lover to me."

It took her a second to realize he was teasing. They'd just had a heated discussion, but he wasn't bothered by their differing opinions. He'd treated her respectfully and was enough of a gentleman to want to lighten the mood.

When he set his paint roller down in an empty tray, Kari grabbed a wet sponge from her bucket and threw it at him. It hit the back of his head with a splash.

That wiped the smile off his face. He straightened, staring at her in amazement.

She started giggling, as surprised by the impulsive action as he was. When he picked up the sponge to retaliate, she let out a little shriek, backing away from him. "I was going for your shoulder," she said, covering her head with her arms.

"You have bad aim."

"I'm sorry!"

He caught her before she could run around the corner, trapping her against the wall while he squeezed the sponge over her head. It was clean, cold water, wetting her hair and shoulders. She put up a token resistance, sputtering with laughter.

Trying not to get paint on her clothes, she stumbled sideways and almost tripped over the curb. Still laughing, she reached out to steady herself, grabbing his arm. Before she found her balance, the edge of her foot was pierced by a stabbing pain. When she'd swept up the shards of glass, she must have missed one.

She gasped, lifting her injured foot off the ground.

Adam stopped soaking her with the sponge and looked down at her foot, which was already bleeding. "Shit," he said, chagrined. In the next instant he'd tossed the sponge aside and picked her up, carrying her toward the storage room.

Kari marveled at how easily he handled her weight. The wound was minor, not warranting this level of chivalry, but she made no protest. While blood dripped from her toes, she clung to his shoulders, enjoying the ride.

"Where are the first aid supplies?"

"Bathroom," she said, pointing.

He sat her down on the edge of the counter and she put her foot in the sink, studying the gash as water rushed over it. She didn't think it needed stitches. He dried her foot with a clean towel, patting it gingerly. "Jesus, I'm sorry."

"What for?"

"I didn't mean to hurt you."

"You didn't. The piece of glass did."

"Well, I feel bad."

"Don't be silly. I'm fine."

He found supplies in the medicine cabinet and bandaged her foot carefully. She started giggling again, picturing the look on his face when she'd thrown the sponge. The corner of his mouth tipped up, and his gaze traveled along her bare legs, taking the scenic route.

She realized that she was sitting on the counter, one knee bent, with her dress hiked up to the tops of her thighs. He hadn't averted his eyes, either. "Are you trying to look up my skirt, Officer Cortez?"

"It's Adam," he reminded her. "And yes."

She drew in a sharp breath. Although the door was open, the space in the bathroom was cramped and she couldn't straighten her knee without brushing it against the front of his jeans. She was very aware of her body in relation to his. Sensuality hummed between them. Her hair was damp from the dousing he'd given her, tendrils clinging to her neck. The front of her dress was wet, too. Her nipples tightened against the cups of her bra.

For modesty's sake, she should rearrange her skirt or cross her arms over her chest. But she didn't want to. She had a shocking urge to lift her dress up higher, to pull him closer. She wanted his hands on her skin, his eyes on her breasts. She longed to feel the buttons of his fly against the cleft of her sex.

Anticipating his taste, she moistened her lips.

His eyes locked on her mouth, and he wrapped his hand around her ankle, taking her foot off the top of the sink. Letting her leg slide down the outside of his, he skimmed his fingertips along her calf, hooking his hand behind her knee. She shivered, tingling at the contact. He moved between her splayed thighs, right where she wanted him. She twined her arms around his neck and tilted her head back, giddy with excitement.

Just before his lips touched hers, she caught a flash of movement in the storeroom.

Maria.

She gasped, shying away from his mouth.

"What are you doing?" Maria asked, sounding shocked.

Adam was just as startled by the interruption, and twice as annoyed. He stepped back, cursing under his breath.

Kari hopped down from the counter and left the bathroom in a hurry, trying not to rub against him on the way out. She could feel heat and tension coming off him in waves. "I cut my foot and he was . . . helping me."

Adam didn't corroborate the story. He was obviously aroused and hadn't recovered enough to turn around yet.

Maria frowned. "Are you okay?"

"Of course," Kari said, her cheeks hot. "There was a lot of blood to wash up."

"Washing up," Adam muttered, slamming the bathroom door.

Kari hobbled toward Maria, lowering her voice to a whisper. "Why are you here?"

"I took a lunch break," she said. "What happened?"

"My store got vandalized last night."

Maria's eyes widened with dismay. "Was it bad?"

"Not too bad. We just painted over the graffiti."

When Adam came out of the bathroom a moment later, Kari didn't know what to say. It was incredibly awkward, juggling her would-be lovers. Maria draped her arm around Kari in a possessive manner, glaring at Adam. "I'm so sorry, *mi amor*," she said, stroking her damp hair. "I will kiss it better."

Kari almost died from embarrassment. Maria's breath fanned her cheek and their bodies were plastered together, full length. But she couldn't tear her gaze away from Adam. He stared back at her, looking somewhere between jealous and intrigued. Like he didn't know if he wanted to pull them apart or watch them go at it.

"I have to leave," he said, shaking his head in regret.

"Thanks for helping me," Kari said.

"Yeah." He rubbed a hand over his mouth, as if trying to recapture their almost-kiss. "See you later."

Maria stopped petting her as soon as he was gone. "Was that okay? I didn't know how much gay to be."

Kari sank into a chair and buried her head in her arms.

"I don't think this is working. He still likes you. What were you doing with him in the bathroom?"

"We were this close to kissing," she said, her thumb and forefinger an inch apart.

"You are not a good lesbian," Maria informed her.

"I know," Kari groaned.

"Are you mad at me for interrupting?"

"No," she said, smoothing her disheveled hair. "I'm glad you came. For all I know, he's investigating me, or snooping for Moreno. And even if he's not, I can't get involved with a police officer right now." She glanced at Maria, feeling dazed. "This is madness."

"He will not give up," Maria said.

"What makes you say that?"

"The way he looked at you. At us. He wanted me to disappear!"

Kari flushed, picturing the scene they'd made. She wasn't sure that Adam wanted Maria to disappear. He probably would have been amenable to letting her stay. "I'll have to do a better job at discouraging him."

Maria took the seat across from her. "Something happened at the hotel."

Her stomach tightened with unease. She'd been too wrapped up in her own drama to notice that Maria appeared shaken. Her baseball cap was missing, her long black hair hanging down her back. "What?"

"Chuy warned me," she said. "If you talk to your sister again, they will do bad things. To your store, your house . . . you."

Kari swallowed dryly, feeling ill. After seeing the vandalism she'd known they meant business, but she hadn't stopped to consider Maria's welfare. "Did he hurt you?"

"No," she said, looking away.

"Where's your hat?"

She lifted her hand to her head. "I don't know. I will try to find for you."

"I don't care about the hat, Maria. You shouldn't go back there."

"Today is payday," she said, stubborn.

"If he touched you—"

"He didn't get the chance. The man from *la migra* was there, and he started a fight with Armando. I got away."

"Who's Armando?"

"Chuy's partner."

"What about next time?"

"Next time I will not get caught. Chuy was angry with me for . . . *como se dice?* Trying to listen to them."

Kari gaped at her, incredulous. "You were eavesdropping?"

"Yes. I heard them say something about Tuesday. New drugs coming in."

"That's the day I go to Mexico," she murmured, her eyes filling with tears. "What am I going to do?"

Maria's expression softened with sympathy. Instead of giving Kari answers, she offered her support, putting an arm around her trembling shoulders and murmuring words of comfort while she cried.

Adam came home from work in the wee hours of Saturday morning, dead tired.

He still didn't know what to think about Kari. If she was a drug smuggler, she was doing a damned fine job of fooling him. And an even better job of appealing to him on every level. There was something about her, a sweetness he couldn't resist. He'd anticipated a sexual attraction, but he hadn't expected to *like* her.

As he pulled into the garage, he noticed a strange presence at his doorstep, a figure slumped over in the dark. Ian. Adam wondered what had brought his friend back again so soon. It was unusual for him to visit while he was on assignment. They went weeks, sometimes months, without seeing each other.

Adam locked his car and left the garage, approaching the lump on his doorstep with caution. Ian was leaning against the side of the house, dozing. Always a light sleeper, he startled awake before Adam reached out to nudge him. The hood of his jacket slipped down, revealing his misshapen face, grotesque in the moonlight.

Adam swore under his breath. "What happened?"

Ian lumbered to his feet, with help from Adam. His left eye was swollen shut and dark with bruises. But he just shrugged, playing it cool.

"Do you need to go to the ER?"

"No, I'm good."

"Come on," Adam muttered, unlocking the front door and watching him limp inside. He went straight to the refrigerator, grabbing a bag of frozen peas. "The DEA can't afford ice packs?"

Ian accepted the bag with a wry smile. "I had one. It melted."

"You need painkillers?"

He put the peas over his eye. "Yeah."

Adam went to the medicine cabinet and shook out a few tablets, over-the-counter stuff. He'd offer something stronger, but he knew Ian wouldn't take it. He handed him the pills and a glass of water, grimacing. "What's the damage?"

Ian took the bag away from his face long enough to swallow the painkillers. "I think I have some cuts on my back."

Adam gestured toward the bathroom, resigned to playing doctor again. Only Ian wasn't half as pretty a patient as Kari. When he pulled his T-shirt over his head, Adam's gut clenched in sympathy. "Jesus, man."

Ian turned, trying to check out his back in the mirror. There were a couple of shallow lacerations and some serious bruises. "Am I that fucked up?"

"Nah," Adam said, finding the antiseptic. "You look like shit, though."

Ian smoothed a hand over his stomach, which was washboard flat. He had always been lanky, and now he really fit the description of an addict. There wasn't an ounce of fat on him. "I could use a plate of your sister's enchiladas," he admitted.

Adam dabbed at Ian's scratches with a soaked cloth. "Yeah, well. Maybe you should have married her."

Ian tensed, either from the sore subject or from his stinging wounds. They rarely discussed his fling with Raquel—it was ancient history. Adam didn't know why he'd brought it up. Frowning, he finished tending to Ian's back and gave him a clean T-shirt.

"Thanks," Ian said.

They went back to the kitchen, where Ian sat down and Adam heated up some soup. "What are you doing here?" he asked, studying Ian's puffy eye. He wouldn't have shown up like this unless he was in trouble.

Ian took a few spoonfuls of soup and pushed the bowl aside. "I got in a scrape with a target," he said, rubbing his bruised jaw. "I'd rather not make a big deal of it."

"You mean you'd rather not report it?"

After a brief hesitation, he nodded.

"Why?"

"There was a girl . . ."

Adam took a seat at the table, cursing silently. He already knew where this was going, and he didn't like it.

"I was outside with a secondary," Ian continued. "My primary dragged her into a secluded location, against her will."

"You couldn't leave and call for backup?"

"Not in time to help her."

"Shit," Adam muttered, understanding the dilemma.

"The other guy was staring me down, spoiling for a fight. He'd warned me away from this girl before."

"Why would he do that?"

"I was looking at her."

"She's pretty?"

"Very."

"Go on."

"I got this feeling that he didn't like what was happening. But he couldn't step up, either. So I just tackled him."

"Jesus, Ian."

"Yeah. He fought hard, obviously."

"Was he armed?"

"He always carries a knife."

"You're lucky he didn't shank you."

Ian nodded. "The target came out to break it up, and the girl got away."

"How did *you* get away?"

"I told him the other guy was taunting me. We both pretended like the fight had nothing to do with the girl. He bought it."

"Are you sure?"

"No. But I'm a good customer, so maybe he cut me some slack."

Adam leaned back in his chair, mulling the story over. "Okay, but why not report it? You took a gamble and it paid off. The girl is safe."

"If I make a report, my judgment will be questioned. I'll be taken out of the field for a psych eval and a physical exam. Maybe even reassigned."

Adam glanced at Ian, wondering if that would be for the best. He didn't say it, because he knew his friend had worked hard to get close to these guys. Ian wouldn't give up before he brought them down.

"There's another complication," Ian admitted.

"What?"

"The girl . . . I know her."

Adam straightened in his chair. "You know her?"

"It's Maria Santos. From El Caracol."

"No way."

"I'm sure of it."

"You're crazy," he said, refusing to believe him. "Her face was bruised and battered when you found her."

"The swelling went down after a few days. I recognized her."

He searched Ian's good eye, trying to assess his mental acuity. Undercover work had a way of messing with your mind, eating away at your soul. Adam knew that from experience. "Did she recognize you?"

"I doubt it."

"This is why you stepped in, isn't it? You've always been bugshit over that girl. You left CBP, quit Border Patrol—"

"I hated that job, Adam."

"And you like this one? You enjoy living in a dump, looking like a bum?"

"Do *you* enjoy destroying people's dreams? Keeping families apart?"

"Fuck you," Adam said tiredly. "Fuck you if you think you're doing something more honorable than I am."

Ian went back to his bowl of soup, finishing it with swift, angry motions.

"If this girl from El Caracol remembers you, you're done. She could blow your cover at any moment."

"Thanks for the heads-up," Ian said, his voice laced with sarcasm. "I hadn't thought of that."

"You can't keep this a secret, Ian. You're endangering yourself and the investigation."

Drops of broth clung to his goatee, proving that his manners had become just as raw as his appearance. "Are you really going to lecture me on rules and procedures?" he asked, wiping his mouth with the back of his hand.

"Why shouldn't I?"

"Because you're the sneakiest bastard on CBP," he said, rising to his feet. "And now you're a fucking hypocrite, too."

Adam stood and walked over to the fridge, annoyed. Ian was pissing him off, but he had a point. He grabbed a beer for himself and a soda for Ian, making a peace offering. "Kari's store got vandalized last night."

"Whose store?"

"Kari Strauss's. She owns Zócalo, on E Street."

Ian popped open the soda. "You've been watching her?"

Adam nodded. He might be a sneaky bastard and a hypocrite, but he couldn't lie to his best friend.

"I've seen her before," Ian admitted. "She's nice-looking."

Adam took a pull on his beer, thinking about her smooth, tanned legs. "Yes, she is." He'd seen a glimpse of her panties today, purple with little flowers. He'd have given anything to get inside them. "I think she has a girlfriend."

Ian almost choked on his soda. "Really?"

Adam smiled, taking his beer to the couch. Ian followed close behind, eager to hear the rest. "I helped her paint over the graffiti this morning, and she cut her foot on some glass. We were in the bathroom, cleaning her up, and she was giving me these . . . signals, you know. Like she wanted more than a Band-Aid."

"Then what?"

"Then her roommate walked in."

"And you had a steamy three-way, *Penthouse* Forum style?"

He laughed ruefully. "No."

"What a letdown."

Adam felt disappointed for other reasons. If Kari Strauss was a drug-smuggling lesbian, his instincts were dead. And if she wasn't, he didn't have any reason to follow her. Either way, she was taken, off-limits. Out of reach.

"Why do you think they're together?" Ian asked.

"She said she was seeing someone, and her roommate acted jealous. I thought they were going to start making out. Only, not with me."

Leaning back against the couch, Ian placed the bag of peas over his eye again, settling in. "What does she look like?"

"The roommate? She's hot, too. More your type than mine."

"Dark hair?"

"Yeah."

"Describe what they were wearing."

"No way," he said, offended. "Get your own fantasy."

Ian laughed, shifting the frozen peas again. "I have a tip for you."

"What?"

"Supposedly there's some new stuff coming in. *Blanca nieves*."

"When?"

"Tuesday."

Adam had met Kari on Tuesday. Maybe she made weekly trips to Tijuana. "Shit," he said, scrubbing a hand over his face. "How much?"

"I don't know any other details."

"That's useless to me, Ian. People smuggle drugs every hour, every day."

"Right. But I can't ask for specifics without getting my head blown off."

Adam fell silent, brooding. He hated when Ian talked like that. It was almost as if he didn't care if he lived or died. "Mom's birthday is tomorrow."

"Are you doing anything?"

Adam shrugged. Last year they'd had a big fiesta, with relatives from all over Mexico and California. Ian had been there, looking a damned sight better than he did now. It seemed like a lifetime ago. "Maybe I'll go visit. Take some flowers."

"Give her one from me, okay?"

"Sure," he said, feeling numb.

8

Tuesday dawned bright and hot.

Kari hadn't slept at all the night before. She'd lain awake, thinking of everything she could have done differently. She should have called the police the first day, or on the night she met Sasha at the mall. Her sister had probably been carrying drugs, and she certainly had inside information. An arrest threat would have forced her cooperation.

She should have staged an intervention years ago.

If she could do it all over again, she'd have protected Sasha that night at the club, instead of sneaking away to be alone with her stupid boyfriend. She'd never have taken her to parties or given her that first joint.

Wallowing in regrets, Kari got up early and ran hard, pushing herself, punishing herself. When she came back home, short of breath and covered in sweat, Maria was in the kitchen, making breakfast.

She slid an omelet onto a plate, offering Kari a serene smile.

Kari took the plate and sat down, sipping her orange

juice. The kitchen was warm and cozy with morning light, Maria demure and ethereal in her white nightgown. It was a comforting scene—but this was not how she pictured domestic bliss.

"I always thought I'd be the wife," she complained.

Maria glanced at her, chuckling. "We can take turns, if you like."

Kari wondered if she'd be spending the next few years in jail, forced into a similar but much less pleasant living situation. She shuddered, eating a few bites of omelet without really tasting it. "What will you do if I don't come back?"

Maria sat down with her plate. "Stop saying that. Of course you'll come back."

"I have some cash in my closet—"

"No."

She held her palm to her stomach, hoping it would settle. Sasha hadn't returned any of her calls over the weekend. Adam hadn't come back to the store, which should have been a relief. Instead, she felt abandoned.

Her life was spiraling out of control.

"Tell me about your family," Kari said, needing a distraction.

Maria unfolded a napkin over her lap. "What would you like to know?"

"Anything. Something good."

She nodded. "My father went to the U.S. when I was little to look for work. I was maybe five years old when he left, and seven when he came back. His shoes were falling apart, and his clothes were torn, but he brought me a doll. A beautiful *American* doll. He carried it all the way from Texas. That was the happiest day of my life."

Kari smiled as she pictured the touching scene. She'd had a similar fascination with American toys as a child. "Were you surprised to see him?"

"Oh, yes. I didn't know he was coming. He cried when he hugged me."

"Did he stay home?"

"Only for a few months. By the time he went back, my mother was pregnant with my sister."

"You have a sister?"

Maria swallowed a bite of omelet. "Two. And a brother who just turned fourteen. He's dying to come here. I tell him to wait."

"Where is your father?"

She dabbed her mouth with the napkin. "He fell off a train in the middle of the night. Ten years ago."

"Oh," Kari murmured. "I'm so sorry."

"It is a dangerous journey."

"Why not cross legally and apply for citizenship? Isn't that less risky?"

"Of course, but it is not easy. There is a long wait just for a work visa, and you need a signature from a U.S. employer. Without family connections, it is almost impossible to get a job offer in this country." She gestured down at her plate. "For those who are hungry, the reward is worth the risk."

"So you've been in Tijuana for four years, hoping to cross again?"

"And saving money, sending most of it to my family. My brother has a job now, so he helps to pay bills." A crease formed between her brows. "I also was not eager to pay another coyote to bring me here. I did not want to be hurt by bad men again."

Kari finished her omelet and drank her orange juice, considering Maria in a new light. No wonder she didn't seem distressed by Kari's predicament; she'd been through worse scrapes and survived.

If Kari got caught smuggling drugs, she'd ask for a lawyer and keep her mouth shut. She had no prior arrests, no convictions. That would work in her favor.

And if she didn't get caught, she would be complicit in Moreno's crimes. He would have leverage against her, a dirty little secret to keep her quiet. But once she did this, she'd be free. Sasha would be free.

The reward was worth the risk.

"What about your family?" Maria asked.

"Sasha is all I have."

"Where are your parents?"

"My mother died when I was eight. We moved here a year later. I think my father wanted to start over."

"Did he do well?"

"Very well, for an immigrant. But he worked too hard and didn't take care of his health. He died of a heart attack right after I graduated from high school."

Maria's eyes softened with sympathy. "So your sister is everything to you."

"Yes," she said. "Exactly."

After breakfast, Kari showered and dressed with care, choosing a brief outfit. Showing a little skin hadn't hurt her chances last time. The cutoff jean skirt and skimpy tank top made her look like a party girl. She left her hair down and applied more eye makeup than usual. After putting on a pair of gladiator sandals, she left the room.

Maria was standing by the door, ready. Since she'd

lost her hat, the rest of her disguise had relaxed. Today she was wearing a sleeveless T-shirt and sturdy blue jeans. Although her clothes were boyish and outdated, they didn't detract from her beauty.

"How do I look?" Kari asked.

"*Muy* sexy."

"Is it too much?"

"No," Maria said, her gaze sharp. "Is just right."

Kari grabbed a light sweater anyway, draping it around her shoulders. "I'm so nervous, I feel like I might throw up."

"*Pobrecita,*" Maria murmured, giving her a hug. "If I could do it for you, I would."

She knew that was impossible. Maria would never get through without papers. "Are you sure you want to work today?"

"*Sí,*" she said, determined.

"Let's go, then."

After taking Maria to the hotel, Kari stopped by Hands Across the Border, following her usual Tuesday morning routine. There were bags of clothing, toiletries, and some canned goods to disperse. Kari loaded the donations into her truck, smiling her thanks. She'd been working with the charity for more than a year now, and she loved it. At Christmas, she'd delivered a truckload of new toys. It felt good to make people happy.

She dropped off the goods at the Iglesia de Santo Ignacio in downtown Tijuana and left in a hurry. Dressed as she was, about to commit a serious crime, she wasn't comfortable hanging around in a church. She felt like a sinner. Normally she'd have done some shopping, another pleasant Tuesday task. Instead she went straight to the pickup location. She was much too anxious to stroll through the busy streets or chat with vendors.

Chuy Pena had contacted her with terse instructions. She drove to the unfamiliar address he'd indicated, her heart racing. City traffic was always chaotic, and Mexican drivers committed every violation imaginable without blinking an eye. After thirty nerve-wracking minutes, she arrived at a dusty tile manufacturer called Saltillo Mundo.

By this time it was almost 11:00 a.m. and the sun was blazing. Even so, she wrapped her sweater tight around her body and stayed inside the vehicle, sweating like crazy. A worker approached the driver's side, his shirt stained orange. "Can I help you?"

"I'm here to pick up an order for Carlos," she said.

He nodded, gesturing for her to pull forward. Kari stared into the dark garage with trepidation, wondering if Moreno's plans for her were more sinister than drug smuggling. She got out of the van, her pulse pounding.

"Is there a problem?"

Her hands trembled as she gave him her keys. "I'll stay out here."

Shrugging, he climbed behind the wheel, making no comment about the peculiar request. American customers were always right, apparently. Or maybe it wasn't cool to argue with a woman sent by Moreno. Kari had no idea who was in on the deception and who wasn't.

She stood there in the hot sun, her mind blank and her shoulders trembling, for an interminable length of time. Finally the man backed out and turned her van around, facing the street. "It's all loaded up," he said as he exited the vehicle.

"Thank you."

"Have a nice day."

Right. Feeling light-headed, she got into the van and drove away from Saltillo Mundo, heading north. The next few moments were surreal. She'd anticipated being freaked out, but she was shocked by how intense her anxiety was. Her heartbeat seemed erratic, her breathing too shallow. She clenched her sweat-slick hands around the steering wheel and checked her rearview mirror for police cars, hoping she wouldn't faint.

"I'm going to die," she whispered, approaching the gridlock at the border. "I'm going to have a heart attack and die."

She took deep, even breaths and tried to stay calm. Her skin prickled with heat, and red splotches broke out on her chest, like panic hives. Tossing aside her sweater, she gulped bottled water and prayed for strength.

"I have a plan," she reminded herself. "I have a plan, and I'll get through this."

Her plan involved Adam. She would enter his lane, smile pretty, and make nice. Maybe even hint that she'd reconsidered their date. Surely he wouldn't inconvenience a woman he wanted to go out with. She'd agree to anything—even a ménage à trois with Maria—if he'd let her pass through!

Maybe she was taking an additional risk by involving him. He might not give her deferential treatment. He might already suspect her of wrongdoing. He might be one of Moreno's henchmen.

God.

Pushing a lock of damp hair off her forehead, she made her way toward lane sixteen, where she'd first met

Adam. She couldn't believe only a week had gone by since then. It seemed like months. The closer she got to his station, the worse she felt about using him. She didn't want him to see her at such a desperate moment.

But it was too late to turn back.

The U.S. side of the border began about a hundred yards from the inspection stations. Street vendors stayed in Mexico, walking up and down the aisles of traffic. It was the point of no return. She'd already committed a felony.

Kari couldn't change lanes at this stage of the game, either.

Sweat molded her tank top to her lower back and trickled between her breasts. She rolled the windows down on both sides, letting in hot air and smog. Catching sight of two officers on foot, she froze.

The tactic wasn't unusual. There were always uniformed men and women in the lanes, checking out passengers and monitoring the flow of traffic. Some were with the canine unit, directing drug-sniffing dogs.

A large, alert German shepherd strained at his leash, just two cars down.

Kari's stomach twisted. She might not make it to Adam's station. They could detain her before she got there.

Her attention was fractured by the threats from all sides; her vision closed in on her. There were dogs and camera equipment and law enforcement personnel everywhere, watching her every move. She was so distracted that she failed to notice her lane clearing. The driver behind her honked a warning, and she pulled forward, searching for Adam. It was almost her turn. Maybe when she saw him, she'd feel safe.

He'd wave her on. He had to.

The next two minutes felt like hours. She stared straight ahead, focusing on the Baja California license plate on the car in front of her, afraid to blink. Afraid to glance in the rearview mirror. Finally it was showtime.

She could do this.

Legs shaking, she tapped the gas pedal. As soon as she met Adam's steady gaze, she'd calm down. His presence would soothe her.

In what seemed like slow motion, she stopped the van and turned to look inside the booth. A man in a midnight-blue uniform asked for her paperwork. He had short black hair, a serious face, and a dark complexion, but . . . he wasn't Adam.

He wasn't Adam.

Kari's throat went dry. Struggling not to show her panic, she fumbled for her travel documents, handing them over. "Is Officer Cortez available?" she asked. Her voice sounded shaky and high-pitched.

He flipped through her passport. "Available for what?"

She was too nervous to think. "Um . . ."

"If you need to file a complaint with a lane supervisor, I can give you a form—"

"No," she said quickly. "I just wanted to say hi to Adam."

The CBP officer gave her a closer study, and he didn't miss the exposed flesh at the neckline of her tank top. Kari thanked God for making men predictable. Then he said, "We're not allowed visitors while on duty."

"Oh, I'm sorry!" She let out a nervous giggle, splaying a hand over her décolletage. "Never mind. I wouldn't want to get him in trouble."

The officer ignored her cleavage in favor of inspecting her paperwork. She nibbled at her lower lip, hoping he'd think she was Adam's girlfriend and let her through. After a long, agonizing moment he disappeared into his booth.

Kari wondered how far she'd get if she made a run for it. She pictured a group of officers tackling her to the ground, German shepherds gnashing at her sandals.

"You need to report to the secondary inspection area," the officer said when he came back.

She blinked a few times. "What?"

He pointed to her immediate right, indicating a large section in the carport. It looked like an auto repair shop, only the car wash was really a giant X-ray machine. "Pull over and stay inside your vehicle. An officer will be with you shortly."

Kari's heart plummeted. She was done for.

Adam didn't always work the lanes.

For security reasons, CBP officers rotated stations, dividing their time between pedestrian booths and vehicle lanes, working primary and secondary inspection. Due to his work experience, education level, and bilingual status, Adam enjoyed a higher rank than most of his fellow officers. He was authorized to cover any area of the land port, and often took on a supervisory role.

Today he was in secondary, his choice location. Most of the good shit happened in secondary. The really big loads were discovered here, along with the ever-changing methods of hiding them. Illegal cargo was stopped every day. High-profile smugglers had been apprehended here, and thousands of pounds of drugs seized.

Adam loved being a part of that.

He didn't love the idea of adding Kari to his list of arrest assists. He'd been monitoring the tracking device he'd attached to her van, and although service was spotty south of the border, he knew she was coming.

About twenty minutes ago he'd done a visual sweep of the lanes. Her van was waiting in line sixteen, where they'd met. He didn't think that was a coincidence. "Detain the white Dodge," he ordered Officer Sandoval via CB radio.

"She's on her way," Sandoval radioed back later. "Friend of yours?"

"What do you mean?"

"She asked for you."

Adam broke radio contact, starting to sweat. An attack of conscience had caused him to make the inspection request. He should have sent her to secondary last week. If she told anyone he'd been pursuing her, he'd have some serious explaining to do.

She'd already mentioned him to Sandoval. Fuck!

He tugged at his collar, trying not to borrow trouble. If she passed inspection, he had nothing to worry about. If she didn't, well . . . he hadn't crossed the line. She wasn't his suspect, and he wasn't investigating her officially. Their meetings were coincidental, as far as anyone else was concerned.

He went to the control booth, glancing at the video monitors. Kari exited the vehicle and spoke with a female officer about the search procedure. While her van was X-rayed and inspected, she would wait inside. Nodding her understanding, she followed the officer to the detainment area, hugging a sweater to her chest like a security blanket. She was wearing a short denim skirt and leather sandals with ankle straps. Every male in the vicinity watched her walk away.

Adam felt his jaw tighten with annoyance, although he was just as guilty as the rest. More so.

An inspector drove the van through X-ray. The process was slow and methodical, scanning the vehicle from top to bottom. It looked clean. The tires, a typical hiding place for illegal contraband, were clear. There was nothing in the cargo but stacks of floor tiles in cardboard boxes. Although drug smugglers were clever and they could make a brick of coke look like a brick of clay, illegal substances fluoresced under radiation.

Adam advanced the vehicle to a parking area, where a final visual check of the exterior and interior would be completed. The dogs sniffed the van's perimeter but did not alert. From floorboards to rooftop, it was clean.

He left the control booth, approaching the van on foot. An officer was shining a flashlight under the back bumper. "There's an object attached to the chassis."

"Let's see it," Adam said. The GPS couldn't be connected to him, and it would look suspicious for him to ignore the detail.

The other officer stripped the device from the chassis and handed it to him. He gave the GPS a cursory inspection. It wasn't unheard of for car owners to use tracking devices in case of theft or to keep tabs on a loved one. "Bring her back out."

After the necessary release forms were signed, the female officer led Kari to her vehicle and gave her a copy of the paperwork. Adam waited another minute, studying her pale face. She looked terrified.

Did she think she wouldn't pass inspection?

Frowning, he walked up to the driver's side. She smiled when she saw him, but her gaze revealed darker emotions, an intriguing blend of fear and fatigue.

"How's it going?"

Her smile broke. "Not good."

"What's wrong?"

She shook her head, tears filling her eyes.

"Maybe I can help."

"Whatever you found—"

"What do you think I found?"

She stared at him in misery.

Adam lifted the GPS in his hand, ignoring the jab of guilt he felt for attaching it, and the even stronger punch of sympathy he felt for her. Whatever she'd done, he couldn't believe her to be a bad person. "This was underneath your van."

A crease formed between her brows. "What is it?"

"A tracking device."

"Oh."

"Do you know who put it there?"

She blinked rapidly, her eyes shifting to the left. "I did."

"You did?"

"Yes. I forgot all about it until now."

Adam couldn't call her on the deception. In other circumstances, he might have taken her back to the detainment area and had her questioned in depth. She was on the edge of breaking, brimming with vulnerability.

Instead of pressing for details, he decided to release her. They would finish this later. "Okay, then," he said, giving her the GPS. "You're all set."

Her jaw dropped. "I'm free to go?"

He nodded, gesturing to the exit lanes. "Pull to the left and merge forward."

She stared at him in disbelief.

"Drive safely," he said, and walked away.

9

Ian hadn't been to a buy in days.

He'd taken Chuy's warning to heart and stayed home, lying low. Nursing his wounds. On Saturday morning, after leaving Adam's house, he'd reported to his supervisor, claiming that a couple of thugs had accosted him on the street. It was the first time he'd lied to another agent and he wasn't proud of himself.

He'd been admonished for breaking procedure. Not only had he failed to call for backup, he'd waited an entire day to check in.

Ian explained that he'd felt disoriented and fallen asleep after the attack. This false confession led to a litany of physical exams. He was subjected to a round of blood work, piss tests, and mental health checks, all of which he passed with flying colors. Cleared for duty, he was sent back into the field.

His apartment was a hovel, but he'd been glad to return to it. Adam had asked if he enjoyed living like a bum. In a sick way, he did. He hated the character but relished the role. The stress of his undercover assignment was like a drug to him. He was addicted to the tension, the risk. Without that rush of adrenaline, he didn't feel alive.

Sometimes it was easier to be someone else. To fade in. His fucked-up childhood and drugged-out mom didn't matter to the dregs of society he kept company with these days. Most of them had similar backgrounds. There were no outcasts on the streets.

Nothing shocked these people. Nothing even *affected* them. Ian had spent his formative years trying to act cool and pretend things were normal. Going home at dinnertime, as if there would be food on the table.

Here in dysfunctionville, there was no normal. There was no dinnertime.

Although Ian was accepted in this world, it was a difficult, depressing existence. Hauntingly familiar. Everyone was high except him.

He'd spent the past few days recharging. There was still a dark crescent under his eye, but the swelling had gone down. He felt stronger. Better. More relaxed. Ready to jump back into the fray.

After donning a pair of cheap sunglasses to hide his bruised eye, he left the apartment. Today marked a turning point in the investigation. If Chuy continued to do business with Ian, they were in good standing. Ian could rebuild trust.

He picked up the pace as he walked down E Street, glancing at the Zócalo storefront. There was a CLOSED sign in the window. Ian wondered if Adam was tailing Kari Strauss because he wanted Moreno or because he liked her ass.

Ian hoped it was the second. Adam had been off the

rails since Penelope's death, and he needed to find another hobby. Another woman. Not the kind he met at a bar for a casual, late-night hookup, either.

Ian didn't have the mental energy to worry about his best friend right now, so he concentrated on staying calm for the buy. He felt nervous, anxious . . . excited. Flexing his hands, he approached the Hotel del Oro, visualizing a successful transaction.

Armando was sitting in the alcove outside Chuy's office, poker-faced as always. He rose, gesturing for Ian to turn around. Ian complied easily, bracing his hands on the wall while Armando patted him down in the shade of the trellis.

"How's it going?" Ian asked over his shoulder.

"Fine," Armando answered politely, as if they hadn't beaten the crap out of each other during their last meeting. After determining that Ian was clean of weapons and listening devices, Armando let him into the office.

Chuy wasn't behind his desk. He'd taken a seat on the couch on the opposite side of the room. Lines of white powder were drawn up on the surface of a glass-topped coffee table. *Blanca nieves*.

Armando shut the office door behind him. Chuy offered Ian a seat on the couch, directly in front of the white lines.

His stomach clenched with unease because he couldn't refuse the hospitality. Not at this juncture. "I'm sorry for what went down last week," he began, sitting next to Chuy. "I was fucked up. It won't happen again."

Chuy leaned forward, his eyes narrow.

"I didn't mean any disrespect," Ian assured him.

"My partner says you don't fight like a junkie."

Ian darted a glance at Armando, caught between pride and annoyance. "What's that supposed to mean?"

"Maybe you aren't who you appear to be."

His throat went dry. "Bullshit," he said, whipping off his sunglasses. "Look at my fucking eye! He kicked my ass."

"He has combat training."

Ian swallowed hard. Had his defensive techniques given something away? "I'd smoked a little PCP that day."

Chuy looked at Armando, who shrugged. Angel dust wasn't a commonly used substance, but it circulated from time to time. It made users behave erratically and believe they had superhuman strength.

"I was totally out of it, and I'm sorry. It was stupid."

After a moment's contemplation, Chuy nodded at the lines on the table. "That's the Snow White. Try it."

Ian rubbed his sweaty hands on his dirty jeans. "I don't have my rig."

"Fuck your rig. Snort it."

Ian had been in tight situations with dealers before. Sometimes he had to party with the big boys in order to gain their trust. He knew how to simulate drug use, and ways to decline without giving offense.

There was no way out here. He couldn't refuse, and he couldn't fake it. This was a test he was doomed to fail.

"I always try a small amount of a new batch—"

Chuy stood, pulling a 9 mm from the holster at his waist. He pointed the barrel at Ian's head. "Do it."

Fuck, fuck, *fuck*!

Ian held up his hands and looked straight down at the

table, afraid to make any move that might set Chuy off. "Okay, man, just chill out!" There was a short straw next to the lines. Reaching slowly, he picked it up.

If this was uncut heroin, he'd be dead before it hit the back of his throat.

Leaning over the surface of the table, he plugged one nostril and lifted the tooter to the other, inhaling deeply. The line disappeared up his nose, flooding his mouth with an acrid taste. He didn't have a cardiac arrest. Tossing the straw aside, he settled back against the couch, his eyes watering, nasal passages burning.

"How's it taste?" Chuy asked.

"Pretty good," Ian lied, sniffling. "You gonna sell me some now?"

Chuy relaxed, putting his piece away. Armando exited the office, claiming he had to run an errand, and they completed the exchange with little fanfare, Chuy accepting money for drugs. Ian put the balloon in his pocket, already feeling woozy. He had about five minutes before it kicked in completely.

As luck would have it, another customer showed up as Ian was leaving. He didn't make eye contact with the tattooed gang member on his way out. It was bad form to stare, and he needed to concentrate on walking.

Ian had to get as far away from Chuy's apartments as possible. He was in danger of breaking cover. A seasoned addict wouldn't react strongly to a single line of heroin unless it was 100 percent pure, and this stuff wasn't. If they saw him fall on his face, they'd know he wasn't the junkie he appeared to be.

Instead of crossing the courtyard, which looked sunbright and difficult to navigate, he took a left, lumbering down the shaded walkway. His legs felt rubbery, his knees ready to buckle. He knew he wasn't going to make it back to base. Maybe he could stagger through the parking lot and pass out behind a dumpster.

He tried to walk normally, but his feet refused to co-operate. A pair of vending machines swam into his field of vision, so he focused on moving toward them. It was like climbing Mount Everest. Or wading through molasses.

At last he was standing in front of the soda machine, mesmerized by the shiny façade and whirring refrigerator engine. He knew why people liked opiates; he'd never felt so peaceful. This vending machine was fascinating. He contemplated the vibrant design and perfect colors, wallowing in visual nirvana.

In the corner of his mind, he understood that lingering here was dangerous. Armando might be close by, and he had eyes like a hawk.

Get out of sight, Ian. *Get out of sight.*

He tore his gaze away from the vending machine, searching for an escape. There was a small, nondescript door on his right. Utility closet? He glanced back at Chuy's apartments and saw nothing but a gray blur.

Lurching forward, he grabbed the doorknob. Turned it. Open.

Victorious, he stumbled inside and closed the door behind him, fumbling for the lock. Either there wasn't one or his clumsy hands couldn't find it. The closet smelled like pine soap. He reached out for a mop handle, but it wouldn't hold him upright.

He fell down, into darkness.

* * *

Kari couldn't believe Adam let her go.

Had there been a mix-up at Saltillo Mundo? Maybe the shipment hadn't come in, or they hadn't loaded it into her van. She didn't understand what had happened. If she'd been smuggling illegal cargo, surely the inspectors would have detected it.

Why hadn't she been charged and arrested?

Kari drove to downtown San Diego in a daze, too drained to make sense of the situation. She didn't fool herself into thinking it was over. She'd made it across the border by some kind of miracle, but she could still get caught.

Investigators could be following her, hoping for a bigger bust.

No one was there to meet her at Zócalo. She parked behind the store, her pulse racing. Afraid she'd be tackled by law enforcement the instant she left the vehicle, she stayed inside for a few moments, searching her surroundings.

Everything looked normal.

A delivery truck passed by, carrying stacks of five-gallon water containers. The liquid sloshed back and forth. Kari was struck by warring discomforts: a full bladder and intense thirst. She squirmed in her seat, glancing in the rearview mirror.

Across the parking lot, a man opened a can of soda and took a long drink. Kari couldn't take it anymore. She rolled up the windows and leapt out of the van, locking it quickly before she rushed to the back door. There were no shouted threats, no weapons drawn. Her eyes darted around the parking lot as she disengaged the alarm. Inside Zócalo, she used the bathroom and drank straight from the sink, splashing cool water on her flushed cheeks. As she straightened, she winced at her reflection. She looked like a crazy person. Mascara smudged, eyes wild. Her tank top was damp with sweat.

"Ugh," she said, yanking it off. After a quick toilette with paper towels, she put on the extra shirt she kept under the counter.

A man was waiting for her when she walked out.

Kari let out a muted scream, flattening her back against the wall. It was Chuy's partner, the quiet crew member with the no-frills face.

"Good afternoon," he said, standing still in the hallway. His accent wasn't as pronounced as Maria's, or as pleasing to the ear. With the light behind him, he was a dark outline, almost unrecognizable. "Do you know who I am?"

"Yes," she said, her heart pounding. "Where's my sister?"

"She will be delivered to you, as planned."

"When?"

"When you give us the packages."

"They're in the back of my van."

"Those are just tiles."

Her stomach felt queasy. "I don't understand."

"It was a dry run," he explained slowly, as if speaking to a child.

A dry run. She'd almost gone insane for nothing. Even worse, she had to repeat the experience. "No," she whispered. "That's impossible."

The man remained silent.

"I can't do it again!"

"Would you like to pay the debt another way?"

Kari slid down the wall, shaken. She couldn't come up with that kind of money. Selling her assets would only cover a fraction of the amount.

"We will give you more instructions before the real pickup."

"I want to see my sister."

"After the delivery."

"You're an evil man," she said, her voice breaking. "How do you live with yourself?"

He turned his head to the side, contemplative. In profile, he was only slightly less intimidating. "I'm sorry you are upset."

"Fuck you!"

With a polite nod, he left her alone.

Kari couldn't have guessed how long she sat there, her knees drawn up to her chest. Finally she got up and went to the mini-fridge, staring at the contents blankly. Something gnawed at her belly, but it didn't feel like hunger. She grabbed a yogurt smoothie and drank from the container, hoping to fill her emptiness.

A knock at the back door alerted her that she had another visitor. She went to answer it, not exercising any special caution. She felt numb.

It was Adam.

"What a surprise," she said, crossing her arms over her chest. There was no warmth left inside her, no hint of the coquette.

He gave her a quick survey, assessing her bleak mood. "You forgot your sweater."

She looked down at the garment he offered. The cream-colored knit made a sharp contrast to his dark hands. They were strong, capable hands. An honest man's hands, she thought, even though she didn't trust him.

"Normally we would have stuck it in the lost-and-found," he said.

Her gaze rose to his face. It was compellingly sincere. For some reason she couldn't unfold her arms to accept the sweater. She just stared at him, her lips trembling. The tears that wouldn't come a few minutes ago rushed to the surface, wetting her dry eyes.

He didn't panic at the sight or make any awkward excuses. As if he understood that she was frozen, he shook out the knit fabric and draped it around her shoulders, enveloping her in its soft embrace.

Kari melted at the gesture. Allowing herself to be drawn forward, she pressed her face to the front of his shirt and cried. He wrapped his arms around her, cupping the back of her head and stroking her hair. There were no words of comfort or invasive questions. He just held her until the tears abated.

"I'm sorry," she said, sniffling. Her nose was running, so she shied away from him, grabbing a tissue. "I didn't mean to get so emotional."

"What's wrong?"

She shrugged. "I had a bad day."

"Maybe you should talk about it."

"To you?"

"I'm the only one here."

God, he seemed so earnest. She'd always been drawn to nice men but fallen into lukewarm relationships. Adam was different. He had the good-guy appeal she responded to, along with a mysterious edge that excited her.

Maybe he was the last person she should be baring her soul to. But he was available, and she liked him.

"My sister is a heroin addict," she said, clearing her throat. It was the first time Kari had spoken those words out loud. When the earth didn't quake in protest, she added, "I've always felt guilty about it."

"Why?"

Kari went back to the fridge for a cold drink. This was a long story. "You want one?" she asked, lifting the water bottle.

"No thanks." He grabbed a chair at the table, waiting for her to continue.

She sat down across from him. "My father was poor when we came here, but he worked really hard and saved enough money to buy a furniture store. His business was a runaway success. He lived the American dream, spoiling Sasha and me with expensive gifts. We wore designer clothes and went to trendy clubs. By the time we were teenagers, we both had fake IDs. No one questioned us."

"What about your mother?"

"She died in the Czech Republic. I'm sure that was one of the reasons my dad treated us like princesses. I think he wanted us to have a carefree life, because his had been so full of hardship. But it didn't work out that way."

"What happened?"

"A year after I graduated from high school, my dad had a heart attack and passed away. I didn't know how to be responsible for myself, let alone Sasha. She'd always been wild, and I wasn't a very good guardian to her."

"Why do you say that?"

Kari swallowed hard. "Later that year I met this guy, a club promoter. He took me to all the best parties, and I was . . . easily impressed. One night he introduced Sasha to a friend of his. The four of us went up to the VIP area. Sasha drank too much champagne, which was typical of her, but so did I. Andrew asked if I wanted to go to the next room, and I said yes. I left my sister there, practically passed out, with a total stranger."

Adam didn't have to ask what had happened then. He knew.

"When I heard her scream, I sort of . . . woke up from the champagne fog. I ran to help, but the door was locked. When I finally got in, Sasha was sobbing, her clothes torn. And the guy was so smug, like he knew he'd get away with it."

"Did he?"

"Yes. I took her to the hospital and gave a statement to the police, but she refused to press charges. She said she couldn't remember anything. She was only seventeen at the time. And she's been using heavily ever since."

"Why do you think you're at fault?"

Kari's eyes welled with tears once again. "I introduced her to drugs at a very young age. We smoked pot together. Whatever I did, she did."

"Did you do heroin?"

"No, Adam, I left her to be raped!" Hands trembling, she swiped at the tears on her cheeks. "I was annoyed with her for getting wasted and embarrassing me. So I left her, drunk and alone, to be raped."

"You were drinking, too. Your judgment was impaired."

She looked away. "I will *never* forgive myself."

"What about the rapist? Doesn't he deserve the blame?"

"Of course, but—I should have protected her. I should have known."

"The only person who could have known was the perpetrator himself, and maybe his asshole friend. How old were they?"

"Twenty-five," she whispered.

"I'll bet the club promoter understood the danger he was leaving your sister in and didn't give a damn. Those men exploited both of you."

Kari nodded, miserable. She'd never seen Andrew again.

"If you'd been raped while Sasha was passed out, would you hold her responsible?"

She blinked at him in surprise. "No."

"Jesus, Kari, have you ever talked to anyone about this?"

"Just the police officer."

Adam gave her a level stare, saying nothing. Maybe he didn't think she'd made all the right decisions, but he didn't criticize her or dismiss her feelings. He wasn't offering any false platitudes, either. She appreciated his straightforwardness. Too many men said what they thought women wanted to hear.

"I've enabled her in so many ways," she murmured, hugging the sweater around her body. "I've given her money and kept her secrets. I told her I wouldn't see her unless she was sober, but she's never sober. I couldn't cut her out of my life." Her throat tightened with sadness. She stood abruptly, tipping the plastic chair over. "Now I feel like I've already lost her. I've never been able to help her, and I'm afraid she's going to die!"

Adam's expression softened, but Kari pressed her hand to her mouth and turned away, dismayed by her words. Voicing her fears made them seem too real, too frighteningly possible. She couldn't handle the thought of her baby sister overdosing. After the day she'd had, it was too much.

He rose to his feet and came up behind her, touching her arm. His hand burned through the thin knit, heating her bare skin.

Kari didn't want to cry anymore. She didn't want to let go of Sasha; she wanted to reach out and grab something else. She needed to shut off her emotions for a few fleeting moments and surrender to sensation.

She knew Adam would accommodate her. She could read his desire without even looking at his face. His body was taut with tension, and his chest emanated warmth. If she leaned back a few inches, she'd feel him.

Her breath quickened, and she covered his hand with hers, stroking his knuckles. His fingers tightened on her upper arm, a reflexive squeeze that made her shiver. "Could you get in trouble for being with me?"

His hand stilled. "Maybe."

Her stomach fluttered in anticipation. Moistening her lips, she glanced over her shoulder. "Then why did you come?"

His gaze darkened, from medium brown to espresso black. "Just tell me what you're mixed up in."

Instead of spilling her secrets, Kari turned to face him. She knew Adam would alert his superiors about the shipment. He was too honest to give her the kind of help she needed. But he wasn't perfect. He didn't step back when she closed the distance between them, or pull away when she twined her arms around his neck.

"Let me help you," he said, a muscle in his jaw twitching.

"I can't."

"Damn it, Kari—"

She lifted her lips to his, shutting him up.

10

There was a dead man in the broom closet.

Maria startled when she saw him, smothering a scream. The slumped figure straightened unexpectedly, opening red-rimmed eyes.

Drunk. Not dead.

She knew those eyes, *color de avellano*. She couldn't remember the English word for eyes that muddy shade of green, but she'd recognize them anywhere.

Her inebriated savior frowned, trying to free his arm from a tangled mop head.

She glanced past the vending machines. Chuy's office door was closed. Sonia had just gone in for their afternoon appointment. "What are you doing?" she asked in a low voice, leaning over him.

"Shut the door," he rasped.

"You can't sleep in here."

He thought about that for a minute, grappling with the concept. "Where's Armando?"

"I don't know." She hadn't seen him in the past hour, but that didn't mean he wasn't on the premises. "Are you hiding from him?"

He shook his arm loose from the mop strings, ignoring her question.

Maria realized that he was on something a little stronger than alcohol. He didn't smell like booze, and his eyes were strange. "What will Armando do if he finds you?"

"Kill me," he said, slumping forward again.

She shut the door, her mind racing. Armando wasn't around, as far as she knew, and Chuy would be occupied for about five more minutes. If she left this man in the broom closet, one of the other maids would report his presence within the hour.

Would Armando really kill him? He'd already beaten him to a pulp. His face still bore the bruises.

Maria knew she should walk away. This was a dangerous situation, and she had plenty of other people to worry about. Kari might have been arrested. And the last time Chuy had caught her interfering with his business, he'd been furious.

She didn't want to be dragged into his room again.

On the other hand, this man had saved her—twice. Maybe he'd lost his way and taken too many drugs, but he was still a good person. He was the same man who'd held her hand in the hospital, the handsome agent with the rough-soft voice. She couldn't leave him in such a vulnerable position.

Decision made, she ran to the elevator and pressed the up button, then rushed back to the closet. "Come," she said, tugging on his wrist. "I hide you in better place."

He seemed willing to go, if not quite able.

She crouched over him, putting her arms around his lean waist. "Hurry," she panted. "We go to elevator."

With her help, he staggered to his feet, and they moved

toward the end of the walkway. She supported him on
one side, urging him to walk faster. The elevator doors
sprang open with a noisy jingle. They almost didn't
make it inside.

As soon as the doors closed behind them, he collapsed
against her.

"Levántate," she ordered. "Stay on your feet!"

He nodded, appearing half asleep.

"Don't you dare pass out," she hissed in Spanish, trying to hold him up. There was no way she could do this
if he lost consciousness. For a skinny guy, he weighed a
ton, and he was a head taller than her.

His throat worked as he swallowed. "Okay."

The doors separated, revealing the empty second
floor. Maria breathed a sigh of relief. During the middle
of the week, the hotel was never fully occupied, but a
guest could leave one of the rooms any minute. Worse,
Armando might step out of the shadows.

"Let's go," she said, digging her fingernails into his
ribs. He lurched forward, his mouth set with determination. Although he put forth a lot of effort, his motions
were clumsy. He was a hard man, all sharp edges and
ropy muscles. She had a difficult time directing him.

Thankfully, the hiding place was close. Over the
weekend, one of the rooms had been damaged by a
small fire. A guest had been careless with a cigarette,
igniting a trash can and burning up a section of carpet.
The room had been closed for repairs, and no one had
actually started the work. Chuy's other business was his
top priority.

Maria propped the man against the wall and used her
card key to unlock the door, glancing around to make
sure they were still alone. She helped him inside, wrin-

kling her nose at the smell of stale smoke and burnt carpet fibers. As soon as he saw the bed, he stumbled toward it, falling facedown on the bare mattress.

She shut the door and peeked out the window, seeing no one. So far, so good. He could sleep it off in here while she finished her shift.

Her heart continued to pound, from tension and exertion. She didn't know what would happen if they were discovered. Armando was a cold-blooded criminal. He might not enjoy hurting women, but that didn't mean he wouldn't do it.

He'd kill her quickly, perhaps.

Shivering at the thought, she turned to face the sleeping man. His name suddenly came to her: Agent Foster. He looked so different now. His hair was still dark brown, but medium length, his jaw covered with a scruffy beard. There was a dark circle under his left eye. He was wearing a faded black T-shirt and worn gray jeans. The clothes weren't just old and frayed, they were dirty, as if he hadn't changed them in days.

Despite this evidence of his deterioration, something about him appealed to her. Beneath those dingy clothes, he had strong muscles. Under the overgrown facial hair, he was handsome. Agent Foster was still in there.

She sat at the edge of the bed, sweeping a lock of hair off his forehead. His skin felt cool to the touch, and his breathing was deep and even.

"Thank you," he mumbled, not opening his eyes.

"*Estás bien, señor?* If I leave, will you . . . *como se dice* . . . stop breathing?" She didn't know how to say *overdose* in English.

"I'm okay. Leave me."

But she sat and watched him for several more minutes, reluctant to walk away.

The instant his lips touched hers, Kari's stressful day faded into the background. Her concerns for Sasha were pushed aside.

The only thing she cared about right now was Adam. His mouth, his body, his touch.

He slid his hand into her hair, holding her still. The subtle use of force excited her. It suggested that, although she'd started this, he was going to finish it. She liked that. Letting her eyes drift shut, she tilted her head back, inviting him to continue. When he covered her mouth with his, she parted her lips on a low moan.

The way he kissed was kind of . . . indecent. He didn't test the waters or use a light touch. He just dove right in, filling her mouth with his tongue. There was nothing polite or tentative about it. He used her mouth for his pleasure, delving inside, taking what he wanted.

Kari liked that, too. She pressed her body closer and grabbed handfuls of his shirt, squirming for more. He tasted as good as he smelled, clean and spicy and delicious. His tongue was hot and his lips were firm. She wanted his mouth all over her body. Her sex tingled and her nipples tightened against the cups of her bra.

He broke the kiss, panting lightly. Her lips felt swollen and wet. His eyes dropped from her mouth to her breasts.

Kari indulged him, tugging her T-shirt over her head. His gaze darkened at the sight of her white bra, which barely held in her endowments. It wasn't a push-up, but it squeezed her breasts together in a sexy way.

He groaned, covering her breasts with his hands and taking her mouth again. She kissed him back hungrily, arching at his touch. When his thumb brushed over her taut nipple through the fabric of her bra, she gasped against his lips. Even that slight barrier was too much. She was too eager, too sensitive.

"I need to take this off," she said.

He released her immediately. "Good idea."

She unclasped her bra and let it fall to the ground. He wanted to stare, but she didn't have any patience for that. She brought his hands to her breasts, delighting at the feel of his rough palms cupping her soft flesh. He trapped her nipples between his thumb and forefinger, watching her face as he applied gentle pressure. His hands looked so beautiful on her, dark and strong and long-fingered. Her legs began to tremble and her panties got wet. She bit down on her lower lip, afraid she might come just from this.

He must have understood how close she was, because he glanced around the room, assessing all possible surfaces. The plastic table wouldn't hold their weight. Her work counter was a little too high. He backed her toward the stack of handwoven rugs in the corner, lowering his mouth to kiss her again.

"Wait," she said, holding his arm. Before they lay down, she grabbed a drop cloth, protecting the merchandise.

They both laughed at her compulsive behavior. Then his lips met hers, and all of her concerns drifted away. There was only here, and now, and him. She unbuttoned his shirt and pushed it off his shoulders, her fingertips dancing over his chest. Her mouth made a mew of approval as she explored his taut muscles.

"You must work out," she said, smoothing her palm down his flat stomach.

With a low growl, he grabbed her wrists, holding them over her head as he stretched out on top of her. She could feel the rasp of denim on her tender inner thighs, the jut of his erection against her cleft. It felt big.

Trapping her wrists with one hand, he reached under her skirt with the other, removing her panties. She moaned when he stripped the damp fabric away from her sensitive flesh. The flimsy white cotton snagged briefly on her ankle strap before he tossed it aside.

It felt strange to be naked except for a skirt and sandals. She was completely exposed to him, her thighs parted, sex bare.

He just looked at her for a moment, his gaze on her mouth, her breasts, between her legs. She hoped he liked what he saw. When his eyes met hers, she moistened her lips in anticipation, desperate for him to get on with it.

In no particular hurry, he released her wrists and sat back on his heels, unbuttoning his distended fly. He pushed his jeans and shorts down to his knees, freeing his erection. It bobbed up against his flat belly, heavy and thick.

Kari wanted him inside her. Her inner muscles clenched in anticipation, her body greedy to accept his. Driven by a desire she'd never known before, she fisted her hands in the well-worn denim skirt, lifting it higher. He studied her tingling flesh, his nostrils flaring. She knew she was wet, glistening.

Her nipples were ruddy and puckered, her eyes half-lidded.

He stretched a condom down his length and placed

the blunt tip against her. She barely restrained herself from lifting her hips to seat him. Teasing her, he slid the head of his penis along her slippery cleft, rubbing her clitoris.

She groaned, so close to climax she could taste it. Her chest was flushed, her tummy quivering. "Please."

He gave her what she wanted, plunging his thick cock into her, all the way to the hilt. She cried out as her body sheathed him, grasping tight. He paused a moment to let her adjust, and she needed it. She felt stretched to the limit, full of him. Trembling with anticipation, she wrapped her arms around his neck.

"Okay?" he asked.

"It's better than okay," she panted.

Watching her face, he drew back and drove deep again, wrenching a gasp from her lips. He repeated the motion, hitting the perfect angle, maximizing her pleasure. "Yes," she said, beyond shame. This was too good to feel bad about. "God, yes!"

His hands gripped her hips, sliding her up and down his length. She sobbed out loud, wanting more. Harder. Faster. When he didn't find a pace to suit her, she dug her heels into the cloth and lifted her bottom off the ground, rising to meet him.

"Slow down, honey," he said, trying to still her movements. "You're going to make me come too fast."

Mindless in her own need, she ignored him, sliding her hand down her belly. He watched, transfixed, as she worked her hips in a pagan rhythm, pressing her fingertips to her clit. The combination of sensations hurled her into a bone-melting orgasm. She bucked against him, convulsing in ecstasy.

When she drifted back down to earth, he was gazing at her, an appreciative expression on his face. She might have felt embarrassed about taking matters into her own hands if he hadn't enjoyed the show so much.

His cock pulsed inside her, hard and hot. "Do that again."

She didn't think she was capable of a second orgasm so soon, but when she traced her stretched opening with her fingertips, circling her swollen clitoris, the tension inside her recoiled. He drew himself out and eased back in, rocking against her. This time, the ride to the top was gentler, but no less intense. He felt deliciously stiff. Reveling in the slick friction, she locked her legs around his hips and cried out again, dissolving in pleasure. He followed her this time, his shoulders quaking as he found his own release.

They didn't lie there together, basking in the glory of great sex. Adam was polite enough to lift his considerable weight off her. He withdrew from her carefully and went to the bathroom to dispose of the condom.

Kari's languid satisfaction disappeared with him. She became aware of how she must look, her legs splayed wide and her skirt hiked up to her waist. The back door was unlocked. Anyone could walk in.

She tugged her skirt down and grabbed her sweater, wrapping it around her naked torso. What had she just done?

She didn't even know Adam. This wasn't the beginning of a beautiful relationship. It was a mindless fuck on the floor. With a stranger who would arrest her in a heartbeat if he discovered her secret.

Feeling queasy, she awaited his return.

* * *

After her shift was over, Maria slipped out of her work smock and snuck up to the second floor, keeping her eyes peeled for Armando.

She didn't think anyone had seen her hide Agent Foster. Chuy had been busy with Sonia, and then he'd taken care of some customers. It was business as usual at the Hotel del Oro.

Moving quickly, she used her card key and slipped inside the damaged room, undetected. Her stowaway wasn't on the bed, where she'd left him. Had he wandered off, or been discovered by another staff member?

Pulse racing, she locked the door behind her and entered the room, searching for him. The bathroom door was open. She peeked in.

He was sprawled out on the floor by the toilet.

"*Dios mio,*" she said, covering her mouth with one hand. "Are you sick?"

His eyelids fluttered and his head lolled to the side. He was obviously ill. His T-shirt was damp with sweat, his face wan. Wincing in sympathy, she rifled through her purse. She'd bought a Coke at the vending machine, hoping a bit of caffeine would wake him up. Maybe she should have purchased some crackers to settle his stomach, too.

"Drink this," she said, cracking the top open.

With her assistance, he sat up to take a drink. When the liquid stayed down, she gave him a little more. "Feeling better?"

He settled against her shoulder, drifting off.

"Oh no," she said, putting the Coke aside. "You can't

stay here all night. We have to get you up and walking again."

His eyes opened, bleary and unfocused. "Let Armando kill me."

"You don't mean that," she said, but he was already asleep again. She disentangled herself from him and stood, pacing the bathroom. What was she going to do? She had to get him out of here before they were caught.

Although she didn't have any experience with drug addicts, she knew of two ways to sober men up. The first was with food, which he might not be able to handle. The second tactic involved cold water.

She tapped her chin, considering the shower stall. He was already dirty.

"You need a bath," she said, eyeing his soiled shirt with distaste. When he didn't protest, she knelt to untie his ratty tennis shoes. The socks underneath were clean, oddly enough. She stripped them away, revealing his long, narrow feet. He had nice-looking feet, for a man. She frowned at the thought, shaking her head.

When she tried to unfasten his belt buckle, he roused, locking his hand around her wrist. "What are you doing?"

"Taking your pants off."

He blinked at her a few times. "I can't . . . perform."

"Good."

His head rested back on the floor and he let her continue, staying half alert. His boxer shorts were blue pinstriped and looked new, like his socks. She tugged his jeans down his legs and folded them.

"Don't search my pockets."

"Okay," she said easily. "Sit up."

Groaning, he managed to lift his upper body off the

floor, and she pulled his damp T-shirt over his head. Although his skin was clammy with perspiration, he didn't stink. She'd sat next to men on the bus who smelled worse.

He was also more fit than she'd imagined. His arms were well defined, his stomach muscles etched into hard flesh.

Glancing away from him, she studied the shower area. There was no tub, and he might not be able to stay upright on his own. She'd have to get in with him. "Look away," she warned, taking off her jeans.

He averted his eyes, obedient.

She unbuttoned her shirt and set it aside, making a neat stack. In her plain cotton panties and serviceable white bra, she didn't make a seductive picture. And he was too loaded to care.

"Into the shower," she said, helping him stand. He was cooperative but clumsy. It took every ounce of strength she possessed to get him into the stall, and she felt very awkward, pressing her naked skin against his.

Panting with effort, she reached behind him to turn on the faucet. Cold water hit his back, shocking him fully awake. "Hey!"

"Stay still," she said, hugging him around the waist. "I'm helping you."

He endured the icy spray for a moment, but it didn't have the desired effect. Although they were both soaked, and shivering from cold, he wasn't in his right mind. His hands wandered over her slippery skin, cupping her bottom. He obviously didn't understand what she was trying to wake him up for.

"Stop that," she said, slapping his hands away.

He had the wherewithal to turn the water off, and the

nerve to stare at her dripping body, zeroing in on her wet underwear. The white fabric was now transparent, revealing her nipples and the dark triangle between her legs.

Maria realized that she'd succeeded in rousing him, but not the way she'd intended. "Let's go," she muttered, urging him to step out of the shower. He was harder to manage now, trying to grope her again and almost losing his balance on the linoleum floor. When she finally got him to the bed, he gave up on pawing her and passed out cold.

She sat at the edge of the mattress, filled with frustration. He'd asked her not to go through his pockets, but she had no choice. Storming across the room, she searched his jeans. He had a bag of drugs, a wad of cash, and a cell phone.

She turned on the phone, dialing Kari's number.

"Hello?"

Maria let out a slow breath, relieved. "How did it go?"

"I can't talk right now," she said.

"Are you at the store?"

"Yes."

"Is your sister there?"

"No."

Maria moistened her lips, wondering what had happened. "I'm going to be late."

"Why?" Kari's tone changed from melancholy to alarmed. "Are you okay?"

"Yes, I'm fine. Everything is fine. I'll be home in a few hours."

Kari insisted on coming to the hotel to check up on her. Maria convinced her not to. They ended the call, each worried about the other. Feeling anxious, Maria washed Agent Foster's shirt in the sink and hung it up to dry.

Then she perched at the edge of the bed, propped her elbows on her knees, and rested her chin in her hands.

It was going to be a long night.

11

Adam couldn't meet his eyes in the mirror.

He'd crossed the line. Twice now, he'd let Kari go when he should have detained her. Breaking procedure, he'd followed her for a week. He'd come here to drill her for information and ended up . . . drilling her.

He'd jeopardized his entire career, for what? Five hot minutes.

And he still didn't know what game she was playing. It was likely that a shipment of drugs had been smuggled over the border in another vehicle at the same time Kari came through. He could have sworn by the way she acted at the border that she was doing something illegal. Guilt and fear and anxiety radiated from her. Even while he was on top of her, she'd been keyed up. She'd fucked him like her life depended on it.

He should go home, regroup. Figure out what the hell he was trying to accomplish on this after-hours mission, besides getting her off.

Luckily, Adam had plenty of experience with leaving women right after sex. He knew how to sidestep awkward scenes and messy entanglements. He always had an excuse ready for parting ways.

Avoiding his reflection, he walked out of the bathroom.

To his surprise, Kari wasn't curled up on the mats, drowsy from satiation. She was standing with her back to him, talking on her cell phone.

She'd tugged her skirt down and thrown the sweater over her shoulders, but she hadn't bothered to put on a bra or shirt. Her panties were lying on the floor where he'd left them.

This must be an important fucking phone call.

Don't ask who it is.

Rule number one for getting out fast was no personal questions. Adam waited for her to hang up, unaccountably annoyed. The fact that she was on her cell should have made leaving her easier. Instead, it felt like an insult. Hadn't he been good enough? Was she so bored and restless that she had to get up and check her messages?

Kari ended the call and turned to him, giving him an apologetic look. "That was Maria," she explained. "Sorry."

Oh, it was *Maria*. His attitude shifted from cagey withdrawal to seething outrage in an instant. Her body was still flushed from the pleasure he'd given her, and she had the nerve to mention her other "lover"? This was total bullshit. She was toying with him, trying to make him jealous—and it was working.

Don't react.

"Let's get something straight," he said, ignoring the rules of disengagement. "I know goddamned well that you're not sleeping with your roommate, so you can drop the lesbian act. We just proved without a doubt that you play for my team."

Color rose to her cheeks. "I'm sorry," she said again. "I've never done this before."

Adam glanced at the lacy scrap of panties on the floor, arching a brow. "That's hard to believe, *bella*."

Her mouth made a thin line and she snatched up her undergarments, setting them aside. "Not with a stranger, I mean."

A *stranger*. He raked a hand through his hair, disturbed by that characterization. The truth was that he knew her better than any of the women he'd been with in recent memory. They'd had more meaningful conversations, spent more time together.

"Have you?" she asked.

"Have I what?"

"Slept with a stranger before."

"Yes," he said, knowing the blunt admission wouldn't make her feel better.

"What do you say afterward?"

"It depends if I want to see her again."

She hugged the sweater around her naked torso, uncomfortable. "I can't get involved with anyone right now."

Adam clenched his hands into fists. He'd never been on the receiving end of a brush-off before and it didn't feel very good. Maybe this was payback for all the women he'd used and discarded in Penelope's wake. "Let me give you some tips on how to handle this, for future reference. Never say you can't get involved. What you mean is that you want anonymous sex but would rather have it with someone else. No man wants to hear that. Instead, say you had a nice time, kiss him goodbye, and don't call back."

Her eyes darkened at his harsh tone, but she didn't speak. The sweater at her shoulders slipped down a little, its latticework fabric revealing more than it concealed. A pert nipple peeped through the spaces, the rosy tip framed by soft knit.

With some difficulty, Adam returned his gaze to her face. "I'd also recommend putting on some clothes. The only thing I can think about while you're like that is fucking you again." Turning his back on her, he strode toward the door.

She followed, catching hold of his arm. "Wait."

He paused, impatient.

"Answer one question before you go," she said, lowering her voice. "Are you with Moreno?"

Adam looked down at her slender hand. "Moreno?"

"Carlos Moreno. My sister's boyfriend."

"I know who he is."

"Are you part of his crew?"

He'd never been so insulted by a postcoital interrogation. He could handle questions about his marital status, his general health, and even his sexual history. His professional integrity hadn't been an issue with women.

Then again, he hadn't slept with a drug smuggler before.

"No," he said, removing her hand from his person. "I'm not part of Moreno's crew. I'd quit the department before I accepted a bribe. I don't expect you to believe that, because liars are notoriously skeptical, so I'll spell it out for you in a convincing way."

She recoiled at his fierce expression, shrinking back a step. Her wary eyes cut him to the quick. If she thought he would join a criminal organization or hurt a woman physically, she didn't know him at all.

"Three years ago I was about to marry my longtime girlfriend," he said in a flat voice. "We met in junior college and decided to get engaged right after graduation. I'd just been stationed at the San Ysidro port of entry. She had dual citizenship and a promising career as a reporter for a bilingual newspaper."

Kari waited for him to continue, her face pale.

"She was covering a story on drug violence, interviewing a couple of lowlifes at the Coyote Café in downtown Tijuana. Shots were fired between Moreno's crew and members of La Familia, a rival cartel. One of the bullets hit her in the neck, grazing her carotid artery. She bled to death while the crowd scattered."

"Oh my God," Kari whispered, reaching out to him. "Adam, I'm so sorry."

"Don't," he said, warding off her touch. "For almost two years I tailed Moreno every chance I could get, fantasizing about strangling him with my bare hands. It took a long time for me to let go of my anger and give up on vengeance. I'd still rather kill him than do his bidding. Do you understand?"

She crossed her arms over her chest, nodding miserably.

He took a business card from his pocket and scribbled his cell number on the back. "If you want to talk about *your* involvement with Moreno, I'm available," he said, handing it to her. "If not, this is goodbye. I had a nice time."

After a brusque kiss on the cheek, he left the store.

He'd lied to her, of course. He hadn't abandoned his vendetta or gained control of his anger. Those dark feelings were as strong and corrosive as ever, bubbling up beneath the surface, eating him up inside.

Ian awoke, disoriented.

His throat was dry and he had a mild headache, like a hangover. Although the hotel room was dark, he was vaguely aware of its basic layout. He rose from the bed and stumbled into the bathroom, turning on the light.

Wincing at the harsh brightness, he took a piss and washed his slack face, drinking water straight from the sink. Feeling a little better, he went back to bed.

The details were fuzzy, but he knew where he was. He also knew whom he was with. Maria Santos was lying next to him, one slender arm resting above her head, dark hair spilling across the pillow.

He wasn't clear on why they were here, though he remembered showering with her. Instead of trying to make sense of the past few hours, which were inaccessible, he focused on what they were going to do next.

Leaving the hotel seemed like a good idea. On the other hand, there was a beautiful, half-naked woman in bed with him.

Ian couldn't stop staring at her.

She'd wrapped a towel around her body after the shower, but it had fallen open at some point during the night. Now she was enticingly revealed. Her bra and underwear were plain white cotton, sort of pristine-looking. Damp, the fabric appeared paper thin. He could see the dark circles of her nipples and the shadowy triangle between her legs.

She was slender, but with lovely feminine curves. She had a flat, sexy stomach and gently flared hips. Her breasts were small, delicate. Although they wouldn't fill his palm, he ached to cup her.

Ian's brain wasn't functioning properly, but his cock was working overtime. Blood rushed from his head to his groin, swelling him to an almost painful degree.

He studied her face, the sweep of her eyelashes, her soft, parted lips. His erection throbbed with every heartbeat. The urge to wrap his hand around it and stroke himself off while he watched her sleep was overwhelming.

She sighed dreamily and rolled over, treating him to a view of her heart-shaped bottom. Then she snuggled closer, fitting that pretty backside against his upright dick.

Ian smothered a groan. He knew he shouldn't touch her. Engaging in sexual activity as an undercover agent was grounds for termination, and he didn't even think she was willing. He had a faint recollection of her slapping his hands away earlier.

She hadn't brought him here to ball him.

His sense of chivalry told him to get up and leave the room. But that sense was dull in comparison to his desire. He could smell her hair, her skin, the delicious chemistry of warm female and damp fabric.

She shifted in her sleep, restless.

He leaned forward a fraction, burying his nose in her hair. God, she smelled good. With a trembling hand, he touched her slim waist, skimming his fingertips along her side. Her skin felt like silk.

She moved again, wiggling her cute little bottom, and he was lost. His hips jerked forward, grinding into her. When she didn't protest, he didn't stop. Flattening his palm over her belly, he pressed his erection harder against her buttocks.

She gasped, arching her spine.

One of his hands wandered up to her breasts, finding taut nipples and tender flesh. With a low groan, he pushed aside the damp cotton, teasing the puckered tips. His other hand slid between her legs, cupping her sex. She covered his hand with hers and moaned, practically begging for his cock. He wanted to give it to her. He wanted to yank down her panties and take her like this, from behind.

He might have gone ahead and done it if she hadn't frozen suddenly and bolted away from him, scrambling off the mattress. She stared at him, wide-eyed. The air between them went from hot and steamy to cold and tense.

"*Que haces?*" she whispered, tugging her bra into place.

Ian realized that he'd mistaken her dreamlike state for a pleasurable response. She hadn't given consent; she'd been asleep, unaware.

Several layers of understanding struck him at once, and the repercussions were staggering. The first time he'd seen Maria Santos, she'd been lying in a crumpled heap on the sand dunes near an unofficial border crossing called El Caracol. She'd been beaten within an inch of her life and raped repeatedly.

Last week Chuy had dragged her to his back room, almost assaulting her. That must have brought back bad memories. She'd risked her neck to help him yesterday. She'd tried to sober him up, stayed by his side.

And what had he done to repay her? Groped her while she slept.

His behavior was so inexcusable he felt sick. *"Lo siento,"* he groaned, wanting to crawl under a rock and die. *"Soy bien cabrón."*

She straightened, seeming unfazed by his gross misconduct. "I speak English now, remember?"

Ian knew there was something off about the way she said that, but he couldn't quite put his finger on it. Still disoriented from the opiates, he repeated his apology in English. "I shouldn't have touched you."

Shrugging, Maria handed him a can of soda from the nightstand. "Can you walk, *señor*? We have to leave."

He sipped the Coke with a grimace. It was flat.

She took the soda back and drank from it also, studying him with a curious expression. "You should get dressed."

Although Ian's ardor had cooled, his erection hadn't subsided. After a long dry spell, it was desperate for attention, embarrassingly stiff. He clenched his teeth and thought of ice. "I need a minute."

Her gaze fell to his lap and lingered there, which didn't help at all.

"Maybe you should get dressed first," he said, stealing another glance at her chest. Her nipples poked against the fabric of her bra, taunting him.

"Oh," she breathed, clapping her hands over her small breasts. Whirling around, she grabbed a neat stack of clothing and retreated to the bathroom, giving him some much-needed privacy.

She didn't seem traumatized. Her mild reaction didn't assuage his guilt, however.

He'd always carried a torch for her. At first it was her spirit he'd been attracted to. She'd been battered, but she wasn't broken. Every day he visited her in the hospital, she'd cheered *him* up with her strength and optimism.

As the bruises faded, her beauty shone through, and he couldn't stop staring at her. There was an innocence about her that discouraged lustful thoughts, and she'd just been attacked, so he kept his distance. She was also barely legal, eighteen to his twenty-four. Too young for the hardships she'd endured. Although she appeared to be healing well, he didn't think she'd recover emotionally for months or years to come.

Even so, he was drawn to her. She'd almost died in his arms the day he'd found her, and he felt protective of her.

He wanted to keep her safe.

It was impossible, of course. As soon as she was released from the hospital, she'd been taken back to Mexico on a bus full of migrant workers who'd been caught at the border, attempting to enter the country illegally. He hadn't asked for her contact information, and he'd never said goodbye.

His inability to act on her behalf weighed heavily on him. He hated filing an incident report for a crime that couldn't be investigated in the United States because it occurred on foreign soil. Mexican officials wouldn't scour the desert for rape suspects. They had few resources and even fewer incentives to make hard-hitting arrests. There was no justice for Maria on either side of the border.

Ian rose from the bed, frustrated. With some difficulty he wrestled into his pants, buttoning the fly and securing his belt. His T-shirt was damp and smelled like bar soap. Maria had washed it, he realized, feeling another wave of regret.

She was a sweet girl. And he was a sick, horny mother-fucker.

Wanting to punch himself, he flipped open his cell phone and sent a quick text to his superior, who was probably frothing at the mouth. He made up an excuse about a dying battery and promised to check in later.

When Maria came out of the bathroom, her hair was tied back at the nape of her neck and her cheeks looked freshly scrubbed. He wondered if she knew that her hair had been his undoing. He'd kill to bury his face in it again.

"Ready?" she asked, her brows arched.

He nodded, turning to the window to push the blinds aside. The courtyard was dimly lit, deserted. "Looks clear."

They left the Hotel del Oro without incident.

Ian glanced at Maria as they walked down E Street, thinking that he owed her his life. If Chuy or Armando had seen him stumbling around yesterday, doped to the gills, he'd have been executed on the spot.

He was glad to be here, with her, alive.

It was a beautiful night, warm and breezy. The blister-ing sun and heavy traffic that usually marked his jour-ney didn't exist at this hour. "Thank you for helping me," he said, shoving his hands into his pockets.

She smiled at him, surprised. "You're welcome."

He wished he could take her out somewhere and thank her properly. Denny's was open. But he couldn't risk spending time with a woman who'd known him as Agent Foster. Instead he pulled his money clip out of his pocket. He had two twenties. "Take this."

She closed her hand around his, shaking her head. "Please. It was nothing. You have been very kind."

"No, I—treated you badly."

"When?"

"You know when."

Her eyes softened. "That was not bad, *señor*. You did not harm me." She switched to Spanish, needing the ease to explain herself. "I was startled when I woke up, and I thought it would be better to stop before things went too far."

"You were afraid?" he asked in English, more comfortable in a bilingual conversation. She understood his language better than she could speak it, and vice versa.

"Only that you would expect too much."

He nodded, still conflicted about what he'd done. "You should expect men to listen if you say no at any point."

"What we hope for and what we get are often two different things," she said simply.

He swore under his breath, wanting to throttle everyone who'd wronged her. "It wasn't right for me to take advantage of you. I wasn't . . . myself." That was a bullshit excuse, but he didn't know what else to say. He couldn't admit that she'd haunted his dreams for years, or that he'd been dying to touch her.

She lifted her hand to his face, her expression troubled. "What happened to you, *señor*? You look like a man who has lost his way."

The irony overwhelmed him. He'd finally found her, and lost himself.

Feeling pressure behind his eyes, he walked her to the corner and hailed a cab. Giving the driver a twenty, he let her slip away again.

* * *

After Adam left, Kari opened up her laptop and logged on to the Internet, doing a search for Penelope Mendes.

Her death had sparked public outrage. She was a local girl, born and raised in San Diego, a CSU graduate with a bright future. The media ran with her story, partly because she was one of their own, a member of the press, but also because she was gorgeous. It was a tragedy for someone so lovely to be killed in the crossfire. She had become a symbol for the war on drugs, a talking point for gun control.

Penelope's smiling face had graced every newspaper, every television screen. She was stylish and sophisticated, the ultimate border-town beauty queen.

Kari couldn't find a mention of Adam, although it had been widely reported that Penelope was engaged to her college sweetheart. Perhaps his name had been withheld because he was employed by Homeland Security. There was a picture of her grave site at Chula Vista Memorial, a close-up of a heart-shaped bouquet.

Kari closed the screen, her chest aching.

She didn't know what to do. She couldn't smuggle for Moreno, not after being with Adam, not after seeing this. It would be an unconscionable betrayal. Over the next week she had to figure something else out.

Sasha hadn't been returning her calls. She'd said it was dangerous to go to the police, and Kari believed her. Penelope Mendes's murder had never been solved for a reason. Testifying against a drug lord was suicide.

She wanted to talk to Adam and confess everything. She had to make things right between them. But she suspected that he cared more about nailing Moreno than about protecting her. He might not be sympathetic to her plight at all.

She'd lied to him, used his body, and accused him of being a dirty cop.

"God," she muttered, hating herself. "When I screw up, I don't do it halfway."

Pushing away from the front counter, she grabbed her things and locked the back door, walking out into the balmy night. She drove by the Hotel del Oro but didn't see Maria. Worried and exhausted, she went home.

She took a long, lukewarm shower, her mind numb. Although she should have felt like a sleaze for sleeping with a man she hardly knew, memories of their encounter elicited pleasure rather than shame. She'd never enjoyed sex so much. Wanton need had overpowered her, washing away all rational thought.

She only wished he'd made it last longer.

If she could do it again, she'd have brushed her lips over his hard chest and flat stomach, giving him a sultry look while she sank to her knees. He'd have fisted his hand in her hair, blurring reality as she took him in her mouth.

Kari turned off the shower, her breath quickening.

After she finished him off, he'd have returned the favor, kneeling between her spread thighs and kissing the swollen lips of her sex.

Groaning, she leaned back against the stall and touched herself there, imagining her slick fingertips were his tongue. Her breasts quivered, water droplets clinging to her skin. She rubbed her clit in slow circles, her eyes drifting shut.

She came with a hoarse cry, her hand between her legs, his name on her lips.

A moment later, she stepped from the shower stall, wrapping a towel around her body. Her cheeks were flushed, her eyes luminous. Not bothering to dry her hair, she climbed into bed, naked and wet and alone.

Sometime during the night, a cab pulled into the driveway, its headlights pooling into Kari's dark bedroom. She lifted her head from the pillows and looked out the window, smoothing her damp, disheveled hair. Maria exited the cab and hurried toward the front door, her face calm.

Kari was glad to see her. She rose from the bed, donning a summer nightshirt before she went out to the living room. "What happened?" she asked, letting Maria inside the house. The cabdriver drove away.

Maria collapsed on the couch, rubbing her tired eyes. "You first."

"Are you hungry?"

"Yes, but it can wait. Tell me everything."

Kari nodded, detailing her border-crossing fiasco and the intimidating visit from Moreno's henchman.

"This is terrible," Maria said, frowning. "What will happen if you refuse?"

"They'll probably hurt Sasha. Or burn down my store."

"The man who visited you is the same one who came to your house? Medium tall, *cara de cuero*?"

Kari was amused by the description, which translated as "face of leather." Mexican people rarely minced words. "Yes."

"That is Armando. I will talk to him. Find out."

"Are you crazy? He's a maniac."

"I don't think he's so bad."

Kari shook her head, exasperated. "Don't talk to him. Don't even go back to that hotel. You're stressing me out, Maria!"

Maria gave her an apologetic look. "I'm sorry."

"Where were you tonight?"

"I was with the border agent. Foster, I think his name is."

"Doing what?"

Maria explained that she'd hidden him in a hotel room and stayed there until he was sober enough to walk.

"Why would the dealer care if he was drugged out?" Kari asked.

"I'm not sure. He is very strange, this man."

"What do you mean?"

"He pretends to not remember me. It's almost like he is a different person. Only Agent Foster on the inside."

A thought occurred to Kari. If she hadn't been spending so much time with Adam, wondering if he was working undercover, it might not have occurred to her. "Maybe he's a narcotics officer."

"What is that?"

"A policeman, playing a part. Like an actor. Collecting information."

Her eyes lit up. "You could be right. His clothes are ugly, dirty. Underneath, he has nice muscles, clean skin."

"You saw him without clothes?" Kari asked, surprised.

"I try to wake him up with a cold shower. But it did not work." A crease formed between her brows. "I have a question for you."

"What?"

"Can a man stop in the middle? During sex, I mean?"

Kari's jaw dropped. "You had sex with him?"

"No! I am only curious."

Kari closed her mouth abruptly, realizing she had no

room to judge. She'd slept with a strange man this afternoon, and enjoyed it so much she'd masturbated to the fantasy. "He should be able to stop, yes."

"Even after . . ." Seeming embarrassed, she made a crude gesture, sliding her forefinger into a half-closed fist.

"Yes. Even then. The only time he might have trouble is at the very end, when he's . . ."

"Coming?"

"Right," she said, relieved that Maria understood. "And just because you ask him to stop doesn't mean he will. Some men won't listen."

Maria's shoulders stooped. "I am more familiar with those kinds of men."

Kari rubbed her arms, wishing there weren't so many abusive scumbags in the world. She also wondered if Maria was too innocent to know the difference. Young, inexperienced women were fooled every day.

Kari was tired of being at the mercy of bad men. She hated getting jerked around by Moreno and watching Sasha throw her life away. From this moment forward, she wasn't going to wait for his orders and hope for the best.

For Sasha's sake, and her own, she had to go on the offensive.

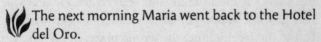The next morning Maria went back to the Hotel del Oro.

She convinced Kari that she'd stay out of trouble, but she planned to keep her eyes and her ears open. Unfortunately, she also had to go back to room 28. Sometime between dragging Agent Foster out of his hiding place and shoving him into the shower, the pepper spray canister had become unclipped from her waist. It wasn't in the supplies closet, near the vending machines, or inside the elevator.

She must have left it in that hotel room.

Maria performed her cleaning duties as quickly as possible, glancing around for Armando. Just because she hadn't bumped into him lately didn't mean he wasn't around. When the coast looked clear, she approached the damaged room with stealthy movements, using her key card to get in.

Safe.

Pressing her back against the closed door, she let out a slow breath, her heart racing. No one had seen her.

Although it wasn't wise to linger, she found herself staring at the bed she'd occupied with Foster.

His touch had been like a very sexy dream, not quite real. She'd responded without thinking, without her normal inhibitions. As she became more alert, she'd been struck by the startling realization that they were two short steps from intercourse.

Letting him continue would have been a disaster. As much as she liked and admired him, Foster was a different person now. The man who'd found her on the dunes and held her hand in the hospital seemed like a distant memory. She didn't know this new Foster. He was still a nice guy, she supposed, but she couldn't sleep with him. It was the wrong time, the wrong place, the wrong situation.

After what she'd gone through at El Caracol, she needed to feel safe and be with someone she could trust.

Maria tore her gaze from the bed and crossed the room, looking for the small black spray canister. The bathroom was the most likely location, so she went there first, glancing in the shower stall, around the toilet, underneath the sink.

It wasn't there.

Frowning, she checked behind the door. Nothing.

Maybe Foster had picked it up by accident and taken it home with him. Or maybe the canister had rolled under the bed. She walked out of the bathroom and knelt beside the mattress, peering into the dark space.

While she was down there, she heard an ominous click. The door!

Acting on instinct, she lay flat, hiding behind the bed. When she heard the faint, almost indiscernible creak of an approaching footstep, she panicked, wiggling her slender body under the bed frame.

It was a hot, airless space. She prayed that Chuy and Sonia hadn't come for an early tryst. The thought of him heaving and grunting on top of the pretty receptionist made her sick. And their combined weight would suffocate her.

The intruder moved through the room *como indio*, without noise. She knew then that it was Armando. Only he could step so lightly. Appearing out of nowhere was one of his talents, like whittling.

She closed her eyes and held her breath, trying to become invisible.

There was a muted thud in the bathroom as the doorknob hit the wall, but no shoe sounds on the linoleum floor. He'd probably just pushed it open to make sure the area was clear. *Chingado!*

She stared at the carpet in her immediate vicinity, her heart in her throat. A pair of black low-heeled boots came into view.

Maria made the sign of the cross. *Por favor*, don't look!

But God wasn't here at the Hotel del Oro. There was only Armando, and he worked for the devil.

He crouched down, meeting her eyes. "Looking for something?"

She glanced at the object he was holding. Kari's pepper spray. Pulse racing, she scrambled out from underneath the bed. Her hair snagged on the mattress springs, yanking several strands from the roots.

Rising to her feet, she smoothed a hand over her head. "I must have dropped it," she said in Spanish.

He stood also. "What were you doing in here?"

"Looking for it."

His *cara de cuero* appeared impatient. "I mean when you dropped it."

"Using the bathroom," she said, moistening her lips. "It's more private."

He didn't believe her. That hard face seemed incapable of revealing what he was thinking, let alone showing an emotion, but she sensed his skepticism. Instead of disputing her, however, he held out the canister.

She stared at his upturned palm, wary. He smiled coldly, daring her to take it. Lifting her chin in defiance, she reached out to snatch it from him.

A mistake.

He locked his other hand around her wrist and spun her around, wrenching her arm behind her back. The pepper spray bounced off the bed. He put a cold blade to her throat, applying a terrifying pressure.

Maria froze, her mind flooded with memories. She flashed back to a man holding her down, another forcing himself on her while she kicked and screamed.

"Maybe you were here with a customer."

"No," she said, her voice hoarse. "I'd die first."

He didn't take the knife away from her throat. His body felt hard and strong against hers, his chest rising and falling with each breath.

Maria was beyond fear, beyond pride. She couldn't bear to be raped and beaten again. She'd do anything to avoid another brutal attack. "If you want something from me, just name it. I'm willing."

And she was. She'd rather *choose* to do this than fight him and lose.

After a long, tense moment, Armando released her.

"That is the stupidest thing I've ever heard a woman say."

She rubbed the marks he'd left on her skin, whirling to face him. "Why?"

"Because there are two kinds of men in the world. The first don't give a damn if a woman is willing. They want to inflict pain no matter what. Why do you think so many prostitutes get raped?"

She swallowed hard, afraid to answer.

Armando sheathed his blade. "The second kind of man, who doesn't like to use force, will agree to your offer. Either way, you're fucked."

His crude words made her flinch. "Which kind are you?"

"The second."

She looked from the empty bed to his dark eyes. "Then why . . ."

"Maybe there's a third kind," he allowed. "The kind who prefers women to be wanting, rather than willing."

She shook her head, wordless. For him, she would never be wanting.

His mouth twisted wryly, as though he could read her thoughts. "Did you have that when Chuy grabbed you?" he asked, nodding at the pepper spray.

"Yes."

"Why didn't you use it?"

"I don't know. I was . . . afraid."

"No defense tactic works unless you practice it."

Maria couldn't believe they were having this conversation. She picked up the canister, clipping it to her waistband. If she had a bit more nerve, she'd practice on Armando's cold black eyes right now.

"Don't come back to this room, little butterfly," he

said, dismissing her with a wave. "And keep that spray can ready. If you continue working here, you'll need it."

Kari's number one priority was contacting Sasha.

Her sister hadn't been returning her calls, and she lived like a recluse. Moreno had curbed her shopping addiction, to some extent, by keeping her on a strict allowance. Drug use and bouts of depression isolated Sasha further. Most days she stayed in bed and didn't leave his house.

But there were some indulgences her sister continued to enjoy. Sasha's hairdresser and manicurist saw her more often than Kari did. She also frequented a New Age spa that did everything from body wraps to "spirit cleansing."

Kari closed up Zócalo and visited all of Sasha's haunts, hoping to catch a glimpse of her sister dashing to or from an appointment. The stylist at Wild Hair was very understanding. She admitted that she'd been concerned about Sasha and promised to call Kari the minute she heard from her.

The manicurist was angry rather than sympathetic. Sasha owed her several hundred dollars. Kari didn't think her sister would dare show her face at this particular nail salon, but she left a twenty and her phone number.

Kari's last stop was Soul Oasis, Sasha's favorite spa. Kari had been there with her just two weeks before, getting a painfully embarrassing bikini wax.

The girl behind the counter smiled. "How can I help you?"

"I'm looking for my sister," Kari said, glancing around

the waiting room. "Can you tell me if Sasha Strauss has an appointment this week? I remember she said something about needing a toxin cleanse or a seaweed wrap."

The receptionist, whose name tag read Tracy, had a delicate dragonfly tattoo on the inside of her wrist. "I'm sorry," she said, closing the appointment book. "We can't give out personal information. At Soul Oasis, our clients enjoy total privacy."

"It's a family emergency," Kari said, lowering her voice. "I'd really appreciate it if you could help me out."

"I'm sorry," Tracy repeated, blinking her pretty eyes.

"You can't bend the rules, just this once?"

"I wish I could."

She sighed, drumming her fingertips against the counter. "Is the owner or manager available?"

"Sure," the receptionist said. "Have a seat and I'll get her."

"Thank you."

As soon as Tracy was out of sight, Kari reached over the divider and grabbed the appointment book, searching through the names. Sasha's was scribbled in for 2:00 p.m. today. Relieved, she returned the book to its rightful place.

She drove her van to the transit station and parked it. The GPS device that Adam had found was still in the passenger seat, and she knew it could be used to track her movements. She'd decided to keep it. Play along— for the time being.

Donning a floppy straw hat and oversized sunglasses, Kari took the bus back to Soul Oasis. It was almost two o'clock when she arrived. She waited near the outdoor fountain, listening to the annoying faux jungle sounds that emanated from the speakers. Sasha was late, but she showed.

Unfortunately, she had a bodyguard with her. Chuy Pena.

"Damn it," Kari said, slipping further into the garden. Dripping springs and frog calls echoed in her ears. After the pair passed by, Kari walked around the back of the building, searching for an alternative entrance.

The receptionist she'd met earlier was there, also engaged in a furtive activity. Tracy was crouched near a dumpster, smoking a cigarette. When the girl saw Kari, she straightened, crushing the butt on the asphalt.

"Sneak me in to see my sister and I won't say a word."

Tracy used hand sanitizer and breath spray, deliberating.

Kari held up a twenty.

Tracy grabbed the bill and shoved it into the pocket of her low-rise jeans. "Come on." She led Kari through the back door and to a private bathroom. "You're not planning anything harmful, right? I don't need any more bad karma."

"I just want to talk to her."

"If you cause a scene—"

"I won't."

Tracy brought Sasha in a few minutes later. Her sister was wearing skintight leggings and skyscraper heels. She skittered forward, frowning at Kari. "What are you doing here? My acupuncturist is waiting."

Just what Sasha needed—more needles.

"I had to see you," Kari said, shutting the bathroom door behind her. "Why haven't you been returning my phone calls?"

She rolled her eyes. "Carlos took my phone away. He has me on a very short leash."

"I saw your escort."

"Exactly."

Kari put a hand on her shoulder. "He wants to get rid of you, Sasha. Chuy said that Carlos would deliver you to me after I brought the packages over the border."

This time Sasha didn't dismiss Kari's claims as silly or unimportant. Perhaps she'd had a rude awakening over the past week. "Carlos is worried about me," she admitted. "He thinks I'm high all the time."

Carlos was right. He was also *responsible*. He'd been a toxic influence on Sasha, fostering her addiction for more than five years. It was a little disheartening to hear that Sasha cared more about his opinion than anyone else's. On the other hand, her sister had almost admitted she had a problem. That was a step in the right direction.

"You need help," Kari said, pressing her advantage. "Let's go right now and check you into a rehab. Please, Sasha. I love you too much to watch you destroy yourself."

She shook her head, her lips trembling. "I can't leave him."

"He's killing you!"

"I'm afraid to leave," she wailed back. "Even if I got sober, I'd still owe him money. He'd find me, Kari. He'd send his dog after me."

"Chuy, you mean?"

"Yes. Carlos wouldn't harm a woman, but Chuy would. I know he would."

Kari was startled by Sasha's vehemence. "Has he done it before?"

Sasha just stared at her.

"Did he kill Penelope Mendes?"

She raised a finger to her lips. "Shhh!"

"Surely you know that Carlos makes the decisions, Sasha. He must have ordered Chuy to open fire."

"No. They argued about it. I overheard."

Kari fell silent, pacing back and forth in the bathroom. Adam would be very interested in this conversation, but it didn't change the game for Kari. Carlos Moreno had deadly intentions and Chuy Pena was a ticking time bomb.

What was she going to do?

"I'm scared," Sasha whispered. "Maybe if you . . . cooperate, Carlos will let me go, and we can talk about . . . rehab."

Kari whirled to face her sister. "What do you mean?"

"Just bring the packages! You won't get caught. They never do. Once my debt is paid, I'll be free. I can enter a treatment program."

Kari wanted to say no. But Sasha was her only sister, and she was in trouble. If Kari turned her back on Sasha and something bad happened to her—again—she'd never forgive herself. "Do you promise you'll get help?"

"Yes! Please, sis. Do this for me. This one last thing."

Kari closed her eyes in frustration, because it was a familiar refrain. How often had Sasha asked her for one more favor? One last loan. And she always gave in. Besides Moreno, Kari was Sasha's greatest enabler.

"Okay, but that's it," she said, making a chopping gesture. "If I go through with this and you refuse to get help, we're done. I will never speak to you again. You'll be dead to me. Do you understand?"

"Yes." Sasha threw her thin arms around Kari's neck, sobbing. "Thank you."

Kari endured the hug for a moment. For the first time, it was she who felt uncomfortable, she who couldn't wait to break away.

13

Kari was too keyed up to sleep in the next morning.

She went for an early jog and ran hard, pushing herself to the limit. On impulse, she headed toward Chula Vista Memorial Cemetery, which was just outside her normal route. The air was still cool with dew as she rounded the front gate, slowing to a stop underneath a sprawling live oak.

The graveyard was neatly tended and sun-bright, its lawns a fresh, brilliant green. Kari wandered up and down the rows for quite some time before she found what she was looking for: Penelope Mendes's final resting place.

The smooth granite headstone was engraved with a simple epigraph: *Nuestra angel. Siempre perdida, siempre amada.*

Our angel. Forever missed, forever loved.

There was a long-stemmed rose at the base of the headstone, its bud slightly unfurled. The edges of the petals showed a hint of discoloration. Three days ago, at the most, this rosebud had been perfect and fresh.

It was a romantic flower, blush pink. She felt certain that Adam had placed it here, and the knowledge was like a thorny stem around her heart.

Forever loved.

Kari stared at the inscription for several minutes, despondent. Had Carlos Moreno ordered Chuy Pena to open fire that day? Even if the bullet hadn't come from the drug lord's weapon, he was responsible for her death. His crew had engaged in a shootout in a public place. They'd gunned down a young, beautiful woman.

Forever missed.

She turned away from the headstone, her throat tight. Kari might be visiting Sasha's grave soon, if her sister didn't get a handle on her addiction. As she trudged toward the path that led to the front gate, another decorated site caught her eye.

More long-stemmed roses. Deep, dark red.

There was a motley collection of other flowers, and they all appeared recently placed. The colorful bouquets weren't quite as romantic, or as tragic, as the fragile pink rosebud. Kari paused at the headstone, reading the name.

Patricia Rosales *Cortez*.

That was Adam's last name.

Frowning at the odd coincidence, Kari looked closer. Her date of birth was July 17. This past Sunday.

"Son of a bitch," she said, straightening. Then she clapped a hand over her mouth and made the sign of the cross, apologizing to the poor woman resting here. Adam had told her he was buying a birthday gift for his mother, who was apparently dead.

He'd lied.

She walked away at a brisk pace, her thoughts in motion. This new development cast Adam in a different light.

The first time he'd visited her store, he'd claimed he was looking for *dia de los muertos* figurines. Although the dancing skeletons symbolized that celebration, they weren't given to the dead as gifts. Besides, the holiday was in November.

He'd mentioned his mother's birthday again the second time he came in, speaking of her as if she were alive.

"Who does that?" she asked out loud.

No one in the cemetery answered.

Adam hadn't come to Zócalo to buy a gift. If his goal had been to get in Kari's pants, mission accomplished. But it was still a strange, sleazy thing to lie about. A real man didn't invent lame excuses for stopping by.

What else had he been dishonest about?

Kari had looked into Adam's eyes when he spoke of Moreno. She believed he'd rather kill Moreno than join him. Perhaps he was a conscientious officer on the job and a lying, cheating bastard at home.

She gasped, remembering the *rebozo*.

"Oh my God," she said, starting to jog again. She didn't slow down until she reached her front doorstep. It was still early, so she started making breakfast, beating Maria to the punch. When her roommate wandered into the kitchen a few minutes later, Kari caught her up on the Adam situation.

"Maybe this is good thing," Maria mused.

"How?"

"Well, he hates Moreno, and he is willing to lie to get what he wants. You can use it to your advantage, yes?"

"I don't know," Kari said, shaking her head. It would be extremely risky to ask for Adam's help.

"We have a saying in Spanish: *el enemigo de mi enemigo es mi amigo*."

The enemy of my enemy is my friend.

Kari studied Maria's deceptively sweet face. "You have a devious mind."

Maria smiled, sipping her coffee. "*Gracías, mi amor*."

After breakfast, Kari picked up her cell phone to call Adam. Her tank top was still damp from her run, her heart pounding anew.

"Yeah," he answered.

Kari's stomach fluttered at the sound of his voice, husky from sleep. If he was married or had a live-in girlfriend, he wouldn't have taken a call in bed. "Can I see you?" she asked, trying not to imagine him naked.

He shifted the phone around; it sounded like the receiver was brushing against his pillow. "I have to leave for work in an hour."

"Tonight, then. We need to talk."

"Fine. I'll meet you at your place."

"No. I'll come to you."

"Whatever," he said, sighing. "It's 732 Grant."

The phone clicked in her ear as he hung up. She scribbled down the address, frowning at his brusque tone. Despite their rocky start, she didn't want Adam as a friend *or* an enemy. She wanted him as her lover.

Adam shouldn't have been looking forward to Kari's visit.

She was a criminal, involved in an intricate drug smuggling operation. He'd taken a sworn oath to protect the country from people like her.

It wasn't a *date*.

But his libido wouldn't hear that. As soon as he got home from work, he made sure the place was spotless. He also took pains with his appearance. After a shower and shave, he put on cologne and shrugged into one of his nicest shirts.

Then he braced his hands on the sink and stared at his reflection in the mirror, wondering what the hell he was doing.

He'd told her he didn't want to see her again unless she told him the truth. But he was edgy with anticipation, and it had a lot more to do with getting dirty than with coming clean. The intensity of his desire for her blindsided him.

Adam had slept with beautiful women before. He'd had hot, meaningless sex with strangers. Even with Penelope, he hadn't always been a gentleman. Tawdry hookups and impulsive acts weren't new to him.

But most of the encounters weren't memorable, either. Only the times with Penelope seemed special. None of the women since had mattered—except Kari. It wasn't just a physical thing between them, either, although her body was incredible. The way she'd responded, tearing off her clothes and lifting her skirt for him . . .

Christ.

It was like she couldn't wait to get fucked.

He knew she'd used sex as a weapon, avoiding his questions by jumping on him. But he also knew she hadn't faked anything. She'd been fantastically wet. He remembered her uninhibited cries, the hot clasp of her body as she came.

When the doorbell rang earlier than expected, he snapped out of his lustful stupor. Buttoning his shirt hastily, he went to answer the door.

It wasn't Kari.

His sister, Raquel, was standing there. Judging by her slinky dress and done-up hair, she was going somewhere fancy. Her husband, Brian, waited in the car. Little Logan and Maya stood next to her, their eyes bright.

"Shit," he muttered, rubbing a hand over his jaw.

"Don't tell me you forgot," Raquel said.

Adam bent down to pick up Logan, who was holding out his chubby little arms. Maya raced past him into the house. "Is it Friday already?"

"I have reservations at Anthony's in an hour."

Adam smiled at Logan. "What's up, buddy?"

"Down, down," Logan said, wanting to run after his big sister. Adam let him go, aware that his radiant toddler energy couldn't be harnessed.

Raquel crossed her arms in front of her chest, looking him over. "Were you getting ready to go out?"

"Not . . . exactly. Someone was coming here."

Her face lit up. "A woman?"

Adam glanced inside, avoiding her question. Maya was dancing around the living room. Logan had crawled under the kitchen table.

"It's a date," she accused, delighted. She turned to her husband. "My brother has a date tonight!"

Brian checked his hair in the rearview mirror. "So do we, babe. Hurry up."

"Who is she? What does she do?"

Adam scrubbed the back of his neck, wincing. There was no way to explain the situation to Raquel, who had been hounding him about his love life for years. When she caught hold of an idea that appealed to her, she was like a dog with a bone.

"She's not one of those hoochies from the club, I hope."

"Logan's getting into my knife drawer," he lied.

"Sorry for ruining your fun," she said, obviously not meaning it. After she said goodbye to the kids, she gave Adam a peck on the cheek and dashed off.

A few minutes later, he had the evening under control. The kids were coloring at the kitchen table and dinner was on the way. He thought about calling Kari to cancel, but decided against it. Maybe they could have their conversation—minus the sex fantasy—while the kids were occupied.

She showed up right on time in a summery blue dress, looking good enough to eat. He liked the way her clothes were all sexy and feminine and easy access. But he doubted that she'd worn the outfit for him. Her face was clean of makeup, her hair in a simple knot at the nape of her neck. She'd probably driven straight from work.

"Come on in," he said.

Moistening her lips, she stepped inside. And stopped short when she saw Maya and Logan. "Are those . . . yours?"

He sighed, pressing his fingertips to the bridge of his nose. She thought he'd invited her over to hang out with his children, whom he'd never bothered to mention? Wow. He hadn't done a very good job of charming and disarming her.

Maya bounded toward them. "Who is it, *tío*?"

"It's my friend Kari."

Maya gazed up at her, curious. "Hi."

"Hi," Kari murmured.

Adam put his hand on Maya's shoulder. "This is my niece, Maya, and that's my nephew, Logan."

She gave him an apologetic look. "They're adorable."

"I forgot they were coming over," he explained.

"Are you going to play with us?" Maya asked. "Uncle Adam always orders pizza and buys ice cream!"

"Maybe I should go," she said.

Logan, who was putting the final touches on his drawing, knocked over a cup of juice at the kitchen table. "Uh-oh."

"Shit." Adam hurried to grab a towel from the countertop as the liquid rushed over the table, chairs, and floor.

"Logan ruined my picture," Maya yelled.

The toddler scrambled out of the chair, trying to get away from the mess, and promptly slipped on the wet floor, bumping his head. He started crying really loud, so Adam figured he was okay. Tossing the towel down, he scooped Logan up. Orange juice soaked the front of Adam's shirt and Logan's wails echoed in his ears.

"He always does that," Maya said to Kari, rolling her eyes.

The doorbell rang again.

"The pizza man is here!"

Adam met Kari's gaze while he patted Logan's back, murmuring soft words of comfort. This wasn't quite the impression he wanted to create. Normally things ran smoothly when his sister's kids were over.

Kari seemed amused rather than horrified. "Do you need some help?"

"Yes." Holding Logan with one arm, he reached into his pocket for a couple of twenties. "Can you pay for the pizza while I take care of him?"

"Sure."

Kari went to the door and Maya started wiping up

the orange juice like a good big sister. "Thanks, *mamita*," he said, whisking Logan off for a quick change of clothes.

Raquel hadn't packed a spare play outfit, so Adam put Logan in his airplane pajamas and called it good. Then he stripped down to the waist, leaving his dress shirt to soak in the sink. When Kari poked her head in a moment later, Logan was sitting on the bed, still sniffling. She looked from the baby to Adam, her eyes lingering on his bare chest.

He opened his top drawer, finding a T-shirt.

"I, um, helped Maya clean up. Pizza's on the table."

"Stay and eat," he said, pulling the shirt over his head.

"I shouldn't."

"Why not?"

She sighed, leaning against the doorjamb. This wasn't how she'd pictured the evening, either.

"Want pizza," Logan said, holding his arms out.

After a brief hesitation, she stepped forward and picked him up. Logan wasn't friendly with everyone, but Adam had noticed that he liked pretty women. The little rascal.

"You're a big boy, aren't you? Can you walk?"

"I can run!" Tears forgotten, he wriggled out of her arms. Showing her how fast he was, he tore across the carpet, heading back to the kitchen.

As soon as he was out of earshot, she said, "I'm sorry. They look like you."

"It's no big deal," he replied. "My sister asked me to babysit last weekend and it slipped my mind."

"Do you watch them often?"

"Not that often. A few times a month."

She seemed surprised by the arrangement. It was unusual, he supposed, but Raquel didn't have any close female family members to rely on. Adam had been her regular babysitter for the past year, since their mother died.

"Hang out for a while," he said. "Maybe we can talk after dinner."

Kari agreed, sitting down to cut up bite-sized pieces of pizza for Logan while Adam got drinks from the fridge.

Both children took to Kari right away. They chattered nonstop, vying for her attention. Adam played moderator, gently reminding them to concentrate on finishing their dinner. About halfway through the meal, Maya came up with a real zinger.

"Are you a hoochie?"

Adam almost choked on his pizza.

"Hoochie, hoochie," Logan repeated, like an owl.

"My mommy says that all of Uncle Adam's girlfriends are hoochies," she added, blinking her big brown eyes.

"Your mommy talks too much," Adam said, scowling.

Kari hid a smile and kept eating, taking no offense. They made it through dinner without any other serious gaffes. As usual, they walked down the block for ice cream afterward. Somehow Maya convinced Kari to stay for her favorite movie, *Beauty and the Beast*. At Maya's request, Adam put a rug over his back and did his best Beast impression, making the kids scream with delight. Logan snuggled up in Kari's arms and fell asleep. By the time the credits rolled, Maya was lights-out, too.

Adam always had fun with the kids, and Kari's presence added that extra spark. He couldn't remember having enjoyed an evening so much in ages. After putting

Maya and Logan down, side by side in his bed, they snuck back to the living room.

He was reluctant to ask Kari why she'd come. Despite his parting words to her at the store, he didn't want to talk about her involvement with Moreno. He'd rather go on as they had for the past few hours, pretending the conflict didn't exist.

"You're good with them," Kari said, sitting down on the couch. Although the kitchen lights were on, the living room was dim.

Adam sat down next to her, making no attempt to brighten the space. "Thanks."

She dragged a hand through her hair. "Do you want kids of your own someday?"

He stared back at her, considering. With another woman, this conversation would have sent him running for the hills. "Just between us, yes."

"Is it a secret?"

"No, but my sister nags me about settling down. I don't want to encourage her."

"How old are you?"

"Twenty-nine."

Kari didn't say that he was too young to start a family. "Sounds like she doesn't approve of the women you date," she said, smiling.

He smiled back at her, remembering what Maya had repeated about his "hoochie girlfriends." Raquel's criticism wasn't quite fair. He hadn't had a girlfriend since Penelope. "What about you?"

"Do I want a family?"

He nodded, though he already knew the answer. It had been apparent the day she'd modeled the *rebozo*. He'd seen it tonight, in every interaction with the kids.

She might not have what his bachelor friends called "baby fever," but there was a lush readiness about her that he found appealing.

"Yes, I do. By the time I'm thirty, definitely."

"How old are you?"

"Twenty-six."

He'd known that, too. He had all of her personal information memorized.

"I hadn't thought about it much until last year," she continued.

"What happened?"

Her expression was troubled. "This is also just between us?"

"Of course."

"My sister had a miscarriage. She didn't tell me until after she lost the baby. I don't think she knew she was pregnant, and I doubt she stopped using." Kari shook her head, saddened by the situation. "Tonight, with your sister's kids, I couldn't help but wonder what it would have been like to be an aunt." She took a deep breath, as if staving off tears. "I'm sure I'd have enjoyed it."

He was caught off guard by the easy intimacy between them. Rather than disengaging, he wanted to get closer to her. Comfort her. "The best thing about nieces and nephews is that they go home when you get tired of them."

She laughed, seeming embarrassed by her sentimental streak. "Your sister must be a great mom."

Adam agreed absently, his eyes drifting down her body. He should be directing the conversation toward her unfortunate criminal activities, not getting personal with her. Or picturing her naked.

"How was your mom's birthday, by the way? Did she like the gift?"

He tensed at the question, lifting his gaze to her face. Her voice was a touch too bright, her posture a bit too stiff.

Damn it. She'd caught him in a lie.

14

Having brought up the subject, Kari couldn't back down.

Adam was handsome and charming. He seemed like a loving brother and a fantastic uncle. He had a good job, a great body, and an irresistible smile. But he was still a liar. "I saw her grave, Adam."

His eyes narrowed. "You visited my mother's grave?"

"And Penelope Mendes's grave," she said, nodding. "Did you put a rose there?"

"Yes."

That admission shouldn't have felt like a dagger through her heart, but it did. Especially since he was acting defensive rather than contrite. "Why did you say you were buying a gift for your mother at my store?"

"Why did you say you were dating someone when I asked you out?"

A flush rose to her cheeks. "It was a polite way to refuse you."

"Pretending to be a lesbian is polite?"

"I never said that," she hissed, keeping her voice low.

"You jumped to the conclusion because you were titillated by the idea."

"Ah. I guess I imagined your roommate stroking your hair and saying she would kiss everything better."

She wanted to slap the smirk off his face. "I didn't tell you Maria was my roommate."

"No, you insinuated that she was your girlfriend. And you're goddamned right I was titillated by the idea! What man wouldn't be?"

"That wasn't my intention—"

"Right," he said, making a scoffing sound. "Every move you've made toward me has been designed to titillate. From the flash of skin at the border to the quick fuck in the storeroom, you've used sex to distract me."

Kari didn't know how to respond to that charge. In some respects she was guilty. On the other hand, it took two to tango, and she'd hardly twisted his arm. "I asked you a question. Why did you lie?"

"To gain your trust. Why did you?"

"To get rid of you!"

"I don't like being played, Kari."

She placed a hand over her chest, sputtering. "Aren't you playing me?"

"I followed you home the first day we met," he admitted, inclining his head. "I saw Chuy Pena leave your house, and I know who he works for. It's pretty fucking ironic that you would accuse *me* of dishonesty."

Kari recoiled in shock. She couldn't believe he'd known the whole time. Every visit he'd made to the store had been calculated. Every conversation he'd initiated had been an attempt to collect information.

"The innocent act is wearing thin, *bella*. Did you

come here to scold me for lying, or is there something else you want?"

She moistened her lips, deliberating. This could be her last chance. If she didn't ask for his help and ended up in jail, she'd have a long sentence to regret her decision. "I want you to wave me through at San Ysidro."

He didn't even flinch. "No."

She turned her face away in shame, appalled by what she'd just done.

He put his hand on her chin, forcing her to look at him. "Even if I wanted to, I couldn't. CBP officers have rotating stations, rotating shifts. I can't guarantee that I'll be at the vehicle booths at a certain time."

"Oh," she said, feeling stupid.

"Tell me why you need a wave-through."

Her eyes filled with tears. "I wish I could."

"You don't trust me."

"Do you trust me?"

"I know you're not a criminal by choice. You wear your heart on your sleeve, and you're a terrible liar. It's only a matter of time until you get caught."

She met his gaze, tears spilling down her cheeks. He brushed them away with his thumb, and she tasted salt on her lips. "I'm sorry for using you," she said, lifting her hand to his. "If it's any consolation, the sex wasn't . . . premeditated."

"It wasn't?"

"No," she said, swallowing dryly. "And I loved every second of it."

He parted her lips with his thumb, his eyes darkening. After a brief pause, he surrendered to temptation and covered her mouth with his. She moaned and threaded her fingers through his hair, kissing him hungrily.

Kari experienced the same buzz of sexual energy he'd created the first time they kissed. Her desire for him drowned out every negative thought, every niggling concern. Her body took over her brain, driving her to seek more friction, more sensation.

His hand slid down her neck, his thumb stroking the hollow of her throat. She practically purred around his tongue, her nipples tightening against the bodice of her dress. He pushed the skinny strap off her shoulder, revealing most of her left breast. Breaking the kiss, he did the same to the other side, baring her upper body completely.

She put her arms down, letting him look.

"You have the most beautiful tits," he said, cupping their soft weight. After rubbing his thumbs over the tips, he dipped his head to taste. She clutched the arm of the couch, gasping while he took one taut peak into his mouth, then the other. With each pull on her nipple, her inner muscles clenched and her sex ached. He slid one hand under her dress, along her thighs, and she spread them eagerly, inviting him to touch.

"I thought of you in the shower the other night," she said, breathless.

His head lifted. "Really?"

"Yes. I fantasized about you . . . kissing me."

He cupped the front of her panties. "Where?"

"There."

Groaning, he laved her nipples and traced the cleft of her sex with his fingertips, grazing her through the damp fabric. She pictured him kissing his way down her belly and moaned. Wanting to feel his skin against hers, she tugged on the hem of his shirt. He jerked the T-shirt over his head and pushed her skirt up to her waist, preparing to take off her panties.

"Wait," Kari said, stilling his hands. She wanted his mouth on her, but not yet. Reaching down, she molded her palm around him, feeling his erection through the denim. "In my fantasy, I did it to you first."

He stared at her. "You fantasized about going down on me?"

She nodded, biting down on her lower lip as she squeezed his turgid flesh. She hoped he didn't think she was too forward. The idea of pleasuring him before she'd had any relief made her squirm with arousal. "Can I . . . ?"

To her delight, he didn't seem capable of denying her. He stood abruptly, tugging at the buttons on his fly. She slid off the edge of the couch, kneeling in front of him.

He freed his erection for her, his eyes glittering with desire.

With a shiver of excitement, she curled her hand around him, stroking his length. He was hard and thick and perfect. His gaze moved from her naked breasts and clenching fingers to her ready mouth. When she moistened her lips in anticipation, he made a strangled sound and plunged his hand into her hair, bringing her closer.

Adam seemed to know what she wanted sexually. He was a nice guy, but not too nice. That dangerous edge excited her.

She touched her tongue to him. Soft licks at first, wetting the tip. He tightened his hold on her hair and she drew him into her mouth, letting him guide her up and down. When she moaned, deep in her throat, he relaxed his grip. They continued like this, mesmerized. His gaze followed the wet slide of her mouth. Hers stayed on his face. Although she was doing all the work, the pleasure wasn't one-sided. Her sex throbbed with every heartbeat.

Then he tensed and pulled her hair, but not in a good way.

She lifted her head questioningly, catching a glimpse of movement by the front window. It was dark in the room, and the blinds were drawn, but they weren't closed all the way. The person standing by the door had seen what they were doing.

Ian was grounded.

He'd told his superior about Chuy's accusations and the subsequent drug use, but he hadn't mentioned Maria's daring rescue. Instead, he said he'd stumbled away from the hotel and nodded off on a park bench for a few hours.

A dirty test was unacceptable for a DEA agent no matter what the circumstance. Twenty years ago, undercover officers had been given more leeway to blend in with the seedy world of narcotics sales. Now, even simulated use was frowned upon. Today's agents didn't mess around with small buys or penny-ante dealers, either. That's what informants were for.

Most agents used informants to set up a buy with a major dealer for a one-time sting. The problem with that tried-and-true method was that Moreno ran a notoriously tight crew. His top guys were untouchable.

Chuy Pena had been on top a few years ago. Something had created a rift between the kingpin and his minion. Moreno had sent Pena to the Hotel del Oro as a punishment and now used him as an errand boy. Pena was no longer involved in the higher-level operations. Although cocaine and methamphetamine were the drug lord's bread and butter, Pena had been put in charge of heroin sales, a smaller trade.

But Pena was an ambitious bastard, and he'd found his way back into Moreno's good graces. He'd thrived in the black tar business. The Hotel del Oro was turning a profit. And Pena had a new drug connection south of the border.

If the alliance flourished, Chuy Pena was poised to become the leading heroin distributor in San Diego. For whatever reason, Moreno stayed away from opiates. He was letting Pena take the lead in this endeavor.

So the San Diego police department was wise to keep an eye on the situation. Ian had been directed to watch the hotel, collect intelligence, and foster a relationship with Chuy Pena. It was a high-pressure, open-ended assignment. His apartment and weekly buy budget were major expenses for the DEA. Results were expected.

He hadn't delivered.

Chuy had put a gun to his head, practically calling him out for being a cop. It was a surprising charge, because informant spies were far more common. Ian knew the situation was dangerous, but he hadn't realized how savvy Chuy was.

For now, the undercover portion of his assignment was on hold. His current duties included surveillance, surveillance, and more surveillance.

The Breezy Shade apartments, his home base, were sandwiched between two other tall buildings that blocked any hint of breeze. A pair of towering eucalyptus trees out front offered very little shade. There were plenty of shady people living here, however. The complex also boasted a direct view into the courtyard at the Hotel del Oro. From his apartment window, Ian could watch customers coming and going from Chuy's office. He had a front seat to the parking lot and laundry facilities. He'd witnessed countless drug deals and room cleanings. The constant hustle and bustle contrasted sharply with his inertia.

If he'd been confined to a wheelchair, he couldn't have felt more claustrophobic. He was supposed to take frequent breaks and not work more than twelve hours per day, but he couldn't go anywhere.

"Fuck," he said, moving away from the window. He hated this shithole apartment. Instead of punching a hole through the wall, he threw himself down on the bed, staring up at the ceiling. His eyes felt strained, the sockets aching. Playing video games was out of the question. It was too early to sleep.

His thoughts drifted toward Maria, the only bright spot in recent existence.

She'd used his cell phone the other night. He'd made a note of the number she'd called, but hadn't followed up on it. Obsessing about her wasn't helpful. He needed to get his head back in the game.

Before he'd managed to scrub her beautiful face and slender body from his mind, his cell phone vibrated.

He took the phone out of his pocket, squinting at the numbers on the screen. It was a landline, easy to trace. "Who is this?" he demanded.

"Maria. From the hotel."

As if he wouldn't know which Maria.

"I need to meet with you."

"No."

"Why?"

"I'm busy."

She was silent for a moment. "I know who you are."

Ian experienced a falling sensation, as if the mattress had been dropped out from under him. Fuck, fuck, *fuck*! This was the last thing he needed. The words she'd said at the hotel came drifting back to him: *I speak English now*.

Not only had she recognized his face, she remembered their conversations in the hospital. Although his Spanish had been awkward, the communication between them hadn't felt stilted. They'd always . . . understood each other.

"What do you want?" he asked, his heart racing. She could put the nail in the coffin of his undercover assignment.

"Just to talk. There is a restaurant I can walk to. Big café, yellow sign."

"Denny's, on Grand?"

"*Sí, eso*. I will be there in one hour."

He agreed to the time and hung up, walking to the kitchen table to open his laptop. Entering the phone number in a database, he waited for it to generate a name and address, drumming his fingers on the table.

When the information appeared, he couldn't believe what he was looking at. Rubbing his weary eyes, he refocused and read it again: *Karina Strauss, 1410 Calle Obregon, San Diego, CA.*

"Holy shit," he muttered, mapping the address and committing the information to memory. Kari Strauss was the subject of Adam's most recent fixation, the pretty owner of Zócalo, sister of Carlos Moreno's girlfriend.

Adam had mentioned a dark-haired roommate who was "more Ian's type." She was his type, all right.

And maybe his downfall.

Kari gasped, scrambling to her feet. The man outside stepped away from the window, hovering near the front door.

Cursing, Adam fumbled with the buttons on his fly.

"Who is it?" she whispered, fixing her dress.

"My brother-in-law."

She stared at Adam, horrified. He put his shirt back on and went to the door, letting the man inside.

"Sorry, dude," he said to Adam. Then to Kari, "I didn't see anything."

Kari closed her eyes, wanting to disappear.

Adam introduced her to his sister's husband, Brian. He seemed as embarrassed as she was. A curvy, dark-haired woman entered the house behind him, her high heels clicking on the front walk.

"I thought you were going to wait in the car," Brian said.

"If both kids are asleep, I'll have to carry one," she said, catching sight of Kari. "Hello there."

"Kari, this is Raquel."

"Pleased to meet you," she murmured, her cheeks flaming.

Adam's sister was gorgeous. Her hair was a little mussed, as if she and Brian had also been having a sexy time. But they were married and in love. She had a diamond ring on her finger and a telltale bump in her tummy.

In contrast, Kari felt like a . . . hoochie.

"Did we interrupt something?" Raquel asked, fluttering her eyelashes.

"Raqui," Brian said, trying to shush her.

She ignored him. "How long have you and Adam been dating?"

Kari fought the urge to wipe her mouth. "Not long."

"Where did you meet?"

Adam intercepted Raquel's question, rescuing Kari. "She owns the store where I bought you that baby thing."

"The *rebozo*? I loved that!"

"I'm glad," Kari said, picking up her purse. "Congrats on the new baby. Your children are angels."

"Oh, thank you," she said, resting her head against her husband's shoulder. "I hope we're not running you off."

Kari inched toward the door. "Not at all," she lied. "I was just leaving."

Adam exchanged a glance with Brian, who cleared his throat.

"Great to meet you," Kari said, making her escape.

Adam followed her out. Jogging to catch up with her, he wrapped his hand around her wrist, his eyes pleading. "Wait. Please."

She didn't want to cause an even bigger scene by jerking her arm from his grasp or running down the street, so she let him detain her. "I'm so mortified," she said, covering her face with one hand.

"Don't be. He won't say anything. I'm sure he didn't really see—"

She peeped between her fingers, gave him an annoyed stare.

He winced, scrubbing the back of his neck.

"I was servicing you with her children in the house, Adam."

"Those kids sleep like rocks. It was fine."

"She must think I'm a total slut."

"No way. You own a successful business, and you're not drunk. She's already planning our wedding."

Kari didn't know if it was the stress of the situation, but they both started laughing. Adam put his arm around her and she leaned on him, giggling uncontrollably. Brian and Raquel came out of the house a moment later, each carrying a sleeping child. To Kari's relief, they buckled the kids in their car seats and waved goodbye.

"I bet they think we're going to go back inside and finish."

Adam smiled. "Aren't we?"

"No!"

He laughed again, knowing damned well that Raquel and Brian's interruption had ruined the mood. "I'm sorry," he said, sobering. "I should have been paying more attention to the front door, listening for their car. It didn't occur to me that Brian might glance through the blinds before he knocked."

She blushed, shaking her head. In a way, she was flattered that he'd been so intent on her that he'd forgotten everything else.

"My sister can be really nosy. She didn't mean to make you uncomfortable."

"It's okay." Kari wouldn't see any of Adam's family members again, so the incident didn't matter. It *shouldn't* matter.

"Where's your van?" he asked, glancing around the neighborhood.

"I took the bus. More incognito."

His brows rose, but he didn't say anything. They stared at each other for a moment, acknowledging the strange context of their relationship.

Relationship?

Well. Whatever it was.

"I'll drive you home," he offered.

She accepted with a nod. The part of town he lived in was quiet and middle-class but not the best place for a single woman to be walking around after dark. She hadn't planned to stay at his house so long.

He grabbed his keys and led her toward the garage. His car was midsized, a basic black, clean and sleek but unpretentious. She could tell that he took care of his belongings, and suspected that he owned the home. On the surface, he was a responsible, respectable guy. Underneath, he was a hard man with a tragic past.

He held the door open for her.

They fell into a charged silence on the way to Kari's house. She had so much to think about, so many questions to consider. Would Adam notify his superiors that she'd asked him to let her pass through? Should she tell him about her sister's debt and repeat what Sasha had said about Chuy Pena?

If he truly couldn't help her, there was no reason to meet him again.

He pulled into her driveway ten minutes later. "Thanks for the ride," she said, reaching for the door handle.

"Hang on a sec."

"What?"

"Am I going to see you again?"

"Why, so I can get you off?"

A muscle in his jaw tightened. "Maybe if you'd tell me what you're involved in, I could help you."

"You already said you couldn't help me."

"No, I said I couldn't wave you through. There's a difference."

She glanced away, feeling cynical. He wanted two things from her: sex and information. And if they hadn't been caught *in medias res* an hour ago, they might not be having this conversation.

He cupped his hand around her face, meeting her eyes. "I like you, Kari. I like spending time with you. Under any other circumstances, I'd want to get to know you better. But the smuggling thing is kind of a deal breaker."

He said the last sentence with a smile, and she couldn't help but smile back. Damn him for being funny, along with devastatingly handsome and killer sexy. There was no defense against a man this appealing. "I have a lot to think about," she whispered.

He traced her cheekbone with his thumb. "Can I kiss you goodnight?"

She studied him for a moment, bemused by his polite query. He had no qualms about being dishonest, spying on her, or urging her down on her knees, but he was enough of a gentleman to ask for a kiss?

She turned her head slightly, brushing her lips over the pad of his thumb. "No."

His gaze darkened at the subtle caress. Never in her life had Kari said no when she meant yes, but he seemed to understand what she wanted. For some reason, a bit of forcefulness turned them both on.

He slid his hand into her hair, holding her in place as he brought his lips to hers. It was a tasting kiss, light and sensual. Instead of crushing their mouths together, he licked her parted lips and teased her seeking tongue.

His earlier kisses had been about thrusting his tongue deep, filling her mouth. This kiss was like oral sex for her.

And if he did that as well as he did this . . . OMG.

"I think I need another shower," she said when he broke contact.

He groaned, glancing at the front of her house. "Let me in."

"No."

His eyes returned to hers. "No, as in 'break down the door and ravage me, bad boy'?"

"No, as in definitely not." Kissing her fingertips, she touched his taut cheek. "Goodnight."

15

Maria glanced in the mirror before she left the house, wondering if she should change back into her old clothes.

The hand-me-down dress was sexy, she supposed, with its black and red floral design and the thin straps that crisscrossed over her back. Although it wasn't Maria's size, the stretchy fabric conformed nicely to her smaller frame. Kari said it suited her coloring better, too.

Shrugging, she put on her "cute" shoes, a pair of simple black flats. Tossing her pepper spray in her purse, she walked out into the sultry night.

She hadn't picked up any new information at the hotel this week. She hadn't summoned up the nerve to ask Armando about Sasha, either. He seemed like a decent person, not an emotionless monster, but Maria didn't feel safe around him.

Even so, Kari needed help, and Maria wanted to do her part. While her friend was feeling out Officer Cortez, Maria could seek advice from Agent Foster. As far as she was concerned, he was an untapped resource.

She had his phone number written down on a scrap of paper in her purse. He hadn't given it to her, of course, and he wasn't pleased by her call. His brusque tone had hurt her feelings a little, but it hadn't surprised her. He was in a dark place in his life. She got the impression that he wanted to hide from her.

Sighing, she picked up the pace, arriving at the café a few minutes early. Foster was already there, waiting by a bike rack outside. His clothes weren't quite as ragged as usual, but he still looked like a rough character, a rawboned thug. His jaw was scruffy and his black T-shirt sported a tear near the hem.

He waited for her to come forward, his eyes wary.

"Let's go there instead," he said, jerking his chin toward a dive bar across the street.

She stared at the low-class establishment, hesitating. Nice girls didn't go to bars like that. Denny's looked so innocuous and well-lit in comparison.

"We can drink soda. No one will bother you."

"Okay," she said, following him.

He put a hand on her bare shoulder, leading her to a booth in the corner. A couple of gray-haired bikers watched her pass by, their eyes bold. Foster ignored them, so she lifted her chin and tried to look classy. After gesturing for her to sit with her back to the bar, he slid into the space across from her. A waitress came to take their drink order.

"Two Cokes?" Foster requested, glancing at Maria.

She nodded at the waitress, a chubby woman with exaggerated makeup. "Fine."

"Any rum for yours, honey?"

"No thanks."

Disappointed, she left to fill the order.

Maria studied Foster while they waited. His eyes looked bloodshot, but the muddy green color was still nice. The keen intelligence was still there.

"I don't have any money," he said.

"I'll pay for the drinks."

He gave her an impatient look. "That's not what I meant."

The waitress appeared with two Cokes, two napkins, and two paper-covered straws. Maria thanked her and turned her attention back to Foster. "I need help, not money."

"Do I look like I'm in a position to help anyone?"

"Agent Foster would not deny me."

He leaned forward, lowering his voice. "Agent Foster doesn't *exist.*"

She unwrapped her straw and slipped it into her glass. "What do I call you?" she asked, taking a small sip.

His gaze rose from her lips. "You don't."

"*Bueno,*" she said, getting annoyed. "I understand now. When you need help, I am there. When I ask for a favor, you are not."

"What do you want?" he growled.

"Advice."

"That's it?"

"Yes."

He glanced around the bar, deliberating. "Have you mentioned my name at the hotel?"

"No! I'm not stupid, *señor*. I would never do anything to danger you."

The corner of his mouth lifted, as if she'd said something funny. "What kind of advice do you need?"

"My friend is in trouble with the law," she said.

"Is she a citizen?"

"Yes. She brought me here. *Entiendes?*"

"*Sí,*" he said shortly. "Do you owe her money for that?"

"No, no. Just *gratitud*."

He rubbed a hand over his shadowed jaw. "Go on."

"She is in debt . . . sort of . . . to a drug lord. But she can't pay. So he asked her to bring something over the border for him."

"Something illegal?"

"Yes. If she gets caught, will she be arrested?"

"Of course."

"What if she fears for her life? She is afraid to go to police, afraid to say no . . . you see the problem."

"People who break the law get arrested, Maria. Unless she has a gun to her head, she will face the same consequences as anyone else."

"What should she do?"

"Go to the police."

Maria sipped her soda, thinking. "There is another person involved. A captive."

Foster smiled. "Sounds like a *telenovela*."

"You don't believe me?"

"If your friend is worried, for herself or someone else, she should go to the authorities immediately. Drug lords can't be bargained with. Even if she cooperates, she'll lose. Women who won't talk to the police are easier to manipulate. And when they disappear, nobody knows what happened."

She frowned at his words, filled with foreboding. "What if the police can't help?"

"This isn't Mexico, Maria. Here in the U.S., we try to protect innocent women."

Although she heard the "we" in the last sentence and

understood its implications, she couldn't prevent the memories that sprang to the surface of her mind. The police in Mexico weren't always helpful. Sometimes they stole innocence rather than protecting it.

Foster was the only lawman she'd ever trusted. Even after what she'd gone through at El Caracol, she wasn't afraid of him. He'd been strong, kind, reliable. It was a shame that he didn't exist anymore.

"I will tell her what you say," she murmured.

"In the meantime, don't go back to that hotel. Some serious shit is going down there, and I don't want you to get hurt."

She made a noncommittal sound. For the sake of appearances, she should continue her maid duties. "If I can't convince my friend to go to the police, I will get more details for you. Could you pass on information? Would that help her?"

"Maybe."

"Okay. I see what I can do."

"You're a magnet for trouble," he muttered, shaking his head. "Do you ever get tired of saving people?"

Her gaze wandered over his face, taking in the familiar lines and angles. Although he looked different with the longish hair and beard, he wasn't unattractive to her. "Someone saved me once," she reminded him.

This dilemma was killing her. Enable Sasha or let her die. Turn her back or go to jail.

No decision felt right.

Pushing away from the couch, Kari walked over to the bookcase, dragging out a thick, leather-embossed photo album. She sank to her knees on the carpet, opening it. Page after page showed a happy family. Baby Kari in her father's arms. Kari as a downy-haired toddler, holding a newborn Sasha with her mother's help.

The two sisters standing in a kiddie pool, smiles as bright as the sun, their tanned arms wrapped around each other.

She flipped to the final pages, drenched in sorrow. There were several of Kari and Sasha in sexy outfits, dressed up for a wild night.

The last good times.

They hadn't gone out and had fun together in years. Not since Sasha had hooked up with Carlos Moreno.

She closed the album, her heart heavy. After her father died, she'd been forced to sell his furniture stores to pay off their debts. She and Sasha had split the amount that was left over. Kari had used the money wisely, investing in her future. Sasha went through her portion in record time and had nothing but a closetful of clothes to show for it.

Maria walked in the front door a few minutes later, wearing the dress from the picture Kari had just looked at. It suited her slim, elegant figure.

"Hot date?" Kari asked.

Maria collapsed on the couch, chuckling. "Not quite. How about you?"

She sighed, biting down on her lip. "Adam has been spying on me. He saw Chuy and his partner leave the house."

Her eyes widened with dismay. *"Hijo de puta."*

"He didn't agree to help me at the border, either."

She muttered a string of Spanish curses. "Why did he lie about his mother?"

"Just an excuse to stop by, I guess."

"That bastard."

"Yes."

"Did you two . . ." She made the hand gesture.

"No!"

"Maybe you should."

"Maybe I should what? Offer him sexual favors in exchange for help?" She placed a palm to her chest, disproportionately indignant for a woman who'd been caught on her knees less than an hour ago.

Maria shrugged. "It's not wrong if you want him."

"Your mother would be appalled to hear you say that."

"Yes," she agreed, smiling.

"Speaking of sexual favors, where did you go in that getup?"

Maria glanced down at her dress. "Do I look like a lady of the night?"

"No, I was just teasing. It's very cute on you."

She rested her arm on the back of the couch. "I saw Agent Foster. He said you should go to the police."

Kari's mouth dropped open. "You told him about me?"

"I didn't use any names. Don't worry."

She thrust her hands into her hair, wanting to pull it out by the roots. "Are you crazy? How can I not worry?"

"Everything will be okay."

"He could find out who I am, Maria."

"That's true, but he won't tell."

"How do you know?"

"Because he doesn't want *me* to tell anyone who *he* is."

Kari stood and paced the living room, filled with nervous energy.

"It's better this way," Maria insisted. "We can't trust men like Chuy and Carlos Moreno. I know Agent Foster is good. Do you think Adam is good?"

Oh, he was *good*, she thought. "He's not as bad as them," she said.

"Maybe you can make a bargain."

Kari stopped in her tracks, nodding. She couldn't bargain with Adam sexually—he wasn't that cheap. And since she'd been throwing herself at him, it was too late to play coy. But she did have something else he wanted: information.

Although it was painful for Kari to acknowledge, because she was developing feelings for him, Adam wasn't over Penelope Mendes. She suspected that he'd do just about anything for details about her killer.

"That's it," she said, forming a new plan.

After Adam returned home, he had another late visitor.

He opened the door for Ian. "What's up?"

"My assignment is fucked."

Adam let him inside, gesturing for him to sit down. There were very few people he cared about outside his own family. Ian was one of them. In fact, Adam was closer to Ian than he was to Gabriel, his real brother. Gabe had been living like a recluse since he came home from Iraq, and no one could get through to him.

Adam didn't want Ian to drift away, too. He would always have his best friend's back. "What happened?"

Ian rubbed his eye sockets. "I don't even know where to start."

"At the beginning?"

"I told you about the fight with my target, right?"

"Right."

"The next time I went for a buy, he accused me of being . . . deceptive. He said I didn't fight like a junkie."

Adam had sparred with Ian and could attest to that truth. "What else?"

"He put a gun to my head and forced me to snort heroin."

"Fuck," he muttered, shoving a hand through his hair. He couldn't think of a worse situation for an undercover cop to be in. Damned if you do, dead if you don't. "Did you test dirty?"

"Oh yeah. I went to HQ for a voluntary and explained the situation. But it looks bad. Especially after that bullshit story I told about being jumped last week."

"Fuck," Adam said again.

"They put the undercover portion on hold. Now I'm doing basic surveillance."

Adam knew how much this assignment meant to Ian. Being relegated to surveillance was a huge demotion, and it must have killed his friend's morale. Even so, Adam was relieved. It was a dangerous job and Ian had been risking his life, taking the role too far. By virtue of his dysfunctional upbringing, Ian fit in a little too well with the criminal underbelly. Adam hardly recognized him nowadays.

"There's more," Ian said.

"It gets worse?"

His friend swallowed. "I told my superiors that I went home and slept off the heroin. That was a lie. I couldn't get back to base. Maria Santos found me stumbling around and . . . helped me. She took me to a hotel room until I sobered up."

Adam jerked his head toward Ian, questioning.

"Nothing happened. Nothing much, anyway."

"Jesus, Ian," he said, stunned. Ian could lose his job along with the assignment if any of this came out.

"Here comes the really crazy part."

"I don't think I'm ready for it."

"Well, you'd better be, because it involves you. And I promise that if you go off on some half-cocked revenge mission, I'll take this to the chief of my department and tell him everything."

"What the fuck are you talking about?"

Ian's gaze was hard. "I'm trusting you with some very sensitive information. I want to work together on a solution, within the bounds of the law, if possible."

Adam found that statement ironic, but he nodded his agreement.

"Maria called me tonight, asking for advice."

"You gave her your number?"

"Hell no. She used my cell phone while I was out of it."

"And?"

"The call came from Karina Strauss's house."

Adam rose to his feet. "You can't be serious."

"Maria works at the Hotel del Oro, three blocks from Zócalo. My target is—"

"Chuy Pena," Adam finished, his mind reeling.

"I met her at a bar an hour ago. She said she has a friend who owes Moreno money."

"Kari," Adam supplied.

Ian nodded. "That's what I figured. She can't pay, so she's smuggling for him. Allegedly, she's afraid to go to the police because of a captive loved one."

"Sasha."

Ian shrugged. "You know anything about Moreno's mistress?"

"She's a drug addict who likes to shop."

Adam swore under his breath, his stress level rising. Walking over to the fridge, he grabbed a soda for Ian and a beer for himself. He popped off the tops of both bottles and brought them to the couch.

"Thanks," Ian said, taking a swig.

"What did you tell Maria to do?"

"Go to the police."

"You think she will?"

"No. She's undocumented—and that's just between us. Your smuggler girlfriend brought her here."

Adam drank his beer, unsurprised. She'd acted suspicious the afternoon they met, and that was before Chuy's visit. What were the odds that she'd been carrying illegal cargo in the form of a slender, dark-haired young lady?

"No wonder she came on to me that first day," Adam said. "She had Mario Santos in the back of her fucking van!"

"Have you seen her lately?"

"She was here earlier," he admitted, tugging on his shirt collar. He tried not to conjure a vivid mental picture of what she'd been doing to him.

Ian arched a brow, making an educated guess. "Really."

"She asked me for a wave-through. I said no."

"You're turning into a regular Boy Scout."

Adam groaned, holding the cold bottle to his sweaty forehead. That was hardly true. "She wouldn't tell me why she was asking."

"Now that you know, what are you going to do?"

"I'll talk to her again and report back to you. I'd rather move forward with her cooperation."

Ian didn't have to ask why. He knew Adam could face administrative action for launching an extracurricular investigation. Crossing the line with her sexually made the situation even more precarious.

His friend gave him a measured look. "I take it that the lesbian theory you were pondering has been disproved?"

"It was a soft theory," Adam admitted.

Ian clinked their bottles together. "Cheers to that."

16

Kari made plans to see Adam again the following night.

It was muggy, even after the sun went down. She showered and changed clothes, donning a pair of white shorts and a loose-fitting animal print blouse. Strappy black sandals completed the outfit.

She was selling information, not her body, but it didn't hurt to look good. Kari applied shimmery lip gloss and a touch of eye makeup, trying not to overdo it. When riding the bus in downtown San Diego, a girl didn't want to stand out too much.

She arrived at his house as the twilight faded from the sky. He answered the door in jeans and T-shirt, his hair damp and his feet bare. She inhaled a quick breath, her heart kicking. He smelled like spicy soap and clean heat.

"Sorry, I just got out of the shower."

She blushed, remembering their last conversation.

His dark eyes traveled down her body, lingering on her bare legs. "Come on in," he said. "Do you want something to drink?"

Bypassing the couch, she sank into a chair at the kitchen table. "What do you have?"

He looked in the fridge. "Beer, soda, water . . ."

"Water's fine."

"I might have some wine around here somewhere."

"I don't drink anymore. Sasha's addiction kind of killed the urge."

He nodded, grabbing two bottled waters and taking the seat across from her. Before handing her the water, he loosened the cap.

She took a sip, wishing he wasn't so damned handsome and polite. It was difficult to meet his searing gaze, so she stared at the base of his throat. The tension swelled between them. "I have information about Penelope's murder."

His expression didn't change, but she felt a sudden chill. Whatever he'd been expecting her to say, this wasn't it. "Go on."

"M—my sister knows who did it."

He leaned back in his chair. "Everyone knows who did it."

"I mean, she knows who pulled the trigger. She overheard an argument about it."

A cold, dark interest sparked in his eyes. He waited for her to continue.

"I thought you might agree to help me in exchange for the details."

He glanced away, drumming his fingertips on the surface of the table. "You'll tell me now?"

She moistened her lips, nodding.

"What's the incentive for me to keep my end of the bargain?"

"An arrest, hopefully."

"Your information is hearsay. It doesn't hold up in court."

"If Sasha made a statement—"

"She won't."

Kari realized she was going to have to spill everything. There was no way he'd agree to her terms blindly. "Is this conversation off the record?"

"I can't answer that."

The blood drained from her face.

"I have ethical obligations—"

"Oh, fuck you," she said, rising to her feet. "Where were your ethical obligations when I was on my knees?"

He cringed slightly, massaging his brow. "Kari, I'm a police officer. If you tell me about a crime in progress or a person in danger, I have to report it. I care about you and I want to help you, but I can't promise anything until I hear the details."

Kari crossed her arms over her chest, her thoughts spinning. What other choice did she have? She didn't trust Moreno. She didn't trust Adam, either, although she knew he was the better man. He might break her heart and use her body, but he wouldn't disregard her safety or risk her sister's life.

"Okay," she said, sitting once again. "I'm sure you're aware that my sister is Carlos Moreno's girlfriend." When he inclined his head, she continued. "Sasha pawned some of the jewelry he gave her to buy drugs. He must not have liked that. Chuy Pena came to my house, put a gun to my head, and demanded I pay her debt."

His shoulders went taut. "Did he hurt you?"

"No, he just scared me. I told him I didn't have the

money. He said that if I brought some packages across the border for them, Moreno would turn Sasha over to me."

"Have you spoken to her?"

"Just once this week. She's essentially being held hostage." Kari explained that she'd seen her sister at the spa with Chuy. "I'm so scared for her, Adam. She told me that Chuy has no qualms about killing women. He opened fire at the Coyote Café, acting against orders. According to Sasha, Moreno was angry about it."

Adam left the table abruptly, walking over to a set of sliding glass doors that led to an outdoor patio. His backyard was precisely landscaped, green and shady. The ideal setting for a family barbecue.

"I was supposed to do the job for them last week," she continued, feeling numb. "I went to the pickup location and brought the cargo as planned."

"What went wrong?"

"Nothing. They called it a dry run."

He turned to look at her. "This Tuesday is the real deal?"

"I think so."

"How will the exchange happen?"

She was encouraged by the questions. His voice was clipped and his manner cold, but he wasn't showing her the door. "I was instructed to park the van behind Zócalo. As soon as they drop off Sasha, I hand over the keys."

He scraped his hand along his jaw, considering.

"If you can arrange for me to get through the border, I'll trade the keys for Sasha, and the police can follow the van to the next location."

"It's risky," he said. "Odds are good that Chuy Pena is using Sasha to squeeze you, with no intention of delivering."

"Then he can't blame me for not keeping my end of the bargain."

He laughed harshly. "That's not the way it works, *bella*. My department wouldn't allow you to be part of the sting, either. If something happened to you, we'd be liable." A muscle in his jaw tightened. "And I'd never forgive myself."

Kari was touched by his concern. Then it occurred to her that his fears had more to do with his tragic past than any tender feelings for her. The realization was like a tiny pinprick, bursting the bubble that shouldn't have formed.

"I have to advise you not to cooperate with Pena," he continued.

"Isn't failing to cooperate just as risky? My sister could die. If we pull this off, I get Sasha back, and you get the bad guys. Everybody wins."

"Unless everything goes wrong."

"Don't involve your department," she said, thinking fast. "Follow me from the border and make sure the exchange happens safely. Then call for backup when the van leaves the area. Say you got an anonymous tip."

The corner of his mouth quirked up. "You have a rudimentary understanding of law enforcement."

"What do you mean?"

"A top-tier bust usually requires an entire task force. Dozens of officers, months of planning."

"You can't help me," she said, crestfallen.

He swore in Spanish, shaking his head. "I might be

able to make arrangements with ICE or the DEA. They can hang back while you do the exchange, and move in on the secondary location."

"Perfect."

"Nothing ever is. I can't ensure your safety."

She swallowed hard. "Fine."

He stared at her for a moment, seeming angry. "My brother was a sharpshooter in Iraq. I'll ask him to be there."

"All right."

"As soon as you park the van, get away from it, but stay visible. Hand over the keys even if Sasha doesn't show. Don't go inside Zócalo, or anywhere else, with Chuy Pena."

A chill raced down her spine. "I understand."

"You still have that GPS device, right?"

"Yes."

"Make sure it's charged and put it in the glove compartment."

"Why?"

"So I can track it. And keep your cell phone on. Any instructions I give, you follow. This is nonnegotiable."

"Of course," she murmured, feeling shell-shocked. He'd planted the GPS, not Moreno. She supposed she should be relieved that Adam was a sneaky, thorough son of a bitch. No mama's boy rule follower would agree to this plot.

They discussed a few more details and he told Kari to call him on Tuesday morning during her jog. She picked up her purse on the way out the door, her hands shaking. She'd been worried about her sister for years but had never taken action. Although the constant hand wringing was unproductive, it had become . . . comfortable. She was used to it. There was nothing comfortable about grabbing the bull by the horns.

After her troubled teen years, Kari had grown up fast. She'd made nothing but sensible decisions since then. Sometimes she felt like she was trying to counterbalance Sasha's screwups. As her sister sank lower, Kari set her sights higher. She'd become a homeowner at twenty-four and a successful businesswoman at twenty-five.

Looking back, the climb had been exhausting. She was tired of being a workaholic good girl. Her scramble for financial stability hadn't led to happiness. Although she knew her father would have been proud, she didn't want to end up like him, a victim of cardiac arrest. What she truly longed for was a close family and a loving relationship.

Adam walked her to the door, hesitating before he opened it. A moment ago he'd been Officer Cortez, stern and serious. Now the hard glint in his eyes had eased a little. "I'm sorry for lying about my mother," he said, surprising her. "That was over the line."

"Did she really collect those figurines?"

He nodded slowly. "I added the new one to her collection. My dad keeps everything in the house the way she left it. He . . . misses her."

Kari's throat tightened with sympathy. Judging by his hoarse voice and pained expression, Adam missed her, too. How painful it must have been for him to lose the two women he loved most. "How long has she been gone?"

"Less than a year."

"My mom died when I was eight," she said, commiserating. "I still miss her."

"I'm sorry."

"So am I."

He raised his hand to her face, brushing his thumb over her cheek. She wanted him to kiss her. Relinquishing control of Sasha's fate had only increased her anxiety. But she knew a temporary way to ease it.

His gaze moved from her mouth to the living room couch, and he dropped his hand. "That was . . ."

Fantastic? Amazing? Incredibly hot?

"Inappropriate."

"Totally," she agreed, taking a step back.

"We shouldn't—"

"I know." She flattened her palms on the wall behind her, a blatant invitation for him to come forward.

He just looked at her, studying her parted lips and half-lidded eyes. Kari was glad she'd worn sexy lingerie. Her nipples pebbled against the cups of her bra and an ache formed between her thighs. When he didn't take the bait, she turned her head to the side, exposing the fluttering pulse at the base of her throat.

He closed the distance between them, bracing his hand on the window frame. When he lowered his head, touching his lips to her neck, she smothered a moan. "I hope your brother-in-law isn't planning to stop by again," she said, breathless.

With a flick of his wrist, he locked the door.

Then they were all over each other. He crushed his mouth over hers and she twisted her fingers in his hair. Their tongues met, caught, tangled. Groaning, he slid his hands over her bottom, cupping her to him. She wrapped her legs around his waist, making mindless sounds of pleasure as he thrust against her.

Maybe what they were doing was wrong. But that was probably what made it feel so good. She should be thinking about her sister, not sex. The stakes for Adam were even higher. He could get in serious trouble for touching her and he knew it.

The fact that he couldn't seem to stop himself excited her. Her shameless mewling excited her. His stiff erection, strong hands, and avid tongue excited her.

"Bedroom," he said, dragging his mouth from hers.

"Yes."

He picked her up and carried her there, just like in the movies. Kicking the door shut, he tossed her down on the mattress. She let out a breathy laugh and clutched the sheets, watching him. When he pulled his shirt over his head, her throat went dry. The man had a killer body. Hard pecs, nice biceps, taut stomach.

She stared at his distended fly, mesmerized.

"Are you going to undress or should I rip your clothes off?"

Her startled gaze rose to his face. Was he serious? Although the idea intrigued her, she was too frugal to allow it. Giggling, she yanked off her shirt and fumbled with the zipper of her shorts, wriggling out of them.

"How's that?" she asked, still in her matching bra and panties. The caramel-colored fabric was very sheer, revealing more than it concealed.

His gaze lingered on the cleft between her legs. "Keep going."

While he unbuttoned his fly, she reached behind her and unfastened the clasp at her back. Her breasts trembled as she freed them, her nipples drawn tight. He shoved down his jeans and shorts, kicking them off.

Again Kari was distracted by his erection. It was impressive.

He put one knee on the mattress and climbed over her before she remembered what she was supposed to be doing. Instead of tearing her panties to shreds or thrusting right through them, he settled next to her, kissing her swollen mouth. Then he kissed her collarbone, her pouting nipples, and her quivering belly.

She was shaking with need, embarrassingly aroused. Her panties were damp, clinging to her sex. When he looked at her there, she snaked her hand down her stomach, cupping her palm over the telltale wet spot.

He didn't seem concerned by her belated shyness. Smiling, he kissed the back of her hand, sliding his tongue between her fingers. A neat trick. In a few seconds, her hand relaxed and her fingers fell open, giving him access. His tongue rasped against her clitoris, teasing her through the gossamer fabric.

"God," she groaned.

He hooked his fingers in the waistband of her panties, stripping them off without damaging a single thread. Lowering his head once again, he licked the bare lips of her sex, tasting her.

Whimpering, she closed her eyes. She wanted to lift her hips and press her pulsing clit against his mouth.

"Show me what you did in the shower."

Her eyes flew open.

He kissed her fingertips, one by one.

Indulging him, and herself, because she was desperate to be touched, she put her hand between her splayed thighs, dipping one finger inside. When she removed it, slick from her arousal, he brought it to his mouth, sucking gently.

Her sex throbbed, demanding the same attention.

She rubbed two wet fingers over her ultrasensitive clitoris, straight-up masturbating right in front of him.

"Wait," he said, replacing her fingers with his tongue, mimicking the exact motion.

Oh God. She spread her legs wide and raked her hands through his hair, caressing the base of his skull. Never in her life had she felt anything so pleasurable. He slid one of his own, larger fingers into her tight sheath and continued to flick that clever tongue against her. She screamed out loud, shattering into a thousand pieces.

When she opened her eyes, he was studying her. "How was it?"

"Horrible."

He laughed, his teeth flashing white against his dark complexion. His erection prodded her thigh, leaving a pearly drop on her skin. She wrapped her hand around his shaft, stroking him up and down. He was deliciously hard.

Groaning, he gripped her wrist. "Don't make me come in your hand."

Another bead of moisture seeped from the tip. She bent her head to him, licking it away. "How about my mouth?"

He sucked in a sharp breath, shaking his head. "I won't last a minute that way."

"So?"

"Please. Let me have my dignity."

Laughing, she rolled away from him, toward the nightstand. "Condoms?"

"Top drawer."

She opened it. And found a framed photo of Penelope Mendes, staring back at her. The candid head shot depicted her lovely smile and warm brown eyes. Her pretty perfection was like a slap in Kari's face.

"This is an interesting contraceptive device," she said, glancing over her shoulder. "Very effective."

Adam's gaze moved from Kari's naked bottom to his nightstand drawer. The lust in his eyes faded a little, and his head fell back against the pillows. "Fuck," he said, clenching his hands into fists.

"Suddenly that's the last thing I feel like doing."

"I can explain."

"Don't bother," she said, fumbling for her shirt. She tugged it on and tried to rise from the bed.

He threw his arm around her waist, holding her down. "Wait."

Kari wasn't in the mood to be dominated. "Let me go."

"Give me two minutes. Please."

"Let go!"

Cursing in Spanish, he released her.

She scrambled off the mattress, throwing his jeans at him. "Make it quick."

"The last woman I went home with looked like her," he said. "After she fell asleep, I kept staring at her. Thinking about Penelope."

"This is supposed to make me feel *better*?" Kari asked.

He arranged his pants over his lap, sighing. "It was a breaking point. I stopped tailing Moreno and picking up women. I didn't want to sleep with anyone unless it meant something. Until I was over her."

She crossed her arms in front of her chest, looking away. "How long has it been?"

"Six months. That's why the condoms are underneath the picture, Kari. I haven't used them, or looked at her face, since before Christmas. I was so caught up with you just now that I forgot the photo was even in there."

Taking a deep breath, she met his eyes. "Are you still in love with her?"

"I thought I was," he said, holding her gaze, "until I met you."

Her anger dissolved, replaced by a terrifying elation she couldn't suppress. He rose from the bed, wrapping his strong arms around her. She felt his heart thumping hard against hers. "Don't hurt me again," she whispered, looking up at him.

He didn't make any promises. That was good, because she wouldn't have believed him. Instead, he soothed her with a simple kiss. If nothing else, his passion was sincere. She knew he wanted her, and badly. This wasn't an emotionless one-night stand.

They fell back into bed together, hands grasping, tongues dancing. His erection was a hot brand across her belly. He reached for the condoms this time, slamming the drawer shut. Keeping his eyes on Kari, he rolled it over his length.

She pushed against his shoulder, climbing on his lap. He conceded easily, groaning as her body enveloped him inch by inch. The last time, he'd been on top, but she'd raised her hips to meet his thrusts. This time, he controlled the depth of the penetration. Gripping her hips, he worked her up and down on him.

Kari moaned, wallowing in pleasure. Although she was still wearing her shirt, she was naked below the waist, her bare legs and slick sex completely exposed to him. The sensual contrast sent shivers along her spine. Her nipples rasped against the silky fabric and her clit tingled with each bump of his pelvis.

Panting, she pulled her shirt over her head.

"Touch yourself," he ground out.

Oh God. Apparently he liked to watch. As luck would have it, she liked to perform, and his hungry gaze aroused her beyond belief.

She squeezed her breasts together, pinching her stiff nipples. He stared at the rosy tips, his throat working as he swallowed. Smoothing her hand over her belly, she touched the place where their bodies were joined, feeling him piston in and out of her.

His eyes darkened as she raised her fingers to her mouth, tasting them.

"Fuck," he groaned, moistening his lips.

She moved her hand back down, stroking her clitoris in a circular motion. Oh God, she was so close. When he held her up, balancing her on the tip of his cock, she came with a keening cry, her sex clenching. He muttered a suitably dirty phrase in Spanish and slammed her down, driving deep as her body convulsed around him.

She was still rioting with aftershocks when he sank his hand into her hair, bringing her mouth to his. Kissing her hotly, he found his own release, his hips jerking, arms trembling. They shuddered together, sweaty and spent.

After a long moment she rolled to the side, letting him get up to dispose of the condom. "How was that?" she asked when he came back to bed.

"Horrible," he murmured, his mouth on her neck.

Chuckling softly, she snuggled against him. She'd never felt so languid in her entire life. At the same time, she couldn't help but wonder if she was deluding herself. Instead of relaxing her guard, she should be tensed for the blow.

17

On Tuesday morning, she called Adam before her jog, giving him the details.

Maria had relayed a terse message from Chuy: same time, same place. Kari would return to the tile manufacturer for the pickup.

Adam's manner was brusque and businesslike, no friendlier than she expected. She left the house and ran like the devil was at her heels, studying every passing car with trepidation. The occupants could be undercover officers or a drug kingpin's spies.

At the corner of her block, she hit an uneven section of sidewalk and went sprawling into a brick flower planter.

Crying out in pain and shock, she rolled to a sitting position in her neighbor's hydrangeas. Both of her elbows were scraped and one knee was skinned badly. "Shit," she muttered, glancing around. There was no concerned citizen in her immediate vicinity, no secret agent rushing to help her.

Good.

Brushing away crushed petals and loose dirt, she got

up and limped home. By the time she arrived at the front door, a trickle of blood had snaked down her shin, staining her ankle-high athletic sock.

"*Pobrecita*," Maria exclaimed, turning off the stove. "What happened?"

"I fell."

"Are you okay?"

"Yes. I'm just going to shower off."

Maria looked doubtful but didn't argue. It occurred to Kari that she was more like a mother than a wife. Which was odd, considering their respective ages and Kari's tendency to take care of everything. Shaking her head, she walked straight to the bathroom and turned on the shower, stripping off her dirty clothes.

Her elbows were fine but the knee looked ugly.

Groaning, she stepped into the shower and closed her eyes. Although she felt a strong urge to cry, she didn't give in to it. This was not the time to break down. Tears could come later, when she held Sasha in her arms.

She toweled herself dry, moving the terry cloth gingerly over her raw knee. After applying four bandage strips from the medicine cabinet, she wrapped the towel around her body and walked to her room. The outfit she'd described to Adam was laid out on the bed: loose-fitting jeans, a red tank top, and white tennis shoes. Sex appeal wasn't getting her across the border today. She put on the comfortable clothes and fashioned a quick ponytail before checking her appearance in the vanity mirror.

She had dark circles under her eyes, her pupils were huge, and her face was pale. "I'm a drug smuggler," she said out loud, staring at her reflection. "I'm a crazy drug smuggler who talks to herself."

In the kitchen, Kari sat down to a healthy breakfast she couldn't eat. Her stomach roiled with tension, rebelling at the smell of food.

"Are you sure you want to do this?" Maria asked, taking the seat across from her. She sipped coffee, her face full of concern.

"What choice do I have?"

"We can run away."

She smiled at the idea. "To where?"

Maria thought about it for a minute. "Canada!"

Kari was afraid to laugh. She couldn't show any emotion, high or low. The only way to survive this day was with an even, pervasive numbness. After choking down a few bites of toast, she left the table to finish getting ready. It was just shy of ten o'clock when she dropped off Maria at the Hotel del Oro.

Chuy had insisted that Maria work today.

"Are *you* sure you want to do this?" Kari asked.

"Of course."

Kari studied her pretty face, wondering if she had a few screws loose. "You don't owe me anything, Maria."

"Now you make insult," she said. "I have other reasons."

"Like what?"

"You brought me to this country, but God brought me to you. He sent Agent Foster to save me when I was in the desert. I am here by His grace. When the choice is to help or not help, I always know what to do."

Kari's chest tightened at the words, and she wasn't even religious. She envied Maria's straightforward outlook, but she couldn't imagine choosing right from wrong with such certainty. Much less acting on it.

What Kari could imagine, far more easily, was losing

Maria. She'd lost her sister to drugs, her mother to cancer, and her father to a heart attack. This not-so-simple girl from Mexico had filled an empty place in Kari's heart. She was struck by the crippling fear that she'd never see Maria again.

"Be careful," she said, clearing her throat. "And I—I love you."

Maria chuckled, hitching her purse on her shoulder. "*Ay, amor.* Now you are really scaring me."

"I mean it."

"I know," she said, kissing Kari's cheek.

Kari watched Maria walk across the courtyard, her dark hair shining in the sun. If—*when*—they got through this, she was going to help Maria apply for citizenship and offer her a job at Zócalo.

As soon as Maria was out of sight, Kari drove away from the hotel and crossed the border into Tijuana. The sleepless night and constant anxiety wore her down, leaving her frayed nerves on edge. Her eyes felt grainy; the sun was too bright. The entire situation seemed surreal, like a bad acid trip. She'd tried mushrooms once with Sasha and spent the night in the bathroom, her head swimming with vertigo.

She needed a vacation. She'd planned to take some time off to get Sasha settled at an affordable rehab. A few of those days could be spent at the beach, recuperating. Kari visualized pounding surf and clean saltwater, washing away her troubles.

She turned down the gravel road that led to the tile manufacturer, her hands clenched around the steering wheel. Just before she pulled into the parking lot, a man standing next to a dark blue SUV gestured for her to slow.

Heart hammering against her chest, she pressed on the brakes.

"Park there and get out," he said, pointing at the side of the road.

She followed his orders, handing him her car keys when he held out his palm. He was a short man with small hands. Not friendly, but not menacing. She crossed her arms over her chest, watching him drive away.

She didn't dare call Adam to tell him of the slight change in plans. What did it matter where the drugs had been stashed? Maybe the tile store wasn't one of Moreno's Tijuana-based strongholds.

For a few bleak minutes she stared down the dusty road, half hoping the man wouldn't come back.

But he did return, slowing to a stop and hopping out. "It's ready."

Kari murmured a thank-you, as if he'd done her some great favor by filling her van with illegal substances. Shaking her head, she climbed behind the wheel and turned around, heading north, toward the border.

She hadn't thought her tension level could increase, but it did. Her last trip had rated a ten out of ten, anxiety-wise. This one was off the charts. As she entered the traffic gridlock, her heartbeat surged erratically and black dots danced before her eyes.

She pinched her hand, terrified she would pass out.

Breathe. Breathe. Breathe.

Kari tried to think good thoughts. Images from her last night with Adam danced in her head, but they failed to calm her. When the metallic tang of blood filled her mouth, she realized she'd bitten her lower lip.

Her empty stomach lurched in protest. She grabbed a plastic trash bag and heaved into it quietly, her back bowed toward the passenger side, vision blurring with tears. Finally, the nausea passed. She found a tissue in her purse to wipe the blood and bile from her mouth. Shuddering with distaste, she tied a knot in the trash bag and tossed it on the floor on the passenger side. Then she drank a small amount of bottled water, spitting the first sip out the window.

Yuck.

The lines moved fast today, which was both a blessing and a curse. She pulled into the shade at the inspection booth before she felt composed, her wary eyes darting toward a CBP officer who wasn't Adam.

"Citizenship?"

"U.S.," she murmured, handing him her passport.

"Anything to declare?"

Her heart kicked against her ribs. She pictured it exploding like a firecracker, obliterating her chest cavity. "No," she said. "Nothing."

"What's the reason for your visit?"

Although the question was standard, Kari wasn't prepared for it. She'd thought she was picking up tile crates. Instead, there were a couple of large shipping boxes in the cargo space, the same kind she'd smuggled Maria in. What should she say was back there, television sets? Did it matter what she said?

As long as Adam had kept his word, she should pass inspection.

"Shopping," she said quickly. "I was shopping."

Dark sunglasses covered the officer's eyes, but she sensed his scrutiny. "Just a moment, ma'am." Taking her passport with him, he stepped inside his cubicle at the inspection booth, touching the radio at his shoulder.

Had something gone wrong?

She moistened her lips, tasting blood again. Shit! Pulse racing, she glanced around for Adam. He wasn't there.

The officer reappeared at her window. "Move forward to the secondary inspection area," he said, pointing to the right.

Kari's stomach dropped with the realization that Adam had betrayed her.

It was a quiet morning at the Hotel del Oro.

Although there were few guests and fewer rooms to clean, the air crackled with energy. Maria felt certain that the shipment Kari was smuggling over the border would end up here. Maybe it was a bigger haul than usual, or a more lucrative deal. Chuy paced the courtyard, his ear stuck to a cell phone.

Armando whittled away at a piece of wood, unconcerned.

Sonia, the receptionist, called Maria into the lobby at noon. One of the guests had dropped a six-pack of beer near the front desk, leaving foam and broken glass all over the tile. Maria swept up the glass and mopped the floor, placing a yellow caution sign at the entrance. Before she left, Sonia snapped her fingers. "Take care of that, too," she said in Spanish, pointing out an orange stain behind the potted plant in the corner.

Maria nodded, grabbing a spray bottle from her supply cart. The lobby was Sonia's responsibility, but she was too much of a princess to empty trash cans or scrub floors.

Maria didn't mind. She felt sorry for Sonia, who seemed desperately unhappy. The pretty receptionist could do a lot better than Chuy Pena. He wasn't rich or handsome or even that powerful. And he certainly didn't treat her well.

Sonia was probably aware that Chuy had dragged Maria into his room last week. She seemed to know everything that went on at the hotel, despite her ambivalence toward the lesser employees. She'd given Maria several warning glares, letting her know that she wouldn't tolerate any poaching on her man.

As if Maria wanted that *cochino*.

Wrinkling her nose, she knelt behind the potted plant and sprayed the tiles with cleaning solution. It looked like melted candy, thick and sticky. She sat back on her heels, giving it a chance to soak. She was thinking about getting Irma's gum scraper when Chuy walked into the lobby. He didn't notice her, which wasn't unusual.

Good maids were invisible.

If Sonia remembered Maria's presence, she didn't care. When Chuy sat down in a chair behind the reception desk, Sonia started massaging his shoulders and pressing her cleavage against his arm. "You're so tense," she murmured. "Want me to relax you?"

"I don't have time," he said, but his voice sounded rough. Tempted.

"When is the delivery?"

"Soon."

Sonia must have taken that as an invitation to proceed. She walked around the front of his chair and sank down, out of sight.

Maria stayed behind the potted plant, shocked into silence. It was a poor hiding place. Although Chuy had his back to her, he could turn his head and catch sight of her at any moment. If she got caught eavesdropping again, he'd be furious. She held her breath, waiting for the opportunity to sneak away.

"I don't know why you wouldn't let me be the decoy," Sonia murmured. Maria detected the faint rasp of a lowering zipper.

"You don't want that job, baby."

"Why not?"

"It doesn't pay."

"What's she going to get?"

"Exactly what she deserves."

"You're so clever," she cooed.

"Shut up," he said, ever the suave gentleman. There was a slight choking sound that Maria supposed meant Sonia had gotten down to business.

Time to go. She crawled out from behind the potted plant and crept toward the open front doors, keeping her body low. Moving carefully around the caution sign, she slipped through the entrance.

When he didn't chase after her, she figured she'd made a clean escape. Racing to the laundry room, she found Irma. "Can I use your phone?"

"What for?"

"It's an emergency."

Irma's expression was doubtful, but she rummaged through her purse, handing Maria a battered-looking cell phone.

"Thanks," Maria said, running out the back door to make the call. She punched Ian's number with shaking fingers, listening to the abbreviated trill. Maybe she should have tried Kari first. *Chingado!*

He answered on the second ring. "Who is this?"

"Maria," she said, glancing around the mostly empty

parking lot. "I just heard Chuy say that Kari is a decoy. I think she's in trouble. You have to help her."

"Slow down—"

"I can't! They're coming across the border right now."

"Where are you?"

"At the hotel."

"Be more specific."

"Outside the laundry room."

"Shit," he said, his voice rising. "I can see you from my apartment window."

"What's wrong?"

"You need to get the fuck out of there! Go toward the parking lot. Take the phone with you and run, right now."

Although Maria understood his warning, she didn't follow his orders. She couldn't steal Irma's cell phone. Besides, fleeing the hotel suddenly might make Chuy suspicious and put Kari in danger. Then she heard the click of a safety release behind her and realized that the short hesitation might have cost her her life.

This operation was about to go down in the clusterfuck hall of fame.

Making arrangements for today had been complicated, to say the least. Adam couldn't waltz up to his superior and tell him that he'd organized a sting with a civilian. After Kari left his house the other night, he'd called Ian to brainstorm some ideas.

Luckily, his friend was willing to do just about anything to bust Chuy Pena. Together they'd come up with a basic plan.

Adam had approached Pettigrew this morning with

the story. He'd said that his best friend, an undercover DEA agent, had been given a tip by a credible informant. This agent suspected there was a leak in his department, so he'd come to Adam.

The tip from the informant was simple. And true. Kari Strauss had been threatened and coerced into smuggling a large shipment of heroin for Pena. She would trade the cargo for her sister at her place of business.

Adam was risking his job by lying to his supervisor about the informant, but he hoped that success would smooth any ruffled feathers. Takedowns like this didn't usually happen on the fly, so Adam was concerned about the outcome. It was almost impossible to orchestrate a high-profile arrest at the last minute.

And if they failed, his ass was on the line.

Ian was also going to catch hell for claiming there was a rat in his department, though it wasn't far-fetched. Moreno had dirty cops everywhere. Adam could only pray that none of them were involved in this ragtag op.

So far, nothing had run smoothly. Adam had been scrambling since dawn. The mobile X-ray equipment had been delayed in Tecate. Kari was already waiting in line at the border when the M-VACIS arrived, and it took time to set up. They barely managed to get into position before she arrived at primary inspection.

When Adam saw the scan of Kari's van, his chest seized with panic. The contents changed everything.

"Fuck," he said under his breath, studying the screen. A figure was crouched inside one of the boxes in the cargo space.

The M-VACIS rays didn't harm humans, but it wasn't designed to detect them. Adam could only see the vague outline of a person. An assailant, most likely. He didn't appear to have a weapon, but he could jump out and attack Kari at any moment. No one on the team would be able to prevent that. Not even Adam's sharpshooter brother, who had reluctantly agreed to set up on top of a building adjacent to Zócalo.

Before Adam could decide what to do, his cell phone rang. It was Ian.

"I just got a call from Maria," he said. "She thinks Kari's a decoy. The real shipment is coming in at the same time."

Adam's stress level skyrocketed. Could this get any worse?

"Pena interrupted our conversation," Ian continued. "He's got a gun on her. I just saw the whole thing from my apartment window."

Adam stared at the scanning screen, his blood pumping with adrenaline. "What are you going to do?"

"This op is fucked, man! My cover is blown. I'm going in."

"You need backup," Adam said.

"No shit!" Ian said, ending the call.

Adam paused for a moment, trying to collect himself. He had to push aside his concern for Ian and focus on the task at hand.

Putting his phone away, he turned to his crew. Pettigrew had brought in two ICE agents and four CBPs, including the lane supervisor, to consult with. "Apparently the shipment is coming in a different vehicle," he said. "We need to mobile-scan all suspicious cargo. Someone tipped off the target, so they already know we're on to them. Every officer in the lanes needs to be on high alert."

"What about Strauss?" the line supervisor asked.

He deliberated for a moment, drumming his fingertips on the table. Pena was expecting Kari to cause a distraction. "Send the van to secondary and detain her as an arrestee. I'm going to open up the back."

Two of his coworkers joined Adam as he left the central observation area. The rest stayed behind to continue the mobile scanning process.

The next few moments were an agony of tension. Adam thought of Penelope, and the Tijuanero police officer who'd called to notify him of her death. He thought of her funeral, her grave site, the picture in his nightstand.

A secondary inspection officer drew his weapon, shouting for Kari to exit the van. As soon as she came out, her arms raised high above her head, she was ordered to get down on the ground. Two officers handled her roughly, cuffing her wrists behind her back and dragging her upright.

As Kari was guided to the detainment area, she caught sight of Adam. She had blood on her lips, probably from being slammed into the concrete by his overzealous coworkers. The real damage appeared to have happened on the inside, however. He'd never forget the look in her eyes: shock, horror, despair.

Adam returned his attention to the back of the van, hating himself. It killed him to see her like this, but he was glad she wasn't seriously injured. Drawing his own weapon, he gestured for the secondary officer to open the rear door.

The boxes in the cargo space were motionless, undisturbed.

"Come out with your hands up," he shouted in English, then repeated the command in Spanish.

Nothing happened.

Rather than waiting for the assailant to act, Adam climbed into the back of the van. Advancing quickly, he kicked the side of the box, ordering the person to get out. When he got no response, he directed his fellow officers to remove the rest of the cargo, giving him space to maneuver. As the men stood at the rear of the vehicle, guns ready, Adam holstered his weapon and shoved the box onto the asphalt.

Sasha Strauss fell out, her thin arms akimbo, face pale with death.

18

Chuy was standing a few feet away, his gun trained on Maria's forehead. "Give me the phone."

She did, her hand shaking.

Agent Foster had hung up, but his number was visible in recent calls. Chuy appeared to recognize it. "Motherfucker," he said, pressing redial. Predictably, Foster didn't answer. "Motherfucker!" Chuy chucked the phone against the asphalt, his mouth twisted with fury. It shattered, electronic parts flying.

Maria cringed, flattening her back against the wall. She couldn't think of a worse outcome than this one. In trying to help Kari, she'd just betrayed Foster. Chuy had overheard the conversation and put two and two together.

He was ugly, but he wasn't stupid.

"You're dead," he said, pressing the gun to her temple.

Maria closed her eyes and begged God to grant her an instant death, her lips moving in silent prayer.

The blast didn't come.

She winced as Chuy ground the barrel of the gun into her scalp and fisted his hand in her hair, guiding her forward. "I should have known you were a fucking snitch," he said, directing her toward his office. "Where's Fuller?"

Maria almost stumbled over a bump in the sidewalk. Her entire body was trembling, her mind blank with terror. "Who is Fuller?"

"The guy you were just on the phone with! What the fuck is his real name?"

"I don't know English very well—"

Chuy opened the door to the office and shoved her inside. She fell to her hands and knees on the carpet, crying out in pain.

She should never have come to the United States. Her mother hadn't wanted her to leave home. Virginia Santos had accepted her genteel poverty without complaint, claiming that the meek inherited the earth.

Why hadn't Maria listened?

"Don't give me that bullshit," Chuy said, ready to execute her. "Your English was fine a second ago."

"I don't know," she repeated, sobbing the words.

Chuy grabbed her by the hair again, pressing the gun to the nape of her neck. "Tell me his name or I'll kill you."

She swallowed hard, wondering if she should go for her pepper spray. Armando had told her to practice with the canister, and she'd taken that advice to heart. She'd worn down the pocket of her jeans, whipping it out.

But she couldn't think—couldn't move—with a gun at her head.

"I'll make the call to have your friend killed, too," he warned, yanking her hair. "I'll kill your whole fucking family, you wetback bitch! Now tell me his name!"

"Foster," she said, whimpering. "Agent Foster."

Chuy released his grip on her hair and eased up on the weapon. He was breathing heavily, his eyes wild. "Is he FBI?"

"I don't know."

With a strangled growl, he kicked her in the stomach. Maria slumped forward, writhing in pain. Black spots danced at the edge of her vision. "Last time we met he was with *la migra*," she gasped, holding a palm to her burning midsection. "That's all I know."

Armando came into the office unexpectedly. Although his expression was flat, as always, there was a hard set to his mouth. He glanced from Maria's crumpled form to Chuy's clenched fists. "Why did you hurt her?"

"She overheard me talking to Sonia about the decoy."

"So?"

Chuy bared his teeth in menace. "So she called that fucking junkie, Ethan Fuller, otherwise known as Agent Foster, and told him everything!"

Armando inclined his head. "Ah."

"That's all you've got to say about it? Motherfucking *ah*?"

"No, I have more. Mr. Foster is in the parking lot right now. He's carrying a very accurate-looking semi-automatic pistol."

"Fuck!" Chuy said, his face dark with fury. Holstering his weapon, he took out his cell phone, stabbing a few buttons. "*Jefe*, we have a problem," he muttered, turning his back on them to explain the situation to Moreno.

Armando stepped away from the door, inching closer to Maria.

Chuy caught the motion, looking over his shoulder. His gaze darted from Maria to Armando, sharpening with suspicion. After a few terse, one-word responses, he said, "I'll take care of it," and ended the call.

"Is there a new rendezvous point?" Armando asked.

"Yeah," Chuy said, picking up a black duffel bag. He crossed the room, tearing a picture off the wall and opening the safe behind it.

"You can't go there."

He shoved cash into the bag, his jaw clenched. "This is my deal, my setup, my decoy. I'm not going to give up my cut."

"If the police follow you, no one will get a cut."

Chuy slung the bag over his shoulder, drawing his weapon again. "You fucking bitch," he said, pointing his gun at Maria. She covered her head with her arms, cowering on the floor. "I should fucking smoke you right now!"

"Don't be a fool," Armando said, putting his body in front of hers. "You can't shoot an innocent woman with the feds outside."

"Who's going to stop me?"

Armando drew his own weapon, a move that spoke volumes.

"I don't need your permission, *puto*. You think any-one gives a fuck about a common Oaxacan guerrilla *como tú*?"

"I'm from Chiapas," Armando corrected.

"Whatever. You're just another dime-a-dozen *mo-jado*."

"And you're just another trigger-happy drug dealer who can't keep his mouth shut."

Maria trembled uncontrollably, her stomach roiling. These two were going to shoot each other, and kill her in the crossfire!

"I was big-time before you came," Chuy said.

"Yeah, I know all about the TJ fuckup. The boss sent me here for a reason. He doesn't trust you with the ladies."

Chuy continued to hold the 9 mm steady, his nostrils flaring. "Fuck him," he said. "And fuck you."

Armando stood his ground. "We can settle this after we get away from the hotel."

"You're a dead motherfucker, Villarreal," he said, wavering.

"Kill me later, *cabrón*."

Chuy dropped his arm, acknowledging the wisdom of Armando's words. Cursing, he walked to the window, parting the vertical blinds with his fingertips. "Head to the laundry room. As soon as you're clear, I'll take her to the lobby and ditch her. There's a guy waiting for us on Flores Street."

Armando glanced at Maria, deliberating. "She'll slow you down."

"She'll keep me alive. They won't fire on me if I have a hostage."

With a terse nod, Armando agreed to the plan. "*Bueno*. But remember what I said. You hurt her, I hurt you. *Comprendes?*"

Chuy smiled coldly. "If I didn't know better, I'd think you were in love with her."

Armando made a dismissive sound on his way to the door. "Women are your weakness, not mine."

Chuy shrugged, guilty as charged. *"Cuando te veo."*
Until I see you again.

Armando didn't respond to the threat. Creeping forward, he turned the doorknob and stepped out, holding the gun at his side.

As soon as he was halfway down the walkway, Chuy grabbed Maria by the arm, jerking her upright. "Let's go, *puta*." Instead of waiting for Armando to get clear, as promised, he dragged Maria through the open doorway, pressing the gun to her temple.

His next move was even more horrifying.

Taking the gun from Maria's head, he pointed it toward Armando and pulled the trigger, shooting his partner in the back.

Adam knelt beside the body.

Rigor mortis had set in, indicating that Sasha Strauss had been dead for more than four hours. Her arms were contorted in a zombie-like pose, her hazy blue eyes open. He searched her slender form for signs of a struggle or cause of death. There were no wounds at all, unless he counted the track marks.

His radio sounded. "Officer Cortez."

Adam touched his shoulder. "Yeah."

"The M-VACIS has located a gray panel truck with heavy fluorescing. Looks like the load you were after."

"Which lane?"

"The driver is at inspection booth twelve. We are ready to pursue."

Adam straightened, glancing toward the group of vehicles ICE had gathered for the mission. Normally he didn't assist in arrests outside the port of entry, but today Adam was acting as a liaison between CBP and ICE. He couldn't stay at San Ysidro and console Kari, or even give his supervisor a quick rundown of the situation.

When the smoke cleared, he might lose his job . . . and her.

"Fuck," he said, leaving the secondary inspection crew to process the scene. Hopefully Kari wouldn't be arrested for murder before he returned.

Adam climbed into the backseat of a black-on-black squad car just as the truck from lane twelve passed through inspection. Two unmarked vehicles led the pursuit. The driver of the car Adam was in, an ICE agent, followed at a short distance.

"We know we're he's headed?" the agent asked.

"No," Adam replied, putting another call in to Ian. His friend didn't pick up. "It's a basic stop-and-go."

A stop-and-go operation was typical in drug enforcement. Agents followed the vehicle to the drop-off location and arrested all involved parties on the spot. Adam didn't think they were going to nab Chuy Pena, but it would be a major bust regardless. If nothing else, they were taking a large shipment of narcotics off the street.

While they were en route, Adam sent his brother a text message, telling him to abort. He suspected that Gabe had been struggling with PTSD since his last tour. Adam hoped he wasn't having flashbacks of Iraq.

The panel truck cruised through a business district in downtown San Diego, pulling into an open garage at an auto parts warehouse. And just like that, it was go time.

The lead vehicles jerked to a stop behind the truck, blocking it in, and several patrol cars weaved through the midday traffic, sirens blaring.

Adam wanted to get in on the action, but this phase of the operation was out of his hands. The supervisor directed them to circle around the block, securing the perimeter. As soon as they rounded the corner, a trio of men in dark clothing walked away from the back door of the warehouse, heading toward a silver Mercedes.

One of the suspects stood out from the others. He was tall and lean, a baseball cap covering his hair. After tracking this man's movements for two years, Adam recognized his gait, his bone structure, his . . . aura.

"That's Carlos Moreno," he said, stunned.

The driver notified his superior of this unexpected development and stepped on the gas, racing down the street. Unfortunately, Moreno spotted the black-on-black squad car just before he climbed into the Mercedes. His eyes darted to the crowded intersection at the end of the block. Perhaps he decided that leaving by automobile wasn't the best choice, because he turned around and fled the scene on foot.

The instant the squad car pulled up to the Mercedes, Adam was out on the street, his weapon drawn.

While his fellow officers dealt with the other two men, Adam took off after Moreno, running hard. The cartel leader was surprisingly fast. They raced down two blocks at full speed, dodging cars and street signs. Moreno pushed a trash can over, littering the sidewalk with debris. Adam leapt over the mess, clearing the trash barrel. Moreno lost a few seconds to the failed maneuver. When Adam started to gain on him, Moreno went into overdrive. In a burst of energy, he darted between two buildings, his legs pumping.

Adam couldn't believe he was running down Carlos Moreno. He hadn't expected to see him at all today. Moreno rarely got his hands dirty with drug shipments—it was too risky. Maybe the screwup with Chuy Pena had forced him to take over the delivery.

It was an incredible stroke of luck for law enforcement.

Adam followed Moreno into the narrow alleyway, where he caught another break. It was a dead end. Moreno slowed to a stop at the brick wall, his posture bowed with defeat, chest heaving from exertion.

"Put your hands up," Adam shouted, pointing his gun at the back of Moreno's head.

Moreno lifted his arms, surrendering easily. He also glanced over his shoulder, giving Adam a quick perusal.

"Face forward," Adam ordered, moving closer.

"I thought you looked familiar," Moreno said.

Adam came to a halt a few feet away. "Brace your hands against the wall and shut the fuck up."

"I know you, Cortez."

"You don't know me."

Although Moreno's head was turned, Adam could see the edge of his smirking profile. "Yeah, I do. You're the cop boyfriend of Penelope Mendes."

Shock and fury washed over him. The barrel of his gun wavered, the trigger slick against his fingertip.

"You thought I didn't know you were stalking me? How . . . cute."

"Fuck you," Adam said, rage narrowing his vision.

Moreno looked back again, his expression almost

pitying. "You should have kept her out of trouble, *hermano*. A woman like that belongs in a man's bed, not on the streets of Tijuana, asking dangerous questions."

Adam decided he could shoot Moreno right now and get away with it. His fellow officers would never know the drug lord hadn't resisted arrest or reached for a weapon. There were no witnesses.

It was just him and Adam.

For several long, drawn-out seconds he wanted to do it. The bloodlust Adam thought had receded over the past six months pumped fresh and new, reaching a powerful crescendo. The urge to pull the trigger was almost overwhelming. With relish, he pictured Moreno's head exploding.

He knew Penelope wouldn't have approved of his vigilantism, but that mental argument had always failed to sway him. It wasn't what stilled his hand now. He didn't picture a ghostly, dark-haired angel frowning down on him from heaven. Instead he conjured a very real Kari, staring at him like he'd killed her heart.

If he went through with this, he'd never be able to look her in the eye again. He wouldn't deserve a chance to make it up to her. If he murdered someone in cold blood, he couldn't live with himself.

His soul would die.

"Put your hands behind your head and interlock your fingers," he said, reaching for his cuffs. Just as he touched the metal, a shot rang out behind him. Not the heavy blast of a handgun but a hissing round from a high-powered rifle.

Apparently Moreno had a sharpshooter on his team as well.

Adam felt the bullet rip into his left side, penetrating his uniform and slamming against one of the armor plates in his ballistics vest. CBP officers were required to wear a Level IV vest, the maximum protection. The body armor was a weighty nuisance, damned near unbearable on hot days—and he'd never been so glad for the burden.

Even with the vest on, getting shot hurt like a bitch. The impact reverberated through the protective plate, rattling his teeth. He stumbled sideways, barely maintaining a grip on his weapon. His handcuffs clattered to the sidewalk.

"Motherfucker," he muttered, whirling into a defensive stance. He searched for the shooter on the rooftop, locating him immediately. Heart racing with fear, he wrapped his left hand around his right wrist, needing both arms to hold his revolver steady. Although he managed to squeeze off a shot, his Beretta was outmatched. The rifleman fired again, hitting Adam in the upper part of his chest.

And that was all she wrote.

He fell back against the building, stunned into utter uselessness. His right arm felt like a slab of meat. He couldn't draw breath. Adam wasn't completely sure that his gear had held up. Contrary to popular belief, bulletproof vests couldn't stop every type of ammunition.

Then his lungs expanded, sucking in oxygen, and he knew the bullet hadn't penetrated his chest cavity.

But the point was moot. Because Moreno had turned and drawn on him.

Adam tried to bring his gun arm up to protect himself, and failed. A deep ache radiated from his collarbone to his fingertips, making him nauseous. The first hit hadn't incapacitated him, perhaps because his lateral muscle had absorbed more of the impact. The flesh on his upper chest wasn't as meaty.

Moreno stepped closer, looking down at Adam with cautious curiosity. How easily their roles had reversed. Adam could almost read Moreno's thought processes as he contemplated pulling the trigger. His indecisiveness surprised Adam. He hadn't expected the drug lord to have a conscience, let alone struggle with it.

They stared at each other like equals.

"I didn't kill your girlfriend," Moreno said finally.

Adam drew in another sharp breath, his chest burning with two kinds of pain. "Did you kill yours?"

Moreno's face revealed an emotion Adam recognized well: anguish. He holstered his weapon in an angry motion, jerking his chin toward the sharpshooter above. "My associate will shoot you in the head if you make a move."

Adam could only lie there, watching his nemesis walk away.

Kari's knee was bleeding again.

She couldn't believe Adam had set her up. When they dragged her away in handcuffs, he'd looked right through her. He hadn't appeared sad, or conflicted, or coldly satisfied. His face was a mask. He didn't even acknowledge her.

Bastard.

She was sick with worry for Sasha, shaking uncontrollably. The detainment area was made up of four walls, a locked door, and a concrete bench. With her wrists locked behind her back, she couldn't do anything about her knee. The bandages had been knocked askew when she'd been forced to the ground. Beneath the fabric of her jeans, blood oozed from the wound, dripping down her shin in an agonizingly slow crawl.

The only thing that sustained her was anger. She felt like a wild animal, ready to pounce. If Adam was in front of her right now and her hands were free, she'd rip his face off.

Her fear was too sharp, too painful. So she focused on the rage instead.

He'd lied to her. Over and over again. And she'd bought it because she was a lonely, pathetic fool. Her hungry heart had eaten up every word, every gesture, every pseudo-sincere expression.

She must have had *sucker* written on her forehead. Right next to *fuck me*.

Why had she believed him? Because he was handsome and exciting and fantastic in bed? He'd said he cared about her, that she was special to him, and he didn't love Penelope anymore. What bullshit!

She understood that he was a lying son of a bitch, but she didn't know what had gone wrong with the plan. Why would they arrest her and give up the chance to take down Moreno's crew members? More important, what would happen to Sasha? If her sister had been harmed because of Adam's deception, she'd never forgive him.

Kari was still shivering, and seething, when a female CBP officer came into the detainment room. She had short, dark hair and a midnight-blue uniform. "Ms. Strauss? I'm Officer Li."

Kari just stared at her, teeth chattering. She couldn't extend her hand, and she sure as hell wasn't pleased to meet her.

"Come with me."

She stood, allowing Officer Li to guide her out the door. There was a small room nearby with a table and three chairs. When the woman removed her handcuffs, Kari massaged her aching wrists. Her arms felt like rubber.

"Have a seat," Li said.

There was a bottle of water on the table. Kari unscrewed the cap and took a long drink. "Can I use the restroom?"

"Sure." Li pointed to the nearest door.

After Kari used the facilities, she bent over the sink, washing her hands and face. Her mouth tasted like blood. Pulling up her pant leg, she cleaned her knee as well as she could, blotting the scrape with a paper towel. Under the fluorescent lighting, her skin looked ghostly, the shadows beneath her eyes like purple bruises.

She left the bathroom, taking a seat across from Officer Li. Although she knew that asking for a lawyer was in her best interests, Kari was more concerned about Sasha's well-being than her own. She also didn't give a damn if Adam got in trouble.

"Do you know why you're here?" Li asked.

"I assume there were drugs in my cargo space."

"You're not sure?"

After a brief hesitation, she explained that she'd made a deal to smuggle some packages across the border in exchange for her sister's debt.

"It didn't occur to you to call the police?"

"I was afraid for my sister's life. That's why I approached Officer Cortez."

"Officer Cortez," she repeated, arching a brow.

Kari nodded. "We met at my store and . . . hit it off. He agreed to help me. Obviously he didn't follow through."

"What is your relationship with him?"

Kari knew she could cause Adam a lot of grief by telling the truth, but she was too proud to admit she'd been screwed by him in more ways than one. "There is no relationship," she said, lifting her chin. "Can I call my sister?"

Officer Li's expression revealed an emotion that Kari didn't want to recognize. It was part revulsion, part pity.

"Is Adam available?" Kari asked, tamping down her anxiety.

"Officer Cortez is not on site."

Tears of anger and frustration filled Kari's eyes. Wasn't that just like a man? He'd used her and ditched her.

"I have some bad news for you," Li said.

Kari's heart dropped. "No."

"Your sister was found in the cargo space of your vehicle."

"Is she okay?"

"No, ma'am. She's deceased."

Kari stared at Officer Li, her lips trembling. Tears poured down her cheeks, unchecked. "No. Please, no. It's not true."

"I'm afraid it is. Would you like to identify the body?"

After taking a moment to let the finality sink in, she rose to her feet, swaying a little. "Yes. Let me see her."

Officer Li led her out to the secondary inspection

area, guiding Kari by one arm as if she were an invalid. When the crime scene investigator unzipped the body bag, revealing Sasha's frozen face, Kari was glad for the support.

She collapsed on the blacktop, devastated.

19

Maria screamed, trying to yank her arm from Chuy's grip.

He held tight, placing the smoking barrel against her temple once again. It burned, sizzling her hair and skin. Her ears were ringing from the shot, her eyes watering. Armando lay on the ground, motionless. A pool of blood began to form underneath him.

Agent Foster appeared at the edge of the courtyard, about twenty feet past Armando. His face was taut and alert, the muscles in his arms flexing. He looked taller than she remembered, stronger and more formidable. "Let her go," he said, pointing his gun at Chuy.

"Stay back or I'll blow her fucking brains out," Chuy replied. "You know I will."

Foster kept moving forward, like a man-machine.

Chuy pulled her toward the lobby, shouting obscenities, promising to kill her. Maria knew he wouldn't—not yet. If he shot her right now, there would be no bargaining chip, nothing to prevent Foster from opening fire.

"Let her go!" Foster repeated.

They arrived at the lobby entrance and Chuy's body

tensed for action. Maria knew he was about to make a move. The instant he took the gun away from her temple, shoving her inside, she reached for the pepper spray at the waistband of her jeans. Heart pounding, she gripped the canister in her sweaty fist.

Using the lobby entrance as cover, Chuy aimed down the walkway, shooting at Foster. As the agent returned fire, Maria lifted the canister, blasting Chuy in the face. She hoped she wasn't too late.

"*Pinche puta!*" Chuy yelled, swiping at his eyes. With his left arm, he swung at her, striking her across the cheek. Crying out in pain, she fell backward, sprawling across the floor. The caution sign she'd placed in the lobby less than an hour ago clattered beneath her body, digging into her hip.

Chuy stumbled away from the entrance, coughing like a sick dog. His eyes were squeezed shut, tears streaming from them.

Maria lifted a hand to her stinging cheek, shuddering in fear.

In an awful twist of fate, Sonia crept out from behind the counter where she'd been hiding and rushed to Chuy's aid.

He fired the gun again, shooting Sonia in the stomach.

She crumpled like a puppet, landing in a pitiful heap on the just-mopped floor. Her head lolled to the side and her eyes glazed over. Blood dripped from the corner of her mouth and blossomed across her midsection.

Maria stared at the horrific scene, afraid to move. Afraid to breathe.

Although Chuy's vision was obstructed, his instincts were still good. He seemed to realize the mistake he'd made. Choking out Sonia's name, he made a sign of the cross. Then, with a strangled sob, he fled the scene, crashing out the back door.

Foster appeared at the entrance a moment later. When he saw Maria, terrified but unharmed, his eyes darkened with an indefinable emotion. "Where is he?"

She pointed the direction Chuy went, her mouth trembling.

Foster limped inside the lobby, his hairline dark with sweat. His jeans were torn at the thigh, his pant leg bloody. Glancing at Sonia's crumpled form, he advanced toward the exit. Chuy must not have been visible, because Foster didn't pursue. He came back inside and took out his cell phone, requesting an ambulance.

Maria was so relieved to see him alive that tears sprang to her eyes. She wanted to run to him, to wrap her arms around him and never let go. But Sonia was bleeding, perhaps dying. "Will she live?"

"I don't know," he said, his mouth tense.

"Are you okay?"

His brows rose. "I'm fine."

"Your leg . . ."

"It's just a fragment."

Maria didn't know what that meant, but he didn't seem worried about the injury. "I will get some towels."

He crouched down beside Sonia. "Be careful."

She rose to her feet, walking through the lobby doors. To her surprise, Armando wasn't lying facedown in a pool of his own blood. Maria followed a series of crimson splashes to the laundry room.

He was inside, pressing a towel to the wound. "What happened?"

"Chuy shot Sonia on accident. Then he got away."

"Where's the cop?"

"In the lobby. His leg is shot."

Armando winced. "Tie this around me."

Maria secured an apron around his taut midsection, holding the towels in place. She didn't think the improvised bandage would last long . . . and neither would he. His breathing was labored and he'd lost a lot of blood. Unlike Foster, Armando appeared to be in serious trouble.

"Wait here," she said, grabbing a short stack of towels. She raced back to the lobby, leaving red shoeprints on the concrete. When she handed the towels to Ian, he pressed them to Sonia's ruined stomach. She glanced at his thigh, noting that the puncture was seeping rather than gushing. "I have to help Armando."

His focus was on Sonia, who appeared critical. Nodding, he spoke into his phone, giving the emergency operator details on her condition.

Maria returned to the laundry room, her heart pounding.

Armando's face was ashen, his black eyes unnaturally dull. He took an envelope from his pocket, smearing the surface with red fingerprints. "Get this to my daughter. Please. There's an address."

Maria shook her head, holding the envelope in his hand. "Don't try to run, Armando. You can barely walk."

"Promise me," he demanded, shoving the envelope at her.

"You have to get to a hospital."

"No."

She put the paper in her pocket and glanced past him, through the open back door. "Where will you go?"

"Somewhere safe."

After a second's deliberation, she slipped her arm around his waist, letting him lean on her for support. The sound of approaching sirens spurred them into motion. Maria didn't want to leave Foster, but she was terrified to talk to the police.

Armando wasn't in any position to argue. He let her guide him down the back alley, lurching forward with awkward motions. As they rounded the corner, a rash of squad cars descended on the scene, tires squealing.

"That way," Armando gasped, picking up the pace.

Maria knew he wouldn't get far, even with her assistance. She stumbled across the street, holding him upright, praying she wasn't signing his death certificate.

"There," he said, indicating a small business with a white stucco exterior. La Canada Veterinary Clinic, the sign read. The office was closed for lunch, the waiting room empty. "Go around the back."

Arms trembling from exertion, she took him down a narrow alleyway. Behind the building there was an open field and an aqueduct. She stopped short, knowing she couldn't drag him across the space.

"Leave me here," he ordered, gesturing at the back door of the veterinary clinic.

Maria gaped at him. "You'll die."

He pushed away from her, using the building for support. Resting his shoulders against the wall, he slid down to a sitting position, collapsing in an ungainly heap. The apron and towels she'd tied around him were soaked red.

Maria bit at the edge of her fist, horrified.

"I'll be okay," Armando insisted, his lips pale.

She followed his gaze to a woman walking a dog in the field. Her auburn hair was tied in a ponytail, her white jacket flapping in the breeze. There was a shiny name tag on her lapel. "Will she stitch you up?" Maria asked.

Armando didn't answer.

"You're not a dog," she pointed out.

He rested his head against the building. "True. Dogs are loyal."

"What if she refuses?"

"I won't give her a choice," he said, pulling a gun from his waistband.

"No," Maria whispered, crouching next to him. "You might hurt her on accident."

Armando gave her a dark look, but his gaze wasn't steady, as if he was seeing more than one disapproving face. With a flick of his thumb, he ejected the clip and removed the bullets, fumbling to put them in his pants pocket. Then he returned the empty clip to the chamber, shoving it back into place. "Better?"

Maria hesitated, tears filling her eyes. She shouldn't have helped him.

"I can't go to jail, *mariposa*. I'll never survive there."

She knew he wasn't exaggerating. His rift with Chuy would have grave consequences, and Maria felt partly responsible for them.

"Go on," he said, gripping her hand. "Don't forget the letter."

"*Vaya con Dios,*" she replied, kissing his rough cheek.

He didn't bother to say that he wasn't on a path to heaven. She'd just assisted him in the opposite direction, in fact. Smothering a sob, she stood, running down the alleyway before she could change her mind.

Returning to the Hotel del Oro wasn't an option. Removing her bloody apron, she tossed it aside and smoothed her hair, walking along the street. Tears coursed down her face as she headed south, toward the border. Away from God.

Although Ian had wanted to stay on the scene at the Hotel del Oro and help mobilize the manhunt, he was required to seek emergency treatment for his gunshot wound.

The injury was minor, caused by a bullet fragment, but it had made all the difference in the chase. He'd stumbled sideways when hit, slowing down for the extra few seconds that Chuy Pena needed to get away.

Motherfucker.

Sonia's body had been the second obstacle to his pursuit. Ian couldn't let a woman bleed to death while he limped after a fugitive. The hell of it was that he probably could have caught Chuy. Ian's hurt leg wasn't as much of a handicap as Chuy's temporary blindness. And Ian hadn't been able to do a damned thing to help Sonia.

By the time backup arrived, Armando had disappeared with Maria.

Ian couldn't believe he'd let both suspects flee the scene. Armando was half dead, and Chuy's vision had been seriously impaired. It was a fucking embarrassment, like two senior citizens outrunning a beat cop.

He suffered in silence while his thigh was X-rayed, explored, and irrigated. Hollow-point bullets created an expanding path of destruction, ruining a shocking amount of tissue. Ian was lucky to have been hit by a ricochet. At full speed, the hollow-point might have destroyed his leg, even taken his life.

This wound was nothing. When the numbness wore off, he'd probably be able to walk out of the hospital.

While he was in the recovery room, wondering if Chuy or Armando had been apprehended, and hoping Adam's side of things had gone better than his, Special Agent in Charge Michelson appeared at the doorway. Judging by his grave expression, this conversation wouldn't end well.

"Sonia Barreras died in surgery," Michelson said, taking a seat in the only chair.

Ian let his head fall back against the pillow, closing his eyes. "Fuck," he whispered, wishing it had been him. If he'd just waited for backup, or proceeded with a little more caution, she probably wouldn't have been shot. Instead, he'd chosen an aggressive approach. After he watched Chuy drag Maria to his office, a gun to her head, he'd completely lost his mind. He hadn't been able to focus on anything but saving her.

"I want to apologize to the Barreras family," Ian said, wracked by guilt. Before this, he'd only thought of Sonia in an insulting sexual context.

"I'll let you know if we locate anyone."

"The suspects . . . ?"

"Not in custody." He gave Ian a quick rundown of the situation, explaining that Moreno's crew had been shaken up by the bust. Several of his top guys had been arrested, and many others had scattered. This kind of discord created a very dangerous situation, in which upstart crews and ambitious drug dealers scrambled for positioning.

"I've spoken to Officer Pettigrew of the CBP," Michelson continued, "but I'd like to hear your side of the story."

Ian stared at his superior, feeling pressure behind his eyes. Michelson was usually a hard-ass, tough to the point of unkindness. Ian had anticipated scalding words and a hot temper, not this quiet calm.

Ian started at the beginning, explaining his past with Maria and detailing every mistake he'd made over the course of the undercover investigation. It was a slow, awkward confession. Maybe he was digging his own grave, but he didn't care. His reckless bumbling had led to a civilian's death. The least he could do now was take full responsibility.

Michelson accepted Ian's disclosure with few questions and almost no visible reaction. "Do you have any idea where Ms. Santos went?"

Ian shook his head. "She said she was going to help Armando. Maybe she's afraid to speak to the police. I hope she didn't get taken hostage."

"She's a primary witness, so her cooperation would be helpful. Even if Pena didn't mean to shoot Sonia Barreras, as you suspect, we want him prosecuted to the fullest. A statement from her could make a difference in the case against him."

"Assuming he's caught."

"He'll be caught," Michelson promised, his eyes narrow.

"I can find Maria. I'll talk to her."

Michelson's mouth turned down, as if he was about to say something distasteful. "Tomorrow I'll need you to write up everything you just told me and sign a sworn statement. And, although it kills me to do this, because you're a damned good cop, I have to ask for your resignation."

The request was nothing less than Ian expected, but it stung. It stung hard.

"I'm sorry, Foster. You disobeyed a direct order by not waiting for backup. Failing to communicate integral details and lying to your fellow officers about your undercover activities are also grounds for dismissal. Although I believe your intentions were good, I just can't excuse the behavior."

Ian's throat tightened. He could only nod, resigned to his fate.

Officer Li walked Kari back to the detainment area and left her there, alone.

She was offered a meal, which she declined. She didn't know if she was under arrest or under suspicion. She was in limbo. Over and over again, she pictured Sasha's face. Her hazy blue eyes and birdlike limbs, distorted in death.

Kari's heart twisted with grief. She pushed aside her misery and concentrated on loathing Adam. Hate was an easier emotion to deal with. He'd used her. Every kind word he'd spoken was a lie, every touch a manipulation. If she hadn't gone to him for help, Sasha might still be alive.

After what seemed like days, Officer Li returned for her.

"Am I under arrest?"

"No," she said, taking her back to the interrogation room. "I've been asked to explain the situation to you and wait for further instructions."

"I'm not free to go?"

"No, ma'am."

Although Kari didn't feel like sitting, she took the chair across from Li.

Li cut to the chase. "While you were in the lanes, officers mobile-scanned the cargo of your van and found a figure. The equipment isn't made to detect humans, dead or alive, so only a vague shape was visible. Officer Cortez assumed it was an assailant."

She stared at the surface of the table, numb.

"At the same time, Maria Santos contacted another officer. She had overheard Chuy Pena say you were a decoy."

"A decoy," she repeated flatly.

"Pena set you up to be a distraction. We had no choice but to detain you."

She lifted her chin. "Did he kill Sasha?"

"I don't know. She didn't have any obvious wounds. It looks like an accidental overdose, but we're waiting on the autopsy."

Kari shook her head, refusing to accept that. Moreno must have found out she'd talked to a border cop, and he'd ordered Chuy to get rid of Sasha. "I shouldn't have asked Adam for help. I wish I'd never met him!"

Officer Li's eyes softened with sympathy. "I'm sorry for your loss, but I don't think that your sister's death was part of the plan."

She buried her face in her hands, reeling from the impact. It was too much to process, too disturbing to fathom. Her natural instinct was to assign blame. She wanted to indict Adam, Chuy, Moreno . . . herself.

Kari's baby sister was dead. Someone was responsible. Someone had to pay.

"Where's Adam?" she asked, straightening.

"He left the port with a group of drug enforcement

agents. They scanned another suspicious vehicle and found the real shipment within minutes. The team followed the suspects to the delivery location and made a series of important arrests."

"Was Moreno one of them?"

"No."

"That figures," she said, bitter.

Li gave her an even stare. "Officer Cortez tried to take down Moreno and was shot by a sniper in the process."

Kari's lungs seized. She couldn't draw breath. "Is he okay?"

"I know he's been hospitalized. I don't have word on his condition."

"Oh my God," she said, clapping a hand over her mouth.

"There was another shootout at the Hotel del Oro. An undercover officer and a civilian were wounded in the crossfire."

Her vision swam with tears. "A civilian?"

"The receptionist. She died in surgery this afternoon. Pena and his partner, Armando Villarreal, got away. Maria Santos is still missing."

"Oh my God," she repeated, overwhelmed by the back-to-back blows. Her sister dead, Adam shot, Maria gone.

"Until the suspects are apprehended, your life may be in danger. My supervisor has recommended secured lodgings."

"What does that mean?"

"We want you to stay in a safe room at the police station. They're designed for witnesses who need temporary protection."

"Temporary?"

"At least for tonight."

The devastating trauma of the past few hours, paired with Officer Li's irritatingly reasonable attitude, made Kari snap. She leapt to her feet, pacing the small room. This was all her fault. She'd put Maria at risk.

She'd bargained with her sister's life—and lost.

Smothering a sob, she turned to face the wall, wanting to beat her fists against it. Her grief was so heavy she almost couldn't hold herself up. She wanted to destroy Chuy Pena, to tear Carlos Moreno apart with her bare hands. She wished for superhuman strength to match the intense rage and relentless sorrow that welled up inside her.

"Is there someone you'd like to call? A close friend or relative?"

"No," she said, staring at the blank space. Sasha had been her entire world. Their parents were dead. All of her living relatives were strangers in the Czech Republic. Everyone else had drifted away. "There's no one."

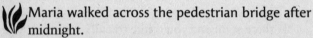Maria walked across the pedestrian bridge after midnight.

She entered Tijuana with extreme caution, hugging an oversized sweatshirt around her trembling body. After a long day of dodging police cars and watching out for Chuy, she was exhausted. She'd bought a change of clothes at a thrift shop and boarded a random bus, riding it through a chaotic blur of strange neighborhoods.

Sonia's face haunted her. Armando could die from his wounds. Foster had been shot.

Maria felt awful. She should have left the hotel and called Agent Foster from a pay phone. She should have been more careful. She should never have come to the United States. Both of her visits, though short, had ended in tragedy.

Keeping her head down and her feet moving, she headed toward the bus station. She had nowhere to go but home.

Although the circumstances were far from ideal, she was looking forward to the reunion. She missed her brother and sisters. She hadn't seen her mother in four years. While she was there, she could see about delivering Armando's letter. It was addressed to a school in Taxco, about a day's travel from Maria's hometown.

The transit center was only a few miles from the border. She skirted around drug dealers and prostitutes, minding her own business. The city's seedy underground didn't bother her; she'd lived here for several years and knew how to avoid trouble. Traveling on foot at night was dangerous but necessary. She couldn't risk being spotted.

Chuy wasn't the type of man who took responsibility for his actions. If he was still on the loose, he'd be looking for revenge. She'd given Foster the tip, caused the rift with Armando, and tagged him with pepper spray.

He'd shot Sonia because of her.

Shivering, Maria picked up the pace, hurrying to the dubious sanctuary of the bus station. Maybe Chuy was in jail, or otherwise engaged, rather than searching for her. She hoped she could get a quick ticket to the capital, because she felt like an easy target in Tijuana, Moreno's stronghold.

It was late when she arrived, the darkest hour of the night. There would be a dozen buses leaving for central Mexico at dawn. Resigned to wait, she put a few quarters into a pay phone near the women's restroom, calling Kari.

Her cell phone went straight to voice mail. Glancing around warily, Maria left a short message. "I'm okay. I hope you are, too. I'm sorry for not calling sooner." After a moment's hesitation, she whispered, *"Te amo,"* then and hung up, her eyes moist. Kari had been a good friend and Maria would miss her.

For the next few hours she dozed on a plastic bench at

the station. Her cheek felt swollen and her stomach ached from the blows Chuy had dealt her, but the pain was distant. So were her emotions. Maybe, once she boarded the bus, or fell into her mother's arms, she would let down her guard and weep.

At dawn she bought a ticket to Mexico City. The girl at the counter gave her a curious look but didn't ask questions. In places like Tijuana, domestic violence victims weren't uncommon and most people looked the other way.

She walked down the terminal and into the loading area, eyes averted. A group of uniformed drivers were gathered in the parking lot, puffing on cigarettes. The smell of smoke and motor oil and smog made her dizzy with nausea. She realized that she hadn't eaten since breakfast—yesterday.

She thought about turning around to grab a snack, because she had twenty minutes to kill before departure. But she also became aware of approaching footsteps, the distinctive shuffle of a man's worn boot heels. Pulse accelerating, she made a sharp detour, ducking between two buses. The man in the cowboy boots passed by, paying no attention to her.

Maria placed a hand over her heart, relieved.

She was about to come out of her hiding place when another figure appeared, blocking her exit. This one hadn't made a sound. Gasping, she whirled around, ready to run in the opposite direction.

Chuy Pena was standing there.

His cohort rushed forward, grabbing her by the arms. She was trapped between them, bracketed by tall buses on both sides. She didn't dare cause a scene. If she called out for help, they would kill her and anyone who came to her aid.

"Where's Armando?" Chuy asked, stepping close enough to touch the mark on her face.

Maria turned her head to the side. "I don't know."

While the other man wrenched her arms behind her back, Chuy yanked the purse off her shoulder, breaking the thin leather strap. After a rudimentary search, he tossed it aside. Change spilled out, rolling under the buses.

Maria stared at the silver coins on the stained asphalt, thinking about how hard she'd worked for every one.

"I know you helped him get away, *puta*. Your apron was in the bushes across the street from the hotel."

"I tied it around his waist to stop the bleeding," she said, meeting Chuy's gaze. He looked mentally imbalanced, as if the past twenty-four hours had taken its toll. Did he feel bad about shooting Sonia, or were all women interchangeable to him?

"Don't lie to me," he growled, clutching her throat. His thumb dug into her larynx, silencing her. With his other hand, he reached into the waistband of her jeans, finding Armando's letter. "What's this?"

Although it was futile, Maria twisted sideways, trying to free her arms.

Chuy stopped choking her long enough to tear open the envelope. He scanned the contents with interest. Maria had memorized the address but she hadn't read the message, so she had no idea what it said. "Shady, two-faced bastard," he muttered, putting the letter in his pocket. He smiled at Maria, sending a chill down her spine. "I'll deliver this to his daughter. Might even give her a little something extra."

"No," she whispered, tears rushing to her eyes.

He jerked his chin toward the back of the bus, indicating that their conversation was finished.

The man holding her dragged her down the narrow space between the buses. Chuy's SUV was parked nearby. She kicked her legs and screamed for help, too terrified to worry about innocent bystanders. He shoved her into the backseat, unfazed by her struggles. Someone covered her face with a wet rag, smothering her cries. Chemical fumes burned her eyes as the hand clamped down harder over her nose and mouth, suffocating her brutally.

Her body went limp and darkness took her.

Kari woke up in a strange bed.

She sat forward, blinking at her surroundings. The safe house looked like an anonymous hotel room. Groaning, she pushed the tangled hair out of her face. Her eyes were swollen from crying and her head ached.

Sasha was dead.

She'd finally surrendered to emotional exhaustion around two in the morning. Now it was seven o'clock.

Sasha was dead.

Just like yesterday, the realization kept hitting. Every few seconds the horrible awareness would wash over her. It was like a monster's footsteps in her psyche, an approaching Godzilla. Soul-rattling, relentless.

Dead. Dead. Dead.

The secured lodgings were bland and sanitized, with twin beds and an adjoining bath. She'd showered last night and washed her undergarments. Her panties fluttered by the air-conditioning vents, hanging from the window blinds.

She reached for the cell phone on her nightstand, noting that there were no missed calls from Adam. Instead of dialing his number, she listened to a message from Maria, becoming frantic with worry. If Maria was okay, why was she calling from an international location at four o'clock in the morning?

Tossing the phone down, Kari rose from the bed and turned off the air conditioner, grabbing her dry underwear on the way to the bathroom. She wrinkled her nose as she put on her outer clothes, which were still soiled. The image of Sasha in a body bag came rushing back to her, along with the faint smell of death and latex.

Her stomach lurched and she stumbled sideways, light-headed.

She'd been given a meal last night, courtesy of the San Diego Police Department, but Kari had only choked down a few bites. Now she felt a gnawing ache in her empty belly, a warning that she needed to eat something to get through the day.

Leaving the bathroom, she proceeded to make do with the only provisions available: two single servings of coffee. She was glad she'd managed to get a few hours of rest, but she couldn't say she felt better.

While she was having coffee, a uniformed officer delivered breakfast. Again, it was standard fast-food fare. Kari ate most of her microwaved eggs and half of a soggy pancake, trying to refuel.

A short time later another officer came to visit, introducing himself as Special Agent Nolan. He wore casual clothes and a badge on his belt. They sat down at the only table, which was round and off balance. Kari didn't offer him coffee.

Nolan cleared his throat. "We've received intelligence that both Carlos Moreno and Jesus 'Chuy' Pena have crossed the border into Mexico. Wanted criminals, especially drug cartel members, tend to do that. There's always the possibility that they'll return to the U.S., but it's not likely while the heat is on."

"Does that mean I'm not in danger?" Kari asked.

"No, but it means the risk is lessened. The recent arrests have broken up Moreno's crew and he can't control things as easily from a distance. Some of the cartels, including his, also have strict codes against killing women, but there are exceptions."

Kari swallowed hard, trying not to picture Sasha's dead body again.

"Ordering a hit against you would be frowned upon in their circles. I personally don't believe Moreno would jeopardize his tenuous position by making such an unpopular move. Chuy Pena is another story. His behavior is hard to predict."

"Can I go home?" Kari asked.

Special Agent Nolan nodded. "For the time being, we'll have an unmarked car stationed outside your residence. If you need to leave the house, we ask that you notify our officers. We also recommend that you rent or borrow a different vehicle because your van is so easily recognizable."

Kari didn't want to see that deathmobile ever again, let alone drive it, so she accepted the agent's terms without complaint. "What about my sister's autopsy? I need to make funeral arrangements."

"Her remains should be released today."

When Nolan inquired about Maria, Kari handed him her cell phone, watching him listen to the barely audible message. "I'll have the number traced," he promised, thanking her for the information.

She set the phone aside. "Have you heard anything about Adam?"

"Adam?"

"Officer Cortez. He was shot yesterday."

"Oh, right. The CBP officer. No, I'm sorry. I haven't been updated on his condition."

She rode home in a squad car, feeling numb. The first thing she did was head straight to the shower, tearing off the clothes she'd never wear again. When she felt clean, she donned her robe and threw the garments in the trash.

Going back to sleep was out of the question, so she made a fresh pot of coffee. Then she stared at her cell phone, willing it to ring. If Adam was alive and conscious, he had no excuse for not calling.

Maybe he was dead.

Or maybe he was just done with her. He'd seemed pretty cold-blooded at the border. What had he told her about handling no-strings affairs? Kiss the person goodbye, say you had a nice time, and walk away.

Hands trembling, she picked up the remote control and turned on the news. Sure enough, yesterday's shootout was the top story. They flashed a mug shot of Chuy Pena, looking like a bulldog, along with a surveillance photo of Moreno. Even from a distance, he was lean and handsome. If he ever went to prison, he'd have plenty of lonely, troubled women writing to him. Bastard.

Kari wanted to throw her coffee at the screen.

The next picture was of Armando Villarreal. He was barely recognizable in sunglasses and a windbreaker, his inelegant face turned to the side. Black hair, dark skin, medium build. Half of the men in San Diego fit that description. Including Adam.

The newscaster said that Armando had been found in a ditch near the border. He was in critical condition.

"Good," Kari muttered, sipping her coffee. Of the three men, she hated Armando the least, but she wasn't going to cry a river for him.

There was almost no information about the two officers who had been injured in the melee. According to the report, both had been working undercover and were hospitalized at an undisclosed location. Their identities were not revealed.

"Damn it," she said, switching off the TV.

This was bullshit.

Setting her coffee aside, she snatched her phone from the counter and dialed Adam's cell phone number. His voice mail picked up, crisp and controlled. "If you're alive, fuck you," she said after the beep, her voice shaking. "And if you're not—"

She ended the call, appalled by the sob that rose up in her throat.

"If you're not, fuck *me*," she whispered. She couldn't handle her sister's death or Maria's disappearance. Being kept in the dark about Adam was an additional torture. She wanted him alive so she could hate him.

Her sister was dead.

Leaving the coffee behind, she went into the bedroom. Heart aching, she crawled under the blankets, cradling the phone beside her.

* * *

When Maria came to, she was slumped in the backseat, her arms tied behind her back.

She lifted her face from the leather seat, smothering a moan as the interior of the car spun out of focus. Her mouth tasted awful and her stomach roiled with nausea. Squeezing her eyes shut, she took a few steady breaths, hoping she wouldn't throw up.

After a few seconds, the dizziness passed. She opened her eyes and looked around again, trying to orient herself.

She didn't recognize her surroundings. They were parked on a dirt road in front of a ramshackle house. It was a rural area, probably the hills of east Tijuana.

The car door was open and Chuy Pena stood outside, his back to her. Two other men were with him. They appeared to be waiting for someone. Judging by Chuy's defensive stance, his feet braced wide, it wasn't going to be a pleasant meeting.

A silver Mercedes came to a stop behind the vehicle she was in. The man who climbed out was angry. His lips curled into a grimace as he strode forward, clenching his hand into a fist. His greeting for Chuy was a punch in the mouth.

This was Carlos Moreno.

Chuy fell down to his knees in the dirt. He spat out blood but didn't retaliate in any way. Instead of getting up, he stayed there. Although he was obviously not top dog, his posture didn't indicate submission. He reminded her of a mongrel who would wait for a better time to bite. After he was fed, perhaps.

Moreno didn't seem to think Chuy's demeanor was

respectful enough, either. He kicked him in the face, snarling.

The other men stepped back, giving Moreno more room to play.

Chuy rolled over, pressing a hand to his flayed cheek. The first blow had merely insulted him; the second really hurt. "I'm sorry," he said, breathing heavy. "Give me a chance to explain."

Moreno's bunched shoulders relaxed a little, but he didn't offer Chuy a hand to get up. "It better be good."

Chuy maneuvered into a sitting position, resting his shoulders against the wheel well. "Armando is a rat."

"Bullshit," he said succinctly.

"He was working with an undercover agent. Some guy named Foster."

"How do you know?"

"I caught him on the phone, talking about the shipment."

"This Foster was a customer of yours, I assume."

Bracing himself for another blow, Chuy nodded.

"Who shot Armando?"

"I did. He was running away from me. The fuckup at the hotel was his fault. As soon as I pulled the trigger, his cop buddy came out of nowhere."

"I heard a woman was killed."

Chuy stared at the ground, swallowing. He didn't have to pretend that this detail bothered him. "She got caught in the crossfire."

"Do you remember what I told you the last time that happened?"

"Yes," he said, his voice hoarse.

"Why should I keep you alive?"

"Because I'll even the score," Chuy said, meeting his gaze. "I'll make Armando pay for betraying you."

Moreno crouched down, fisting his hand in Chuy's shirt. "You should have done that yesterday, you stupid fuck. When you shoot a man like him in the back, you'd better make sure he stays down."

"I'll find him," Chuy promised.

"Too late, *cabrón*," he said, giving him a hard shake. "He's already been found. According to the news, he's in the hospital, comatose."

Maria couldn't hold back a tiny gasp of distress. She was glad Armando was alive, but appalled that Chuy would lay all of the blame at his former partner's feet. If Moreno believed Chuy's outrageous lies, he was a fool.

The boss glanced into the backseat of the car, noticing her prone form. Maria stared off into space, feigning semiconsciousness. "Who's that?"

"A maid from the hotel. She helped Armando get away."

"If he was a rat, why would he try to get away from the police?"

"I don't know. I think he was working with *los otros* as well."

Moreno shoved Chuy down in the dirt, disgusted. "You're a fucking liar," he said, straightening. "He'd never go back to his old crew after what they did to his wife."

"I have proof."

"Where?"

Chuy removed Armando's letter from his pocket, handing it to Moreno. He read the message, his expression skeptical. "This doesn't prove anything," he said, keeping the envelope. But perhaps the letter hinted at

Armando's divided loyalties, because he dropped the subject. "You've got some balls to bring a beaten woman here, Pena. Are you incapable of taking direction, or do you enjoy taunting me?"

"Armando likes her. So does Foster. I thought she might be useful."

"You thought she might make a statement to the police, you mean."

He inclined his head. "Yes. But I can take direction, *jefe*. If not for your orders, I would have just gotten rid of her."

Pulse pounding, Maria closed her eyes. She felt Moreno's dispassionate gaze wander over her slack face. "Even you wouldn't waste such a pretty one," he said. "Bring her in until I decide what to do with her. And if you lay a hand on her, or anything else, I will cut your fucking dick off, *comprendes*?"

Chuy said he understood. One of his comrades pulled her out of the backseat and carried her into the house. She was taken to a basement or wine cellar, some kind of underground room. The man cut her bonds and left her on a dirt floor. Before she could get a sense of the place, the only door slammed shut, casting her new world into darkness.

21

Over the next two days, Maria searched every inch of the cramped cellar for an escape route or an impromptu weapon.

To no avail.

The amenities consisted of a thin sleeping mat and single blanket. A large bag of tortilla chips and a small bag of oranges offered sustenance. She'd been given a gallon of drinking water and a plastic bucket.

Although the walls and floor were dirt, it was hard-packed. She had no tools to dig with and no way to pick the lock. She was stuck.

Listening to the men was her only form of entertainment, so she spent hours on the stairs, looking through a sliver of space under the door. She could hear muted conversations and watch their booted feet pass by.

She wanted to signal Moreno somehow, to tell him that Chuy was lying. He seemed more sympathetic to women, less likely to kill her. But he was never alone and she didn't want to risk Chuy's wrath by shouting out his secrets at the wrong moment.

An opening came during the third afternoon of her

capture. It was Friday, by her estimation, although the meager light made it difficult to keep track of time. The claustrophobic conditions didn't help. She felt like she'd been trapped forever.

Last night the men had sat at the kitchen table and played poker until late. The tension in the room was palpable, underscored by the clinking of liquor bottles and taut silences. At one point Moreno accused Chuy of being high. Chuy denied it but Moreno pushed the table over anyway, sending the cards flying. "Fucking heroin," he'd said, furious. "I didn't want to dirty my hands with it, so I let you take over. Worst mistake of my life."

When he stormed out of the kitchen, no one said a word. Chuy and the rest of the men picked up the mess and resumed their poker game.

Maria assumed they were sleeping off hangovers, because she hadn't heard any footsteps since they retired. After an endless day of lying on the stairs, drowsing on and off, she noticed Moreno's telltale shuffle. He wore expensive tennis shoes like an American. She held her breath, watching under the door while he looked in the refrigerator and sat down at the table. He rolled an object along the surface, back and forth, back and forth. When it fell over the edge, clattering to the floor, she saw that it was a syringe.

Maria shoved her fingers through the space under the door, wiggling them frantically. She was afraid to make noise but desperate to speak with him.

Moreno rose to pick up the syringe and approached the cellar door, standing close. "What do you want?" he asked in Spanish, his voice flat.

She leapt to her feet, pressing her cheek to the door. "Don't do it."

After a long moment he opened it, just a crack. The eye she could see was bleary, bloodshot. "Don't do what?"

"That," she said, gesturing at the syringe.

"Why not? Quitting didn't help."

"You have to stay alert. Chuy is lying to you."

Moreno rubbed a hand over his scruffy jaw, unsurprised by the charge. Or perhaps *unconcerned* was a better word. "This is a business of liars."

"Not Armando," she insisted, her pulse racing. "He didn't betray you. I overhead Chuy tell Sonia that Kari was a decoy. I was the one who told Foster about the shipment. When Chuy tried to shoot me, Armando stopped him."

Moreno processed this information without reacting. "Did you see Armando get shot?"

"Yes. I helped him walk to an animal clinic. He thought the vet might fix him up."

"Where was he hit?"

"In the side."

"The bullet went through?"

"I think so."

"Hmm."

"Let me out," she begged.

"Not yet. I have an errand to run."

Maria tried her luck by shoving against the door, but he was blocking it. "Please. Chuy will kill me."

He locked her in again, extinguishing her last ray of hope. But a moment later, he slid the unused syringe under the door. Maria would rather have a knife or her trusty pepper spray, but beggars couldn't be choosers.

"Wait," she said, her lips almost touching the door.

"Can I have Armando's letter back? He asked me to deliver it."

After a moment's hesitation, he slid the envelope under the door.

"*Gracias*," she whispered.

"*Por nada*," he returned.

She put the letter in her pocket, along with the secret weapon, and crept down the stairs, praying for the opportunity to escape.

Kari still hadn't heard from Adam directly, but she'd received a cryptic text message about his condition from Ian Foster.

According to Foster, Adam was recovering in an undisclosed location and unable to contact her for professional reasons. Foster stressed that this was very sensitive information, not to be shared with *anyone*. He also expressed Adam's condolences for Sasha's death and asked for an update on Maria.

Kari had no word on her friend's whereabouts. An officer had traced Maria's last call to a pay phone at a Tijuana bus station. Kari could only guess that Maria was traveling back to her family and would get in touch as soon as she arrived.

The hours passed by in a blur. She couldn't stop worrying about Adam and she didn't understand why he hadn't contacted her in person. Whatever the reason, she'd never forgive him for leaving her hanging. Unless he was in a coma or wrapped in bandages from head to foot, he had no excuse for not calling.

He might be alive and well, but he was dead to her.

She'd been sleeping a lot since she came home, which

felt odd. Insomnia and hyperactivity were more her style. She prided herself on being a workaholic, a clean freak, an exercise enthusiast. Type A all the way.

But she could hardly drag herself out of bed since Sasha's death. The sense of loss was enormous, oppressive. Carrying it exhausted her. After a few minutes of wandering around the house, she needed a nap.

Along with the sadness, she felt a tremendous amount of guilt . . . and an almost equal measure of relief. For years she'd failed her sister, and enabled her, and worried about her. An awful, ugly little part of her was glad the fight was over.

She'd never spend another sleepless night wondering when Sasha would overdose.

The final toxicology results would take a few weeks, but the initial autopsy report suggested accidental death, with no indication of foul play. Sasha had died by her own hand and been dumped in the back of her van by Moreno's men. There were multiple track marks but no signs of a struggle.

Kari made funeral arrangements quickly and quietly, seeing no reason to delay. Her parents were dead, and none of her far-flung relatives would be able to attend. She wanted to get it over with. The service was scheduled for this morning. Maybe, after taking the weekend off, she could go back to work, her only sanctuary.

An hour before the service, she riffled through the contents of her closet, listless. The navy business suit was somber enough for the occasion, but she reached for the burgundy silk gown Sasha had encouraged her to buy. It wasn't appropriate for a funeral. She dropped her towel and turned to the mirror anyway, holding the dress up to her body. Sasha's raspy, irreverent voice told her to wear it.

She put on the gown, along with sedate underwear and a pair of simple black pumps. Because she wasn't as daring as Sasha, even when delirious from grief, she added a black wraparound tunic. It was thin and light-weight but offered decent coverage, camouflaging the dress's plunging back and low neckline.

Her wan face didn't match the outfit, so she stood at her vanity mirror and applied makeup with an unsteady hand. Eye shadow, waterproof mascara, lip gloss. She stepped back to study her appearance. The accessories toned down the sexy gown without making her appear matronly. Sasha would approve.

Grabbing her purse, she went outside and climbed into her rental car, nodding at the officer parked across the street. He knew where she was going. She'd been assured that there would be a police presence at the funeral.

Not that anyone figured Moreno would be stupid enough to show up.

The parking lot at the funeral parlor was almost full, which surprised her. Maybe another service was wrapping up. As she walked toward the entrance, she realized the crowd was there for Sasha. Friends she hadn't seen in years had gathered to offer their condolences. Sasha's wacky New Age health care providers were milling about, along with her favorite hair stylist and the disgruntled nail technician. Even Kari's ex-boyfriend, Brendan, had come to pay his respects.

She was touched by the outpouring of support. In the waiting area, there were flowers everywhere. Someone had set up a table for pictures. A dozen dazzling photos smiled up at Kari, reminding her that Sasha had loved to strike a pose. She'd been brash, irrepressible, and impossible to dislike.

Warm hugs and polite handshakes greeted Kari as she made her way through the crowd. The funeral director, whom she'd met once before, guided her to a seat in the front row. There were no other blood relatives in attendance. Kari felt awkward, sitting there by herself. After a moment, Sasha's best friend from high school came to fill the space. Beth was married now, with two young children and a frazzled-looking husband.

"If the baby fusses, I'll take him outside," she whispered to Kari, squeezing her hand.

"Don't worry about it," Kari said, glad for the company. "Thanks for coming."

Beth's baby fussed a little during the ceremony, but Kari didn't mind the distraction. She wasn't comfortable showing emotion in front of so many people, most of whom she hardly knew. Instead of breaking down in tears, she merely endured the service, listening to a simple speech about greener pastures.

For a nonbeliever like herself, it was cold comfort. She'd rather have heard about Sasha's real life, her struggles and mistakes.

But Kari had chosen this instead. An impersonal, closed-casket service.

When it was over, she stood by the entrance, accepting condolences and murmuring thanks to everyone who approached her.

Then the crowd moved to the cemetery to watch the burial. Again, Kari felt self-conscious about her solitude. Since her dad died, she'd been more driven than ever to succeed. Men and relationships had taken a backseat.

Now she needed someone to lean on, a strong arm to steady her, a comforting presence by her side.

She wanted Adam.

After the service, she drove home, but she couldn't escape the small group of well-meaning friends who followed her there. They helped her carry in the flower arrangements she didn't want, and brought more food than she could eat. When a young man delivered a beautiful, elegant bouquet of calla lilies, Kari rose to sign the confirmation. She checked for a card, aware that her guests were curious about the ostentatious display.

She felt an absurd moment of elation, wondering if Adam had sent them. Then she realized the flowers were from an anonymous source and her heart went cold. Only Carlos Moreno would throw his money around this way.

Finally the crowd dwindled and Kari was left alone. She crawled into bed, exhausted. But for the first time in days, she couldn't sleep. Daylight mocked her. The smell of fresh flowers and warm casseroles drifted in, their cloying fragrances assaulting her senses. She buried her face in the pillow but found no peace.

Needing a different kind of release, she kicked off the sheets and rose to her feet, grabbing her workout clothes. She hadn't gone for a jog since Tuesday. Her body felt weak and her mind sluggish. Running always helped her wake up.

She nodded to the officer in the black-on-black squad car, letting him know she was leaving. He watched over the house, not her, so he didn't follow. She started off slow but gained momentum, feeling stronger than she had in days. Detouring from her normal route, she returned to the cemetery, slowing to a stop at Sasha's grave.

There were flowers on the mound, creamy white roses and baby's breath. The headstone didn't have an epitaph, just a name and date. Kari hadn't been able to decide on a suitable saying for a troubled young woman who had never valued her life.

She brought a fist to the center of her chest, where she ached. The tears that refused to fall during the service came rushing to her eyes, spilling down her bewildered face. Why had Sasha refused to get help for so long? Why hadn't Kari stepped in sooner?

Now it was too late.

She knelt in the grass beside the grave and wept bitterly, unable to escape the pain. She wished she could see Sasha one last time. The sight of her sister in a body bag would haunt Kari for the rest of her life.

When she lifted her head, wiping the tears from her eyes, she noticed a man standing in the shadows. He was tall and lean, his identity almost disguised by beard stubble, casual clothes, and a Padres cap.

It was her sister's captor, lover, murderer: Carlos Moreno.

Kari scrambled to her feet, her pulse racing. There was no one else in the cemetery. If any police officers had been present at the funeral, they were long gone now. Sprinting to the main road and flagging down a car would take less than a minute. But she was frozen with shock and her legs refused to move.

How dare he come here?

While she stared at him, horrified, he lifted a hand to his face, pressing his thumb and forefinger to his eye sockets.

He was crying, she realized with astonishment. This man had introduced Sasha to heroin, kept her locked away in his mansion, and facilitated her death. As far as Kari was concerned, he might as well have shot her in cold blood. And he had the gall, the unmitigated gall, to show his despicable face at her grave? He'd treated her like a possession, a trophy to be traded away when the shine wore off.

He had the nerve to *cry*? Bastard.

"Did you bring these flowers?" she asked, gesturing at Sasha's grave. "And the lilies?"

Nodding, he dropped his hand.

She swept a dozen long-stemmed roses from the top of the mound and strode forward. Unleashing several years' worth of fury, she attacked him with the flowers, striking him across the face and neck. White petals flew everywhere, like loose bird feathers, and wicked thorns scraped his cheek, cutting deep.

He endured the blows without complaint, making no move to defend himself.

His lack of reaction enraged her. She threw the ruined flowers at his feet, breathing hard. "How could you come here?"

The scratch on his face welled with pinpricks of blood, jewel bright against his dark complexion. "I came to show my respects."

"You never respected her! You used her and threw her away."

"No," he said simply. "I tried to help her."

"By threatening and manipulating me?"

He glanced around the cemetery, making sure they were still alone. "You were the only person she really loved," he said, meeting her eyes. "I hoped that involving you would scare her into getting clean."

"You control the illegal drug trade, Carlos. Couldn't you keep her clean?"

His mouth thinned with regret. "I can't control every dirty doctor or small-time dealer. Sasha was very clever about getting her fix."

"Whose fault was that? You got her addicted."

"For this, I take full responsibility. I wanted her to quit with me. She refused."

"She needed rehab."

"I agree. I asked her to get help, repeatedly."

"Liar."

He gave her a quiet look. "I thought she would go if the stakes were high enough. Chuy's plan was to use your dedication for each other to our advantage. I never should have listened to him."

Kari pressed her lips together to keep them from trembling. "I hate you."

"I'm sorry."

"You're sorry," she repeated, smothering a sob. "You took everything from me! You stole my sister, my only family member—and you shot Adam. How can you stand there and look me in the eye?"

"I didn't shoot anyone."

"Go to hell," she said, sick of his bullshit. "If he dies, they'll lock you up and throw away the key."

"He's not dying."

His certainty gave her pause. "How do you know?"

"I was there when he was hit. I could have killed him, but I didn't, for reasons I still cannot fathom. Maybe I'm losing my touch. At any rate, he was wearing a bulletproof vest. He wasn't seriously injured."

"I don't believe you."

"Do me a favor."

Shaking her head, she turned to walk away. "Drop dead."

"I have Maria," he called after her.

Her blood turned to ice. Although she suspected he was playing her again, she couldn't force herself to keep moving.

Like a fool, she stopped to listen.

"Go to the hospital and visit Armando Villarreal. I think you will find your border cop there in his place, lying in wait for me."

She whirled to face him. "How do you know?"

"It is just a hunch," he said, shrugging. "And evading arrest is my specialty. The room will be guarded, but you shouldn't have any trouble getting in. Call me afterward and tell me who you encountered." He took Sasha's sparkly cell phone from his pocket, handing it to her. "In exchange, I will release Maria."

Kari stared at the object in her hand, tears filling her eyes. "I could just call the police, right now."

"You could," he agreed.

She lifted her chin. "Put Maria on. I want to hear her voice."

He placed the call from his own cell, giving a terse order to the person who answered. A moment later, he turned the phone toward Kari.

"Maria?"

Her friend's voice was hesitant. "Kari?"

"Are you okay?" she asked, leaning closer to hear her.

"I think so."

"Where are you?"

"I'm in a basement—"

Moreno pressed a button, ending the call.

Kari recoiled in shock, her mind screaming a shrill warning. What was she going to do? She didn't trust this man, or his crew of violent criminals, at all. He'd already betrayed her. Their last collaboration had been a disaster.

"I give you my word that she'll be returned to you, unharmed."

"That's what I was told about Sasha. But you couldn't keep her safe."

He flinched, bothered more by this truth than by the blows she'd dealt him earlier. "She was her own worst enemy."

Kari crossed her arms over her chest, staring at the dirt mound that her sister had been buried under. If only Sasha had faced her traumatic past instead of self-medicating. She'd never learned to deal with her emotions or take responsibility for her actions. Kari hadn't known how to be a parent, a friend, and a sister.

"What happened at the end?" she asked.

His gaze followed hers to the grave and then moved away, across the grassy sprawl. "We went to a nice hotel in Rosarito. I wanted to spend some time together, just the two of us. I was rationing her drugs, giving just enough to stave off withdrawals." His eyes were bleak. "Sometime during the night she found my stash and did it all."

Kari studied the mark on his cheek, feeling hollow. She didn't want to speculate on Sasha's state of mind before her death. The possibility that she'd taken her own life on purpose was too disturbing to contemplate. Even more unsettling was the idea that Moreno had killed Sasha with the most powerful weapon at his disposal: love.

Taking a ragged breath, she changed the subject. "What excuse will I give for wanting to visit Armando? We're hardly friends."

"Say you came to ask about Maria. He was the last person to see her."

She nodded, steeling herself for the task. Once more she would do his bidding. But she would never, ever feel sympathy for him. It didn't matter how much they had in common or how devastated he seemed by Sasha's death.

"I'll do it for Maria," she said. "But I hope you come to a bad end."

He gave a slight bow. "I expect nothing less."

22

Kari jogged home to retrieve the rental car, her thoughts racing.

She told the officer she was going to the grocery store and left, driving to the closest area hospital. The heat of the day had receded, leaving a pleasant breeze in its wake. She parked at Scripps and walked across the lot as the sun dipped lower in the sky.

A receptionist greeted her at the front desk. "May I help you?"

Kari didn't know how to proceed. Should she sneak around, hoping to stumble into the right room? That could take hours in this enormous building. "I'm here to see Armando Villarreal."

The receptionist checked her database. "He's in ICU. No visitors allowed."

"Oh," she said, crestfallen. After a moment she asked, "Is there a vending machine around here? Or a cafeteria?"

"It's at the end of Hall B." She handed Kari a folded pamphlet with a map of the facility. "On the west side of the building."

Kari thanked her and headed in that direction, her pulse kicking up. Bypassing the cafeteria, she continued to the intensive care unit, peeping through the double doors at the entrance. There were at least a dozen rooms in the unit, but only one had a uniformed police officer sitting outside, reading a magazine.

She hung back, loitering near the restrooms. How was she going to get by him? While she tried to think of a better idea than stealing a set of scrubs and playing doctor, he rose from his chair and walked toward her.

Trying to act cool, she bent to drink from the water fountain and watched him pass by on his way out of the ICU. After he disappeared into the men's room, she strode forward, doubting she'd get a better opening. Heart pounding with anxiety, she hurried down the hall, ducking into the room the officer had been guarding. It was dark inside. She waited for her eyes to adjust, standing silent, her fingertips tingling with awareness.

The first bed was empty. A curtain divided the room, blocking her view, but the steady beep of a pulsometer indicated a quiet presence. She stepped closer, peering around the curtain. A man in a hospital gown was lying on his back, his eyes closed. He was connected to an oxygen machine and an IV drip.

It was Adam.

Although his face was partially obscured by a breathing apparatus, she recognized him. Perhaps someone who didn't know him on an intimate level might mistake him for Armando, but Kari had no doubt.

The sight of his slack body made her stomach twist with distress. She'd just buried her sister, and her sanity was hanging by a fine thread. Seeing Adam so close to death pushed her right over the edge.

While she stood there, trembling like a leaf, he opened his eyes and sat forward, pointing a gun at the center of her chest.

As she drew a breath to scream, a figure burst from the bathroom, grabbing her from behind. Her high-pitched shriek was cut short as he clapped his palm over her mouth, silencing her with crushing pressure.

She struggled to break free, twisting back and forth in his arms. He stumbled sideways but didn't release her.

Adam ripped the oxygen tubes away from his face. "What the fuck, man? Were you going to let me shoot a defenseless woman?"

The man holding her eased his grip. When Kari stopped kicking, he took his hand away from her mouth. "How am I supposed to know she's defenseless?" he asked, flipping the light switch. Under the harsh fluorescent glow, Adam didn't appear sick or injured in the least. Her concern for him evaporated.

"She's clearly unarmed," Adam said, setting down his weapon.

The man checked anyway, skimming his hands along Kari's sports top and jogging pants. Her cheeks heated with embarrassment, because he was thorough. "You're right," he said. "She's clean."

Adam gave his partner a warning look, as if he hadn't liked the way he'd touched her.

"Why didn't you call me?" Kari asked, itching to slap them both. "This whole time I thought you were dying, you son of a bitch."

The man beside her coughed with surprise.

"Take a break, Ian," Adam said.

Ian left the room without an argument, favoring his right leg a little on the way out. Kari thought he looked familiar, but she couldn't quite place him. He was tall and dark-haired, sort of scruffy-looking, with intense eyes. Not as handsome as Adam, but attractive.

"Is that Agent Foster?" she asked.

"Yes."

"Were you two in on this together? He was trying to get close to Maria while you were working on me?"

"Of course not," Adam said, scowling. "He was there to bust Chuy Pena. Maria was a distraction he didn't need."

Kari crossed her arms over her chest, uncertain. She didn't know whom to trust anymore. Every man she'd come in contact with lately had lied to her and manipulated her. "Is there a reason you couldn't return my calls in person?"

His expression softened. "I've been ordered not to contact you."

"By who?"

"My boss. After everything went wrong at the border I was interrogated about my relationship with you."

"You were honest?"

He gave a curt nod.

She stared at him, still reeling from shock. "Did you ever think of me? Wonder if I was up late every night, worrying about you?"

"Yes," he said quietly. "I thought of you. I'm sorry I couldn't go to your sister's funeral. I wanted to be there."

As if she hadn't cried enough today, fresh tears rushed to her eyes. She turned her back, hiding them from him. He rose from the hospital bed, yanking off the remaining tubes and monitors. But when he put his hand on her bare arm, she snapped.

With a strangled sob, she rounded on him, pummeling his chest with her fists. She felt like she was dying inside, imploding in fury and frustration. He'd let her down at the most critical time of her life.

Her sister was dead and she'd never be whole again. "I hate you!"

Although her strikes were a release of miserable energy, not a serious attempt to injure him, they made more of an impact than she'd figured. He fell backward onto the bed, pressing a palm to his midsection.

"What's wrong?" she asked.

"Nothing," he replied, schooling his expression. "Bruised ribs."

"I thought you'd been shot."

"I was wearing a bulletproof vest."

"Doesn't that protect you?"

"Not always. High-powered rifle fire can penetrate the plates. I was lucky."

She covered her trembling mouth with one hand, disturbed by the close call. After the hell he'd just put her through, she didn't want to care about him. She wanted to walk away and never look back. "I just came to see if you were okay," she said, dropping her arms to her sides. "I won't bother you again."

He stopped cradling his ribs and reached out to her, wrapping his strong fingers around her wrist. "Don't go. Please."

"You're not supposed to talk to me."

"I want to explain."

She studied his handsome face, torn. Her heart was too tender to absorb another blow right now. "Make it quick."

He cleared his throat, searching for a starting point. "When I saw you at San Ysidro the first time, I knew you were Sasha's sister. I didn't send you to secondary inspection for selfish reasons."

"Such as?"

"I suspected you were involved in Moreno's smuggling operation, especially after I saw Chuy Pena at your house." His gaze was steady. "I thought I might be able to get close to Moreno through you."

"By sleeping with me?"

"Yes."

She wasn't impressed by his honesty. He couldn't win her over by telling her something she already knew.

"Then I began to feel conflicted," he said. "I liked you, on a personal level, much more than I expected to. Your store got vandalized and I realized that I cared about you. I wanted to protect you."

Her temper sparked at his words, fueled by pain and loss and adrenaline. "You cared more about catching Moreno than protecting me and you know it. You asked me out because you wanted *him*, not because you wanted me. You attached a GPS to my van to track my movements." She jerked her hand from his hold, counting his sneaky actions on her fingertips. "You lied to me and spied on me and played me like a pawn."

A muscle in his jaw flexed. "You lied to me, too."

"I lied in self-defense because I didn't know what else to say. You did it as a strategy, planned and premeditated."

He rolled his left shoulder, appearing guilty. "You're right, and I'm sorry."

She didn't accept his apology.

"After Sasha's body was found at San Ysidro, we followed the real shipment to the drop-off location. Moreno was there. I chased him for a few blocks and we ended up in an alley, just the two of us. I could have taken him out. Before his sharpshooter got into position, we were alone. He mentioned Penelope, baiting me. I had my gun pointed at his head and I was very, very tempted to execute him."

"Why didn't you?"

"Because of you. I pictured the way you looked at me after they cuffed you, like you were dying inside. I know I caused that, and I didn't want to be . . . consumed by hatred anymore. Killing him wouldn't solve anything. It wasn't worth it."

She waited for him to continue, her throat raw.

"For the past few years, I've fantasized about that moment a thousand times. I lived for the chance to take him down. But when the opportunity presented itself, I couldn't stop thinking about you. I'd already lost Penelope. I didn't want to lose you, too."

"I don't understand."

"You mean more to me than vengeance."

"So . . . you let him go?"

"No, I took out my handcuffs to detain him and came under fire. After the second shot, he got away."

Kari couldn't believe what she was hearing. Waves of sorrow and frustration crashed over her, scattering her already turbulent emotions. "You had him right there in front of you, and you couldn't pull the trigger?"

Adam frowned at her, as if she was missing the point. "I was tired of living in the past, fantasizing about murder. I wanted to move beyond that, let go of the memories. Don't you see? I did it for you."

She ran a shaky hand through her hair, laughing harshly. "You shouldn't have."

He seemed to think she should feel honored by his

decision. "Would you rather I'd murdered him in cold blood?"

"Yes," she said, lashing out at him. "He ruined my sister's life! He fed her addiction, and fed it, and fed it. He's responsible for dozens of drug overdoses and street killings! You decide to go soft on him after an attack of conscience—your first, by my account—and I'm supposed to be happy for you? Well, I'm not, Adam. I wish you'd killed him. I wish you'd done it a long time ago. Then my sister would still be alive. The fact that she's dead and you let him get away makes me sick."

"It makes you sick," Adam repeated, his brow furrowing.

"Yes. How could you think I'd be proud of your restraint? You lied to me and used me for *nothing*."

"Damn you," he said, his teeth clenched. "That was the hardest thing I've ever done. And it wasn't for nothing—it was for you. I let go of the past because I wanted a future with you."

Kari couldn't process anything beyond his failure to apprehend Moreno. It felt like a dousing of ice water, a shock to her system. Cold sadness filled every inch of her heart, leaving no room for forgiveness. "You shouldn't have," she repeated.

He studied her for a long moment, pain etched into his face. She felt distanced from his misery but strangely satisfied by it.

She'd wanted to hurt him.

Before she could change her mind or start to feel guilty about her own dealings with Moreno, she muttered a terse goodbye and walked away.

* * *

Ian came back into the room as soon as Kari left. "Did she say anything about Maria?"

Adam shook his head.

"How did she know you were here?"

"She never said."

"Jesus, Adam. What did you two talk about, the weather?"

He reclined in the hospital bed, his ego still smarting from her harsh words. "You didn't have to pat her down."

Ian gave him a disgruntled look. "Are you serious? I'm here to protect you in the likely event of an assassination attempt. I'd have patted down your *sister* if she'd showed up unannounced."

Adam knew Ian was just using Raquel as an example, but he was in a very dark mood. He'd hated the sight of Ian's hands on Kari, and didn't appreciate the reminder that those hands had once been on Raquel. "Don't talk about my sister. Ever."

"Now you're starting to piss me off. I didn't disrespect your girlfriend or your sister. I have no interest in either."

"If you had no interest in Raquel, maybe you should have stayed away from her."

"Oh, shut up. She jumped on me after getting drunk at her best friend's wedding. It didn't mean anything. The only reason we went out a few times was to make it seem less like a one-night stand."

Adam hadn't known that, and he wanted to punch Ian in the face for sharing personal details about Raquel in such a glib manner. He supposed he was a hypocrite, but he hated the thought of anyone treating his sister the way he treated most women—casually.

"We knew it would never work, anyway," Ian muttered. "Because of you."

"Because of me?"

"Because of our friendship, yours and mine. She didn't want to come between us. Now can we move on, for Christ's sake?"

He shrugged, feeling surly.

"What did Kari say?"

"That I make her sick."

Ian's brows rose. "Do you care?"

"Of course I care! I'm—" Adam broke off, shaken by the realization.

"You're what?"

He was in love with her. "I wish I could have called her."

The corner of Ian's mouth tipped up. "This is ironic, isn't it? You've spent the past few years sleeping with women you never speak to again. Then you find one you actually want to call back, and you can't."

Adam's chest ached from the blows Kari had dealt him. "I suppose I should have avoided sex altogether, like you," he said, annoyed with his friend's self-righteous attitude. "You've spent the past few years pining for a woman you've never even slept with. How's that working for you?"

"It's not," Ian admitted, checking his text messages. "According to the reception desk, Kari asked for Armando."

Adam straightened. "What?"

"That's why we got a notification to be on alert."

"Well, fuck!"

"Do you want me to follow her? She's probably in the parking lot. I can't run fast, but I can still run."

"Go," Adam said.

Ian rushed from the room, his limp barely noticeable. Adam wanted to leave with him, but he couldn't abandon his post. Ian was a free agent, his own man. He'd offered his bodyguard services as a favor to Adam.

After everything had gone to hell at the border, Adam's boss had been furious. While Adam was in the hospital getting chest X-rays, Pettigrew had hatched a new plan. He'd ordered Adam to play the part of Armando Villarreal in hopes that one of Moreno's crew members would come back to seek revenge.

Adam was offered one chance at redemption—and he took it. He knew that Pettigrew would suspend him, maybe even fire him, if he declined.

It was a very sensitive operation. He'd been allowed one phone call, to Raquel. There was no way he could have spoken to Kari in person. He'd taken a huge risk by asking Ian to send her a message. If word of his unnecessary hospitalization got out, it could have jeopardized the mission. Adam was supposed to be lying low.

Kari would probably hate him forever, and he didn't blame her. When he'd agreed to Pettigrew's plan and promised not to contact Kari, he'd known there would be grave consequences.

"Goddamn it," he muttered, wishing he'd had more options. He was probably going to get fired anyway. Ready to walk out on his professional responsibilities, he paced the room. If Kari was in danger, he couldn't sit tight.

Ian called a moment later.

"Where are you?" Adam asked.

"On the freeway. She lives in Bonita, right?"

"Right."

"She passed that exit. Looks like she's headed toward the border."

Adam clenched his cell phone in a death grip. His mind raced with possibilities, none good.

"Maybe she's working with Moreno."

"No," Adam said, refusing to consider it.

"Because she's never done that before?"

"She didn't have a choice!"

They both fell silent as a disturbing thought occurred to them simultaneously. What if Moreno had manipulated Kari again, using the last person in the world she cared about?

"Maria," Ian breathed.

"Don't do anything crazy," Adam warned, his stomach roiling with tension. "Keep following her and stay in contact with me."

"What are you going to do?"

He yanked off his hospital gown and pulled on a pair of jeans. Kari needed him. Ian needed him. To hell with Pettigrew. "I'm leaving right now."

23

Maria found a chance to use her syringe later that afternoon.

While the cat was away, the mice were definitely at play. Since Moreno left to run his errand, Chuy and the rest of the crew had been using drugs openly and discussing an uprising. There was a lot of big talk and nervous laughter. Chuy thought Moreno should step down. The current boss was in mourning, unable to rule with an iron fist.

Chuy's comrades didn't argue with him, but there was something lukewarm about their responses. They didn't laugh as loud as Chuy, or as long. Maria got the impression that they were just humoring him.

Later, when Moreno returned, there would be hell to pay. If Maria could hang on until then, she might get out of this alive.

Unfortunately, she was the only woman in the house and Chuy hadn't forgotten her. "Here's a perfect example of his lack of balls," he said, disparaging Moreno again. "We've got a sweet-looking *muñequita* downstairs and we can't touch her."

They men grumbled a vague agreement, ribbing each other about who needed to get laid the most.

"What's he going to do with her?" Chuy continued. "No one has ever been held there and come out alive."

This statement was met with silence. Suggesting rape was all fine and good, but none of these men wanted the stigma of murdering a helpless female.

"She's been listening to us. I know this girl. She's a fucking rat."

"Another rat?" the man they called Juanito replied. "Your hotel had a lot of those. Maybe you needed an exterminator."

They all burst into laughter at Chuy's expense.

Maria kept her eyes glued to the kitchen floor as he pushed back his chair, its wooden legs scraping along the cheap linoleum.

"I'll do some exterminating," he warned.

"Sit down, *güey*," Juanito said. "Wait for *jefe* and have a drink."

"I don't think he's coming back."

"What if he does? I heard he went crazy when he found his girlfriend dead. He tore the hotel room apart with his bare hands. You want him to do that to you?"

"I'm not going to kill her," Chuy said, making a concession. "I'll just make sure that if she leaves here, she never talks."

Maria didn't like the sound of that. She scrambled down the concrete steps, her heart hammering in her chest. There was no place to hide, no corner to wait in ambush. She couldn't even stand behind the door without drawing notice.

Moving quickly, she overturned the sleeping mat and blanket, creating a visual distraction. It didn't really look like a person hiding, but perhaps the disarray would draw his eye. Then she raced back to the stairs and stood beside them, clenching the uncapped syringe in her ready fist.

The instant he came through the door, she struck, plunging the needle into his ankle. It penetrated his sock and pant leg, sinking in all the way to the hilt.

She wished the syringe was full of heroin, or better yet poison, but the cylinder was empty.

The sharp point made an effective weapon nevertheless. Maybe the needle hit a nerve, because Chuy hollered like a madman and lifted his foot, trying to shake off the dangling syringe. She used that opportunity to grab him by the ankle and pull. He fell forward, crashing down the stairs. His heavy body bounced along the unyielding concrete and landed in a crumpled heap on the dirt floor.

For a few seconds she just stared at him. She couldn't believe the tactic had worked. When she snapped out of her stupor, she made a break for it, leaping over him and racing up the stairs. The men in the kitchen actually moved aside for her, their mouths agape. She ran by them and found the door in record time.

It wouldn't open.

She twisted the knob and yanked, rattling a half-dozen locks. Her stomach filled with dread as she realized she'd never escape this way. She whirled around, searching for another exit. Three men were watching her with a mixture of amusement and admiration.

"What a wildcat," Juanito said, and they all laughed.

Chuy roared for help from the bottom of the stairs.

Before Maria could decide where to go next, Juanito stepped forward to detain her while the other two men,

Beto and Ronnie, went to assist Chuy. They brought him up the stairs and put him in a kitchen chair. He wasn't badly injured, just humiliated. His dark gaze promised an unpleasant payback for Maria.

Juanito tightened his grip on her arm, but it felt protective rather than menacing. When his cell phone rang, the tension in the room ignited.

He took the phone out of his pocket. *"Bueno,"* he answered. "Yeah, everything is fine." After listening for a moment, he moved the receiver away from his ear so that the other men could hear.

"Chuy," Moreno said, requesting his attention.

"Yes, *jefe*." Glaring at Maria, he massaged his ankle.

"I've confirmed that Armando is at Scripps. I'd like you to pay him a visit. Finish what you started."

Chuy flinched at the command. He'd just been ordered to assassinate his former partner. His reluctance was obvious, and not because he had any qualms about shooting an injured man. The danger of getting caught was sky-high. "Whatever you say, boss."

"Juanito, I want you to take Maria to Bob's Big Boy. Drop her off in the parking lot and get the hell out of there. Don't come back to the house."

"Yes, *jefe*," he said, his thin chest puffing out with importance.

Maria's heart leapt with hope. They were letting her go!

"Leave now," Moreno said, ending the call.

Juanito put the phone back in his pocket and headed for the door, pulling Maria with him. She went along easily, eager to be free.

"Hold on, Juanito," Chuy said in a low voice, and the

tiny hairs on the back of her neck prickled with unease. "Let's talk about this."

Don't listen to him, she urged silently.

"No," Juanito said. "I'm following orders. If you don't want to, that's your problem."

"Let's all go together."

He shook his head. "Sorry, *amigo*. You're on your own."

Chuy drew his handgun. "I don't think so. *Amigo*."

Juanito froze. He was just a kid, no more than twenty. With his slender frame and boyish face, he was no match for Chuy.

Even so, he didn't back down. Shoving Maria aside, he reached for his own weapon. Chuy fired before he could brandish it, and his aim was true. Juanito collapsed against the door, leaving a red smear as he slid to the floor.

Maria watched in horror as he took a few hitched breaths, blood bubbling from his lips. Then the light in his eyes faded and his head lolled to the side.

"You monster!" she said to Chuy. *"Vete al diablo, cabrón!"*

Ignoring her curse, Chuy glanced at his remaining comrades, Beto and Ronnie. "Anyone else want to argue with me?"

They fell silent, choosing the devil over death.

He put his gun away. "Good. Roll him up in a carpet and throw her back in the cellar. We're going to Big Boy."

Kari felt nauseous from the confrontation with Adam, but she was more determined than ever to help Maria.

She also hoped that the information she gave Moreno would keep Adam safe. Surely he would call off his revenge mission. There was no point in assassinating a pseudo-Armando. And if he'd wanted to kill Adam, he'd have done it already.

Letting out a nervous breath, she passed the last U.S. exit, lifting her ponytail off the nape of her neck. Maybe all of those trips across the border had given her nerves of steel. She'd just argued with a drug lord and won.

Moreno had wanted to drop off Maria at the tile manufacturer, but Kari had insisted on a public place.

Bob's Big Boy was a casual restaurant in downtown Tijuana that catered to people from all walks of life. Petty criminals mixed with police officers and ordinary citizens. Families with small children sat alongside cartel members. Everyone enjoyed the American-style shakes, fries, and burgers.

Kari parked her rental car in the huge dirt lot and walked inside. At dinnertime on Friday night, the booths were packed. She grabbed a small table with a good view of the parking lot and sipped a Cherry Coke, watching patrons come and go.

The longer she sat there, the more conflicted she felt about her conversation with Adam. She hadn't meant what she'd said. He'd tried to open up to her and she'd shut him down. Maybe he deserved it.

She just . . . wasn't ready to forgive him. She'd buried her baby sister this afternoon. Her heart was closed.

Although she couldn't imagine getting back together with Adam, she didn't really blame him for sparing Moreno. She wouldn't have been able to pull the trigger, and she hated the drug lord with a passion.

Her words to Adam were like poison barbs, designed

to inflict the most damage. She needed to push him away, to protect herself.

While she was waiting for Maria, a dusty black SUV pulled into the parking lot. She straightened, recognizing it as Chuy Pena's. The back door opened and a rolled-up carpet tumbled out. It was thicker in the middle, with a large dark stain on one side.

"Oh my God," she said, leaping to her feet.

Maria was in that carpet. Bleeding to death, most likely. While she watched, her hand clapped over her mouth, the SUV drove away.

Cursing Moreno and his entire crew, she left her soda on the table and rushed outside. Time staggered and she felt like she was in a nightmare sequence, running through wet concrete, slow as molasses. The carpet shuddered in the distance, as if the person inside was having a seizure. Or maybe it wasn't moving at all. The rhythmic motions of her feet on the gravel made it seem like the world was shaking.

She reached the bundle and dropped to her knees, gasping for breath. The carpet was tied with duct tape. Clawing desperately, she screamed Maria's name. The body inside the carpet was still warm, the bloodstain sticky.

So much blood. God.

She managed to rip through one layer of tape, yanking open the top of the roll. A slack face stared at her, his eyes opaque.

It was a young man. Not Maria.

Kari jerked her hands away from the carpet, wiping them on the front of her shirt. She was in shock, her thoughts jumbled and her movements uncoordinated.

Letting out a strangled sound of distress, she rose to her feet, stumbling away.

The black SUV roared back into the parking lot. Before she could regain her equilibrium, it sped by her, almost clipping her elbow. The driver stopped on a dime, sending a choking cloud of dust into the air. A man climbed out of the back.

Kari turned to run, too stunned to scream. Before she could take two steps, the man from the SUV grabbed her by the hair and jerked her backward. Locking his arm across her midsection, he dragged her into the vehicle.

Ian's vision darkened with rage as he watched the cartel member shove Kari Strauss into the back of the SUV.

He couldn't prevent the kidnapping or do a damned thing to help her. Even shooting out the tires would be a bad move, because there was no way he could win a gunfight against three heavily armed men.

Cursing under his breath, he slowed his truck to a stop next to the bundle of carpet, retrieving Kari's purse from the gravel-strewn ground. Leaving the dead man unattended, he stepped on the gas, taking off after the SUV.

Adam was going to lose it when he heard about this late-breaking development.

"Fuck," Ian muttered, tightening his hands on the steering wheel. Luckily, Chuy wasn't weaving through traffic like a maniac or taking unnecessary risks. Ian followed at a safe distance, his senses reeling.

He'd been parked across the street, doing surveillance, when the SUV pulled into the gravel lot. His world had come to a grinding halt when the carpet tumbled from the back of the vehicle. Like Kari, he'd assumed Maria was the lifeless form inside.

Rather than staying to make sure, he'd pursued the SUV, unwilling to let her murderers get away. He'd intended to kill every one of those motherfuckers. Then he realized Chuy was circling the block, not speeding away, and a chill traveled down his spine.

Ian returned to the parking lot as fast as he could, but he was too late to save Kari. When he saw that the body in the carpet wasn't Maria, he was overwhelmed with relief. He thought of Sonia Barreras, the last woman to die on his watch.

No way was he going to let that happen again.

His cell phone rang a moment later, startling him from his thoughts. "I have bad news," he said to Adam.

"What?"

He summarized the situation, emphasizing that the SUV was within sight and that Kari was still alive.

Adam swore in two languages, sounding like he was having a nervous breakdown. "I'm on my way to the border right now."

Ian was glad Adam had left his post, because he needed backup. He was outnumbered and the cartel members had the upper hand. They might take Kari to a secluded location where they could kill her without any witnesses. Although Ian would do his damnedest to help her, he was only one man.

The odds favored Pena.

To his credit, Adam didn't ask Ian to abandon pursuit. Ian would rather die than quit, and he was glad his best friend knew that.

If he was racing to his end, so be it.

"Are you going to notify CBP?" Ian asked.

"Not until I get across the border. They might try to stop me."

The Mexican authorities would probably do the same. U.S. police had no jurisdiction here, and many of the local cops were on Moreno's payroll. Ian and Adam were on their own, outgunned and outmanned.

"Just stay on them," Adam said. "But not too close."

"Yeah."

"And—and be careful."

Ian's throat tightened. "I will."

They ended the call on that sentimental note. He continued after the SUV, wishing he'd brought an arsenal of weapons. His Glock had fifteen rounds in the chamber and he wasn't carrying an extra clip.

When he glanced in the rearview mirror, he noticed a late-model silver Mercedes. It was keeping up with him, changing lanes when he did. Ian's pulse skyrocketed. If the driver was working with Chuy, Ian could kiss his ass goodbye.

Kari's purse jingled in the passenger seat. He reached inside, finding a red cell phone with glittery crap all over it.

Carlos, the caller ID read.

Ian answered. "Hello?"

"Who is this?"

The man on the other end was either Carlos Moreno or a hell of an impersonator. Educated in Mexico City, he spoke English with a distinctive accent.

"This is Ian Foster," he supplied.

"Agent Foster?"

He ignored the question. "Where's Maria?"

"She's supposed to be with Kari. I'd arranged for her to be dropped off."

"Your arrangement fell through," he said flatly, not believing him. "The only thing your men dropped off was a dead body."

Moreno didn't respond. He'd already known that.

"Your associate just kidnapped an American woman from a public parking lot," Ian said. "The heat is going to come down on you like a fucking firestorm. No one will want to do business with you."

"I didn't give him that order."

"It doesn't matter. He's your responsibility."

"And he'll pay for his mistake," he said, hanging up.

Ian tossed the phone onto the seat, hoping that was true.

24

Kari gave the men in the back of the SUV a run for their money.

She kicked one in the face and another in the groin. For a split second she was free, scrambling across the seat. Before she could open a door and throw herself out, Chuy's man yanked her by the hair and shoved her down on the floorboards.

"Tie her up," he told his partner, holding her still.

She struggled for a few more moments but her efforts were in vain. They wrenched her arms behind her back and secured her wrists with coarse rope. Then her ankles were bound the same way. Panting from exertion, she twisted her wrists, succeeding only in scraping them raw with the abrasive rope fibers.

When she settled, the men in the back of the SUV returned to their seats while she stayed facedown on the floorboards. The stocky one kept his boot on her bottom. They both examined her body with greedy eyes.

"This one's even prettier than the other one."

Kari looked away, feeling nauseous.

Chuy spoke from the driver's seat. "Tell me what you did for Moreno."

"Fuck you," she said, her teeth clenched.

He laughed without humor. "We'd love to. Beto just got out of prison, so he can go first."

The man with his foot on her butt grunted in anticipation.

"Then again, Ronnie's married," Chuy mused. "He might be even more desperate."

Ronnie's nose was bleeding and he had a shoeprint across his cheek. His dark, vacant gaze promised no mercy.

"Did you make a deal with Moreno?" Chuy asked.

Kari hadn't really been following him until now. Panic had gripped her brain, scrambling her thoughts. "What do you mean? I'd spit on him if I saw him."

"You didn't give him any information?"

Apparently Moreno hadn't relayed the news about Armando yet. She didn't know what to think of that. "I spoke to him about Maria. He said I could pick her up at Big Boy. That's all we talked about."

"He didn't ask you for a favor in return?"

"No."

"I find that hard to believe."

Kari wasn't sure there was any benefit to lying, but intuition told her not to cooperate. Chuy had plans for her, and nothing she did or said would change them. He didn't intend to question her and let her go. "Moreno ordered you to deliver Maria?"

Chuy didn't answer.

"He's going to kill you."

"He's not in charge right now, *muñeca*. I am."

"No one will accept you as a leader," she said, short of breath. "You have a bad habit of shooting innocent women."

"Gag her," Chuy said.

Beto punched her in the stomach, making her gasp for air. Ronnie used that opportunity to shove a dirty rag in her mouth. Tears leaked from her eyes as he tied a knot at the nape of her neck. The gag was taut, unforgiving. Her vision swam with dark spots. She inhaled through her nostrils and tried not to throw up.

"You ever had a blonde before?" Beto asked.

Ronnie moistened his lips. "No."

Kari closed her eyes, blocking out their disturbing visages. She couldn't bear to imagine them brutalizing her.

After what seemed like hours, the vehicle shuddered to a halt. Beto jerked her off the floorboards and her stomach rebelled. He untied her gag just before the contents came up, sickly sweet and acidic.

When she was finished, Chuy scolded Beto for letting her puke in the back of his truck, and they carried her into a small house. It appeared to be a rural area but Kari was too disoriented to get a good look at her surroundings. She ended up on a scuffed linoleum floor, her head spinning.

"I changed my mind," Chuy said, looming over her. "I think I'll go first."

A muffled scream rang out, rising from the bowels of the house. "Maria!" she cried, searching for her friend.

Chuy turned his head toward a closed door. "Shut up," he yelled. "You're next!"

"No," Kari protested, shuddering with revulsion. "Please."

He closed his hand around her neck. "Talk."

"I don't know anything!"

"Talk," he said, applying steady pressure.

A few seconds of choking was enough to make her change her mind about cooperating. When she nodded, he relaxed his grip, and she sucked in a lungful of air, desperate to get oxygen to her brain.

"What did you do for Moreno?" Chuy asked again.

"I went to the hospital to visit Armando," she croaked. "Moreno wanted me to make sure it was him."

Chuy's thumb brushed over the hollow of her throat in a menacing caress. "Was it?"

"No," she said.

He released her and rose to his feet, pacing the kitchen. The tattoo on his cheek stood out in harsh relief. He appeared pale and unbalanced, close to lunacy. "I knew that motherfucker was setting me up!"

Kari stared at the door Maria was behind. Slender fingers wiggled through a crack at the bottom, signaling that she was unbound, maybe even unharmed. Kari felt a surge of hope, even though she couldn't imagine how they would escape.

Beto and Ronnie stood near the doorway, listening to Chuy rant like a madman. His ring tone sounded, disturbing the chaos.

"Fuck," he said, checking the screen.

The other men looked anxious as Chuy answered the call. After a terse exchange, he agreed to something and hung up. "The boss is coming right now. Put this bitch in the basement with her friend."

"What are you planning to do?" Beto asked.

"I'm going to take him out."

Ronnie dragged Kari toward the basement door. "Please," she said, but he ignored her. When Beto opened the door, he pushed her forward. If Maria hadn't been there to catch her, she'd have fallen down the concrete stairs.

The door slammed shut, leaving them both in the dark.

Maria didn't seem to have any trouble seeing her. "*Ay, amor,*" she said, tugging at the coarse rope at her feet and wrists. "Did they hurt you?"

Tears rushed into her eyes at the sound of Maria's voice, the feel of her tender hands. "No. How about you?"

"I'm okay. A little dirty, a little hungry."

"I'm so glad you're alive!" As soon as Maria worked the bindings loose, Kari threw her arms around her friend, sobbing. Maria felt even more slender than usual, but just as strong. "How long have you been here?"

"Three days."

"With no food?"

"Tortilla chips and oranges. Want some?"

Kari laughed through her tears, on the edge of delirium. Once her eyes adjusted to the lack of light, she saw that they were in an underground room with a dirt floor. Four concrete walls, a mattress in the corner.

"Oh my God," she whispered. "This isn't fit for an animal."

"No," Maria agreed. "We have to break out."

"How?"

She took a sliver of plastic from her pocket. It looked like a needle cap for a syringe. "I was using this on the lock. When they are busy, I will try to open the door."

Kari hugged her again. "Maria, you're a genius."

* * *

Adam was on the fence about calling his superior at CBP.

Pettigrew would order him to wait for backup. He would request a SWAT team and air support. The Mexican authorities would have to be notified. A tactical collaboration of this scale couldn't be organized in minutes.

He was already skating on thin ice professionally. Going rogue might put an end to his career at the port. But Kari was in danger, and saving her was the only thing he cared about. Every second counted.

As soon as he crossed the border, Ian called with a location. "We're heading east on the 1100 block of Salsipuedes."

Adam entered it into his navigation system. He was only twenty minutes away.

"I've got company," Ian added.

"Who?"

"Moreno. He's right behind me."

"Shit!"

"He must have been at Bob's, watching to see how the drop went down. He says he ordered them to deliver Maria to Kari."

"You talked to him?"

"He called on Kari's cell. I picked up her purse in the parking lot."

Adam clenched his hands around the steering wheel, his blood pressure skyrocketing. Ian was trapped between vehicles on a two-lane road. Moreno's men might be heading to a remote area to execute him.

"Hang on," Ian said. "It's ringing again."

"Put us on speaker."

There was a moment of fumbling while Ian set up the three-way call. Then Adam heard Moreno's voice. "Chuy will turn right on the next street, Calle Oscuro. He's going to a house a few miles down the road."

"Why are you telling me this?" Ian asked.

"Because we both want the same thing."

"What's that?"

"To take him down. If you work with me, it will be done quickly, before the women are harmed."

"How?"

"Pull over and we can discuss our approach. I know a safe place."

"Just a second," Ian said, putting Moreno on hold so he could talk to Adam privately. "What do you think?"

Adam went with his gut. "I think we can trust him."

"Jesus," Ian said, letting out a shaky laugh. "I can't believe you're saying that about Carlos Moreno."

"I can't either. Do you disagree?"

"No, I'm with you. We need all the help we can get."

"Stay in your car and wait," he said, adding the new location to his navigation system. "I'll talk to him first."

Ian switched the phones back to speaker. "My friend Adam Cortez is going to join us. You might remember him."

"The border cop?"

"I'm here," Adam said. "I'm coming alone."

"No backup?"

"Completely off the books."

"Very well."

"I'll be there in ten minutes. And if you shoot my friend, I'll fucking kill you. Do you understand me?"

Moreno promised he would save his bullets for Pena and hung up. Adam's navigation system didn't recognize Calle Oscuro, so he stayed on the phone with Ian, listening to his description of the exact location. He didn't want to end the call. As long as he could hear Ian's voice, he knew his friend was all right.

Adam drove as fast as he dared on Salsipuedes, passing cars like they were standing still. He found the dirt road with a handmade sign and turned right. A moment later he came upon a gravel pullout beneath a copse of trees. Moreno's expensive silver Mercedes was parked in front of Ian's economy car.

Adam slowed to a stop next to Ian, his heart pounding. He'd pulled on some street clothes at the hospital, but he was still wearing his protective vest. The T-shirt underneath was damp with sweat.

He got out of his car and approached the driver's side of the Mercedes, nodding at Ian to cover him.

Moreno waited for Adam with his window down, drumming his fingertips against the steering wheel. "We have to stop meeting like this, Officer Cortez." Although his lips curved into a smile, it didn't reach his eyes. He looked like he hadn't slept in days. His run-down appearance made a sharp contrast to the elegant façade he usually cultivated.

"What's your plan?" Adam asked.

"He's expecting me, so we can use my vehicle. You should crouch down in the back. I'll go in first and cause a distraction."

Adam thought it was a ballsy move, borderline suicidal. "What's to stop him from shooting you before you get inside?"

"*Codigo,*" he said, using the Spanish word for code of honor. "There are rules to follow in a succession. If he wants to be the new boss, he has to challenge me openly. Cowards can't take the reins."

Adam studied Moreno's face, evaluating his sincerity.

"I don't expect you to believe me, but I have standards about killing innocents. Pena has crossed that line twice. I will not allow him to do it again."

"Where are the women being held?"

"In the basement. There's a door in the kitchen."

"Describe the layout of the house."

Moreno did, in simple terms. There were three rooms and two exits, a front door and a back door.

"What are we up against as far as weapons?"

He listed a number of pistols and semiautomatic handguns. "There are also enough explosives to blow the place sky-high."

"Jesus," Adam said.

"If I thought there was a better way, I would leave it to the police force. But time is of the essence and Pena has a taste for rape."

Fury rose up within Adam, blackening the edges of his vision. He could cooperate with Moreno, but Adam would never forgive him for associating with a sick bastard like Chuy. Anyone who touched Kari deserved to be cut into bloody little pieces.

"Let's go," he said, gesturing at Ian to come along. While they got into the Mercedes, crouching behind the seats, Adam gave him a rundown of the situation.

They traveled the last stretch of Calle Oscuro with

their heads down, cloaked by tinted windows, under the cover of dusk.

Maria worked on the lock with intense concentration, her slender fingers clutching the tiny piece of plastic in a tight grip.

"Almost," she whispered.

Kari was lying on her stomach at the top of the stairs, looking under the door. There was no one in the kitchen. She had no idea where the men were, but she hoped they couldn't hear Maria picking the lock. "Still clear."

"Got it!" With a dull click, the mechanism released. Maria shoved the needle cap back into her pocket and reached out to turn the knob, her hand trembling.

Kari grabbed her ankle, delaying her. "Wait. Someone's coming."

Maria sank to her belly beside Kari, peering underneath the door. Together they watched Chuy's slip-on Adidas come into focus. He sat down in a chair at the kitchen table. Another man took the seat across from him.

"Moreno," Maria mouthed, confirming Kari's suspicions.

Although Chuy's feet were wide apart, his slouch suggesting indolence, the air between the two men was bone-chilling. They were ready to kill each other. It wasn't a good time to attempt an escape.

"You didn't follow orders," Moreno said.

Chuy made no excuses. "What's done is done."

"Let the women go. They won't risk testifying."

He tapped his foot, contemplating. "What do you offer for them?"

"A smooth transition."

"You really want out?"

"It's time," Moreno said. "I don't have the stomach for murder anymore."

Kari realized that he was making Chuy an offer he couldn't refuse. The top position in his drug empire, handed over without a fight.

"What about Armando?" Chuy asked.

"Forget him."

"Give me his letter."

"I don't have it."

Chuy seemed displeased by the answer. He leaned back in his chair, putting distance between them. "You haven't promised anything I can't get on my own. You say you're done with killing but I know you're armed. Do you think I'm stupid?"

"I think you're reckless," Moreno admitted.

Chuy didn't respond.

"The receptionist you shot . . . she was very beautiful."

His nervous foot went still. "So?"

"Were you sleeping with her?"

"What difference does it make?"

"She was pregnant."

Chuy's hand crept down toward his ankle. "Who told you that?"

"One of my sources."

"The same one who confirmed Armando was in the hospital?"

Kari grabbed Maria's shoulder, clutching it tightly. They both dreaded what was coming. She didn't know whether to warn Moreno or get away from the door.

"Perhaps," Moreno said.

Chuy's next move was as quick as lightning. "Liar," he growled, snatching a pistol from his ankle holster. Moreno leapt to his feet, knocking a chair over. There were two earsplitting blasts as their weapons fired simultaneously.

Chuy staggered to the side, letting out a strangled sound.

Moreno fell to the ground and stayed there.

Kari clapped a hand over her mouth, smothering her scream. She started to scramble down the steps but Maria held her still, shaking her head. Wide-eyed, she pressed a finger to her lips, gesturing for Kari to be quiet.

Chuy shifted his feet, struggling to stay upright. Crimson drops splashed on his shoes and peppered the dirty linoleum.

Another man entered the kitchen, reaching down to disarm Moreno. The former drug lord lay motionless. "We've got movement outside," Ronnie said. "I don't know about you, but I'm getting the fuck out of here."

Chuy was bleeding, but he wasn't down. "Where's Beto?"

"Covering the front. Let's go."

The instant Ronnie walked out the back door, more gunfire erupted. Chuy muttered a string of curses and slammed the door shut, leaving Ronnie to his own devices. "Motherfucker!" he yelled at Moreno's lifeless body, exiting the kitchen.

Kari stared at Maria, her heart hammering against her ribs. They couldn't try to get away during a shootout. It was too dangerous. "What should we do?"

"Let's wait."

She nodded her agreement, relieved. Hand in hand, they started walking down the concrete staircase.

They'd gone only a few steps when the house exploded.

Ian had been braced for action from the moment Moreno pulled into the driveway and parked beside Chuy's SUV.

He'd anticipated a gunfight in the front yard. When Moreno wasn't shot on sight, Ian let out a slow breath, exchanging a surprised glance with Adam. They'd both expected the worst.

Although Chuy had allowed Moreno to come inside, Ian doubted the drug lord would walk out alive. This mission had kamikaze written all over it. Ian didn't know why Moreno would make such a sacrifice and he didn't care. His entire focus was on saving Maria. Everything else was peripheral.

"When it's go time, head around to the back of the house," Adam said in a low voice. "I'll cover the front."

Ian didn't argue. The kitchen was in the back, along with the door to the basement where Maria and Kari were being held.

As soon as they heard the shots, Adam moved out of his hiding position, shoving open the car door and tumbling across the dirt lot. He crouched behind the hood, his weapon drawn.

Ian exited the vehicle through the same door, glad for the approaching nightfall as he circled the back bumper with his head down. Staying low, he ran across the front yard, heading toward the far corner of the house.

For a few seconds he was out in open space, completely vulnerable. Blood pounded in his ears and pebbles crunched under the soles of his boots. He tightened his grip on the Glock, praying he wouldn't get hit.

As soon as he got clear, he raced along the side of the house, flattening his back against the stucco wall. Before turning the corner, he paused, listening for movement. Someone was trying to leave.

Ian burst into motion, flying around the corner. "Get down on the ground," he shouted, ready to shoot.

The man coming out the back door reached into his waistband, pulling out a semiautomatic handgun.

Ian fired twice, hitting him in the shoulder and the center of the chest. The man fell against the open door, his handgun peppering the dirt with bullets. Judging by the way he went down and stayed down, he was dead.

Ian didn't have time to reflect on his first kill, because Chuy Pena appeared in the doorway before Ian could squeeze off another shot. Ian ducked behind the corner of the house, narrowly avoiding Chuy's return fire.

Jesus! That was close.

Although Ian was ready for him, Chuy didn't advance. The shady bastard slammed the door and retreated inside, leaving his fallen comrade on the back step. Once again, Ian didn't hesitate to move in closer. Rushing forward, he picked up the dead man's handgun and shoved it in his waistband.

Sweat dripping in his eyes, he waited beside the door. No one came out.

More gunfire erupted in the front of the house. Ian identified the report of Adam's Beretta along with that of a semiautomatic machine gun. His friend was in trouble. Making a split-second decision, Ian left the back door and rounded the corner again, knowing that Adam needed assistance *now*.

Hopefully he'd get a chance to save Maria later.

As he ran toward the fray, an explosion knocked him off his feet. He felt the stitches in his leg separate, and gritted his teeth against the pain. Rolling over, he brought his arms up to protect his head as burning debris rocketed across the dark landscape.

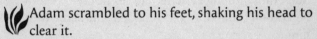Adam scrambled to his feet, shaking his head to clear it.

The explosion had thrown him against the car, smashing his bruised rib cage against the open door. Ignoring the fierce ache in his side, he took a sharp breath and concentrated on protecting himself from another round of bullets.

Whoever had been shooting at him from the front window was no longer firing. Flames spread up toward the roof, lighting the night sky. Adam couldn't see the south side of the house, where Ian had gone, but the north side had a hole in it the size of a truck.

While he watched, still disoriented, two figures emerged from the flames, their arms around each other.

Adam's vision blurred. He blinked at the brightness, recognizing that Chuy Pena was one of the figures. The other man fell to the ground and stayed there. Pena, who appeared injured, didn't waste any time helping him. Holding one hand to his midsection, he stumbled away from the burning house.

Adam glanced at the inferno, aware that any remaining explosives would be set off by the fire. The entire building could collapse in seconds, trapping Kari and Maria inside. Ian might be hurt, even bleeding to death.

And Pena was getting away.

The torch of hate that Adam had carried for Moreno hadn't been extinguished, but neither had it transferred to Chuy Pena. Adam didn't give a damn what happened to him. He just wanted to find Kari.

If Pena had any brains, he'd run away from the blaze, across the dark hillside. Instead he closed the distance between Adam and the SUV, challenging him to open fire. And, although Adam had no desire to shoot Pena, he couldn't allow a cold-blooded murderer to pass by him.

Adam would rather kill him and be done with it, but professional ethics dictated that he attempt an arrest first. Which was a fucking hassle that he didn't need right now. He'd abandoned his quest for revenge. It was infuriating to have to deal with this worthless scumbag while the people he loved were in danger.

Cursing under his breath, he strode toward the SUV and trained the barrel of his Beretta on the back of Pena's shaved head. "Get down on the ground or I'll kill you."

Pena opened the driver's-side door, ignoring him. He was gut-shot and covered in sweat. Even if he got away, he wouldn't get far.

"I'm not fucking around, asshole! Get down now."

Pena had a pistol in his hand in the blink of an eye. A bullet hissed by Adam's left ear as he fired three times, connecting with his opponent's chest and neck. Pena slumped against the driver's seat and crumpled to the dirt.

Adam stepped forward and kicked the gun away, crouching down to check for a pulse. Nothing.

Although Pena never would have survived the stomach wound, Adam was furious with him for forcing his hand. A year ago he might have enjoyed this violent end. But the man he'd become was disturbed by the experience, rattled to the bone.

He'd let go of his bloodlust and overcome the past. Pena, in his final act of defiance, had cast Adam in the role of vigilante again.

Dead or alive, he was a ruthless bastard.

Making the sign of the cross, Adam straightened and turned away from the corpse, running toward the inferno.

Kari rose to a sitting position, coughing uncontrollably.

Maria was lying on the dirt floor beside her, unconscious. When the explosion propelled them both down the stairs, Maria had fallen first and taken the brunt of the blow. Kari thought she'd hit her head on the ground as they fell.

She shook her slim shoulders, trying to rouse her. "Maria, wake up!"

Maria moaned, insensible.

Panicking, Kari searched the dark basement for an escape route, trying to see through the smoke. The ceiling had fallen through in some places, leaving burning beams and hot ash. There was a swirling vortex of flames overhead, blazing a giant hole. They had to get out of here before the roof caved in.

She grabbed the gallon container of water and doused Maria with it, wetting her from head to toe. Maria sputtered a weak protest, her eyelids fluttering. Encouraged by the sight, Kari poured the rest of the water on her own head and grabbed the blanket from the corner. Draping it over her shoulders, she crouched down next to Maria, slipping an arm around her waist. "I'm not going to leave you," she promised. "But we can't stay down here. If you don't get up right now, we'll both die."

Maria wrapped her arms around Kari's neck, murmuring her assent. With Kari's help, she staggered to her feet. Kari dragged Maria up the stairs, holding the blanket around her body. For a skinny girl, Maria weighed a ton. By the time Kari reached the top of the stairs, she was gasping for breath, coated in sweat.

Unfortunately, the flames were hotter at this level and the smoke thicker. Kari couldn't find a way out. Tossing the blanket over both of their heads, she crawled across the kitchen floor on her hands and knees, pulling Maria along with her. She expected to bump into Moreno's body at any moment.

It wasn't there.

Kari wondered if she'd made a wrong turn at the top of the stairs. She couldn't see her hand in front of her face or get a clean breath to clear her head. Maria collapsed on the sweltering linoleum, her strength sapped.

They were going to die here. Inches from a door, probably.

Kari stuck her head out of the blanket and tried to scream. Her lungs filled with smoke and she coughed instead, her throat burning.

Then a man appeared before her, yelling Maria's name. She shoved Maria's blanketed form toward him, almost weeping with relief. "Take her," she gasped, dizzy from lack of oxygen. "Come back for me."

Agent Foster was strong, but he couldn't carry them both. He nodded and lifted Maria into his arms, disappearing into the flames.

When Kari tried to crawl after him, a ceiling beam fell down, blocking her path. Disoriented, she curled up under the kitchen table. Every time she coughed, her lungs contracted, desperate for air. Her wet hair was steaming. She was too exhausted to move, too hoarse to cry out. And she was so . . . sleepy.

She closed her smoke-irritated eyes, letting the black fog envelop her.

Adam found another corpse by the corner of the house.

The man who'd helped Chuy escape the blaze had a large splinter of wood lodged in his upper thigh and appeared to have bled out very quickly.

Running past him, Adam shouted Ian's name, searching for a way inside. The front entrance was engulfed by flames. After the explosion, Pena and his buddy had come through a gaping hole on the north side.

Adam headed in that direction, spotting Ian. He was carrying a slender bundle in a charred wool blanket. Maria.

"Where's Kari?"

"Still inside the kitchen."

While Ian took Maria to safety, Adam ran into the burning building, calling Kari's name. The smoke was so thick he couldn't see anything but vague shapes. He started coughing instantly. Lowering his head, he continued toward the back of the house, where the kitchen was supposed to be. Flames licked along every wall and the ceiling was crumbling.

Praying that Kari was still alive, he covered his mouth and nose with the crook of his arm and ducked under a fallen beam.

The kitchen was almost unrecognizable, sizzling with heat. Adam saw her running shoes beneath a card table. It was clear from the position of her body that she was unconscious. Refusing to consider the possibility that he'd arrived too late, he shoved aside the table and bent down to pick her up.

His ribs screamed a violent protest as he hefted her over his shoulder. She wasn't easy to carry and he was already short of breath. But failure wasn't an option. Summoning the last of his strength, he rushed out of the kitchen, staggering through the blazing obstacle course. He almost stumbled sideways as another beam crashed from the ceiling.

Gritting his teeth, he picked up the pace and ignored the pain, emerging from the house in a final burst of energy.

A second later, a series of explosions rocked him off his feet. He fell on top of Kari, covering her body with his. The house went off like a bag of popcorn, staccato blasts echoing through the night.

Ian came forward, risking his neck to help Adam. Fearless as always, he waded through the fireworks, grabbing Kari by the arms and dragging her away from the danger. Adam followed close behind, army-crawling across searing debris. When they were safe, Ian began rescue breathing. Adam could only watch, trying to drag air into his own lungs, while Ian gave Kari some much-needed oxygen.

She responded immediately, gasping and wheezing. Ian rolled her onto her side as spasms wracked her body. After a long moment, she quieted, tears streaming down her soot-darkened face.

She appeared dazed and exhausted . . . but she was alive.

Maria, who had also regained consciousness, put her arms around her friend and sobbed with relief. Adam patted Ian on the back, praising him for a job well done. He couldn't believe they were all okay.

It was the happiest moment of his life, by far.

"Moreno didn't get out," Ian said.

Adam glanced back at the house, which was burning down to the studs. Anyone inside would have been incinerated.

The four of them left the scene, injured but upright. Ian helped Maria walk and Kari leaned heavily on Adam. His ribs ached with every step, but the pain was bearable, almost insignificant. Ian limped along beside him, content.

After they called the authorities to report the fire, Adam loaded Kari into his car and took her to the emergency room in downtown Tijuana. Ian followed close behind with Maria. Kari needed some oxygen to clear her lungs and mild painkillers for her sore throat. For Maria, who had a minor concussion, the doctor prescribed rest. Nothing could be done for Adam's bruised ribs, so he didn't complain. Ian's treatment was the most intensive. He winced as his wound was stitched up, enduring the procedure stoically.

Adam was glad their injuries weren't serious. Both women denied being sexually assaulted, much to his relief.

It was almost midnight when they left the hospital. A pair of detectives had asked them to stay in the city while the crime scene was processed. Too exhausted to do otherwise, Adam booked a couple of rooms at a nearby hotel. He doubted the Tijuana police would launch a thorough investigation. When drug cartel members were involved, it often made more sense to look the other way.

Adam's main concern was breaking the news to his superior officer, who might fire him for insubordination. But that could wait until morning.

Right now the only thing he cared about was sleep . . . and Kari.

Kari stood in the shower for a long time, rinsing away the remains of the day.

The steam soothed her sore throat and the hot water relaxed her battered body. She washed her face and arms repeatedly, using plenty of soap, lathering every inch of skin. Finally the water ran clean.

She turned off the faucet and stepped out, drying off with a fluffy towel. This was a nice hotel. Gentle soap, soft towels. After finger-combing her hair, she found a complimentary bottle of moisturizer. She applied the creamy lotion to her freshly scrubbed skin, taking special care around her abraded wrists.

When she was finished, she felt almost human again.

She walked out of the bathroom, surprised to find Adam sitting at the table instead of Maria. The room service dishes had been cleared away. Less than an hour ago, Kari had enjoyed cool gazpacho and orange flan while Maria feasted on a heartier meal of *arroz con pollo*, with chocolate cake for dessert.

"Do you mind?" he asked, rising to his feet. "I thought Ian would rather share a room with Maria."

Kari nodded, figuring that Maria had jumped at the chance to be with Ian. They'd held hands at the hospital and gazed into each other's eyes all night. Kari wasn't as sweet with Adam, though he'd stayed by her side the whole time. She wasn't opposed to sharing his bed; she was uneasy about sharing her *feelings*. Over the course of the evening, she'd come to a frightening realization: she was desperately in love with him.

His eyes traveled along her bare legs, lingering at the hem of her towel. When she shifted her feet, he pulled his attention back to her face. "I don't expect anything," he said, clearing his throat. "I brought my gym clothes from the car, if you want to use them as pajamas. They're clean."

Kari glanced at the clothes on the bed, touched by his thoughtfulness.

"I just need to shower."

He didn't have anything clean to sleep in, either, so she left the shorts for him. While he ducked into the bathroom, she put on his large T-shirt and knee-high socks. Feeling cozy, she slipped under the covers. He came out of the shower five minutes later, smelling delicious and looking even better. There was a fist-sized bruise on his chest. As he turned to switch off the main light, she saw another painful-looking mark on his back.

The sight filled her with a disturbing mixture of emotions. Helplessness, because he had a dangerous job. Guilt, because she'd brought more danger to him. And fear, because she'd just lost someone she loved.

She couldn't bear to go through that again.

"I want to talk to you," he said as he settled in beside her, "but it can wait. I know you need to sleep."

She turned the other way, letting him cuddle her back. He slid his arm around her waist and buried his face in her hair, inhaling as if her scent comforted him. "I'm sorry for what I said to you this afternoon," she whispered, her voice raspy.

"Don't worry about it. You were upset."

"I didn't mean it."

He kissed her shoulder, silent.

"When I saw you in the hospital bed, I thought you were hurt. I'd just buried my sister. It was too much for me to handle."

"I'm sorry I couldn't call. I wish I'd been there for you."

She covered his hand with hers, stroking his knuckles. "I felt so alone at the funeral, and I was so angry with Moreno. I wanted to blame someone for my sister's death. But I know it wasn't your fault."

"It wasn't your fault, either."

Tears filled her eyes. "I'm glad you came after me."

"Always," he said simply.

Kari didn't want to think about gunfire or explosions. She was too traumatized to process what had happened earlier. Her heart was still broken from her sister's death, her feelings too complicated to sort through.

"None of the men hurt you?" he asked.

She shook her head. There was no reason to tell him about the punch in the stomach. He would only get upset.

He pressed his lips to her hair. "I know you told the

doctor they didn't touch you, but I wanted to make sure."

Letting her eyes drift shut, she stroked his arm, enjoying his strength and protectiveness. There was more to say, but her throat was tender, and words didn't seem important right now. She was safe, and he was here, and everything was okay.

26

Maria waited for Ian, her stomach fluttering with anticipation.

She'd leapt at the chance to switch rooms. Kari needed to work things out with Adam, and Maria wanted to be with Ian. She doubted she'd be able to return to the United States, so this might be her last opportunity to spend time with him.

When he came out of the bathroom, a towel slung low on his hips, he did a double take, surprised to see her. His hair was damp and still a little shaggy, but his face was clean-shaven. Although Maria had seen him shirtless before, she gave his chest a close study.

Very nice.

"What are you doing here?"

She lifted her gaze to meet his. "Adam asked to stay with Kari."

He didn't seem bothered by his friend's tricky maneuver or alarmed by Maria's presence. The rooms were spacious, with two large beds in each, so he could keep his distance if he wanted to.

"Have you eaten?"

She nodded.

"I'd offer you some clothes, but I don't have any."

"I see that," she said, her eyes drifting south again. "I'm comfortable in this." The towel she was wearing felt too brief. She wished she had a nightgown.

While she rose to get a drink of water from the bathroom, he limped over to the bed, sitting down and shoving a couple of pillows behind his head.

"Can I sleep with you?" she asked, taking a sip from her cup.

"Next to me, you mean?"

"In your bed."

He examined the fluffy bath towel, which covered her from chest to mid-thigh. "Sure."

Smiling, she set her glass on the nightstand and grabbed a pillow from the other bed, settling in beside him. It felt good to be clean. "Thank you for resuscitating me," she said, resting her head on his shoulder.

"I didn't resuscitate you. You never stopped breathing."

"I mean saving me. I do not know the right word."

"Rescue," he supplied. "But Kari did most of the work. She got you up the stairs and almost out the door."

"She said she wouldn't leave me," Maria remembered, her eyes becoming misty. "She is a good friend."

He murmured a vague agreement, staring at her bare legs.

"Adam is a good friend to you?"

"Uh . . . yeah. We've known each other forever."

"Is he in love with Kari?"

"I think so."

Maria hoped they would be happy together. "I will miss her."

When he straightened in surprise, she was forced to lift her head off his shoulder. "What do you mean?" he asked. "Where are you going?"

"Home."

"Why?"

She frowned at him. "Because I'm illegal."

"That didn't stop you before."

"I also haven't seen my family in four years." She decided not to mention her third reason for staying in Mexico: Armando's letter. Ian might be scruffy-looking, but he was still some kind of cop. "I want to visit them."

He examined her face for a long moment, his expression grave. "You don't have to be illegal, Maria."

She tilted her head to one side, curious.

"You could marry me."

Maria wondered if her English had failed her again. Surely he hadn't just asked her to marry him. "What?"

A flush crept up his neck and his eyes blazed with intensity, more green than brown. But he didn't swallow his offer. "Marry me."

"As in husband and wife?" she asked, pointing at the bed underneath them.

He nodded once, his mouth tense. Without the unruly beard, his face appeared twice as angular, all smooth and chiseled. Her fingers itched to touch the skin along his jawline. "It can be in name only."

"What does that mean?"

He didn't beat around the bush. "No sex."

"No sex?" she repeated, her voice rising. "Why would you want that?"

He laughed, massaging the bridge of his nose. "I wouldn't."

Maria blinked a few times, not following. Then everything became clear and her stomach filled with dread. He was asking her to marry him out of a sense of obligation. He would make her a citizen and not even demand that she have sex with him. It wasn't an offer but a sacrifice.

"No," she said, shaking her head. She wouldn't get married for a green card or because she was desperate. They would both regret it. Especially when he found a woman he truly wanted to be with. "You're very kind, but no."

Ian didn't appear relieved. He flinched at the word *kind* and clenched his jaw, acknowledging her refusal without speaking.

Uh-oh. She'd caused insult by turning him down too quickly. "I'm sorry."

"It's okay, Maria. Forget about it."

She couldn't bear to end the night this way, with his ego bruised and her heart aching. Lifting her hand to his face, she touched his cheek, feeling the freshly shaved skin beneath her fingertips. His eyes met hers, guarded. "I can't marry you for the wrong reasons. And if I did, I would not want you in name only."

He seemed to understand what she was getting at. His gaze dropped to her lips, which were just inches from his.

Maria felt warmth spread through her belly, the same tingling excitement she'd experienced at the Hotel del Oro. Only now she was totally awake and aware of what was happening between them.

She brushed her mouth over his, light as a butterfly.

He moistened his lips, as if tasting her on them, and she followed suit, licking where he'd licked. Then she studied her handiwork. His mouth was wet from her tongue and that looked sexy to her. She wondered if her mouth looked sexy to him. He was staring at it, enthralled.

She touched her lips to his again and he reacted instantly, lifting his hand to her hair and crushing his mouth over hers. He thrust his tongue inside, plunging between her parted lips. The kiss was intimate, possessive, erotic.

Maria twined her arms around his neck, giddy with pleasure. His fingers tightened in her hair and his arousal swelled against her hip, persistent.

That part of him concerned her. She knew that men were dangerous in this state. Although she felt safe with Ian, she didn't want to whip him into a frenzy. Her towel slipped down, pooling around her waist. When he cupped her small breast, groaning as if her meager endowments were male fantasy material, she knew he'd gone off the deep end.

"Ian," she murmured, breaking the kiss.

He rubbed his thumb over her hard nipple in a slow circle.

She moaned, arching her spine. Then she realized that she was squirming against his erection, playing with fire. When he tried to lower his mouth to her breast, she dug her fingernails into his forearm. "Wait."

His eyes met hers, still smoldering with intensity. He was breathing heavily, his body hard and ready. But he didn't seem angry or displeased. As promised, he could stop anytime, controlling his desire.

That, as much as his heroic actions earlier and the

strong emotional bond they'd created, made her want to continue.

"I'm sorry," he said, his throat working. "Those bastards raped you, didn't they?"

"No. Moreno told them not to touch me."

The concern on his face didn't clear, but it eased considerably. "You hit your head."

"It doesn't hurt anymore. I'm fine."

His gaze dropped to her exposed breasts. They swelled at his attention, the dusky nipples puckered. He moistened his lips, distracted.

Maria didn't know whether to cover up or disrobe completely. "I've never done this before."

"Done what?"

"Been with a man. By choice."

Understanding dawned. "Do you want to?"

"Yes, but I can't."

"Why not?"

"I'm afraid."

"Of what? Me hurting you?"

"No," she said, confused. He would never harm her on purpose. "I don't like to feel . . . *atrapada*."

"Trapped, as in held down underneath me?"

She nodded.

His lips curved into a smile. "It doesn't have to be that way, Maria."

"No?"

"You can be on top."

"No," she said, her cheeks burning.

He chuckled at her shyness. "We don't have to do anything that makes you uncomfortable. I'd be happy just to kiss you."

"Really?"

"Yes."

She cast a worried glance at his lap. His erection strained against the damp towel, its outline intimidating.

"I can't make that go away," he said ruefully. "You're half naked and so beautiful I can't stand it."

Tears filled her eyes. Taking a deep breath, she pushed aside her own towel, revealing herself completely.

He stared at her breasts, her belly, the dark triangle between her legs. "Jesus," he said, swallowing hard.

"Is this okay? You can stay calm?"

He tore his gaze away from her. "I can promise that I won't put anything inside you unless you want me to. But I can't control my hard-on, and I'm extremely excited right now. I could come just looking at you."

A thrill raced along her spine. She almost didn't recognize the unique sensation for what it was: power.

Ian had put the reins in her hands. They could take this as far as she wanted. If she told him to hold still while she trailed kisses all over his beautiful chest, he wouldn't complain. He would like it. He would let her do it.

Heat tingled between her legs and gooseflesh broke out over her skin. Her nipples, already tight beads, seemed to quiver in anticipation. She slipped her arms around his neck and pressed her breasts to his chest, careful not to bump against the bandage on his thigh. He splayed his hands across her back, stroking her sides.

With a breathy little moan, she lowered her mouth to his.

This kiss was even more exciting than their first, probably because she was naked. He also let her control the depth. She threaded her fingers through his hair and drew his tongue into her mouth, sucking gently. Although he was an active participant, kissing her passionately and caressing her bare skin, she had the upper hand.

Writhing against him, she grasped his wrist, bringing his palm to her breast. He squeezed her soft flesh, brushing his thumb over the sensitive tip.

She arched into his touch, wanting more.

When he dipped his head again, she didn't stop him. She watched as he flicked his tongue over one taut nipple, then the other.

"Ay Dios, que rico," she moaned, amazed that her small breasts could give either of them this much pleasure. Every rasp of his tongue made her sex pulse with awareness. She squirmed against him, trying to ease the ache.

He splayed his palm over her belly, feeling it quiver.

"Please," she said, pushing his hand lower.

Groaning, he traced the cleft of her sex with his fingertips, finding her moisture. She spread her legs wide, whimpering as he touched her. True to his promise, he didn't dip his fingers inside. He merely circled her opening, whispering in her ear about how much he wanted to taste her. When he drew her earlobe between his teeth and strummed her sweet spot with his fingertips, she exploded in ecstasy.

"God," he said, gritting his teeth.

Before she could catch her breath, he tugged her hand toward his lap, closing it around his erection. He watched her with lust-dark eyes, helping her stroke him up and down. She marveled at the steely softness, the creamy bead at the tip. His shaft jerked in her hand and he let out a hoarse cry, spilling himself across her stomach.

When he was finished, she released him and he fell back on the bed, gasping for breath. She looked from her hand to his groin in amazement, pleased with her performance. He'd clearly enjoyed that. So had she.

He cleaned her tummy with a wet towel and climbed under the sheets, gathering her into his arms. A few seconds later, she burst into tears.

"I'm sorry," he said, as if he'd done something wrong.

She was too choked up to tell him that they'd just shared the sweetest, most intimate experience of her life. He'd made her incredibly happy. But she was also sad, because she knew they couldn't be together again.

Instead of trying to explain it, she curled up in his arms and clung to him, savoring their last embrace.

27

Adam woke just before dawn.

Kari was a warm, soft weight beside him. He'd stayed up late, watching her sleep. Aching for her.

Although he knew he shouldn't touch her, he couldn't stop fantasizing about it. Her naked bottom was inches from his lap, torturing him. He wasn't supposed to engage in any "vigorous activity" because of his injury. More important, *she* was hurt. She'd lost her sister, gotten kidnapped, and almost died in a burning building.

He wanted to show her that he was serious about their relationship by exercising control. Kari was special to him, not just a temporary bed partner. He cared more about her emotional needs than about his physical discomfort.

But she looked so sexy in his T-shirt. During the night, the hem had ridden up in the back, revealing her shapely curves.

Smothering a groan, he tore his gaze away. His cock didn't have any lofty ideals about treating Kari with respect. It was straining at the front of his shorts, demanding attention. Thanks to his sore ribs, he'd had no release all week.

After a few more moments, she stirred. Pushing her hair off her forehead, she reached for the water on her nightstand, taking a drink. "Want some?" she asked, gesturing with the glass.

He accepted the water, trying to stay cool.

She set the glass aside when he was finished drinking and snuggled against him, her bare bottom brushing his distended fly. He clenched his teeth, praying for strength. She made a humming sound and pressed closer, teasing him.

"Make love to me," she said, lifting his hand to her breast. As he cupped her soft flesh, her nipple pebbled in his palm.

He wanted to say no but his body wouldn't let him. She sat up and tugged the T-shirt over her head, her full breasts jiggling from the motion. His erection throbbed at the sight of her. She twined her arms around his neck, touching her lips to his jaw. "Please, Adam," she said. "Chase the nightmares away."

Although he tried to kiss her chastely, she wouldn't have it. Smoothing her palms over his chest, she dug her fingernails into his pecs and panted against his mouth, flicking her tongue against his.

"Baby, wait," he said, gripping her upper arms.

She slid her hand into his shorts, undeterred. "I want your cock."

"Christ," he muttered, inhaling a sharp breath as she stroked him. "You have a dirty mouth."

Murmuring her agreement, she pushed his shorts aside and lowered her head, enveloping him with that dirty, sexy mouth. His hand rose, as if by its own volition, cupping the nape of her neck to guide her. Her wet lips parted, stretching around his shaft. She moaned with pleasure, her eyes half-lidded, mouth full.

He'd never felt anything better, nothing, ever. He threaded his hand through her hair, directing her motions. Her cheeks hollowed as she took him deeper. His balls drew up tight, ready to explode.

Although he longed for her to finish, he couldn't let it end this way. He wanted to show her some tenderness and win her heart.

"Stop," he rasped, tugging her head up.

"Am I hurting your ribs?"

"Yes," he lied.

She was perplexed. "What can we do, if not that?"

His eyes drifted south, lingering between her thighs. "Lay back, *bella*."

Complying easily, she reclined against the pillows. Her hair was mussed, her mouth swollen and damp. Wearing nothing but his knee-high sweat socks, she looked like a locker room pinup.

"Spread your legs."

Her eyes widened at the command but she followed it, parting her sleek thighs for him. Above the lips of her sex, she had a tawny triangle of closely cropped hair. Below, she was bare, glistening. Beautiful.

He wanted to lick every inch of her. "*Quiero comerte.*"

She moaned, throwing her head back. Her hand slid down her stomach, making a V with her fingers.

"You're so delicious," he said in Spanish, lowering his mouth to her. She tasted sweet, like tangy honey, and she smelled like a woman should, earthy and fragrant and female. He drew his tongue through her slippery folds, loving the way she squirmed against his face. When he settled his mouth on her clit, sucking gently, she bucked her hips, begging to come. He eased back, surprised by her eager mewling. His own control had ebbed away. He was so hard, he might go off against the sheets.

But he wanted to feel that hot little pussy around him, see it taking every inch of his cock. "I need to be inside you."

Her eyes flew open. "I thought you couldn't."

"Turn over."

She rolled onto her side, which was good enough. He hooked his arm under her knee and took his cock in his hand, entering her from behind. As he slipped the head of his penis between the lips of her sex, rubbing it back and forth, a terrible thought occurred to him. "I'm not wearing a condom."

"Don't stop," she panted. "It feels so good."

Even in this position, which was fairly comfortable, he couldn't thrust hard without exacerbating his injury. So he moved with short strokes, sliding in and out of her slick heat, dying from the need to go deeper.

"Oh God," she said, gripping his forearm.

He cupped her breasts roughly, pinching each stiff nipple while she groaned. She was fantastically wet, and he was hard as iron. He smoothed his hand down her belly, finding the taut nub of her clit. With his mouth on the nape of her neck, he bit down gently and stroked her to completion. She cried out his name and shattered in his arms, her inner muscles clenching around him, her hips jerking against his.

Adam couldn't hold back a second longer. Ignoring the twinge in his side, he urged her onto her hands and knees and thrust forward, penetrating her all the way to the hilt. She gasped and moaned and shuddered, still coming. He could feel the tremors of her orgasm as he pumped mindlessly, driving deep.

At the last possible moment, he pulled out, pushing her down on her belly. Cock jerking in his hand, he came all over her quivering buttocks, painting her passion-flushed skin with ribbons of semen.

He collapsed next to her, hoping he hadn't just fucked himself to death. His ribs ached like he'd been shot again.

"Are you okay?" she murmured, her voice muffled by pillows.

"Yeah," he said, playing it off. "Fine."

He had the vague notion that he should get a towel or some tissues for her, but he simply could not move. While he lay there on his stomach, taking shallow breaths, she rose from the bed. He heard water running in the bathroom. When she returned, crawling across the mattress, he tried to relax his face.

Unsuccessfully.

"You're hurt," she accused.

"It was worth it."

He thought about apologizing for his lack of finesse. She'd wanted him that way, and it was difficult to regret something that felt so goddamned good, but he wished he'd touched her a little more lovingly.

"I should have used a condom," he said, disturbed by his negligence.

"Since I begged you to continue, I deserve at least half the blame."

They would have to disagree on that point. Adam had always considered protection a man's job.

She stretched out beside him, tucking one arm behind her head. "Are you sure your injury isn't serious?"

"Of course. It's an annoyance, nothing more."

"I don't know what I would do if you got shot again."

"It's unlikely," he said, touched by her concern.

"It was reckless of you to chase after Moreno."

Adam didn't say anything. Yesterday afternoon she'd criticized him for being too soft. That had been a blow to his male ego and it still smarted.

"I'm glad you were wearing a bulletproof vest."

"So am I," he replied.

"Did it hurt terribly?"

"It didn't feel good."

She traced the bruise on his back with her fingertips, her expression troubled. "I don't want to go to your funeral, Adam. I just buried my sister. I can't survive that kind of pain again."

He knew exactly what she meant. His fear of loss had prevented him from entering committed relationships for years. He'd built a wall around himself, an emotional border. Somehow Kari had slipped past his defenses.

And now that she was inside, he wanted to keep her there.

Adam couldn't leave this room without telling her how he felt. Experience had taught him that his world could collapse in a flash. He might not get another chance to say these words. "Last night, I almost went crazy worrying about you," he said, moving onto his side. "I thought Pena was going to kill you. I was terrified that you were going to die inside that house."

Her eyes became clouded. "If you hadn't carried me out, I would have."

"When you started breathing again, I felt like I'd won the lottery. It was the single greatest moment of my life."

She glanced away, swallowing.

"You mean the world to me, Kari. I'd run into a dozen burning buildings for you, take a hundred bullets, walk through a thousand fires. There's nothing I wouldn't do for you." He cupped her chin in his hand, forcing her to meet his gaze. "I love you."

Kari wasn't ready to hear that.

The last thing she expected from Adam was undying devotion. He'd given her a great time in bed, but he wasn't her boyfriend. This confession was premature. They'd never even gone out on a real date.

Trying not to panic, she scrambled out of bed, putting his T-shirt back on. Maybe she'd heard him wrong. He looked calm and comfortable, resting against the pillows with his weight braced on one elbow. "What did you say?"

"I love you," he repeated easily.

"You can't."

He arched a brow. "Why not?"

Moistening her lips, she racked her brain for a few good reasons. Maybe she'd encouraged this revelation by mooning over his injury. It wasn't as though she didn't return his feelings. She just wasn't prepared to deal with them yet.

"I'm emotionally disturbed," she said.

"You're grieving."

"I—I smuggled Maria over the border."

He rubbed a hand over his face, chuckling. "I know. I won't tell anyone."

She stared at him in astonishment, her heart racing. How could he think this would work? They'd gotten off to a shaky start. He'd lied to her about his mother. Their attraction was based on danger, escape, and illicit thrills.

A drug lord had brought them together. That didn't bode well.

Kari also hadn't even started to process her sister's death. It didn't feel right to have this bubbly sensation in the pit of her stomach less than a week after Sasha died. At this point, sorrow was the only acceptable emotion.

Besides, she and Adam didn't have a solid foundation for a relationship. They'd been through a series of traumatic ordeals and enjoyed a few rounds of hot, ill-advised sex. This was not the stuff happily-ever-afters were made of.

"You don't have to say anything," he said, leaning back against the pillows. "It's not an interrogation."

"I have the right to remain silent?"

He linked his hands behind his head, sighing. Her eyes were drawn to his bulging biceps, the tufts of hair under his arms, and the etched musculature of his smooth, dark chest. "I didn't mean to put you on the spot."

"Let's back up a few steps," she said, disconcerted. "We just had unprotected sex. Maybe we need to talk about . . . diseases."

There. If that didn't kill the mood, nothing would.

A muscle in his jaw flexed. "I'm safe. I haven't been with anyone but you since my last checkup."

"Same goes for me."

"What about birth control? Pulling out is hardly fool-proof."

Heat rose to her cheeks. Not only had she encouraged

him to enter her au naturel, she distinctly remembered feeling a twinge of disappointment when he withdrew. Momentary insanity? "It's the wrong time of month," she said, counting the days of her cycle. "The possibility is very low."

He glanced down to her flat stomach, unconvinced but not particularly alarmed. "Okay."

She wondered what they would do if she got pregnant. A strange mix of dismay and longing washed over her, confusing her further. Although she wanted a family someday, it was a huge responsibility, not to be entered upon lightly.

And yet, Adam's steady gaze and calm manner felt reassuring. He wanted to see where this was going. He wasn't going to abandon her. Maybe she should relax her guard and trust him to stay the course.

Before she could decide what to say, someone knocked at the door. "Kari?"

It was Maria.

Adam sighed, staring up at the ceiling. Kari tugged down the hem of his T-shirt and went to the door, opening it partway. Maria was standing there in a white bathrobe, her feet bare, hair mussed. "I need to talk to you."

"In here?"

"No, outside. Bring your purse."

Kari nodded and closed the door, saying she'd be ready in a minute.

"Do you want me to go back to Ian's room?" Adam asked.

"No," she said, grabbing his shorts from the bed and slipping them on. She had to tighten the drawstring waistband so they wouldn't fall off. "We're going down to the lobby for coffee," she said, picking up her purse.

On impulse, she leaned in to kiss him goodbye. He returned the kiss with relish, cupping the back of her head to prolong the moment. But when she pulled away, he let her go. "I meant what I said," he murmured, meeting her eyes.

Her throat tightened. "I know."

When she opened the door again, Maria glanced inside, getting an eyeful of Adam. With his chest bare and the sheet riding low on his hips, he made an alluring picture.

Blushing, Kari pulled the door shut and they walked down the hall together. "Did you have a good time with Ian?"

Her expression was secretive and a little sad. "Yes."

"What happened?"

"He kissed me," she admitted.

She smiled at Maria's demure confession.

"How was your night with Adam?"

"It was . . . nice."

Her nose wrinkled. "Nice?"

"Okay, it was fantastic," she said, her emotions in turmoil. Maybe this was what she deserved for jumping into bed with him too soon. She'd wanted mindless orgasms and he'd given her complex feelings.

"What's wrong with that?"

"I guess I feel guilty. My sister is dead."

"But you are not."

She nodded, aware that Sasha wouldn't have begrudged anyone a good time. Her sister had been unabashedly hedonistic. She'd have pushed Kari into Adam's arms and told her to wear him out.

As they stepped inside the elevator, Maria said, "I need you to do me a favor."

"Anything," she said, setting her troubles with Adam aside.

"I left money in a drawer at your house. Can you send it to me?"

"What do you mean? Send it where?"

"I'm going home."

The elevator doors opened before Kari was ready. She entered the quiet lobby, her thoughts spinning.

"I want to see my family," Maria explained. "And I have to deliver a letter."

"To who?"

She pulled a crumpled envelope from her robe pocket. Its surface was stained with dried blood. "Armando asked me to give this to his daughter."

"You can't put a stamp on it?"

"Her school is near my hometown. It's no trouble."

"It's no trouble? He's a psychopath!"

She put the letter back in her pocket. "When Chuy pointed the gun at me, Armando stepped between us. He saved my life."

Kari studied her friend's serene face and felt like bursting into tears. She didn't want Maria to get mixed up in another dangerous situation. Not only that, she couldn't bear to lose her again. "Please don't go, Maria."

Her eyes softened with sympathy. "I'm sorry. I can't stay."

"Yes, you can. I'll sneak you across the border."

She took Kari by the hand. "I need to see my mother," she said, her voice trembling. "Do you understand?"

Of course she understood. Kari's mother had been

gone almost twenty years, and she still missed her. She would always miss her.

Maria had left home at a young age. She'd suffered a terrible experience trying to cross the border the first time. Over the past few days she'd witnessed several violent deaths and been trapped in a dark basement.

Anyone in her state of mind would want her mother.

So Kari pulled herself together, holding the tears at bay. "What can I do to help?"

Maria hugged her tight. "I love you, Kari."

They visited the hotel gift shop, where Kari bought them each a new outfit. Maria chose a sleeveless top and a basic black skirt with ballet flats. Kari found an aqua tank dress and a pair of beige sandals. Outside the hotel, she made a withdrawal from the ATM machine, giving Maria a wad of cash.

"Don't tell Ian for a few hours," she begged.

"You didn't say goodbye to him?"

"I could not bring myself to."

"Will you come back?" Kari asked.

Maria's eyes narrowed with determination. "I promise I will try."

"Call me, okay? I can help you get a visa. There will always be a place for you at my house, and at Zócalo."

Her mouth trembled. "Thank you."

Kari embraced her one last time. They clung together, each not wanting to let the other go. Then Maria jerked away, as if too choked up to stay another second. She hurried across the street, tears streaming down her face.

Kari watched her friend's dark head disappear into the crowd, feeling like she'd lost another sister.

28

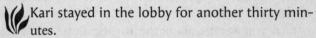Kari stayed in the lobby for another thirty min-
utes.

Reluctant to return to the hotel room, she sipped coffee and nibbled on a complimentary breakfast pastry.
She wasn't certain she'd done the right thing by helping
Maria. The police had asked them all to stay put. Adam
wouldn't be happy. She didn't know Ian very well, but
she'd seen the way he looked at Maria, and she could
imagine his reaction. The woman he cared about had
snuck away from his bed like a thief in the night. He'd
take it personally.

Palms sweaty, she stepped into the elevator, going up.
She wasn't ready to face her relationship issues with
Adam, either. She wanted to go home, crawl into bed,
and sleep for another twenty-four hours.

The hotel doors locked automatically and she didn't
have a key card, so she couldn't slip back into the room
without waking him. He answered her knock, a sheet
wrapped around his waist, his thick black hair disheveled.

Her stomach fluttered with unease.

"Nice dress," he said, noticing her new outfit.

"Thanks. I bought something for Maria, too." She handed him his workout clothes, watching while he put them on.

"Ian called to ask where she was."

"Did you want coffee? I forgot to bring you a cup."

"I'll get one on the way out," he said, putting on his shoes.

"Are we leaving?"

"Yeah. The Tijuana police are meeting us at the port. I don't want to talk to them without my superiors there."

He seemed tense, as if he wasn't looking forward to reliving the ordeal.

"Are you worried about the investigation?" she asked, surprised. "You and Ian were heroes yesterday. Surely they'll believe your version of events."

"My credibility isn't the issue."

"What is?"

He dragged a hand through his hair, trying to tame it. "I abandoned my post at the hospital, acted outside my jurisdiction, and took on a crew of top-tier cartel members without backup. Not only did I fail to notify the Mexican authorities, I didn't even contact my own department." Shoving their dirty clothes into a plastic bag, he leveled with her. "Vigilantism is illegal, Kari. Cops get fired for it."

"Oh," she said, feeling small. "Is there anything I can do?"

"You can tell the truth. Maria, too."

She sat down on the bed, biting the edge of her fist. This was bad.

"Ian was released from duty for entering a gunfight at the Hotel del Oro, so I'm expecting the worst."

"He got fired?"

"From the DEA. He might be able to work for another federal agency, but I don't know. Everything is up in the air right now."

"That's awful," she said, her heart pounding with anxiety.

A knock on the door interrupted their conversation. Adam went to answer it, letting Ian inside. "Is Maria here?"

"No," Adam said, frowning.

"Where is she?"

Kari swallowed hard, looking back and forth between them. "She left."

Ian's eyes darkened. "Where did she go?"

"Home," she said, taking the address from her purse. "I gave her money for a bus ticket."

He snatched the scrap of paper from her hand. "How long ago?"

"Less than an hour."

Although the station was only a few blocks away, Ian's chances of catching up with her there were slim. Mexico's public transit system was popular and reliable. Buses to the capital left every thirty minutes.

Kari twisted her hands in her lap. "There's something else I should tell you."

"What?"

"I think she's going to deliver a letter for Armando first. She had an envelope addressed to his daughter's school. She said she promised to help him because he stepped in when Chuy tried to shoot her."

"Which school?" Ian demanded. "Did you see the address?"

"No," she said, tears filling her eyes. "I'm sorry. She mentioned that it was near her hometown."

He shoved the paper in his pocket. "How much money did you give her?"

"Two hundred dollars."

"Do you have any idea how much danger she's in?"

Kari shook her head, mute.

Cursing under his breath, he paced the room. "Moreno's drug cartel is finished. Everyone associated with them is a target. Men will be gunning for Armando, maybe even using his daughter to get to him."

She felt the blood drain from her face. "I didn't think of that."

"You didn't think at all!"

"Hey," Adam warned, placing a hand on his shoulder. "Watch it."

"Get the fuck off me," Ian muttered, shoving him away.

"You can't go after her right now," Adam pointed out. "We have to be at the port in twenty minutes."

"Yeah, I can't wait to be told that I'll never work in law enforcement again."

"They won't go that far, Ian. You could get reinstated on border patrol. CBP isn't as strict as DEA—"

"Fuck CBP," he said, storming from the room. "And fuck you."

Adam gave Kari an apologetic look and followed him out the door. Although Ian wanted to go after Maria, he agreed to accompany them to the border for Adam's sake. Ian couldn't save his own career, but he could stand by his best friend.

Kari felt sick about her mistake. She'd never imagined that Maria's disappearing act would cause this much trouble. She also hadn't realized that Adam might lose his job. Last night she'd been kidding herself.

Everything was *not* okay.

In the harsh light of day, reality set in. They still had to deal with injuries, and emotions, and consequences. Her sister was dead. Maria was gone. Kari couldn't handle any more upheaval.

As soon as they reached the San Ysidro port of entry, she was separated from Adam and Ian for questioning. Mexican police interviewed her extensively. A CBP officer and an ICE agent took a detailed statement.

After what seemed like hours, she was released from custody. One of the police officers brought her rental car to the detainment area. Exhausted, she got behind the wheel and drove around aimlessly, reluctant to go home.

She couldn't face the flowers, the aftermath, the emptiness.

Instead of heading back to Bonita, she took the dusty trail to Border Field State Park. Parking near the monument, she strolled down to the beach, wind whipping at her skirt. The wall that separated the United States from Mexico ended here, extending a hundred feet into the sea. Slats of treated wood rose from the water like jagged teeth.

Kari stared at the waves crashing against the fence, wondering what to do about Adam.

Imagining a life without him wrenched her heart in two.

The interrogation process was even worse than Adam had anticipated.

They'd revisited the crime scene for a walk-through

and found out that Moreno's body hadn't been recovered. Either his bones were still buried in the smoldering ash or someone had taken his charred remains.

This strange discrepancy, paired with Maria's very inconvenient disappearance, cast a shadow of doubt on their version of events. It was difficult for Adam to defend his actions; he'd worked with Moreno during the takedown. His boss, Pettigrew, grew more taciturn as the afternoon progressed.

At the end of the day, Adam and Ian were led to Pettigrew's office and seated across from him. Another intimidating figure, ICE Special Agent in Charge Mark LaGuardia, accompanied them.

Drenched in sweat, Adam waited for the ax to fall.

"The Mexican police are pissed off, and rightfully so," Pettigrew began. "Rambo officers make everyone look incompetent. There's no way either of you can take credit for what went down in the shootout."

Adam exchanged a hopeful glance with Ian. "We'd prefer that, sir."

"I don't give a fuck what you prefer, Cortez. I'm just telling you how it's going to be. You two were never there. An unknown assassin, probably someone within the organization, executed the attack. Is that clear?"

They both nodded, relieved. This way, no disgruntled family members would be coming after them for revenge.

"I can't keep you in the lanes," Pettigrew said, looking at Adam.

He understood the implication. If he couldn't do inspections in the vehicle or pedestrian lanes, he'd be useless at San Ysidro. Dead weight.

Pettigrew's mouth tightened in anger. "The only reason I didn't fire you on Tuesday was because your ragtag op shook up the Moreno cartel and led to several key arrests. But I can't overlook the fact that you involved a citizen without my knowledge, and failed to disclose your relationship with her."

"I'm sorry, sir."

"I was going to demote you to a lower ranking and put you on administrative leave. That option is no longer on the table. You went too far off the reservation to come back. There's no way I can let this one slide."

Adam had to force himself not to shift in his seat or look away.

"I don't need cocky hotshots in my department, Cortez. I want levelheaded soldiers who know when to fall in line."

"I can do that, sir."

"All evidence points to the contrary."

"I love my job," he said from between clenched teeth.

"I know you do, son. But you don't belong in CBP and you haven't for a long time."

Adam stared at Pettigrew in silence, sensing Ian's frustration beside him. Now they were both unemployed.

Pettigrew addressed Ian with his next statement. "I spoke with Special Agent Michelson about your past performance. He said you were one of the most dedicated agents he'd ever worked with."

"Thank you, sir," Ian said.

He drummed his fingertips on the surface of his desk, looking back and forth between them. "Because you both did well in the academy and have exemplary records otherwise, ICE has offered to take you on."

Ian straightened at the unexpected news. Adam glanced at Special Agent in Charge LaGuardia, who inclined his head. Working for ICE was no demotion. The division handled most of the border-related drug arrests and smuggling investigations.

They were top-notch.

"When your unpaid leave is over, Cortez, there's an entry-level opening for you on the task force in Otay Mesa," Pettigrew continued. "If you do well, you might be able to transfer back to San Ysidro. As an investigator, not an armed guard."

"I'm grateful for the opportunity," Adam said.

"You should be." Pettigrew turned to Ian. "ICE has a unique assignment for you."

"On the line?"

"No, across it," LaGuardia said, taking over. "Are you familiar with the International Affairs division?"

"Of course," Ian said, his brows lifting. DEA handled undercover operations within the United States, but ICE was responsible for those types of investigations in foreign countries, especially border areas.

"We need an ICE attaché to go after a fugitive in Mexico."

"Why isn't USMS on it?" Ian asked.

"Normally a deputy marshal would be called to duty, but because the fugitive is a cartel member involved in smuggling operations, it falls under our jurisdiction. You're being offered first crack at the case because of your experience with the target." LaGuardia passed him a photo of the wanted criminal.

"Armando Villarreal?"

Pettigrew made a grunting noise. "We took a chance on that phony news story and it came back to bite us in the ass."

"What do you mean?"

LaGuardia handed Ian another photo. A pretty brunette in a navy graduation gown smiled brightly, holding her diploma. "This is Caitlyn Weiss. She's a relief vet at La Canada Pet Clinic, near the Hotel del Oro. No one has seen her since Tuesday."

"When was she reported missing?"

"This morning. She wasn't scheduled to work again until today."

"Signs of a struggle?"

"Not that anyone noticed. Blood is a common sight in an animal hospital. Her surgeries and appointments were finished by noon, so the other employees assumed she went home while they were at lunch."

"And you think Armando took her?"

"We have footage of her driving across the border on Tuesday afternoon. There's a dark-haired man in the passenger seat."

Ian gave back the photos, satisfied. "What do you want me to do?"

"Find them."

"Can I leave now?"

LaGuardia glanced at Pettigrew, smiling wryly. "You've got a couple of live ones here."

Pettigrew's response wasn't as warm. "If either of you boys strays from procedure again, you won't have to worry about being transferred to another department. The only place I'll recommend after this is the brig."

When the meeting was over, they stood, shaking hands across the table. Adam was confident that he could keep himself in line as long as Kari stayed safe.

Ian, he wasn't so sure about.

29

Kari went home and slept for twelve hours straight.

On Sunday morning, she wrote thank-you notes to everyone who'd attended Sasha's funeral. The food and flowers were given to a local soup kitchen. On impulse, she made arrangements for her van to be repainted and donated to charity. Zócalo was doing well enough now that she could afford to have her purchases shipped directly to the store. Her weekly trips to Mexico would probably trickle down to once a month, if that.

She loved the crafts and the culture, but she wasn't looking forward to visiting Tijuana anytime soon. The thought of waiting in the lanes at San Ysidro made her stomach ache. She would always associate the border crossing with death.

That afternoon, Adam showed up on her doorstep, holding a simple bouquet of violets. For Sasha, he explained.

Her heart melted at the sight.

She accompanied him to the cemetery, her face crumpling as he placed the flowers on her sister's grave. He held her for a long time afterward, stroking her back while she cried. When her tears abated, she rearranged the bouquets and gathered up fallen petals. Adam accepted her obsessive-compulsive tidiness without complaint.

He also stayed by her side for the next three days.

His bruised ribs were far more serious than her minor scrapes, but he waited on her hand and foot. As much as Kari hated to admit it, she was glad for his help. The psychological trauma of her kidnapping and assault, paired with the loss of her sister, had really taken its toll. She needed the downtime. She needed *him*.

They took long walks together, shared quiet meals, and spent more than a few hours in her bed. Although they kissed and cuddled, they didn't make love, choosing to let the wounds heal instead. Mostly they just slept.

Adam told her about the job offer with ICE, admitting that the new position would be just as dangerous as his current one, if not more so. She was concerned for his welfare but appreciated his honesty. He didn't use the L-word again or press her about their relationship. The days drifted by in a dreamlike haze.

About a week after Sasha's death, she decided to go back to work. Adam tried to talk her out of it, but she was determined to return to her regular routine. He made her a light breakfast and kissed her goodbye.

"I've been thinking," he said before he left.

"Have you?"

"We've been at your house for several days."

She leaned her elbows against the kitchen countertop. "This is true."

"Would you like to stay at my place tonight?"

Pushing away from the counter, she reached for her coffee mug instead of answering.

He pressed on, undeterred. "Why don't you move in with me?"

Kari felt a sharp tug of longing in the middle of her chest. She wanted to say yes, even though it was too soon, and he'd made the offer for the wrong reasons. "Are you asking because you want to keep me safe?"

His steady gaze met hers. "No. I'm asking because I'm in love with you, and I want you in my bed every night."

She filled her mug, flushing with a mixture of pleasure and discomfort. "Adam, I like being independent. I can take care of myself."

He remained unyielding. "I want to take care of you."

"And when you go back to work?"

"I have another month off."

"Yes, but after that I'll be unattended. You should get used to the idea."

A crease formed between his brows. Clearly, he didn't agree.

She set aside her coffee and twined her arms around his neck, soothing the sting of her words with another kiss. "Let's make a deal. I'll sleep at your place tonight if you'll let me take care of *you*."

His throat worked as he swallowed.

"Are you up to it?"

"Yes," he said, though the swelling against her stomach was proof enough.

"Okay then." She nipped at his lower lip, very gently, and stepped back. "I'll see you later."

Adam gave her a dark look, aware that he'd been bamboozled. He must have decided that the arrangement suited him well enough, because he dropped the subject and headed to the door. "Don't work too hard."

"I won't," she lied.

"Call me at lunchtime."

She nodded dutifully.

He paused, as though he wanted to say something else. Then, with an almost imperceptible shake of his head, he left.

As soon as he was out the door, she regretted her abrupt dismissal of his offer. Her thoughts were troubled as she drove to work and parked her rental car behind the building. Instead of making any rash decisions about her relationship with Adam, she cleaned the store from top to bottom, immersing herself in the task.

Being at Zócalo always calmed her nerves.

She dusted the shelves, polished the inventory, and mopped the floor. Cardboard boxes were piled high in the storage room and she had dozens of mail orders to fill, but she wanted to wash the front window first. Dirty glass was her number-one pet peeve. Smudged fingerprints and smog residue, her enemies.

Kari took a bucket outside, frowning as her squeegee sailed along the glass. Her new sign would be delivered tomorrow so she really wanted the storefront to sparkle. When she was finished, she studied the shining surface, looking for spots she'd missed.

A squeal of tires at the closest intersection diverted her attention. She glanced down the street, concerned.

The noise was caused by minor traffic congestion, not even a fender-bender. But her tummy twisted with panic. Memories of Chuy's hands on her throat assaulted her senses. She closed her eyes, seeing flashes of blood and fire. She heard the roar of the SUV, the report of gunfire, the deafening blast of explosives.

Taking a deep breath, she opened her eyes. The commotion cleared and her anxiety eased, but her knees felt wobbly as she ducked back inside the store. After she put away her cleaning supplies, she paced the aisles, unable to relax.

The impulse basket looked a little disorganized, so she rummaged through it, sorting baby booties and stocking caps. For some reason, she lingered over the *rebozos*. She'd left one of the shawls tied in baby-sling style to demonstrate its purpose. With a small frown, she slipped it over her shoulder, sticking her hand in the empty pouch.

Since Sasha's miscarriage, she'd been too focused on work. She realized that now. As much as she loved Zócalo, she longed for more. She wanted a family, close friends and a vivid personal life.

She wanted children.

That desire had been vague and open-ended, more of a hazy wish than a distinct plan for the future, until the day she'd modeled the *rebozo* for Adam. That act, in his presence, had set her biological clock into motion. His niece and nephew were cute as buttons. Kari could easily picture a black-haired infant sleeping against her chest.

The door signal sounded, startling her from her thoughts. She turned to see Adam walking through the entrance. When he saw what she was wearing, he stopped in his tracks. "Making plans?" he asked, smiling a little.

She jerked her hand from the pouch and pulled the

sling over her head, tossing it away like a live snake. "Of course not."

"I thought I'd take you to lunch."

"Is it noon already?"

He arched a brow. "It's two o'clock."

"Oh," she said, perplexed. "I guess I lost track of time."

"Why don't we spend the rest of the afternoon at the beach? I have a blanket in my car. We can go for a swim or take a nap in the sun."

"I have to work."

He gave her a measured look. "You should be resting."

"I'm fine," she insisted, but the tears that filled her eyes said otherwise. Hiding them from him, she turned and rearranged two clay figurines on a shelf. Because her hands were shaking, she succeeded only in knocking one over. It tumbled to the floor and shattered. Her vision blurred as she knelt to pick up the shards.

Adam crouched down beside her, grasping her wrists. "Leave it."

"I can't."

"Come away with me."

She wanted to go with him. Her desire to cling to his neck and collapse in his arms was so strong that she almost tucked her head against his chest, wilting with relief. But something held her back. One last thread of resistance.

Everyone she'd loved had left—or died. She couldn't bear to lose him, too. If she could just put a little distance between them, she wouldn't feel so vulnerable. A protective barrier would keep her from getting hurt.

"I think I need some space," she whispered, avoiding his gaze.

He didn't let her go immediately. After a long, painful moment, he released her and straightened. She picked up the clay pieces and took them to the trash. He shoved his hands into his pockets, staring out at the light midday traffic. "Should I wait for you to call then?"

She glanced away, her throat tightening with emotion. He was referencing their conversation about how to let a man down easy. The irony rose up, threatening to choke her. There was nothing easy about this. "Yes."

A muscle in his jaw clenched. She thought he might give her a curt nod and walk out the door, but he didn't. He had the strength to school his expression and come forward, kissing her stunned cheek. "Goodbye," he said in a husky voice, and left.

Kari watched him go, her heart breaking. She knew she'd hurt him but she couldn't bear to imagine the alternative. For a few minutes, she stood behind the glass counter, feeling numb. Then customers started trickling in, offering a welcome distraction.

She'd sold two pricey stoneware items when Adam reappeared.

Although Kari didn't want to have an emotional scene in public, he didn't give her any choice.

"Sorry, but I have to do this," he said, coming behind the counter. She retreated a step, bracing her palms on the glass surface behind her. He slid his hand around the nape of her neck, lowering his mouth to hers for a thorough kiss.

Then he got down on one knee, and really stole her breath away. "Kari, I love you. If you really need space,

I'll give it to you. But I know from experience that time is precious and I'd like to make the most of it."

"What are you saying?"

He took a black velvet box from his pocket and opened it, revealing a vintage diamond ring that must have cost a bundle. "I want to marry you."

"You don't even know me!"

"I know that you're the love of my life."

Her stomach fluttered at his words. When he laid his heart on the line, he didn't do it halfway.

"I love you, Kari. I love how passionate and dedicated you are. I love the way you work hard and stay strong and never give up. You fought for your sister, for this store, even for Maria. You'll do anything for your friends and family."

Tears filled her eyes and she blinked them away, flustered.

"I understand that you're mourning your sister and I'll wait as long as you want me to, but I can't walk away without telling you how I feel." Rising to his feet, he cupped her face, rubbing his thumb over her cheek. "I need you, *bella*."

Her lips parted under his and he gave her a toe-curling kiss that was totally inappropriate for work. Pressing her against the counter, he plundered her mouth with his tongue while she squirmed against him, grabbing fistfuls of his shirt.

When he was finished, they were both panting.

The trio of women standing by the entrance twittered at their sensual display. Kari gasped and pushed away from him, blushing.

"I'm going to leave now and let you think it over," he said, pressing the velvet box into her limp palm. Wrapping her fingers around it, he kissed the back of her hand. On his way out, he acknowledged the gaping customers. "Ladies."

The women came in and browsed her shelves while Kari clutched the ring box, her entire body trembling. She probably looked like she'd been screwing Adam against the front counter. But she wasn't worried about her mussed appearance or her lack of professionalism. A sudden realization swept over her, and it rocked her to the core.

Losing Adam wasn't the worst thing that could happen. It would be far more devastating to let him slip through her fingers because she wasn't courageous enough to hold on to him. Avoiding his love wasn't going to keep her from feeling pain. It would prevent her from feeling *alive*.

"Excuse me," she said, striding to the front window and turning the sign around. "I'm closing early."

Two of the women seemed annoyed about getting ushered out the door, and rightly so, but the third winked at Kari. "Go get him, honey. If I had a man like that chasing after me, I wouldn't hang around here, either."

"Sorry for the inconvenience," she said. "Come back and I'll give you half off anything in the store."

After locking up, she hurried down the street, searching for Adam's retreating form. She caught sight of him next to his parked car. "Wait!"

He paused, turning to face her.

"Take me with you."

When she started running, he strode toward her. She launched herself into his arms, clinging to him. "I love you, too."

"What?"

"I love you, Adam. I've loved you since that night we spent with your sister's kids. I was afraid to admit it, even to myself. I'm sorry I didn't tell you sooner. It's just that I've lost everyone I loved, and I've never loved anyone the way I love you. I think I'll die if I lose you, and that terrifies me."

He hugged her closer. "I feel exactly the same way."

"What can we do about it?"

"Live every day like it might be our last."

"That sounds . . . financially irresponsible."

He laughed, kissing the top of her head. "I mean that we can try not to take our time together for granted, not that we should stop paying the bills. I want to build a life with you, Kari. A family, if you want one."

"I do," she said, looking into his eyes.

They spent the afternoon at the beach, sharing a picnic lunch and walking hand in hand along the shore. She tried on his ring, which was a perfect fit. At sunset, he drove her to his house, where she agreed to spend the night.

He lifted her off her feet, carrying her across the threshold like a bride.

"Adam! What about your ribs?"

"They're better."

She pressed her lips to his neck. "I love you."

Kicking the door shut, he took her straight to the bedroom, where they made the most of the evening—and then some.